Part One

Diamonds and Rust

First published in Great Britain 1997 by
Silver Moon Books, 68 Charing Cross Road,
London WC2H 0BB

Phototypeset by Intype, London
Printed in Great Britain by
The Guernsey Press Co. Ltd, Guernsey, C.I.

Copyright © 1997 by Jane Thompson

No part of this book may be reproduced in any form without permission from the publisher except for the quotation of brief passages in criticism

ISBN 1 872642 373

A CIP catalogue for this title is available from the
British Library

This is a work of fiction. Names, characters, places and incidents either are the product of the author's imagination or are used fictitiously. Any resemblance to events or persons, living or dead, is entirely coincidental.

Silver Moon Books, London
& Silver Moon Books of Leeds
are in no way connected

JANE THOMPSON

Diamonds and Rust

S·M·B

Dedication

For Jay with love

One

It is eleven o'clock. The answer machine in Mattie's flat is stacking calls – like dominoes in the game her father used to organise at Christmas. As soon as you push one, the rest collapse in sequence. Mattie had given up answering the phone ten years ago when invitations came flooding in from universities and arts centres to do readings of her poems. When people from work rang up about breakfast meetings and when palace revolutions were simmering in response to petty jealousies and arguments over tenure. When the complications of her love life provoked 4 a.m. confrontations. She preferred not to be too instantly available. But now it isn't a question of preference. She is incapable of answering the phone. Even the disembodied voices in the hallway, when she re-plays the tape, leave her feeling anxious and quite unable to respond. Like falling dominoes they crash into each other until her therapist sounds like her mother. Emily from the Women's Sub Committee sounds like Marcia from the office, who sounds like Marjorie, the woman in the States who wants her to lead a seminar on 'reclaiming the feminist agenda'.

Except for Jess. No one sounds like Jess.

'I left some of my CDs and my copy of Sarah Schulman. Could you leave them in the porch and I'll pick them up later?'

Mattie thumps the stop button in a mixture of anger and distress.

'Fuck Sarah Schulman! You also left the bathroom filled with the scent of your perfume and your dirty knickers in the laundry basket. Why not take everything that's yours? And your fucking cold. You left me with your cold.'

The flat is showing signs of being partially but relentlessly vacated. Nothing but the indentation on the carpet and the layer of dust along the skirting board remains of the elaborate stack system that once filled the space with music. Jess has also taken the black sheets that make her feel sexy, the connection to some secret fantasy. The camera. The prints of Frida Kahlo they bought last year in Mexico. In the bedroom the wardrobe door swings open to exaggerate the empty space where until last week Jess used to keep her increasingly outrageous collection of lace and lycra dresses, her studded, skin tight trousers and shiny metal belts. All bought with money she acquired from Mattie and spent recklessly on style.

Mattie also has a taste for shopping. She likes the kind of clothes that carry simple but expensive labels. She likes to dress for the occasion. But only in the best possible taste. She approves of words like elegant and handsome. Black jackets and linen shirts. Waistcoats made from silk. Ankle boots, in every kind of colour. Cut only from the softest leather. But there is none of it, not even from the boutiques of Greenwich Village and San Francisco, that can compete with Jess. Sometimes she looks to Mattie like a storm trooper. Sometimes she looks like a tart. Mattie grows to feel like crimplene and cashmere by comparison. Her dogged addiction to Levi 501s and shirts from Gap mark the moment when Jess starts to weigh the advantages of having a wealthy lover with a full time salary against the embarrassment of being coupled to a dinosaur.

'No one wears that kind of stuff any more. Don't you know that it's the contradictions that make style sexy?'

'Doc Martens and leather ties are hardly conventional academic gear when you're forty-five.' Mattie takes pride in dressing to disregard the men at work.

'Neither are Jesus sandals, stringy beards and pony tails. Why should radical feminism, the movement that fashion forgot, be any more exciting?'

Mattie knows what she means. The girls who are her students all look like re-incarnations of Madonna, or whoever else is currently in vogue, wearing little more substantial than nose rings and thick stockings under shorts. It is getting much more difficult these days to tell who is and isn't gay. Except that all those who look like boys are usually straight. And those who look like bimbos are usually dykes. It's the excess of lipstick that seems to make the difference. The lipstick or the shaven heads.

'Dressing like a het, when you're not is really subversive. That's the whole point. Subvert the subversion'. To Jess the logic is obvious.

'Why adopt oppressive kinds of conventions? I don't understand.' Mattie is truly out of touch.

'Because seeming to go along with all that stuff, when you don't, is wild! And when you show your bra or shave your head or wear something like a collar . . .'

'When you wear a bra and burn your brain', Mattie interrupts.

'. . . people freak.'

'I freak', Mattie says.

'That's the problem.'

After this conversation, Jess takes another mental leap towards the door and wonders who, amongst her contemporaries, can provide the best means of escape from this increasingly boring woman. Three months later, she is gone.

On her own again, Mattie pours herself another glass of wine. She needs to stop drinking during the day. She needs to stop drinking at night. She needs to stop drinking.

Mattie's relationship with Jess began in the classroom. She turned up on a bus from Battersea, with some sandwiches and a thermos flask in a plastic shopping bag, and registered for English. She didn't smile for three weeks. She yawned a lot and watched Mattie with the kind of directness that signifies suspicion. Truculence. A reluctance to take seriously the kind of woman who becomes an academic. Until she knew for certain Mattie wouldn't take the piss.

She always placed herself in the front row in lectures. Scribbling at random into a red exercise book and watching with the kind of concentration that Mattie found both disconcerting and exciting. Of course Mattie noticed the way her skin looked warm and silky, like the blush on a ripe peach. And the way her yellow hair was pushed back from her face in a tangle of unruly curls. But if Mattie hadn't been at a loose end herself, she would have probably taken no further action. As it was, she was feeling bored. And, as so often in this frame of mind, susceptible to flagrant indiscretion.

Forty something is a difficult age. She has given up expecting dangerous liaisons with her friends. Most of whom have settled into comfort and for early nights with a glass of cognac and a lurid thriller. The endless battles over alternative lifestyles and multiple relationships have taken their toll of Mattie's generation. Too many emotional extremes and complicated arrangements around kids and other lovers, that need ground rules, rotas and therapy to sort them out. In the end it seems altogether easier to stick with matrimony. Especially when mortgages, jobs in middle management and sanity are at stake.

Mattie watches the lifestyle change as she clings defiantly to her belief in personal freedom. As a minor star of women's writing and performance in the 80s, the opportunities to prove her point are plentiful. Travelling in Europe and North America, she behaves much like the proverbial sailor, with a girl in every port. Securing just sufficient friendship and flattery and occasional intimacy along the way to stop her feeling like a tourist. To keep her feeling like part of the vanguard in the war against patriarchy.

Sometimes she gets her fingers burned. Straight women with husbands who don't appreciate their wife's defection. Women who don't listen too intently when Mattie lectures about jealousy and the politics of possession. They think she means in general. And not in the particular. Not in relation to them, for example.

Across the years Mattie's passionate intensity has always flourished in direct proportion to her own autonomy. She is capable of the wildest extremes of generosity and romantic extravagance, so long as she retains the balance of control. She can be loving, outrageous and exciting – so long as she doesn't feel relied upon or trapped. As soon as she detects the first shadow of dependence steal across a lover's face, as soon as she registers the first emotional demand that implies responsibility for another's happiness, she begins to sound out her retreat. Like crack troops who desert the front line just as the battle seems intent on escalation. To conserve their energy and their freedom to manoeuvre.

Sometimes she stays a little longer than is usual. Or falls a little further into love than she expects. Occasionally her heart is broken for a while. Until resilience and the priorities of personal survival pull her out of trouble. Until somebody or something else turns up to concentrate her attention, in ways that hide her inability to sustain relationships.

Jess was in her middle twenties when they met. A mature student in the language of the university. And with a life of poverty and mediocrity behind her that she finds it quite impossible to disclose.

'I feel like I'm on a psychiatrist's couch', she complains defiantly.

'I only want to know some more about you.' Mattie's voice is earnest and sincere. 'How do I know where you're coming from or what you're feeling if you don't talk to me about it?'

'I'm not used to talking about it. It was just something to endure. To get over. To get on with. I don't claim to be an intellectual.'

In tutorials Jess lounges in the chair with the kind of ostentatious lethargy that resists interest or engagement. As though to look too eager, to demonstrate serious intention, will mark her out as some kind of swot. The kind of kid at school that everyone despises. Her contribution to discussion is non existent. Her answers to direct questions prised out of her. In monosyllables, like teeth or blood from stone.

But her written work is brilliant. Whatever else her glass and concrete comprehensiveness and dysfunctional family have done to her, they haven't tampered with her brain. Privately she enjoys the feelings of connection and control as pages of carefully constructed argument fall from her pen. A few years on drugs and a couple of abortions are no big surprise these days to girls of slender means. But for Jess, getting back in touch with her intelligence and turning up to education are something of a long shot — and one that could easily misfire. The kind of gamble that naturally appeals to Mattie's missionary intention, and mirrors what she likes to think of as her own salvation. She gives Jess a signed copy of her poems.

'In case you're interested', Mattie smiles. 'Not my best. But formative.'

Jess takes the poems home and studies them for information about Mattie. Are they fact or fiction? Mattie writes a lot about sex and introspection. Before — at school – Jess thought that poems were for sad people, to be resisted. Now she begins to see the attraction.

Once Jess allows herself to feel engaged in learning, less dubious and panic stricken, she comes to reckon Mattie. Quite considerably. The woman is a genius. The other students like her. She makes them laugh with her irreverence. She likes the limelight, Jess can tell. But she always asks lots of questions, and she does a lot of listening. For Jess this is a novelty, no one in her life before has asked Jess questions. Other than the obvious, like 'Want a shag?' 'Or 'Where's my dinner?' No one has asked how she's feeling or ever listened when she speaks about her fears. Or about her dreams of getting out from under.

Jess has never thought about doing sex with a woman before. But she can feel the urge to do something physical when she looks at Mattie in this way. Something more significant than simply screwing your tutor – which does have its perverse attractions. Men she can take or leave without much bother. But this – this is altogether more exciting. Plus, she's been around long enough to know that Mattie fancies her. Mattie doesn't make a secret of her sexuality, in fact, she likes to confront her students with their prejudices, and make being gay something of a litmus test of their correctness. There are always three or four who take her rhetoric to heart and become like groupies. Turning up much too eagerly for lectures, inviting her to parties, adopting the odd mannerism or buzz word she cultivates for this effect. But Jess is not one of them. She is not interested in being part of the crowd. She'd rather have Mattie to herself. For a little undivided attention.

Of course they go to bed. In Mattie's flat in Islington she makes love to Jess with tenderness and passion. She has grown used to taking the initiative. Anticipating inequality of experience and establishing control. In return she wants confirmation, adoration, dedication. Another conscript for her cause, another acolyte.

Jess is shy at first but not the kind of girl to be a doormat. She is bold in bed and doesn't wait around for practical instructions. Or political considerations. She couldn't care less what Lilian Faderman has to say about romantic friendships, or Sheila Jeffreys about heresy for that matter. Acting on her instincts, in the pursuit of pleasure, is not the intellectual occasion for her angst. She doesn't have a line about significance. A lot of Mattie's eloquence, her elaborate repertoire of stories and debates, go on outside her sphere of interest, and sound too much like another faded lecture from a former era.

'Why do you go on so much about your early lovers and about other situations?' Jess has no equivalent stash of secret bodies and discarded experiences in her short life. At least none that she wants to remember. And without competing anecdotes to swap, she feels at a disadvantage. Like an ingénue.

'Do I? I'm sorry. Just my misguided sense of history.' Mattie laughs and rolls over on her back so that Jess can drift across her body like a soft cloud in an otherwise blue and settled sky.

None of Mattie's friends can imagine why she lets Jess move in. The only conceivable reason must be sex.

'But she's so much younger', Rose says. 'Whatever do you find to talk about? She was probably still in school when you were climbing on the fence at Greenham'.

'Born on 4th July – but not before I was arrested at the American Embassy in Grosvenor Square', Mattie laughs. 'She thinks the Vietnam War was something invented by Hollywood to sell movies.'

'That's my point. She's a different generation, one of Thatcher's children. Don't you feel like some kind of political bygone?' Rose still lives with Nancy, a woman she met in 1978, fell out with over child care, and got back in touch with some years later, once the kids had left, courtesy of therapy. Now they live quietly in North London. Rose makes pots and does proof reading for anyone who will pay her. Nancy teaches Tai Chi and is trying to write a novel. Not the kind of serious credentials that can dissuade Mattie from her mission.

'She's a wonderful lover and she's got an excellent brain. It helps to be a student these days, if you're working class and want to be a dyke.'

But at dinner parties Jess is silent and gives no indication of her excellent brain. She doesn't take to Mattie's friends who treat her like a curiosity. And wait for her to sparkle. Mattie is embarrassed by her stubborn disregard for wit and intellect. She stops inviting her friends round and re-starts the occasional fling, when the opportunity arises, to relieve her growing fear of being married. But she doesn't want Jess to go. She is more extrovert and confident when there is no one else around to be middle class and boring. And she is attentive to Mattie's sexual well being, in ways that have become addictive. Though none of Mattie's cronies can quite believe it, the spiky relationship that flares between them is not unequal.

But then, Jess was never in the running to become 'the little woman', or to be tied to Mattie's apron strings. When she moves into Mattie's flat, it is on the understanding that she'll keep on top of the repairs and do the decorating. And when she finishes her degree she will look for a proper job. On Mattie's frequent absences at international conferences and on lecture tours Jess gets used to comfortable living beyond the breadline. In a flat with central heating and a fridge full of food. In which manila envelopes arrive unaccompanied by debt collectors, with statements of accounts paid magically by standing order. And where she can take some time to make her own connections. With girls in bars, and boys on the town. Sex without streams of consciousness. And fashion played for fun and fetish.

By now the two have lived together for about three years. A long time for Mattie. Time to move on for Jess.

'You got me into all of this', she says defensively when Mattie asks about the nights she stays out late. Or doesn't come home until the following day.

'If it's meetings – I'd like to come along some time', Mattie says. 'I don't know much about your politics – except what I read. But I think I would approve – if I could put up with all the men.'

By now Jess doesn't much care whether she approves or not.

'At least they don't just sit in their ivory towers reading', Jess snaps. 'At least they get out on the streets and do something'.

'About what though? About the age of consent for gay men to have more sex? About gays in the army? About "freedom of sexual expression" or whatever else is the latest euphemism for sadomasochism? What's it all got to do with us? Where are the lesbians I'd like to know?'

'Which us? Not you, maybe. Not any longer. But young lesbians. There's a lot of lesbians in Queer Politics, if you haven't noticed. I think we've got a lot to learn from gay men. They know how to enjoy themselves. Unlike some people I could mention.' Jess is getting angry.

Mattie ignites into tutor mode and rails about the backlash, the angers of libertarianism, the false assumption that pleasure leads inevitably to freedom.

'I'm not one of your students any more, you know.' Jess has heard enough. 'How can I take you to meetings when you clearly don't approve of what we're trying to do? Anyway, it's not always about politics. Some of us are bored with politics, haven't you heard?'

'So where else do you go?' Mattie sounds like a jealous wife who assumes she has the right to have an explanation and itinerary.

'What's it got to do with you? I don't ask you where you go all the time. I didn't realise we were supposed to be joined at the hip.'

Mattie feels attacked by her own rhetoric. In ways that don't make her feel too comfortable. Especially as she is also pursuing her own flirtatious inclinations, with little reference to the sensibilities of Jess.

'I'm sorry,' she concedes. 'Let's drop it, shall we? I don't mean to be intrusive. It's just, I don't want you to get hurt.'

Jess is not in the mood for reconciliation.

'Hurt and damage come in many forms, from many sources', she replies. 'Not least of all by slavish devotion to simplistic slogans and by telling lies and using power games. It would be more honest to work it out in bed. But then, you only like sex when it's sweet and soppy.'

'You're talking rubbish!' Mattie can't bear to hear Jess speaking like this. 'You're talking like a gay man.'

'Maybe I am. Maybe it's time you did some up to date research!'

Jess grabs her jacket and slams the door behind her. Leaving Mattie stunned and frightened by her outburst of resentment.

There follows a period of re-adjustment. In which Mattie rarely emerges from beneath her duvet. Getting out of bed becomes a major effort. She rings in sick to the university and lets the answer machine stack calls to which she makes no response. It takes all her determination to raise the corner of her quilt and force her body across the floor in heavy steps towards the kitchen. Loading a tea bag into an indifferent mug, still bruised with yesterday's tannin. To find she's out of milk.

Mattie isn't used to being ditched. And in disgrace, it seems, for being tedious. Rose is not surprised and not supportive. Mattie's other friends require an explanation. Which in itself feels like a measure of their distance.

The days in bed bring intimations of mortality. Of time elapsed. Of years long gone when she could make things happen, in which the world was like a playground for women with decent jobs and independence. And a reason to be listened to. Now shifted onto new agendas without the same commitment. She begins to feel her age, as though what is passed now counts for more than what might come. The future smudged with uncertainty and little of the middle ground to register security. It is a time for calling in the debts and taking stock. For salvage. Not yet for reconstruction.

Two

Outside the window it is Autumn. In regimented roads there are no trees to splash the streets with flakes of rust and amber. Doorsteps confront porches and Victorian bricks in calculated order. Leading into flats and communal houses, basements and maisonettes. No shrubs or flowers soften the façade. Only at number 33. Where Mr Wilkins has lined terracotta pots along a stretch of concrete and filled them full of chrysanthemums and michaelmas daisies. The kind her father used to grow and which make Mattie think of junior school and harvest festival.

The light is yellow now and slightly fading. With the smell of dust and traffic that gets trapped in air in London, like layers of stale perfume. A shroud that soon becomes so familiar you cease to notice it. Until you leave the city.

Meredith is wearing a loose fitting jacket over an Indian cotton dress. She is comfortably middle aged and soft around the edges. Mattie is scrunched into a Lloyd loom chair, shredding a paper handkerchief through thin nervous fingers. The walls of the room in which they are sitting are rag-rolled in midnight blue. A deep purple rug and a scatter of cushions cover the polished oak floor boards. Meredith and Mattie sit facing each other across a low pine table which is empty except for a large box of pale lilac tissues. To the left a vacant seat waits ominously for occupation. Later in the day, as the light fades and as the dampness of the autumn afternoon seeps into the cracks and corners of the room, Meredith will light candles and burn incense. To cultivate calmness in a sea of chaos.

'Tell me how you're feeling?'

Meredith doesn't waste time on pleasantries. She likes to operate a fifty minute hour, which gives her chance to plump the cushions and remove soggy tissues from the waste bin. It allows clients to come and go with less risk of queuing or feeling processed by Meredith's relentless schedule. Her voice is light, like artificial cream. She registers concern.

'You're looking rather little.'

Mattie shuffles in her chair. Tears straying silently across the creases of her skin.

'Oh I'm all right. Just tired I expect.'

'Are you sleeping?'

'Not a lot. Not enough.' She relapses into silence in an effort to retain control.

'It doesn't matter if you cry.' Meredith waits. 'Best not to bottle up distress. It only bursts through somewhere else.'

'I'm not afraid of crying.' Mattie has a strong commitment to emotion. But not her own. Not in circumstances when she's feeling vulnerable.

'I don't mind if you don't want to say anything to me', Meredith smiles. 'But at £45 a time, you could sit more cheaply in a bus shelter.'

Mattie knows she is being ridiculous.

'I don't approve of therapy', she says.

'Then why are you here?' Meredith checks her watch and suppresses a slight yawn. She expects conviction.

'Oh. Because my friends recommended you. Because I've exhausted their tolerance and interest. Because I feel like I'm sinking. Because I don't know what to do.'

'And because your lover's left you?'

'How did you know?'

Meredith smiles. Any fool can tell. The loss of lovers and mid life crises are Meredith's biggest boost to business.

'You look abandoned', she says sympathetically, 'and cut adrift.' Meredith knows how to cultivate the lightness of suggestion that can unlock the most resistant and sceptical of egos.

'Actually, it's not a problem. Things have been difficult between us for a while. It's much better now she's gone.'

Meredith watches the tension gather in Mattie's shoulders like tendrils round a stem. She isn't convinced.

'A mutual decision then?' Meredith is used to picking away at strong defences until they die or bleed.

'She quit. If you require historical accuracy.'

Mattie sounds lost in a mix of sadness and pomposity. She has given few women in her life the chance to leave her. Usually Mattie is the first to disappear. Often without trace. Even Alice, the most important person in her past, fared little better when it came to Mattie's reluctance to concede commitment.

'Tell me about her. Your lover. What is she like? Why did she go?'

'She was my student at one time. I seem to have a weakness around student–teacher relationships. One way and another.' Mattie smiles a wry smile.

'It's happened to you before then?'

'Yes.'

'Once or twice? Or many times?'

'Once or twice. But some things stay with you. Like patterns that shape your life.' Meredith nods thoughtfully, registering connection.

'So what has happened this time?'

'She's grown up, basically. After three years she doesn't need me any more. She's ready to move on. Other people are more exciting. I've become a millstone.' Tears spill again from Mattie's eyes.

'Millstone? You don't seem the kind of woman to call herself a millstone.'

Mattie twists a second tissue round her fingers.

'She reminds me of how I used to be. I want her to flourish in the way I flourished. Put her brains to good use. Become an academic. A feminist.'

'And she doesn't want to?'

'I think that once she knew that she was clever, and didn't really need to struggle, she became blasé. And then, of course, she got distracted. I was away a lot.'

'She got distracted because you were away?'

'She stopped believing in me. She found her own friends. Not my scene, exactly.'

'Did you object?'

'I objected because I didn't like what she was getting into.'

'You didn't approve?'

'No.'

'And then?'

'And then she grew angry and resentful. She stopped caring what I thought. What I wanted. And then she left.'

Meredith is used to women feeling bad about themselves. Feelings of low esteem and masochism are her stock in trade. The motivation behind countless hours of treatment. Designed to dig away at previous relationships. At feelings of betrayal. At ghosts and monsters from the past. Meredith gives her clients permission to regress, to become like children, to identify demands. With Mattie, Meredith weighs the pros and cons of pushing further, against the ticking of the clock. She has left too little time for big disclosures. And settles for distraction. Her calculation is quick and strictly cost connected.

'This chair is vacant now.' Meredith indicates the empty seat. 'But you can invite anyone you like to sit in it. You can make them listen to what you want to say. Hear yourself articulate your pain. The things you'd like to say to them, but don't. For whatever reason.'

Mattie looks sceptical.

'Count me out of silly bugger games. I don't need to talk to an empty chair to find out what I want to say to Jess.'

'Say it then!' Meredith's voice issues her a challenge.

Mattie hesitates. And then concedes.

'How dare you? After all I've given you. Turn your eyes away from mine? Laugh on the telephone to someone, behind a consciously closed door. Designed to keep me out. Look irritated when I ask about your life? Tell me I'm imagining things in ways that make me feel as though I'm going crazy? Leave me – like a whirlwind – when I've grown used to having you around? And just when my life feels lousy. The very time I need you most to take some care.'

'Why do you say your life is lousy?'

'Oh. Because work is boring. I'm boring. I don't have any real friends. My politics are out of style. No one, really, gives a shit.'

Meredith nods her understanding and approval, without comment. To have broken into Mattie's strong defences provides more ammunition for the future. And tips the advantage in Meredith's direction as she abandons Mattie to her own resources for a while.

'I think you should come and see me again in a week's time. In the meantime, I want you to think about two things in particular. The part that power plays in your relationship. And why you never speak about your mother.'

Mattie feels her breath catch in her throat.

'But I have no relationship with my mother. She knows nothing about my life.'

'Precisely.'

Meredith is writing in her filofax. Her voice is now more brisk and organised.

'About the fee. You can pay as you go along, if you prefer. Or, something which might be helpful, a reduction of ten per cent on all sessions paid for in advance.'

She waits. Her pen is at attention.

Mattie hands over £45 in crisp clean notes, delivered

without effort, like monopoly money, from the cash dispenser in the High Street.

Meredith records the fee and closes her filofax to terminate the session. She leads Mattie to the door.

'So, good to see you, Mattie. I think we can make some progress here don't you?'

Mattie feels uncertain. The object of manipulation.

'Stay well in your life'.

The door snaps shut behind her as the dismal grey streets of recently refurbished houses reclaim her for the rat race and the day to day dilemmas of a woman in a mess.

On the streets of London rubbish swirls across the pavements and gathers in the gutters. Rats scurry through the underground. Beggars reach out their empty hands for change. But Mattie passes unaware. Oblivious to other people's desperation. In need of change herself.

At night her dreams bring little consolation. Usually she is naked. The setting is always mundane. The supermarket. A meeting at work. The café where she likes to have breakfast when she is out of milk. Or honey. The dream is never about sex.

Sometimes it is a bus queue. She is standing in line with people she thinks she knows. From somewhere. Young women with hair like petals, her students. Their bright red lipsticked lips encircling their mouths. With boyfriends like bullets, shooting from a gun, never still, or safe. All of them oblivious to the naked woman who bends her shoulders in an effort to be smaller. Hoping she can disappear.

It might be snowing. Rolling into drifts of grey slush

beside the gutter. Where old women in tired and ragged coats, and woolly hats, pulled down around their ears like tea cosies, watch from the shadows. At one time all the drunks were men. But not any longer. Now children – with faces like split peas – trade sex and insults in return for pity.

In this version of the dream a man is begging with his dog. His hair is long and twisted into plaits. A red jewel glistens from his ear. His hand stretches towards her in another kind of desperation. She gives him what she has.

'You have no gloves', he says.

Actually she has no clothes at all.

'Take mine', he says.

Along the main street, lorries cut the snow into ruts and channels, spraying slush into the faces of the dispossessed.

She does not feel the cold. The sharp grey flakes of crusted ice fall like splinters to the ground. Sometimes in the dream she carries a scarf. It is long and black and made of silk. Like the one a woman in her past maintained she stole. A woman who was superstitious in the way that Russians often are. However hard she tries to pull and stretch the silk across her body, it is never dense or wide or large enough to hide her nakedness. In fact, its flimsy inadequacy becomes an additional source of her distress.

The streets of the city run riot with random shoppers and office workers on their determined route to somewhere else. Preoccupied with lists and destinations. Snatched into revolving doors and onto escalators to be whisked away and smuggled out of sight.

When the bus arrives it is already full. She has no money to pay the driver. He stares at her with blank eyes as he hands her a ticket. The girls with red slashed lips have taken up positions on the seats below. Watching like mannequins through plate glass windows as she climbs the metal stairway. Upstairs most of the seats are also occupied by women. Carrying bulging shopping bags of tomatoes. Women have taken to throwing tomatoes much less these days. Not like in the time of her youth. When no one was safe. Not men who beat their wives, or special investigators employed by the state, or private debt collectors. Even social workers had to travel in disguise. Newspaper headlines gave out all the details.

The rest of the space is taken up by elderly men. Their skin loosened and folded around their bones like crumpled paper. Wearing plastic macs and cloth caps. The kind her father used to wear, when he was much younger than she is now. Reading books of poetry. She never knew, until it was far too late, that her father was a poet. She found the secret scribbled in an old exercise book at the back of his cupboard. Soon after he died. Her mother said he was an emotional man but he could never show it.

Packed into the back are bunches of ragged children who could be orphans or refugees. Steered through the streets of Sarajevo between land mines and sniper fire. Never to be seen again.

She fumbles her way to the back of the bus and sits down in the only place remaining. Scrunching her shoulders in the hope that she too might disappear. The bus lurches through the city streets towards the suburbs. People come and go until there is no one left aboard. Except herself and the man with the dog and the red jewel in his ear. At last she recognises the roads. The rows of Victorian houses. Each with their solid red bricks, tall chimney stacks and substantial sounding names –

like Ashburton and Rudbeckia. The bus is stopping now beside her door. The street suddenly sprouting a bus stop where none had grown before. She can see Jess waiting in her yellow shirt like a small daffodil against the snow. The way she looked at first, in the days before she moved in. Her eyes suspicious as they used to be. All the time.

As she gets down from the bus and turns towards the flat she sees Jess disappearing in the opposite direction. She is carrying the dog. And smiling into the eyes of the man with the jewel in his ear.

Three

It's Wednesday and Mattie decides she should be making a better job of her life. But she isn't. In the past she would have simply moved on, physically or metaphorically. Now each direction feels like a blind alley that ends in a brick wall. The plot of ground on which she's standing is getting smaller and smaller, sliced away by desperate remedies that bring no solutions. She survives two or three more sessions with Meredith.

Meredith wants to know about her childhood. About her feelings for her family. Her emotional connections with her mother. Meredith had a narrow repertoire of strategies, which a busy case load and a close affiliation to therapeutic dogma, encourage her to repeat more frequently than might otherwise be expected – given the promise on her publicity of 'individual attention'. She coaxes Mattie to regress. Without success. She becomes irritated with Mattie's reluctance to accept instructions. Meredith's patience is conditional upon the recognition of her wisdom. And whilst she is used to preliminary skirmishes in the battle over will, to establish her control, she expects to win.

'Why do you get so defensive?' she asks accusingly. 'Do you see me as your mother?'

'No.' Mattie is used to clarity. 'You're nothing like my mother.'

'Then why do you resist me like a child? I think you are feeling like a child again. Like a young teenager, maybe. Working through rebellion.'

Mattie watches Meredith defiantly. In stronger mood, she would get up and leave. In another life, she would be anywhere but here, stuck desperately in this Lloyd loom chair, swapping fears and vulnerabilities for psycho-crap and clichés with a stranger, whose concern is calculated by the clock, and costed. Meredith checks her watch and reaches for her filofax. Her mouth set in an irritated line. Her voice professionally brisk and bland.

'I'm afraid I shall be away for a couple of weeks, Mattie. Can we look at dates beginning on 23rd?'

Mattie is relieved.

'I'll let you know', she prevaricates. 'I need to check my schedule at the office.'

'Just as you like.' Meredith recognises the signs of disengagement. 'I can't help you till you agree to trust me.' She turns the pages of her diary, stocked reasurringly with those who do. 'I'm not the enemy, you know. The enemy...' she searches for a suitable conclusion '... lies within.'

Mattie has no energy to argue or to take offence. She passes over her money and heads for the door.

'Stay well in your life.' Meredith's voice collides with the sharp sting of autumn rain that gathers Mattie into its chilly grip and runs her to the bus stop. She waits in line as usual with the rest. And plans her own connections.

The phone sits neatly on a square of crochet. It rarely rings. Days pass. Its unexpected echo in the hallway occasions an event. Mattie waits to give her mother time to answer.

'Hello. Yes?' Her mother's voice sounds cautious, slightly anxious.

'Mum, its me.' Mattie speaks quickly before she loses her momentum. 'How are you? What's new?'

'New? Nothing's new dear, I went to Tescos this morning. Did my ironing. Your brother Billy isn't very happy with himself. How are you?'

'I'm fine', Mattie lies, hoping her mother will catch the slight inflection in her voice, persuade her to come clean.

'That's good, dear. And how's your job? Not working too hard I hope.'

'It's fine.' Mattie always feels her mother would prefer her to be doing nothing. As a way of keeping out of trouble.

'Well then', her mother searches for another question.

'Look Mum, I need to be in Leeds for a few days at the university. I could come over if you'll be around?'

Her mother hesitates. It's a while since Mattie came to stay. Her brief appearances are never easy, but, of course, she likes to see her.

'I don't go very far these days. Not since your father died.' She says it as a matter of regret. Mattie detects the injured tones of martyrdom. 'So when will you come?'

Mattie relays the details of the trains and asks about the weather. The usual disagreement is exchanged about comparisons. Her mother calls it 'sheltered' in East Yorkshire and clings to her uncritical conviction about the wisdom of avoiding all extremes. Unlike in London, where it's always very hot, or very wet, or very cold. Not the kind of climate to be relied on.

'And how is it with you?' Her mother spends a lot of time discussing weather.

'Oh, an Indian summer...' Mattie lies. She has no idea why she bothers to distort the truth. Especially as she's feeling sick to death of London anyway, without needing to be prompted by her mother. But when the rainfall, or the bus service, or the price of a cup of coffee in Regent Street becomes the symbol of one of Mattie's worst mistakes, according to her mother, it's the kind of argument she can't afford to lose.

'No thoughts of coming back up north? The university at York is very nice, by all accounts.' She always asks. As though Mattie can swap jobs like second-hand cars.

'Mother, I like my job. I like living in London. I don't want to come back to Holderness. I'd just like to come and see you for a few days.' Mattie tries hard not to let her irritation show.

'Of course, dear. Just asking. A mother has to ask these things, you know.' Mattie feels about twelve.

'I'll see you Friday, then. Don't worry about sending Tommy to the station, I'll get a taxi.'

'Taxis cost. Tommy will be pleased to come and meet you. He's trying out his new car. A good bargain so he says. It's only had one lady owner.'

'Don't worry about it Mum. I'll see you Friday.' Mattie puts the phone down. 'I could be dead!' she sighs dramatically.

In Holderness the old lady goes into the kitchen to make some tea. Why does a visit from Mattie feel like an inspection by the Queen? To be anticipated with a mixture of awe and trepidation and then endured with clipped politeness. Always terrified in case she says the wrong thing. And always, in the end, believing that she's common.

On Friday morning her mother gets up earlier than usual to change the sheets in Mattie's room. A name plaque, made as a birthday present by her father, is still nailed to the door. Inside the furniture remains the same – 1960s contemporary design – still polished once a week and dusted. She takes out ornaments and photo frames from the top drawer of the dressing table where she keeps them out of reach of little fingers. Now that Tommy's boys have children of their own. And all of them a handful. Are children getting worse? She doesn't know. No one could cause her more concern than Tommy in his day. She never had a moment's peace when Tommy was a boy. Always up to mischief, always in a fight. She was glad when he got married to Julie. Although he was probably too young. And she was no doubt pregnant. Still, they made a proper go of it. Unlike some. Tommy liked to have his own way. Julie had to get used to him. Which she did, without complaining. 'Marriage isn't always easy. You need to work at it, and not expect the moon.' She talks to herself a lot these days. With no one else around to notice the feelings of loss she has grown accustomed to and learned to live with. Like all the other disappointments in her life.

She knows about such things from her experience. She lived with Mattie's father for more than 40 years. Thirty-eight in the same, small terraced house. A marriage that involved a lot of compromise. Like giving up on dancing and learning to mend trousers. In which her husband Henry became as commonplace as custard on her apple dumplings. As everyday as well brewed tea. As ordinary as her own existence. When he retired from the factory, she thought she might go mad, with Henry hanging round the house all day getting under her feet. She found him little jobs to keep him out of trouble. Keeping out of trouble has always been important to Mattie's mother. She and Henry seemed to manage it quite well. But not Mattie or the boys. Mattie was the worst for bringing trouble. She did nothing by the book. Nothing that you might expect. The boys were bad enough, not one of them a patch on Henry for reliability. When he died, she missed his warm, solid back in bed. His collars in the washing basket waiting to be turned. The way he offered every detail of his day for her inspection and approval. Like a child who was more obedient than any child she'd ever known. Certainly more obedient than her own unruly bunch of mischief makers and malingerers.

On the day of his funeral, she sat beside her old friend Elsie in the church, who took her arm and steered her through the ceremony with down to earth detachment.

When Mattie was a child the house was always full of women like Elsie. Her mother's cronies. Popping in and out the backyard door. 'Salt of the earth' was how her mother talked about them. Most of whom survived their husbands – to no one's great surprise.

When Henry died, the proper vicar was away on holiday. Although his stand-in did the best he could, he got into a muddle over names. No one put him right. It didn't seem convenient to object. Not with a second corpse waiting in the wings, and another gang of grieving relatives ready for the off.

'He wouldn't want a fuss', Elsie said with certainty. 'Not after all these years of keeping out of trouble.'

Mattie's mother nodded. She watched the coffin slide behind the curtains and questioned what it all amounted to. A life lived quietly in the backstreets, with little fuss. To be buried by a man he'd never met, who called him Edward. She lent on Elsie's arm and moved from group to group with dignity. She quite understood how mistakes get made. And how death can be embarrassing. Afterwards at home, Mattie passed around the boiled ham and mustard sandwiches. And caught the last train back to London. Her mother didn't cry. Her courage was never measured by the ready demonstration of emotion when it mattered. She squandered her tears lightly on television soaps, and old films from her palmy days, replayed on Sunday afternoons, as antidotes to sport. Tragedies and celebrations she weathered steely eyed.

'Its a pity that our Mattie never married', her mother continues talking to herself as she places ornaments in clusters on hand-crocheted doilies. She studies Mattie's photo in the frame, like butter wouldn't melt in her mouth.' It was taken on a day trip to Whitby when she was ten. Before they knew about the grammar school.

'She was in such a mood that day – because I wouldn't let her wear that old red jacket. You'd never tell, she looks too pretty.'

Mattie's mother smooths the eiderdown and plumps the pillows. She fetches a little vase of plastic roses to put beside the bed. 'That's nice.' She looks around with pleasure.

In the kitchen she switches on the oven and sorts out the ingredients for chocolate cake, the kind that Mattie used to call her favourite when she lived at home.

The train from London arrives in Holderness on Friday afternoon at half past four. It's the first time Mattie has made the journey for some time. The last one was on a bright spring morning, when the weather was out of sorts with the occasion, and the unexpected sunshine shot glints of iridescent yellow through the flat grey landscape, exposing bleak fronts of farmhouses and barns that needed painting. That required some evidence of emotional investment. On that occasion it was her father's funeral.

This time the journey gives Mattie space to think. To wonder why she's choosing to come north. Which brick wall? Which particular blind alley? She can't watch the uneventful farmland flatten to the suggestion of sea, or the wide, sad fields replace the worn out pits and slag heaps of South Yorkshire, without thinking of connections and her roots. And how it is that grey and uncommitted countryside creates worthy, undemanding people. Uncritical when poor. Parochial and self satisfied as soon as hardship is made relative by progress.

She finds the railway station looking much the same as ever, except the bright lights of the buffet now suggest fast food in disposable containers. The newsstand is full of thick paperbacks, wearing letters etched in elaborate gold script, announcing titles like *A Woman of Significance* and *Eastacre*. A place already on the edge of England, it leads to nowhere but the cold east coast and northern sea.

She takes a taxi to her mother's house and rings the bell. Mattie's mother always looks much smaller than she remembers. Her thin body is wrapped in a polyester dress and yellow cardigan. Her hair completely white except for pale residues of mauve and pink from faded perms and former rinses. She smiles, a little anxiously, not sure what to expect.

'Well stranger', she steps back to let Mattie through the door.

Mattie moves to place a light dry kiss on her mother's thin cheek. The tiny house is bright and shiny like freshly minted coins. Each polished surface packed with bric-a-brac and photographs. Hand-embroidered cloths cover hardback chairs, and cushions, clad in nylon fur, stand guard along the sofa like a row of Smarties. Above the mantlepiece there hangs a picture of her father, smudged in crayon by a Spanish fisherman on the beach at Torremolinos. Her mother disappears into the kitchen to take stock, and boil the kettle for some tea. She is worried that her daughter looks so weary.

In the front room Mattie studies the family photographs for clues about her life. Here, in her mother's gallery, she is framed in gilt amongst the rest. At seven, with a pistol in her hand, playing cowboys with her brothers. At seventeen in uniform. An instant smile created by the camera to capture the illusion of her schooldays. Her neatly parted hair all innocent and wholesome. Giving no indication of the sexual turmoil she habitually suppressed throughout her adolescent years, the surprising dreams and passionate obsession she focused on her teacher. In borrowed cap and gown at twenty-one. A first class honours graduate of English, now ear marked for a glittering career. Standing between her mother and father on the day they took a holiday from work, arriving late by train to mark the celebration of her ultimate defection. It was Alice Morrison who took the photograph, as she recalls. Her parents were neither more nor less embarrassed by the teacher's presence at the ceremony, than by all the other representatives of class superiority and education. But then, they didn't know that Mattie and Miss Morrison were lovers. Or that variations on the truth about Mattie's 'way of life' would soon require invention, for the sake of family and neighbours, to explain their clever daughter's adamant determination not to marry, or settle down to breeding children.

'You could do with another shelf for all these photographs. Or have a clear out.' Mattie helps her mother with the tray of tea and home-made cake.

'I could put some of them in albums I suppose, but I like to look at them. They keep me company. Did you notice how Billy's twins have grown? They leave school next year. Both set on College. We've got our fingers crossed. Let's hope it runs in the family – doing well at school'. She smiles at Mattie. 'They might like a bit of good advice, if you're feeling up to it.'

'What do they want to do?' Mattie fingers their photographs with care, hoping for some hint of recognition. The boy looks strong and stupid. The girl could pass for thirty-five.

'You'll have to ask them. Knowing me, I'll get it wrong. I think Jason wants to do something with computers and Melanie would like to be a hairdresser.'

'No chance it could be the other way round?' Mattie

despairs of young women. You'd think that twenty-five years of women's liberation would give them more ambition. Her mother detects an adverse judgement but doesn't want to jump too quickly to the wrong conclusion.

'Maybe it is the other way round. My memory isn't what it used to be'. She cuts Mattie a giant slice of cake.

'Steady on, Mother, I won't be able to manage all of that.'

'But it's your favourite, Mattie. It's very light. Just you try it.'

Mattie has little appetite for anything at present but doesn't know how to explain.

'Oh well', her mother sighs, 'I'm sorry if it's not to your liking.'

'I'm rather full, that's all. There's nothing wrong with the cake. It looks lovely', Mattie tries her best to sound convincing. 'I had some sandwiches on the train.'

'Are you still off meat?' Her mother hopes she's changed her ways. She can't imagine what a person eats who doesn't like meat. Or what to cook for dinner whilst she's home.

'I am a vegetarian, yes. I'm surprised you haven't come around to it yourself by now, with all the bad publicity about mad cow disease and factory farming'.

Her mother can scarcely contemplate a more ridiculous idea.

'This is Holderness, Mattie. It's farming country. You can't be a vegetarian in Holderness. It would be like asking the Pope to become a Protestant. All those who complain on television are just looking to cause trouble. The farmers wouldn't let their animals suffer. They like animals. That's why they do the job.' She gets all her information from television.

'Most of the meat you eat has never seen a farm, Mother. Let alone a farm that's any where near here.'

Her mother feels uncertain of her ground. It's very hard to argue with an academic. Even when you know she's got it wrong.

'But do you get enough to eat, Mattie? That's my main worry when I think about you living on your own. Lack of protein, you shouldn't take your health for granted, you know. Just remember what became of Auntie Eva.'

Auntie Eva went on holiday abroad. Mattie's mother can never quite remember where. Although she tells the story often enough and always ends by saying 'so let it be a warning'.

'When Eva came back home she developed stomach cramps, which left the doctor totally at sea. A month later – she was dead. She was only fifty-four.'

'I don't know what Auntie Eva's death has got to do with anything.' Try as she might, Mattie can never see the logic in this story, or quite remember what point her mother uses it to make.

'The point', her mother says, 'is obvious. She took her health for granted in a foreign climate. And that was that.'

Mattie nods and decides to change the subject.

'I'm thinking of applying for some leave of absence from the University', she says. 'I don't get a lot of time for writing at the moment.'

'No chance of moving back up north? The university at York is always in the papers. What with conferences and important inventions going off. They'd let you do some writing there, I expect.'

'You said that on the phone. But it's not so easy nowadays. There's not a lot of movement in the higher education sector. Unless you've got a short-term contract.

Academics who are at my position on the salary scale cost far too much to contemplate.' Mattie feels like a robot mouthing mumbo jumbo. Her mother is trying hard to concentrate but with little hope of understanding.

'So there's no chance then? I always like to think you'll come back home one day. But I'm probably just a fond old woman who's living in the past.'

'It's called social mobility, Mother. No one of my generation ends up round the corner from her mother, or in the same part of town where she grew up.'

'Your brothers have. But that's different, I suppose. They haven't exactly gone up in the world, like you. Although they're always tried their best...'

'I bet they don't live in each other's pockets though, do they? Billy could never stand Tommy. And Tommy used to bully Billy something stupid when they were kids at school. How often do they see each other now? Be honest.'

Mattie's mother doesn't like to hear this kind of talk. She likes to think of all her children getting on.

'They'd come up trumps in a crisis, soon enough. Same as they would for you. You'd only have to ask.'

Mattie is sceptical. She can still remember Tommy's response when she told him she was lesbian. 'Poofters I can tolerate', he said. 'That means more crumpet on the street for me. But lesbians. That's horrible. With less of it to go around, it means some blokes aren't getting any.'

'Did you tell me on the phone that Billy isn't happy with himself?'

'He's lost his job again. Probably for good this time. No one's taking any body on at present. Except at Tescos in the market place. But even then, it's only women.'

'What's become of the factory where he used to work with Tommy and my father?'

'It was closed down before your father died. Bankrupt, so they say. The land was cleared and turned into a car park. Not much work in that for men with families to feed.'

'Or women', Mattie says. 'Women need jobs just as much as men these days. Especially if they're on their own with kids, or single.' She speaks as though her mother doesn't understand these things.

Her mother wants to put the record straight.

'I've always worked', she says. 'Nothing very grand I must admit. But it made the difference when you were small. It didn't pay for everything, you know, that scholarship to grammar school. There was always extras.'

'I know. I know.' Mattie doesn't want to get into the usual flair of irritation and reprisals. 'And I'm very grateful. Where would I be today without the chance you gave me? Stuck here in Holderness, with a lot of others getting old, who can't find jobs. Still believing that civilisation begins and ends at York.'

'There's nothing wrong with Holderness, our Mattie – that a little loyalty wouldn't cure. Some of us have lived here all our lives and wouldn't thank you for a move to London. Not with all those criminals and drug addicts we hear about. Settling down and having children may not be your way – but it's what the people round here do. Respectable people. Who don't go off at half cock over airy fairy notions'. Her mother clashes the cups and plates into a pile and sweeps the crumbs from the table with her hand. 'You'll be wanting to see your brothers whilst you're here?' The question has an air of accusation. 'They always ask about you.'

Mattie wants to cry. She wants to bury her head into her mother's breast and start again. Admit she's frightened. Admit she's sinking. Try to make some sense of what's gone wrong. See if something can be salvaged. Instead she lets herself be backed into the same old corners and comes out fighting in all the usual ways. Which leaves her feeling distant and disliked. Some kind of misfit in her mother's eyes.

The old lady takes the dishes to the kitchen and washes each in turn. Her eyes are wet with tears. A daughter should be special to a mother. Closer than her sons. Someone to rely on. But not this girl. She shakes her head and sighs.

'It isn't always for the best', she says again, 'to be so clever. But without much common sense. No normal feelings.'

'I've made the bed up in the back.' She means the room that Mattie slept in as a child. But which she has long since ceased to think about as Mattie's room, despite its little name plaque on the door. It's still quite early but the sitting-room is feeling claustrophobic, with conversation growing tense.

'I could do with an early night.' Mattie makes her excuses.

Her mother fetches cocoa and an extra blanket.

'The sheets are aired. Do you want a bottle?' She pulls the flowered curtains shut and runs her hand along the window sill to check for dust. 'Doesn't get much use these days. Will you be warm enough?' She settles for material considerations without a repertoire to talk of feelings. No one touches her these days. She can't remember anyone – besides the toddlers – thinking she might like a cuddle.

Mattie pours herself a double scotch and buries herself beneath a pile of blankets. Her mother hasn't got round to duvets. She considers 'continental quilts' to be some kind of foreign innovation that must be treated with suspicion.

'Duvets mean nothing to us in Holderness', she says. 'We like our candlewick and eiderdown.'

At one time this room was Mattie's sanctuary. During the day a pile of scatter cushions turned the bed into a sofa. She had a kettle and some mugs for coffee, the Dancette in the corner playing Elvis. After school she'd come up here to do her homework, once the kitchen table was required for tea. She'd keep her schoolbooks in the cupboard under padlock and hide her diary in the space behind the headboard. The flowered walls were covered up with Elvis. His sultry eyes and glossy pan-stick scowl consoling her from every possible direction. He was her friend. Not the macho sex machine depicted by the magazines. But someone to confide in. To talk to in the empty night. During all those months when the thought of Alice Morrison made her blush. When she learned to touch herself in ways that made her body burn and wetness gather in her cunt. Her brothers still sharing bunk beds in another room and her parents snoring through the wall next door. Elvis knew. But no one else. Not for ages. Until, of course, she had to tell.

Later, when she became a feminist, Elvis had to be denounced as patriarchal. The exaggerated invention of men's obsession with themselves. The icon of an industry that thrived on turning women into morons. But she could never quite believe it. Not about Elvis. She took his pictures down all right, and put them with his records at the back of the wardrobe. Out of sight. And, for a while, out of mind. But he escaped the general purge of sexist rubbish that got bundled into dustbins with the rest, once her conversion was complete. Her buddy. Her old friend. More like a teddy bear than a phallic symbol. The one who shared her secrets in this room when there was no one else around to understand.

'Your father was the one for poetry. I don't suppose you ever knew that, did you?'

It is the next day and Mattie and her mother are trying hard to find some common ground.

'I did actually. Last time I was here, and we were sorting through his clothes and papers I found his note book. You told me he was an emotional man but couldn't show it.'

'Did I? I don't remember now. I was so busy trying not to cry. Elsie said I should let it all come out. But I couldn't do it. I've cried more since. When I've been on my own. With no one here to see.'

This is one of the few traits that Mattie and her mother share. The fear that crying makes you vulnerable. And gives other people power. 'Tell no one anything about your business', is a phrase Mattie used to think came out of the Bible. Her mother's version of the ten commandments. When Mattie was a child her mother would take the labels off tins of beans and processed peas, before she put them in the dustbin, so anxious was she that any information about the precarious condition of their family fortunes would leak out to the neighbourhood, through the loose talk of the dustbin men. She knew from all the gossip she collected from her cronies that it was a big mistake to trust anyone with your secrets. Someone with a stock of secrets can't help but let them slip. It makes the teller temporarily more interesting and gives them power. The philosophy of the early Women's Movement caused Mattie to rethink her early training in repression. Now she is not opposed to talking about herself – especially if she has an audience and can keep her distance. But in intimate discussions she is still more attuned to other women's fears than making revelations about her own. She claims her sensitivity to others comes from her political commitment to their liberation. But she collects information like a squirrel, to be stashed away and used on some occasion in the future. Not always with integrity. A tendency she makes quite certain not to delegate to others.

'Tell me about my father writing poems.'

'It started when you were at the grammar school. He didn't understand it really. You so clever. He felt so stupid. You never used to tell us very much about your lessons. And we didn't know what questions we should ask. You lived in your own little world most of the time. Up in that back room. Anyway, he met a chap at work who did readings round the clubs. Monologues mostly, and funny tales about the pit. It set your father doodling. And once he'd drunk enough, to give him courage, he'd read a couple out himself. They seemed to go down well, by all accounts. Women weren't allowed in those days so I never heard him do it.'

'What sort of poems did he write?'

'Well, you've seen them I suppose. What you might expect. Poems about his garden and about the factory.'

To be honest Mattie hadn't looked too closely at the notebook. She was feeling hemmed in at the time and just waiting for the chance to shoot off back to London.

'Remind me.' Mattie wants her mother to look at her directly and stop straightening the ornaments.

'He used to think the bosses fixed up the machines to

turn the workers into slaves. He didn't like the job that much.'

'Why did he never complain about it?'

'What would be the point? He had to do it. We needed the money. Your brothers were down there too by then. He wasn't one to make a fuss.'

'Maybe he should have made a fuss', Mattie says. 'Joined the union. Gone on strike for better wages and conditions.'

Mattie's mother sighs and looks beyond the window into dull grey light. Outside the sky is pewter.

'It's a car park now', she says, 'and your father is long past worrying about it, so why should you?'

It was apathy like this that used to drive Mattie to despair, during countless bitter arguments with her parents. In the years before she chose to stay away. No one in her family, including her mother, was very angry. Or critical about their lot. They took what came with equanimity and didn't hold out hope for any change. Outbursts from Mattie put them at loggerheads. Her insults varied over time from lumpen proles to sexist bastards (her father and her brothers) and narrow minded bigots. Arguments about socialism gave way to arguments about sex. They had no words, except those to do with sickness and disease, to make any sense of what she said about herself.

'I can't take it on', her mother said. 'Was it that school that did it to you? All those girls and women without husbands. Where did I go wrong? Was it letting you play cowboys with the lads? Instead of something feminine?'

'Why can't you understand?' Mattie would be shouting now. 'I'm not a freak. This is my choice. Support me.'

Mattie expected her mother's immediate approval.

She didn't care about her father or her brothers. Nothing less would do. She had no time for explanations.

'What you say makes no sense at all to us', her mother's usual response, 'we live in Holderness.'

Twenty odd years later and there is still no easy way of speaking the taboo. Not asking is her mother's way of being tactful. That, and not wanting to hear of 'goings on' she cannot comprehend.

'Is there anyone . . . special? You never say . . .'

Tears gather at the back of Mattie's eyes. She is terrified to lose control. But years of training help to stem the flow. Her mother can see she isn't happy.

'Has it all been worth it then? This life?' She stretches out her hand. And lets it fall. The moment passes.

Soon Tommy is banging on the door to take them for a ride into the countryside. At forty-nine he is already old, his stomach straining at the belt, his red face furrowed in the self same question as his father's. As though life has dealt them each a common hand and reaped a similar response.

'There's a nice little pub at Ribbleswick where they do good bar food. Will that please you Mother?'

Their mother shrugs her shoulders.

'You're the expert Tommy, when it comes to pubs.'

They drive in fractured silence through straggling back roads, between dejected fields of mud and autumn mist. Tommy asks Mattie the odd question about London and what sort of car she drives. He points out landmarks to his mother. At Ribbleswick the pub is almost empty. They wait to be seated by a brown-eyed boy in a striped waistcoat who writes the number of their table on the order. Beyond the kitchen door, the ping of the microwave announces the arrival of the chef's special and a vegetarian lasagna. As Mattie struggles with the pasta the brown-eyed boy plays Pool against himself.

'I could have made a better job of this at home.' Mattie's mother folds her paper napkin with authority. 'And for half the price.'

Somewhere in another city Jess is trying out a new relationship. Her eyes alight with laughter. The feelings of excitement and obsession that always give the game away. When sex is new and unfamiliar. That fills her head with nonsense and distractions. And her body with desire. That leaves little room for kindness or regret when, in the odd moment, now and then, she wonders what's become of Mattie.

Four

Alice Morrison is startled out of her customary after dinner doze beside the fire by the persistent ringing of the telephone in the room next door. Orlando is curled up on her lap snoring loudly. She yawns lazily as Alice climbs stiffly to her feet. The cat arches and stretches her back, flexing and relaxing each delicate limb in turn, before padding in leisurely fashion towards the study, to see what all the commotion is about.

Alice's face is pale. Furrows cut and crease her brow. She pushes capable fingers through black wiry curls that are etched at the temples now with threads of grey and white. She nods in resignation as the voice of the caller stretches on. Orlando can tell this is a matter of some consequence because Alice is looking sombre. Orlando doesn't take kindly to disruption. She likes the lethargy of a quiet evening by the fire with no interruptions. Perhaps a little Mozart. The warmth of Alice's soft woollen skirt and strong gentle fingers twisting in her fur. A substantial bowl of steamed fish around supper time. And no reason to confront the chill and wary streets. Or feel compelled to defend the garden and the boundaries of her territory from intrusion by the marmalade tom from next door. She licks her paws with careful attention, separating each webbed toe in turn with the rough edge of her tongue. Obsessional. But with half an ear attuned to the note of clipped enquiry and obvious anxiety in Alice's voice.

'But I've heard next to nothing from you since Natalia.' Alice says the name with difficulty.

'You know me', the voice says. 'Full of shit. But I'm not like that any more. I've grown up Alice. I've had to.'

Alice looks sceptical.

'Just for a few days. I need to see you.'

After eight years of silence – except for the odd postcard and phone call at Christmas – this is a presumption. A presumption that Alice will feel the same. Will drop everything. Will be available at a moment's notice. Is still alive, for God's sake! After eight years – how can she be so sure? But then, the request is not about Alice. It rarely is. It's as though Alice, on the other end of the telephone, doesn't seriously exist. Is somehow invisible. Is but the metaphor for another's need.

'It's not a good time for me.' Alice tries to live up to the reputation she has acquired for being assertive. Acquired, it must be said, from those who mistake her sensible shoes and steely gaze for an unflinching strength of purpose. 'It's the beginning of term. The new girls need a lot of settling. There's university forms to fill in and references to write.' She sounds panic stricken rather than convincing. Orlando bats her head against Alice's shins, sensing that disaster looms. Recognising the unmistakable assault on Alice's defences by the indefatigable Mattie Reed. She should be saying No with more conviction.

The voice on the phone is pleading now. Orlando can detect the shift into another repertoire. The appeal to old emotions, not yet quite extinguished. The note of calculated desperation working the manipulation. The absolute conviction that Alice, in the end, will never let her drown. Orlando watches in frustration, noting the slight sag and release of tension in Alice's shoulders. Her slide from resolution into capitulation. Against all her better judgement.

'Where are you now?' Alice takes a pen from the desk drawer to scribble a note of train times and a telephone number. 'What time on Saturday? Can you make it a little later? All right then. Oxford station at seven. I'll collect you in the car.'

Alice sighs as she switches off the study light and carries Orlando back into the sitting room, to her chair beside the fire. She is feeling positioned once again. Picked up by Mattie, like a familiar melody, to play along with for a while, without any sense of the disruption it may cause to Alice's routine and self-esteem. And Alice, despite everything she knows about Mattie's strong capacity to cause damage to her own well being, is allowing it to happen. Turned inside out again with little effort, like an old sock.

In London, Mattie pulls the duvet round her head to

obliterate the reticence she can detect in Alice's prevarication. She lies amidst the jumble of pillows and covers that denote the best part of another day spent in bed. She forces herself into the shower, avoiding the dark shadowed eyes that peer back at her from the mirror. Jess's tooth brush still lies abandoned on the bathroom shelf, her towel still betraying the faint smell of perfume and French soap that makes her continuing presence palpable. The tears stream down Mattie's face as the shower water washes over her like flotsam. Alice is her last resort.

At seven as usual the alarm clock on the bedside table signals the end of all reasonable attempts to sleep. Alice takes refuge in her regular routines to contemplate the duties of the day. Orlando is curled at the bottom of the bed sinking her claws into the status quo. She stirs drowsily, widening a quizzical eye in the dim light to gauge the seriousness of Alice's intentions. Now that she's had a night to sleep on it and change her mind. She should phone Mattie back. Orlando represents the voice of sanity. Phone back to say she's changed her mind. Say something has come up around a woman called Jemima or Phoebe or Mary Poppins. Say any name that comes to mind. Say she's in love and cannot be distracted. Say she's married. Say anything, for God's sake. But just say No. Without responsibility – except for her own well being – Orlando is rarely troubled by guilt or by dilemma. Unlike Alice, who has a strong sense of duty. But Alice can't afford another dose of Mattie. Orlando wishes she would be more sensible. Alice shakes her off the bed in irritation.

'What do you know about anything? A geriatric, agrophobic cat...'

This kind of response does not bode well, or suggest to Orlando that Alice has come to her senses overnight. In which case, Alice might just as well jump in the Isis right away, and save the world a bucketful of grief.

Alice carries Orlando, still scowling, still reproaching her about her masochistic, weedy disposition, to the cat flap, and propels her through it, with a careful but determined toe in the region of her bottom.

'Try the Thames by London Bridge before the ice melts...'

She fills her favourite mug with Lapsang Souchong tea and climbs back into bed to listen to the weather forecast and the news headlines. At 7.47 precisely she steps into a piping hot shower. At 7.56 she brushes the tangles from her greying hair and leaves the wiry curls to dry according to their own volition. At 8.10 she makes toast and ginger marmalade whilst Orlando, having finished with the great outdoors and her brief exploration through time, crunches biscuits and diced rabbit from a blue pottery dish. Orlando continually refuses to become a vegetarian, despite Alice's repeated efforts to coax her into ethical eating. She doesn't like vegetarians. She is adamant.

'You're getting fat and lazy.' Alice grumbles as she piles a second helping of diced rabbit into the dish.

At 8.25 Alice goes upstairs to dress. She chooses a Harris tweed skirt, cream shirt and caramel cardigan. Somewhere beneath the elasticated waist and tired folds of wool and cashmere, her body hides from close inspection. Withdrawn and unloved. She sighs, contemplating the disdain with which Mattie will be bound to view her obvious deterioration. She has made it her practice

recently to avoid mirrors, but she won't be able to avoid
Mattie's scrutiny. Or prevent herself from turning off the
light when they make love. They always make love. In
the end. Usually in a precious and greedy moment of
belated intimacy, before Mattie begins to pack her suitcase and check out flight departure times, as she
prepares to continue with her life. Without Alice.

Alice sighs. She throws her toast crusts to the birds.
Plugs in the answering machine, switches on the burglar
alarm and shuts the door behind her. She leaves Orlando
in charge as usual. Watching from the cottage window,
like an old lady who now tastes the world exclusively
through leaded glass, and measures out her life in coffee
spoons. The same scene every morning. And – within a
whisker either way – at exactly the same time. Lending
the illusion of precision and predictability to what is in
reality a very contradictory existence.

Each morning of the school year Alice walks in the
brief distance from the yellow stone cottage where she
lives, to the wrought iron gates of the Independent Day
School for girls where she is the Headmistress.

The trees along the lane are umbra and ochre in the
autumn light. Inside the gates and across the sweep of
lawn, a swirl of beech and chestnut leaves are chasing
the wind towards transitory drifts of red and gold.
Stubbs, the school gardener, is already at work with his
rake and wheelbarrow, intent upon restoring order to the
turbulence of nature. He is losing the battle. A grey
squirrel darts fitfully through the vacant stretch of green
towards the safety of an ancient oak and peers neurotic-
ally from its falling branches to where the gardener's

rake threatens to disturb a secret stash of nuts and berries.

As if on a conveyor belt, smart, brightly coloured cars, of French and Japanese extraction, driven by slightly balding, slightly dissipated dons, or else their harassed wives, pull into the pebbled driveway of the school. And deposit daughters, wearing belted gabardines and boaters, with fleeting waves and hurried kisses, onto the steps outside the main entrance. Alice watches the drivers, as she frequently does, speed back towards the city. To be busy being free or famous somewhere else. A preference she might have chosen for herself had she not got landed with the role of functionary. At the select end of the market, to be sure. But still stuck in the service class.

She watches the cars disappear towards secluded studies in Magdalen and Keble, where research is no doubt under way. And the occasional charismatic tutor draws crowds to early morning lectures about the impact of James Joyce on Irish literature. She remembers the days of Alan Taylor, denounced at Balliol in the fifties as a fornicator, delivering each, perfectly constructed exposition to a tightly packed and appreciative collection of disciples. Without a single note, or interruption. Immaculately timed to begin and end exactly on the hour. One of her few heroes in those unhappy early days of undergraduate existence.

The wives do not return to quiet studies in solid turrets, on the whole. Despite the intervening years of women's liberation. More likely they return to large and dusty kitchens in Jericho and Summertown, where fractured affairs are stopped and started. Where grubby novels get written on scrubbed pine tables and other people's theses are occasionally prepared for publication.

Where those with social consciences still gather to drink coffee and plan poetry readings in aid of refugees. And children tumble home from school at half past three, demanding crisps and beef burgers for their tea. Despite what happens to the forests in Brazil.

Henley Manor is not the most exclusive school for girls in Oxfordshire. But it carries a strong local reputation for exam results and dedicated teaching, despite its somewhat shabby stucco and slightly jaded old world charm. The kind of school that is seriously out of date if your concern is education for the masses. But delightfully nostalgic if what you want is preferential treatment for selected daughters of the chattering classes. It's a reputation which Alice has worked hard to consolidate. During the last eight years or so, the school has become her life. Partly by default. In part by design. She has come a long way since the days she first met Mattie in a dismal, faintly pretentious grammar school, in a nondescript East Riding town called Holderness. Nothing much to recommend it except a rather beautiful church and a harmless population of aspiring white collar workers and factory hands. Surrounded by miles and miles of well regulated fields that turned golden in the late summer and led, in the passage of time, to York. Apart from the occasional oddity like Mattie, St Swithuns Grammar School catered for the daughters of the bourgeoisie – small shopkeepers, accountants and works managers. Alice was twenty-three. It was her first teaching job after leaving home and leaving university. She was up tight, self absorbed and scared to death about what the outside world might have in store. St Swithuns seemed like a safe enough place to make a start. That is, until she fell in love with Mattie Reed.

Since then Alice has moved school three times. On

each occasion to a more senior position. And now, she is in charge. To all intents and purposes she is a formidable woman. Which is what the parents and the governors believe. And why they pay her money. To reflect traditional family values. To keep their girls out of the grip of undesirables. And to propel them into the most lucrative professions, via one or other of the better universities.

Alice lives up to her reputation quite convincingly, most of the time. Made plausible by the sort of voice that can quell an insurrection at five hundred paces, and the kind of attention to detail in her wardrobe that causes Mattie to screw up her face in horror and say 'let's go shopping'. Now the prospect of seeing Mattie again causes Alice more than mere sartorial concern. The façade she uses to face the world, could be revealed as tenuous in the extreme. As when a huge and surging seascape of eccentricity and confusion is held in order simply by the lightness of a vapour. And by Alice's obsession with routines. During recent years she has taken time to shore up and cement her defences, build dams and walls and barriers to withstand the most persistent breaches. But she is not invincible. The strands of weakness, exposed by close association with Mattie throughout a number of emotional disasters, have poignant origins and hidden scars. Memories that get up at night, and stomp around her dreams and nightmares in big hob nail boots.

The pattern is familiar. Mattie arrives, full of energy and big ideas. Alice treads the usual fine line between abject secrecy about her sexuality and dangerous obsession. Mattie berates her, in the process of time, for her hypocrisy. She becomes restless. She turns her enthusiasm to transitory distractions – solidarity with a bunch of women workers on strike for equal pay, the women's music festival in Michigan, pressure on the local council to provide a refuge for battered women. And sex. New sex with the latest of her acolytes and groupies. Most recently, and disastrously so far as Alice is concerned, her virtual elopement with a crazy woman from the Bolshoi called Natalia.

Mattie leaves, full of complaints and accusations. Alice picks over the disaster and remakes her life. Alice, being the kind of woman she is, blames herself. Particularly the fault line in her personality called lesbian. That inner demon, alter ego, suppressed for years but always looking to break free, especially when Alice is distracted by her passions. With each fresh disaster and unfulfilled desire, she shores up her defences even more, so that no one, not even the most assiduous observer of lesbian repression, can guess she has a heart that bleeds, or thoughts that contradict her brisk, professional appearance.

'Good morning, Miss Morrison.' Alice hurries through the crush of girls waiting by the main door to be let in. She pauses to check with Miranda Lawson about her application to Girton and to remind Clancy Williams that purple combat boots do not constitute regulation footwear at Henley Manor School.

'What do your parents think? Am I to tolerate a pupil of mine looking like a boot boy?'

'A what?'

'Never mind. I'm obviously out of touch. What I want to know is whether or not your mother is happy with your footwear and whether I am to continue treating you like the soft, sweet girl I know you still to be.'

Clancy pulls a face. 'She can cope. But you're being sexist, Miss Morrison.'

'Heaven forbid!' Alice allows the merest suggestion of a smile to pass across her eyes.

'Actually Miss Morrison, I was thinking about a nose ring for my birthday. Would that be allowed – in this day and age?'

'Don't push your luck, Clancy. I think it's time I had a conversation with your mother.'

Alice unlocks the door to her study and calls to Hilda to bring a pot of strong black coffee and the morning post. The smell of old books, some of them are first editions, and French polish are like second nature to her now. The mahogany shelves, which line the walls, are as old as the house, which now acts as the administrative block and offices for senior members of the school staff. It was built by the Victorians to reflect the solidity of family life, industry and empire and became a school shortly after the First World War. Previous incumbents of the Head's study have added two oak tables and a large mahogany desk, various leather armchairs, and a richly patterned Axminster carpet, by now a little threadbare at the door and window. Alice's contribution is four oil paintings, each showing enigmatic and flamboyant women, whose eyes look down upon her with amusement. But other than this, nothing. She lets her own eight years of coffee smell and dust settle in the corners with the rest, becoming part of the tradition.

A French window provides the only natural light, opening onto a small terrace, and enabling Alice to keep a careful eye on what she likes to call 'the grounds'. She watches from the window as the usual late comers scurry along the driveway, inventing and rehearsing their excuses about buses that get stuck in traffic and alarms that fail to ring.

Hilda puts the coffee pot on the table by the fire

and takes a suspicious look at Alice. She has been her secretary since Alice became the Head of Henley Manor School. She is a crusty, temperamental individual. A harsh judge of character with an addiction to gossip. Alice tolerates her. And the equivocation is mutual.

'Bad night?' Hilda misses nothing.

'So, so. How about you Hilda? What's new?'

Hilda sniffs, banging down the cup and saucer with her usual absence of grace. She is a small round woman with a button nose and two spots of rouge rubbed hastily into each round cheek. Her red hair – 'auburn lights' according to the description on the bottle – is cropped thick around her face like tufts of hennaed thatch. In her thirties she kept a boarding house for actors and has never quite renounced her end-of-the-pier appearance. Alice knows the signs.

'Trouble at mill?' She tries again.

'Of course, it's none of my business.' Hilda's usual disclaimer. Her eyes sparkle with an impatience to impart her information. 'Apparently Miss Armitage is seeing rather a lot of Steven Rowntree.'

Alice is slow to make connections. 'Could it be the need to work together in preparation for the school concert in January?'

Hilda tuts impatiently, wiping a splash of milk from the corner of the oak table with her index finger.

'You know about his reputation!' Hilda fixes Alice with a knowing look. 'The only man in a staff room full of women. Little boy lost. Struggling with a wife who "doesn't understand" him. A total pushover when it comes to lunatic causes. Preaching revolution. Wendy Armitage – young and gullible. Wrongly convinced that she's a woman of the world. Need I go on'

Alice smiles. 'Steven is an excellent musician. First class examination results. The girls adore him.'

'That's precisely my point', Hilda flounces towards the study door. 'He's dangerous, Miss Morrison. Don't say I didn't warn you!' She bangs the door behind her.

Alice sinks back into her favourite armchair. Its scuffed leather cushions adjusting to the familiar curve and weight of her body. She has grown heavy at the waist of late and a stiffness has settled in her back that wasn't there before. In the mirror her face looks creased around the eyes and a deepening furrow cuts across her brow. She feels stodgy and unfit and out of sorts. Her skin is pale, and in this light, even grey. Last night she didn't sleep of course, which doesn't help the ageing process. She's not in the best of shape to be expecting Mattie. Though why it matters any more, and why she cares about being discovered in a state of quickening decay, is academic. There is nothing much between them now. Except a legacy of occasional delight and lots of sorrow.

At six o'clock precisely, the key turns in the lock and Alice switches off the burglar alarm. Orlando has spent the day padding restlessly from room to room, nursing her wrath to keep it warm. By teatime she's in a miserable mood. A vengeance she has only partly satisfied by disembowelling a fieldmouse.

'You're disgusting!' Alice drops the residual entrails into the dust bin. She carries no particular torch for furry animals but she dislikes murder as a point of principle. Orlando is unrepentant about the consequences of her nature. Something she thinks Alice should understand. She licks her paws. She wants to know why?

'Because!'

Orlando looks sceptical.

'Because it's only for a day or two. Because she sounds in trouble. Because she doesn't have the kind of family she can turn to. Because there's no way she can touch me any more. Because everything is different now. So it's quite safe to be a friend.'

Orlando scowls, detecting bullshit. According to Orlando there's nothing safe about befriending Mattie in her hour of need. It is precisely on these occasions when she should be left to her own devices. Because it's when she's most demanding and self-obsessed. Knowing Mattie from previous encounters, she'd soon latch on to someone else. She isn't noted for a lack of volunteers. Of course, it's just possible that Orlando could be over reacting. It could be that Mattie's changed. Maybe she should try to behave as though this is just a routine visit. Pretend Mattie's like the plumber, simply coming to service the boiler and bleed the radiators. Of no greater significance than a random visit by Alice's brother, on his way to a business meeting in the Midlands. Not worry about Alice's feelings. Or stick her nose in when Mattie tries to get Alice into bed. We have to assume that Alice, being human, must know best. Orlando returns her attention to her paws and to behaving like a normal cat. She sniffs the air disdainfully and exits, stage right, into the sitting room.

On Saturday evening the fast train from London is running late, which helps to exaggerate the state of jagged anticipation that has been tightening its grip on Alice's equilibrium all afternoon. She drinks another coffee in the station buffet. Across the road and by the bus stop she sees two women kissing. The kind of feather light – but consequential – first brush of lips, that takes new would-be lovers by surprise. They are holding briefcases and bags of shopping. Their passion suddenly ignited, amidst the small scale details of an ordinary street. That marks the moment when the dye is cast. The decision taken to make love. At the next, first possible opportunity. Alice watches as the bus arrives and leaves. And as one of the women wanders off alone. The other caught in the steamy blur of windows, that makes Alice wonder what is usual. Already a passenger and once again anonymous beneath her bags of shopping. En route to the suburbs. But having stepped inside the danger zone.

The station tannoy announces the arrival of the London train. Alice watches the thin scratch of metal twist into sight as it curls around the corner and into the home straight. She can remember as a girl, during her time at university, the way the steam and smoke hung in the mists beside the river. The taste of tar and burning coal flaking the station platform with a layer of fine soot. Trains were exciting to her then. Like fuming dragons roaring into life, with no pretence at moderation. Promising adventure. Now they're merely functional and brash. You're lucky if they come on time. And make it to their destination without breaking down.

Alice searches the empty faces, framed in dusty glass, as the train scrapes along the platform to a standstill. She is expecting colour. Brightness unfolding like a peacock's tail. A woman who can cut through drabness and delay – the way a laser beam can slash the black sky into a shaft of light. She is not expecting to find Mattie looking quite so small and insignificant.

'Dear Alice', Mattie says. 'You're looking well! Sorry it's been such an age. I don't know where the years go to any more, do you?'

It's a question Alice could answer with a fair degree of feeling. They disappear in the effort to survive. To pick up pieces. To deal with sadness and not to live amidst regret. In finding satisfaction in a job well done, and watching awkward, often temperamental, teenagers turn into young women with attitude, and with a better stake in the future than Alice has ever found the confidence to feel.

'What's the matter Mattie? You look terrible. Are you ill or something? You've lost so much weight.'

She is clearly trying not to cry.

'I'm having a bit of a rough time, Alice. Desperate really. Drowning – if you know what I mean. I'm sorry to dump myself on you like this – given everything. I thought if I could stay with you for a while ... I know I shouldn't bother you ...'

Mattie's voice trails off into silence. Her eyes fixed on the middle distance, trying to retain control.

Alice takes the suitcase and walks with her to the car. Unsure what constitutes 'a while'.

'You must know, Mattie, that I won't be used again by you, in ways that take me ages to recover. I can't give you any more than temporary shelter. Do you understand?'

Alice is right, of course. And Mattie knows it in her heart. But these are not the words she wants to hear right now. Coming like the smash of more rejection. Tears are spilling down her cheeks as she walks in silence to the car. Against her better judgement Alice takes her arm.

Part Two

Five

If Alice had been born a boy, she would probably be a colonel in the British army by now. Her father and her uncle were military men. All her brothers were schooled for, and graduated to, the officer class. The army was in their blood. So much so, they were at a loss to know what to do with a girl, especially one who had no interest in becoming a soldier's wife. During the earliest years of her childhood the family lived in India and Africa. Wherever Alice's father was required to defend the last rites of the British Empire and its interests overseas. Alice could remember large colonial houses and the kind of heat that scorched the earth and burned the pallid skin of all those who were not genetically – or politically – supposed to be there.

In Africa Alice's mother employed the help of local women as cooks and nursemaids when her brood of toddlers was small. The women kept their distance and she kept hers, living a solitary existence on the fringes of her husband's life. When the boys needed to be sent to school she settled back in Dorset, a short distance from her husband's parents. She woke each morning early, around five, feeling as though her mind was buried under a black cloud that lifted only gradually as the day wore on. Sometimes not at all. In the early days, she cried in private, struggling to keep calm when Alice climbed into her vast white linen bed or when the in-laws arrived to offer advice and issue their instructions.

'The boys must go to Dunstan Lacy. Good army connections. Excellent Head.'

Alice's mother kissed them goodbye on the steps of the house chosen by her husband, as her husband's father sounded the horn impatiently and whisked away her children to somewhere she had never seen. To be cloned as military men by the excellent Head, and tucked into dormitories at night by the excellent Head's excellent wife.

By now Alice's grandmother was in charge.

'When you're old enough', she told Alice, 'we'll find a school that will be suitable for you. Somewhere you can learn music and your alphabet and dancing. Then, when you grow up, you'll fall in love with an army officer or diplomat and become much more useful than your poor dear mother. An asset to your husband, not a source of worry.'

But three boys sent to boarding school soon used up

all the money. Even with the generous allowances and ex-patriot connections. The option found for Alice was a small, fee paying day school in a neighbouring town. Which provided the trappings of tradition, but on the cheap. When Alice was about eight, her mother was pronounced mad. She was rather grateful for the chance to retreat totally into illness, as a way of avoiding her responsibilities, and the total absence of control she felt in every aspect of her life. She spent more and more time in bed. A retinue of nurses came to administer pills and vile looking medicine from an assortment of brown, ridged bottles. Alice was allowed to sit with her for an hour each day. Frequently she watched where her mother's mouth hung open in some absent state of sedated sleep. Other times her mother wept, drawing long velvet curtains across shafts of sunlight, and drifting into darkened rooms to rest. Oblivious to Alice.

Alice also retreated – into a life inside her head, in which she invented buccaneers and highwaymen to talk to. More exciting than soldiers and invalids.

During the holidays, when her brothers came home from school, she could hardly speak to them. They were strange creatures to her – boys. Not to be respected or trusted. They always arrived bringing noise and danger into the house.

'Tie her up', Crispin, being the eldest, was allowed to organise the others into games. 'Alice is the hostage.'

'But who will save her?' Gerald and Tim soon lost interest. 'She's only a useless girl.' Mostly they ignored her or shook salt into her custard when she wasn't looking. Once they made her practice kissing. Crispin demonstrated what he called the French kiss. The smell of Crispin's sweat was overpowering, her breath catching as his thick tongue circled her mouth and pushed in between her teeth. Once, when she was about ten, they made her remove her dress and took it in turns to poke her tiny, pubescent breasts with their grubby bitten finger nails. They laughed at the little spread of hair that was springing unannounced, and quite mysteriously, from the dark place between her thighs.

'Don't think of telling any one about our games or we'll cut your fingers off'. Crispin pushed her roughly through the hall.

It was of slight consolation to Alice that the brothers were equally horrid to each other. Bragging and boasting and trying to be best. They weren't the kind of inspiration to make Alice feel easily impressed. But she envied them what seemed like major privileges compared to her own humdrum existence. They had cricket bats and bicycles with dropped handlebars for Christmas and spoke of schools that sounded serious and exciting.

Girls were a different kind of mystery to her. She wasn't allowed to mix with village children or ask her classmates home to tea, in case her mother's madness became the source of local gossip 'so damaging' to her husband and his family. All the girls at school had names like Sophie, Claire or Caroline. They played on violins and practised elocution. They went to ballet class and dressed in cotton frocks with ribbons in their hair. Alice wanted to be their friend but found she couldn't, somehow, get accustomed to their ways. She watched them in the playground playing skipping games and hopscotch. Usually they didn't ask her to join in and she became quite used to being on her own.

Occasionally her father made fleeting visits home, looking tanned and handsome. He had a dressing room and bedroom at the back of the house. 'Overlooking the orchard and the downs is so soothing after the frenzied heat of Africa', he told Alice.

Alice did not expect to find him in her mother's room. He had no reason to explain. No one could be expected to sleep against the sound of weeping in the night. Alice was made to sleep on her own. Why shouldn't he? She spent the months when he was away longing for his arrival. The one person in the family she hardly knew and seldom saw, she hoped that he might be the one to love her. But on his increasingly infrequent visits home he treated Alice with awkward indifference. Unused to girls, he could not imagine her interests or emotions. He preferred his sons. He knew their ways. Indulged their appetites for sports and competition. 'Why weren't you born a boy, Alice?' he said, 'I'd know better what to do with you then.'

Sometimes the suggestion was appealing. Boys could wear shorts and climb trees. They could drop their muddy boots and discarded jackets on the floor as they raced off in opposite directions. No one stopped them when they interrupted conversations. But as soon as one or other became the centre of attention, the other two got bored, and picked a fight to get back into the limelight. In time her father or her grandmother would lose their patience and pack them off to bed with threats of retribution in the morning. In such moments of adult irritation, Alice, much to her dismay, was held up as the model of obedience.

'Why can't you take a leaf out of Alice's book, you boys? She doesn't shout to get her way. She doesn't leave her bedroom like a pig stye.'

'She doesn't ever open her mouth', Crispin muttered with disgruntled animosity. 'Miss goody, goody, stupid girl.'

Left increasingly to her own devices, Alice took refuge in the countryside and in the play ground of her imagination. Each summer she built a den in the woods. A secret place to go to when her mother was crying, or to escape the attention of her brothers. Here she could invent conversations with her friends and write stories. The bracken grew high in the early summer, its tight furled buds unwinding into light green fans of feathery leaves. Here she could strip shoots from sycamore and willow to make bows and arrows. And gallop through the bracken at full tilt as though she was on horseback. Usually an outlaw. Beyond the woodland was the sea. Cut off from the land by white chalk cliffs. Here ancient ledges twisted their precarious route along the edges of the rock, where a fearless child like Alice could become a pirate, inching her way to hidden caves and squats of outcrop. On her back, in an old leather satchel, she carried homemade lemonade, cheese and bread, which she had raided from the kitchen in the night. And which tasted so much better out of doors, gulped down hungrily against the smack of ocean and the screech of herring gulls, flying with the wind like paper kites.

'What are you good at?' Alice's father asked, before returning his attention to the newspaper. 'It's time you went away to boarding school. To make something useful of yourself. I'll ask your grandmother to make enquiries.'

She couldn't answer his questions. She had no idea what good or useful meant. The boys were neither, so far as she could tell, but yet her father was clearly proud of them.

'When you're an officer of the Queen . . .' he would say to each in turn, followed by some exciting promise about the kind of world they could expect to inherit. It made them even more unbearable. And Alice even more convinced she'd never be allowed to win her father's approval.

In fact she saw him less and less after this. He went to live with a blond-haired woman in Switzerland whose name she didn't know. At some point there must have been a divorce. Alice found herself dispatched to Devon to be groomed for girlhood in a boarding school beside the sea, renowned for routine, playing cricket and lacrosse. And for turning tomboys into lady wives.

Once Alice was at boarding school, making friends with other girls was still quite difficult. Increasingly, it seemed, they talked exclusively of sex, and arrived back from holidays at home with red, puffy eyes and frames filled with photographs of sweaty looking boyfriends, not unlike her dreadful brothers. They spent inordinate amounts of time writing love letters on pale blue note paper and rushing down to breakfast to see whether or not the post had arrived. They attached pictures of Mario Lanza and Marlon Brando to the lids of their desks and went into the shrubberies beyond the tennis courts to practice smoking and the professional application of mascara. Alice, on the other hand, received few letters and wasn't looking for a hero. In the fantasies inherited from her childhood she *was* the hero. Secretly, Alice still pictured herself as a brave romantic figure, dressed in britches and long boots, escaping from convention, saving the underdog with flamboyant but solitary daring. An androgynous creation which allowed her all the freedoms of a man, without the stupidities. And all the emotions of a woman without the compulsion to be pretty. As she grew older, Alice's secret image of herself shifted. She became more Byronic, more Rupert Brooke, more Virginia Woolf. Still figures of passion and emotion, who would not look out of place with flowing locks and wearing cloaks and britches, but now more cerebral, more driven, more touched by melancholy and mortality.

During her time at boarding school Alice's interior cast of characters, her mad mother, her absent, careless father, her rough and noisy brothers, all helped to direct her towards more solitary pursuits. She became introspective and obsessive. Still inventing alter egos to talk to in her head. She backed away from tentative affection before it could attack and undermine her precarious defences. She became bookish and just a little bit pretentious, cultivating a flamboyant interest in obscure and ancient philosophies and writers who struggled with life's mysteries and complexities.

Although she won many accolades and countless honours she made few friends. At Founders Day, in her final year, no one turned up to celebrate her triumph. Her grandparents were too old, her mother was too confused and her father sent a brief message of apology from a hotel in Geneva which arrived three days after the event. She had come to despise him.

By now nowhere less than Oxford was good enough for Alice to complete her education. Her teachers agreed she should do well and packed her off to Somerville for an interview. Alice arrived early, wearing her school uniform. She was not intimidated by the other candidates who were just like the girls she'd met at school. Called names like Sophie, Claire and Caroline. But they arrived with mothers who accompanied them to the interview. They came in neat costumes, stockings and slightly heeled shoes. In turn they fussed and groaned as they emerged from their ordeal, leaving Alice feeling on her own and suddenly quite nervous.

'What are you good at?' The bird like creature behind the large desk scrutinised Alice with curious intensity. Unlike Alice's father, she waited for an answer.

'I'm good at Latin and English Literature. I can play the cello reasonably well and I can write poetry a bit.'

The small woman smiled.

'The cello is an exquisite instrument. We're very fond of chamber music at Somerville. After dinner. In the library. A little Elgar or Haydn to purify the soul and feed the thoughtful mind.'

Alice nodded, feeling at last a reference to the spirit, a spark of intellectual challenge. She found it hard to sort her tentative opinions into coherent sentences.

'Tell me about your reading, my dear. Who is your favourite writer?'

'I like Virginia Woolf particularly, and Jane Austen.'

'Both women? That is unusual. What about Chaucer? Dickens? William Shakespeare?'

'I think there is often too much concentration on the literature of men. I don't discount the genius of Chaucer or the greatness of Shakespeare or the cleverness of Dickens but I am concerned that serious women writers do not receive their proper attention or respect.' Alice did her best to sound considered. She did not yet appreciate that in 1959 in Oxford circles, her views were probably contentious.

'What about Simone de Beauvoir? Are you familiar with her relationship to Sartre? Does she add to, or detract from, our understanding of existentialism?'

Alice had no idea.

'I'm not ready to judge, I'm afraid. But would it be possible to ask instead about Sartre's relationship to de

Beauvoir? Must we assume that it is *he* rather than *she* who is the dominant intellect? I think she has said some interesting things about women as "the other" in relation to men . . .' Alice struggled to continue, aware she was reaching the limits of her knowledge and beginning the kind of discussion she did not yet feel confident to pursue.

'Perhaps you will develop these ideas in your undergraduate studies, my dear', the little bird emerged from behind her desk and kissed Alice unexpectedly on both cheeks.

'If you can fulfil all the necessary requirements I shall be delighted to offer you a place at Somerville. I think you will be happy here.'

No one missed Alice very much when she went to Oxford and she was ready to move on.

'I suppose you'll end up as an old maid teacher', Crispin said. 'Isn't that what they say? Those who can't – teach!'

'Can't what?' Alice thought she loathed her elder brother more than any one she'd ever met. He already had the derisive twinkle in his eyes of his arrogant, handsome father. Slightly flirtatious. Even with Alice. He liked to consider himself a ladies man. 'Can't hardly think for themselves so they have to play at soldiers!'

Her father sent a card of qualified congratulations.

'Your cousin and your uncle were Oxford men, Alice. One of the major colleges, I'm sure. Worcester, I think. Or Balliol. But probably Somerville also has its enthusiasts.'

With no one left to impress, Alice made a promise to herself. As obsessive as it was destructive. If she did not find spiritual fulfilment or the admiration of her generation – some sexual affirmation or celebrated recognition – by the end of her first year at university she would leave. There would be no further point to it. No reason to continue. At Oxford she expected to realise both ambitions as soon as possible.

The work she found exciting, the men more difficult. Her first attempt to discover the truth about sex involved learning a pattern of behaviour which did not come easily to her. She wasn't good at small talk or affecting interest in conversation that was patently inane. The rugby and rowing types were too much like her brothers to be taken seriously. The debating society and all the main political clubs, which she visited in sequence, were immensely male preserves. Occasionally women stood out, those who came as political animals with brothers and fathers already in the House of Lords or Commons. Others acted as an attendant audience, with their intellectual aspirations distracted by the more pressing concern to achieve social and matrimonial advantage. Alice did not fit well into either category. She cared little for the good opinion or potential connections afforded by her family. And although she wanted to have sex, she did not want to disengage her brain or disappear into premature retirement as a useful asset to some self-important man.

She met Jack on a park bench by the river. He was reading Proust, or some one similarly symbolic. Trying to appear pre-occupied, in case any one should suspect he was inept. Alice offered him a cigarette and blew smoke across the silence as though she too was deep in meditation.

'Which College are you?' she tried again. 'What subject are you reading? Do you think much of Alan Taylor as a popular historian?'

Jack was a tall, pale young man who wore a black

cloak and velvet trousers. He had long delicate fingers and curly blond hair which convinced Alice he was Hungarian. In fact he came from Manchester, the only child of elderly parents who saw no strangeness in his gentle manner and singular preference for eccentric clothes and romantic poetry. At night they wandered beside the dark river, hand-in-hand, comparing the imagery of Keats and Shelley. She told him about her passion for Virginia Woolf. Jack listened and did his best to understand. He gave her a book of paintings by William Blake. She gave him *Orlando*.

After three weeks Alice decided they should become lovers. Jack nodded and did his best to acquiesce. His room in Worcester College was on the corner in a tower. Below, the mellow stone quad stood solid in its self assurance. Across the neatened lawns young, pink-faced students clustered like ripening grapes around draughty snickets and idled in the pale October sunshine by the lake.

They decided to wait until the evening. Jack bought some wine. Alice chose a cotton dress and sprayed her breasts with perfume. The wine was sweet and heavy on their breath. It made Alice's mouth feel dry and her head feel like her mind was swimming out to sea. She felt an unfamiliar pulse pounding in her neck, a slight shiver of anxiety. She wasn't sure what happened next. She was too proud to ask Caroline Barnes, the girl who shared her room in Somerville, for information, but supposed that Jack would be more experienced than she. Probably kissing boys would be less suffocating when the exponent wasn't Crispin. Jack with his beautiful, elegant fingers and sweet musky smell was nothing like her brother.

Shyly he took off his clothes and waited for Alice to do the same. She lay on the narrow bed feeling the damp chill of the night air. She heard the clock ticking on the stone landing outside. Somewhere in the distance a train was rumbling towards London. When he kissed her, his mouth was hard. For such a pale and gentle boy, she was surprised. She could feel the sharpness of his teeth against her lip. His tongue pushing in to stop her breath. She wondered if tongues were compulsory. This was her second experience of their intrusion and she liked them no better the second time around. She could feel her heart pounding – but with reluctance rather than passion. Her shoulders grew tight. Her body rigid. His hands on her breast were sweating. He fumbled with her nipple like a clumsy adolescent, like Tim or Gerald, as if to twist and turn it like a handle would secure some point of entry. Mostly she felt sick.

Alice closed her eyes in concentration, wishing that the ordeal could be over but determined to continue. Making love, she reflected later, was probably something of a trial for Jack as well. He was, like herself, greatly troubled by the fear of failure. His penis was extremely pale and knotty. She couldn't bear to take it in her hands. It would be like holding gristle, she imagined. Or guts or sinews. It stood out from his body in a way that made him look ridiculous. How could such a perfect beauty so quickly be transformed into such a fool? She closed her eyes so as not to see. As he tried to slip inside, her body tensed, her hymen refusing to give way. His coming was quick and brief and insignificant, leaving his sticky wetness along the shadow of her thighs. Jack hurried to wipe the mess away and to hide his shrunken penis beneath the sheet. Its business done.

Still neither of them spoke. Outside an owl hooted and late night revellers began to stumble their noisy way along the corridor to bed. Jack got up and dressed, turning his back on Alice, busying himself with making tea and arranging Garibaldi biscuits on a china plate. She knew, as she watched him from behind, that he was ambivalent about sex. But like herself was trying to ignore it. She smoothed out her petticoat and frock. Drank Jack's tea with some references to Proust. Kissed him shyly on the cheek. And left. Alice crept silently down the stairs and out into the starless night. After that she didn't try to contact him again. She saw him once or twice around the town. His lean body wrapped in black and purple velvet. Sometimes with a silver cane or flowing scarf. He was never with a girl. But sometimes with a brown-eyed boy, lost deep in conversation.

The corridors and halls of Somerville were lined with portraits. All of them women. All of them formidable. An inspiration. Alice spent long hours in the library, her head bent in concentration over a sea of spidery writing, making additions, adjustments, footnotes to her argument. She had set herself a tight deadline – to become the author of some definitive interpretation of the literary influences on Virginia Woolf by the age of twenty. Miss Emily Winthrop was her tutor, the small bird-like woman who had greeted her with such affection at her interview. As a tutor she was critical but kindly. She always referred to students as 'my dear'. Often she provided tea and chocolate cake or a glass of Madeira in her rooms to lighten the intensity of critical engagement. She advocated excellence but assumed that scholarship should induce feelings of pleasure rather than of pain. She worried most about the frown of concentration that settled across Alice's expression as Miss Winthrop picked away at her written tendency towards hyperbole and purple prose.

'Surely the beauty of Virginia lies in her language? In the delight she takes in using language like a poet. But sparingly, precisely, surprisingly, with a delightful economy of style? She is the creator of literary influences. Not their creature.'

Alice returned to the library, beside the window, scarcely pausing to consider how the line of poplars, that marked the boundaries of the kitchen garden, had shed their autumn leaves and stood like pencils, sharp against the blue black sky. She drew thick, angry lines through reams of densely crafted, spidery analysis and resolved to start again.

'It is unlikely, my dear, that you will achieve the goal you are setting yourself so young, and if I may say, so relatively inexperienced. Scholarship is the journey of a lifetime. A journey which for you is just beginning. To have produced your best at twenty would leave very little pleasure in anticipation from your future intellectual development!'

Alice listened in silence, the frown gathering in her brows. Miss Winthrop reached for the bottle of Madeira and poured out two large glasses. She smelled of lavender.

'As you know, I am something of a student of the philosophy of Sartre. At your interview you turned around the question I asked about his relation to de Beauvoir in a way which made me think afresh about *her* influence on him. That was the observation of an intellectual, a thinker, my dear. Never underestimate the capacity to ask about the unexpected. To look not simply for what is obvious, but for what is hidden or absent in the text. It will set you apart from the hoi polloi. What de Beauvoir has to say about the concept of "other" is well worth your consideration. It may provide insights into the character of your heroine Virginia. You cannot enjoy the humour and eloquence of Orlando without considering the source of Orlando's inspiration Vita. And as a young woman who has grown up herself, if I might make the personal comparison, like Virginia, in the company of brothers, under the eye of a powerful father – I hope I'm not intruding – it might be relevant to consider what can be gleaned from de Beauvoir's notion of being "other" in terms of such experience'.

Alice could remember very little in her later life about the conversations she had at Oxford. The three years melded into a series of sensations that left a mixture of emotions. Only some of which she associated with happiness. But she remembered these words of Miss Winthrop's in virtual detail. They were the first words which any one had spoken to her which provided both personal and intellectual insight. And which were offered with such generosity and careful attention to her sensibilities.

Miss Winthrop's sharp blue eyes twinkled in the firelight. Her face a little flushed from a second glass of Madeira.

'You will come to understand all of this in time, my dear. Please don't hang yourself from the nearest rafter if it isn't clear by the end of the year. Our nature's are a complication, which only the imagination to ask about the unexpected and the courage to live one's life accordingly, can satisfy.' She kissed Alice on both cheeks. 'And don't forget, the other reason for being up at Oxford is to fall in love!'

Caroline Barnes was stretched out on her bed applying a second coat of pink varnish to her finger nails.

'Do you think that all the tutors here are lesbians?'

It was the first time Alice had heard the word and didn't know what Caroline meant.

'You know inverts, spinsters, queer. Women who fall in love with each other. And then have sex together in secret.'

Alice couldn't imagine Hester Gray, the Principal of Somerville, or Clara Drake or even Miss Winthrop, having sex with anybody.

'I don't think you can say that, Caroline. It's just because they're scholars. Career women with a commitment to intellect and women's education.'

Caroline shrugged her shoulders. She looked unconvinced.

'Everyone does sex with somebody. Unless they're very peculiar. It's part of human nature. Mostly, of course, they do it with the opposite sex. But from what I've read, some people don't really know what sex they are. Something gets mixed up, or the wrong way round inside. They end up in a dreadful mess.'

'Do you know of such people? Where did you read about this?' Alice could feel a kind of tightness in her chest.

'Psychology books. Oh I don't know. I just thought it might explain why no one here is married. Mind you, who would want to marry Drake? It would be like wrestling with a bulldozer. Are you going to the Christmas Ball?' Caroline soon lost interest in her speculations.

'I don't have anything to wear.' Alice knew that nothing in her meagre wardrobe would be remotely appropriate.

'Or anyone to go with, I suppose? What happened to

Jack? You are fickle, Alice. He was besotted with you, or so I heard.'

Alice blushed and looked away. She pulled a face. 'Not my type', she tried to sound relaxed. 'How about you?'

'Oh, I'll probably end up with Teddy. He says he's got the tickets already. But there's three full weeks to go yet. I'd like to keep my options open'. She dropped the empty file of varnish into the waste bin and continued to blow onto her nails until they dried. 'I'll come and hunt for dresses with you, if you like. You'd look absolutely stunning in something long and deep and dark. Match your mood of secrecy and stillness.'

'Is that how you see me?' Alice wasn't sure if this was meant to be a compliment or judgement.

'I do. You're very enigmatic, Alice. Men will like that if only you can learn to make the most of it.'

Alice wasn't altogether sure she cared what men would like. But she guessed that someone, with more experience than Jack, might need to help her come to a conclusion.

Rupert was a postgraduate student with a passion for Wagner. Alice ought, perhaps, to have been more wary of a man who could enjoy Wagner. His hobby was collecting virgins. At least his conceit was such. Alice had been observing Rupert in the Bodleian, in the debating chamber and the bar for some weeks before she decided he would become her lover. For a man who claimed to know everything, he was, as yet, completely unaware of how he fitted in to her intentions. He only noticed pretty women. His hair was like a splash of ripe corn. He wore it long, in curls around his collar. His eyes were brown and steady with self confidence. He was usually at the centre of a crowd, expounding a favourite theory, embellishing an amusing anecdote. He drank only champagne and carried a leather case, made somewhere in the East from alligator skin. He was the kind of man a more contemporary generation would think of as a poseur.

Alice was unclear about how best to attract his attention. She felt large and angular and boring. Not remotely like the pretty, laughing women whose light dresses and pastel colours floated on the periphery of every group she had watched him cultivate. She decided that music could be the only point of contact. She played the cello tolerably well and he played violin in his college string quartet. She had noticed how his face lit up with ostentatious concentration when a visiting ensemble played Mozart in the Holywell Music Rooms one evening after dinner.

'I've got a spare ticket for the Wagner concert this week end.' She heard herself speak to him through the random conversation of some acquaintances they had in common. His eyes watched her with interest, encouraging the blush that gathered at her throat. He guessed now that he was being propositioned. His vanity flattered. His predilection for consuming virgins of prominent consideration.

Rupert was at first a generous lover. He could afford to be. He was confident and familiar with the delicacies of touch, the nuances of illusion, that could usually be relied upon to please. He cultivated romance and was careful to take his time. He considered sex to be an art, and his own, virtuoso performance its chief delight.

But Alice was something of a challenge. She did not respond easily, if at all, to his flirtatious banter. There was a determination about her to have him as a necessary experience, rather than become his conquest. He grew to resent her strength of will. A forcefulness he did not usually encounter. It suggested she might also have a mind of her own.

In consequence the exchange was a joyless and somewhat brutal affair. Alice watched passively as her body was persuaded to moisten and move to his instruction. As if she stood on the outside, observing a performance. Her eyes remained resolute. He couldn't persuade her to relinquish her control. Her hymen continued to resist. Her muscles straining to impede his entry. And this, despite her willing commitment to what she had decided was inevitable. Finally he got impatient, bored and angry. His eyes blunted by determination. His hands becoming rough and careless. His penis more insistent. For Alice there was by now no chance to change her mind. His coming was long and hard and angry – her body collapsing against the force of his determination to have the matter done. She cried in pain. Steeled her aversion. Waited till he fell away exhausted. Oblivious almost to her existence.

'That's more like it', Rupert said. 'Something to remember when you're old and dry. The glory of a good fuck.'

She lay motionless on the bed for some time after he had dressed and gone. Her cunt was throbbing, her body bruised from the grasp of his fingers on her flesh, her mind detached.

In melancholy mood she considered suicide as the only real alternative she had left. She was persuaded that the life she was living had no meaning and no possibility. She was estranged from her family. Her mind felt deadened – here at the self-proclaimed centre of intellectual rigour. Miss Winthrop had dismissed her fervent efforts to become a genius. Her capacity for sexual passion clearly non-existent. No lovers. No family. No friends. No one to care whether or not she might live or die. Fortunately for Alice, the door burst open, closely followed by her room mate Caroline Barnes, whose plans to be away for the evening had taken a serious nose dive due to 'the miserable inconsistency of men.'

'Come on, Alice, let's go out and get ourselves sloshed. I think champagne's in order. And a generous dose of intelligent, reliable female friendship! Oh do get up Alice! You can't lie in your grubby little bed at seven in the evening. The night is young and so are we!'

The remainder of the time which Alice spent at university passed with little incident. She took no further interest in men – unless they were dead poets or sensitive intellects. She stayed friends with Caroline Barnes. She went to her weekly meetings with Miss Winthrop. After a glass or two of Madeira at the end of her tutorial they would often throw another log on the fire and spend a cosy hour together deep in conversation. Miss Winthrop listened kindly whilst Alice poured out stories from her childhood and the years she spent at boarding school, stories she usually reserved for interior discussion with the latest incarnation of her alter ego.

'You should consider writing, my dear', Miss Winthrop passed Alice a second slice of chocolate cake. 'Your head is bursting with reflection, observation, questions about reality. These are the stuff of poetry and literature.'

'The stuff of neurosis and obsession more like. You asked me once to think about de Beauvoir and her notion of "woman as other". I feel profoundly like an "other" in almost every aspect of my life. Even in the company of "other women".'

'How do you mean exactly? Can you put it into words?'

'I'm not sure. Outside, I look like a woman. I am a woman. Compared to men, I must prefer the company of women. But inside, I don't feel like a woman. I don't want a boyfriend. I don't care too much about how I look. I don't think anything of marriage'.

'Neither do I', Miss Winthrop smiled. 'Is that a problem?'

'But you are clever. You write books. You have a leather armchair and rooms in Somerville. In the holidays, for all I know, you travel to the furthest corners of the world. You are independent.'

Miss Winthrop fingered a cigarette into a small gold holder and offered another to Alice.

'No thank you. I'm trying to give them up.'

'Such self-control!' Miss Winthrop's bird like eyes were twinkling with amusement. 'What are you afraid of?'

'I'm afraid that somehow I am wrong inside. The wrong sex, maybe. I spend massive amounts of time having conversations in my head with odd characters in velvet cloaks who incite me to be more rebellious.'

'Rebellious?'

'You know, break out of my routines. Breakfast at 8.30. Library till noon. A sandwich made on wholemeal bread, containing five thin slices of cucumber and a chopped tomato. Two lectures a week. An hour with you. A daily walk across the water meadows to get some air – lasting no longer than forty minutes. Dinner at 7. The library till 10.30. Bed at 11. I'm like an automaton.'

'So what are you saying Alice? How would you prefer to be?'

'I don't know. I don't want to be afraid of passion. I'd like to be famous. I'd like to be like you, in a way. I'd like to be independent.'

'You'd like to swashbuckle your way through life, dressed in a velvet cloak!'

Alice was laughing now. 'Yes. Maybe I would!'

The year that Miss Winthrop retired Alice was awarded a good second class degree which did not, of course, satisfy her aspirations.

'You are a clever and a principled young woman Alice, who has much to contribute to the growth of intellect and education', Miss Winthrop told her. 'See what life will bring, my dear. The world is changing for women. I feel it in my bones. No longer the same stuffy old stereotypes. The same silly frivolous preoccupations. See what you can make of it. Listen to the inner voices and have the courage of your convictions.' She kissed her fondly on both cheeks. 'I'll think of you often, from the comfort of my leather armchair, planning your adventures in the furthest corners of the world.'

Six

'Does your father always wear a plastic bag when it's raining?'

Suzanne Haliday shouted from the safety of a clutch of girls, gathered by the school gate.

'What?' Actually Mattie did hear what she said the first time.

'I saw you on Saturday. In Woolworths. You in your faithful gaberdine. Was it your father in a flat checked cap and plastic bag? How versatile!'

'Tell her to get stuffed!' Joyce took Mattie's arm and bundled her through the gauntlet of girls at the end of the drive, waiting for their friends to turn up on bicycles or by car from the neighbouring suburbs. She waved two defiant fingers at Suzanne and her smirking cronies. 'Bloody snobs!'

Mattie wished her father wouldn't wear a plastic mac for precisely this reason. She knew as she watched him smooth it out on the kitchen table, fold it meticulously into a neat parcel, the exact size of his pocket, and secure it with an elastic band, that when it rained, he'd whip it out and wear it. Totally oblivious to the affect this would have on her credibility at school if spotted by the likes of Suzanne Haliday.

She also wished she didn't have to catch the self same bus every morning as her father. They hurried down Ceylon Street side by side. His plastic mac sticking from his pocket like a flag. Her bottle green beret with the red badge crushed into the front of her satchel until she was near enough to school to put it on. They waited at the bus stop for the number 29 to swing round the corner and trundle up the hill.

'You O.K. Jimmy? See the fight last night?'

The new black-and-white television in the front room, with a twelve-inch screen protected from the sunlight by a lace cover, was her parents' pride and joy. On Sunday evenings the whole family, including Tommy and Billy, sat down after tea to watch 'Sunday Night at the London Palladium'. Her father took his slippers off and put his feet up on the leatherette pouffe. Billy lined a row of Guinness along the sideboard.

'Those Tiller Girls have extra long legs.' Mattie's mother always said the same thing. 'That's why they're chosen.'

'It's the high heels and feathers that makes them look so tall.' Her father always disagreed.

They watched transfixed as rows of white legs kicked out in unison from stiff, sequin studded swimming costumes. A line of spectacular dolls with plumes like circus horses. Their routine reaching its familiar climax as the girls dipped their heads in sequence, like a tidal wave of candy floss, and dropped, one after the other, onto a single knee, their painted smiles flashing into the audience.

'They have to be at least six foot two. It's in their contract.' Mattie's mother was now an expert, having read the TV Times from start to finish.

'They're certainly a bunch of big uns', Tommy winked at Billy who passed across a bottle of Guinness.

Top of the bill – Dickie Valentine.

'He's got a lovely voice', Mattie's mother was a fan.

As the final curtain fell, and the amazing revolving stage of the London Palladium made its final awesome revolution in the sitting rooms and kitchens of breathless millions, Mrs Reed got up to make a cup of tea.

'Time for bed, our Mattie. You've got Grammar School in the morning.'

'But Mum . . . it's only nine o'clock. Can't I watch the play?'

'No you can't. Too much television is bad for growing eyes. Think of all that reading you have to do. Anyway, your father wants to watch the big fight. Put the cover back on when you've finished Henry. Don't forget about the sunlight.'

Mattie and her father met up with Jimmy every morning at the bus stop. And Frank and Mrs Kirby from the end terrace. The conversation was usually the same. Last night's television. The state of the weather. What the floor manager at work had to say to Stan the shop steward about the length of tea breaks.

'Our Christine isn't going in the factory', Mrs Kirby said to no one in particular. 'She's got the chance on an office job. I've told her to grab it while she can. What do you say Mattie? I don't expect we'll see you working round here once you've got those exams under your belt.'

'Don't know.' Mattie knew better than to answer Mrs Kirby honestly. She didn't want to sound too 'hoity-toity' – her mother's phrase.

'People round here don't understand about brains, Mattie.' Her mother's warning carried the authority of one who'd lived in the same street all her life. In the same house for the last fifteen years. 'Better to keep your plans to yourself. They'll know soon enough when it all turns out.'

The bus was almost full by the time it got to Ceylon Street. Just enough room for a few more standing in the lower deck. It smelt of petrol and work clothes and sweat. Following the same route every day that Mattie, after five and half years, now knew like the back of her hand, the bus plunged through the rows of terraced streets and small factories of East Holderness, towards the town centre. Dropping off her father and Jimmy at Metal Box, Frank at Pearson's Bakery and Mrs Kirby at the Laundry. As the bodies thinned and seats became vacant on the top deck, Mattie climbed up the metal stairway, to be hit by the smell of stale smoke and steamy windows, en route to her preferred seat at the front. It was still only 8.15.

At Bessie Street, Joyce got on. Stumbling down the gangway as the bus lurched towards the bus station in the middle of town.

'You've done your hair!' Mattie was impressed. 'What *will* Miss Tate have to say about that?'

Joyce took out a mirror from her satchel and patted her home bleached bouffant into shape.

'Too late to say anything. It's permanent', Joyce grinned. 'I had a moment of panic, thinking I'd left it on too long. My sister's went peculiar because she forgot to wash it off in time.'

'I thought she did it red last week.'

'She did', Joyce said. 'Didn't like it. Decided to go ash blonde instead. Only now it's more like moss green.'

Joyce lit two Park Drives and passed one to Mattie.

'Have you done that homework for English? I couldn't tell what she was on about.'

'I've sort of done it', Mattie said. 'It was a bit boring.' She didn't want to sound too keen.

'Let's see', Joyce said, getting out her blue exercise book and fountain pen.

Mattie handed over her neatly written essay entitled 'The character of Anne Elliot in *Persuasion* – as portrayed by Jane Austen.'

'Ooh this is good! Clever old stick aren't you Mattie? Mind if I just slip a couple of these sentences into my own words?'

She began to scribble furiously as the bus swung back and forward through the traffic. When they reached the bus station, the number 14 was waiting as usual. They had five minutes to dash across the road, buy some chewing gum or fags from the station kiosk, fling an acid or suggestive insult at the boys from King Edward's and run upstairs to the front seat. Joyce got out her ruler and pencil to finish off some geometry whilst Mattie peered out of the window, wondering what Miss Morrison would make them do today.

Mattie was unlikely material for St Swithuns Grammar School. Both her brothers had gone to East

Holderness Secondary, queuing up to leave at the first legal opportunity. Everyone assumed she'd do the same. No one knew that Mattie was clever until the fat brown envelope slapped onto the door mat, offering her a scholarship. Her parents were dumbfounded. Neither realised that the paper which she brought home to sign was anything other than the usual invitation to a parent's evening they couldn't bring themselves to attend, or an announcement about Harvest Festival. No one in the family knew of anyone else who passed for grammar school, except for Elsie's sister's next-door neighbour's girl. The one who got thrown out in the fifth year for being pregnant. Mattie's fees for the new school would be waived because of the scholarship and a school fund would pay for her uniform and games equipment as an act of charity. She cried to be allowed to go. Her father was resistant. Her mother was afraid. Afraid she'd become conceited, ashamed, unreliable as a helper with the housework and as a necessary contributor to the family income.

'It's probably the chance of a lifetime, Henry', Mattie's mother thought it through for three days before coming to a decision. 'I think we should let her do it. There's not a lot going off round here otherwise. It could make all the difference.'

The number 14 soon carried Joyce and Mattie into unfamiliar territory, through tree-lined avenues and quiet crescents where the lower middle classes had come to count on their security and comfort being recognised. Where Ford Anglias and Morris Minors waited patiently in ordered driveways, daffodils clustered round ornamental bird tables in the spring and Greek urns sat on neat patios. Where policemen could ride along on bicycles without being shouted at or cheeked.

St Swithuns was on the very edge of town sheltered from the road by a belt of trees and a secluded shrubbery. A wooden gateway led into a leafy drive that twisted round towards the new science block and gym, and to the rows of solid red brick classrooms. Joyce and Mattie stubbed out their Park Drives on the bus floor and rummaged in their satchels for their berets.

'I don't think we should have to wear these bloody things now we're in the lower sixth', Mattie complained.

'Especially when I've just back-combed my hair.' Joyce did her best to perch the battered beret on the top. 'Does it look ridiculous? Stupid question. Of course it looks ridiculous. God knows why I'm still coming to this dump.'

'You could be engaged to a twit like Malcolm Smith, saving up to have a baby!'

'No thank you! Get me out of Holderness say I. There's got to be more to life than Malcolm Smith. Even if means poxy A-levels and long green knickers till we're 18.'

Across the road Suzanne Haliday and her snotty friends were trying to appear contemptuous.

'Does your father always wear a plastic bag when it's raining?'

'What in heaven's name has happened to your hair?'
'I dyed it, Miss Tate. Do you like it?'
Mattie waited expectantly for Joyce to be expelled. The others in the class exchanging smiles.

'You could have fooled me, Joyce. I'd have sworn you were the unfortunate casualty of an electric shock.'

The goody-goodies, who always sat at the front, even for registration, tittered their approval of the joke. Joyce and Mattie, and those who liked to consider themselves either more sophisticated or more rebellious, maintained a stony silence.

'Would you be so kind as to put your beret on so that I can be sure the school badge is properly displayed', she hesitated, 'though why we should want the world to know you belong to us I can't imagine.'

The goody-goodies turned to enjoy the spectacle of Joyce's humiliation.

'It's in the cloakroom Miss Tate, with my coat.'

'Then go and get it, Joyce.'

Joyce banged her way along the row of desks to the dais at the front. Miss Tate always made sure she was well positioned on the dais. At five foot nothing in her laced up brogues the wooden platform provided extra height Joyce towered in front of her, her yellow bouffant slightly out of kilter.

'I suppose this fashion is intended to attract the boys.' Frances Tate always managed to make at least one comment out of three refer to sex. The girls at the back raised their eyebrows. Mattie tried a noisy yawn.

'I dress to please myself, Miss Tate.' Joyce knew she was on shaky ground.

'Then I must remind you Joyce, that whilst you are a member of my form, and a pupil at St Swithuns, you must also dress to please the rules and regulations of the school. Do I make myself clear?'

Joyce grunted ungraciously.

'I suppose we may have to live with the rather lurid colour of your hair – at least until the usual black roots decide to re-emerge. But could you make some adjustment to the style? Into something which will not constitute a fire risk should you decide to lean over a Bunsen burner? Go back to your seat. I shall expect to see a difference in the morning.'

Joyce returned in silence to her seat. She was saved from any further comment about the slight odour of tobacco about her blouse and cardigan because Miss Tate smoked like a chimney and was completely useless when it came to spotting illicit smokers. She returned her attention to the register, reading each name out loud in alphabetical order. At 9.15 the bell for Prayers sounded in the lobby.

'In orderly fashion, young ladies if you please. As pupils of the lower sixth you have a responsibility to set a good example.'

Joyce winked at Mattie as she passed.

'Mean old cow', she whispered with a fair degree of venom.

The first lesson after Prayers was double English. Alice Morrison was introducing that part of the A-level syllabus concerned with poetry – Percy Shelley, Robert Browning, Thomas Hardy.

'Thomas Hardy is probably best known as a novelist', she said. 'Can any one tell me the names of any of his novels?'

Mattie shot up her hand.

'*Jude the Obscure. Tess of the D'Urbervilles* . . .'

'Good. Any other?'

'*Far From the Madding Crowd.*'

'Well done. And what are the major themes which we associate with Hardy?' Alice looked around the classroom with an air of expectation. She had begun teaching at St Swithuns Grammar School a year ago when she finished university. It was not quite the 'furthest corners of the world' recommended by Miss Winthrop but it felt a long way east of England. The kind of place you had to come to for a reason, not a place for passing through. Her first job and as good a place as any to make a start.

Mattie raised her hand again.

'I think he writes quite a lot about fate', she said, 'and self improvement.'

Alice nodded her encouragement.

'You could say that Mattie. And what about his view of women? Is it generally positive or negative?'

'I don't know Miss Morrison', Mattie blushed, 'I've never thought about it'.

Mattie was sitting nearer to the front of class than was her usual habit. Reluctantly Joyce agreed to join her, as an act of solidarity. She watched Mattie now with curious attention. All this energy she was wasting on the search for answers. All this going red when Alice Morrison looked her in the eye. As Alice's attention returned to the book of poems on the desk in front, Joyce poked her spiky elbow into Mattie's arm.

'You look just like a beetroot!'

Usually in lessons both Joyce and Mattie answered as few questions as possible. Partly to proclaim their disaffection. Partly to protect themselves from facetious comments by other girls about their 'rather quaint use of language'.

'I'll do for these snotty cows one of these days.' Joyce was not averse to confrontation in the face of provocation. Mattie much preferred the silent satisfaction she derived from always getting better marks than any of them, especially Suzanne Haliday.

She waited now for Alice to begin. Her voice quietly intense.

Dear Lizbie Browne, Where are you now? In sun, in rain?
Or is your brow past joy, past pain? Dear Lizbie Browne?

Dear Lizbie Browne I should have thought, 'Girls ripen fast'
And coaxed and caught you ere you passed, dear Lizbie Browne!

But Lizbie Browne I let you slip, Shaped not a sign, touched never your lip with lip of mine, Lost Lizbie Browne.

'Do you notice how her eyes goes misty when she reads out poems?' Mattie asked Joyce when the class was over, 'as though she's going to cry'

Joyce said she hadn't noticed.

'What's her accent, do you think – apart from posh? She obviously doesn't come from round here.' Mattie seemed unusually concerned. The Dorset Coast, Home Counties, London... for a girl who'd been no further south than Cleethorpes on a day trip, Mattie knew as little about the south of England as she did about abroad.

'Don't know', Joyce said. 'Probably it comes from growing up in a place where there aren't any factories. And not in a house beside a railway line with an outside toilet.'

Having crushes on the teachers at St Swithuns was no big deal. Although most girls had out grown the habit by the lower sixth. By now they were more concerned with sex and boys and trying to get their hands on the pill. Miss Becket, the second mistress in the games department always had a trail of younger pupils offering to put away the hoops and bean bags in the cupboard after gym. Or carry messages to Sergeant Major Bolt, the Head of Games. When they found out she had got married, otherwise resilient girls were seen to crumple.

Miss Bolt, on the other hand, was a frightening woman that no one had a crush on. Least of all Mattie. Mattie wasn't fond of sport. She didn't seem to have the necessary class attitude to nebulous concepts like 'team spirit'. She often felt as though she'd been let in to St Swithuns by the back door, so to speak, on sufferance, pending a cultural transfusion. But singing school songs which, it turned out, had been appropriated from Eton, about the playing fields of England ringing to be 'the tramp of the twenty-two men' didn't make a lot of sense to a working-class girl, born and bred in Ceylon Street, down wind from the fish docks.

Sergeant Major Bolt had black plimsolls; strong white legs in long woollen socks; grey, pleated, knee-length shorts, and a Fair Isle cardigan buttoned securely across her chest. She was not a total stranger to feminine pretensions, however. She attacked life from behind a slash of bright red lip stick and wore her long brown hair permed to the shoulder in waves of corrugated iron curls. She got her nickname from her energetic disposition, and the kind of voice that could sink a battle ship. She was probably the major reason why Mattie could never really get to grips with hockey or tennis, and exercised her creative imagination instead on the forgery of spurious letters from her mother, about the intricacies of her allergies, excusing her from games.

Rumour had it, in the sixth form common room, that Miss Bolt lived discreetly on a smallholding with a woman who bred dogs. Mattie saw them once in town, with Yorkshire terriers in tow, buying armfuls of flowers at the covered market. Miss Bolt was laughing like a drain. Her friend looked rather jolly. Mattie watched with curious devotion as the friend stretched gaily onto her toes and planted a swift fond kiss on Miss Bolt's sturdy cheek. Mattie smiled. The incident made her feel much better about Miss Bolt after that. 'I'm glad somebody likes her enough to buy her flowers', Mattie thought. But it didn't make her any more inclined to chase little red balls round a wet and windy hockey pitch with a wooden stick.

When Mattie was in the fourth year the French Assistante was another mistress who had lots of fans. She wore brightly coloured dirndl skirts and floaty chiffon scarves. Sometimes she sped along the school drive in an open top sports car with a handsome man who looked like an actor. The craze for extra conversation classes surprised everyone. It's true she spent a lot of time giving out jam and croissants, and re-enacting scenes from *Brief Encounter* set in pavement cafés and railway station ticket offices. But her attraction was also something else, something which induced idolatry. And a lot of discussion about French kissing in the lunch breaks behind the bike sheds. Mademoiselle le Bon called her special favourites *cherie*. Even Suzanne Haliday was said to shed a tear or two when she returned to Paris at the end of term, though she'd eat rocks rather than admit it now. A noisy rendition by Joyce, in her best Yorkshire accent, of *Non, Je ne Regrette Rien* was still enough to reduce Suzanne to silence, if ever she felt tempted to pass comment on Mattie's increasing, and rather unexpected, devotion to Alice Morrison.

The school staff room at St Swithuns smelled of nicotine and boiled cabbage. It occupied a central location to the right of the lobby and the Headmistress's room, next to the old biology lab and across the playground from the school kitchen. Each morning a troop of determined women arrived by bus and bicycle at the kitchen, divorced themselves from their individual identity under turbans and beneath white overalls, and set out to transform fat slabs of beef, crates of greens and stacks of flour into metal trays of meat and potato pie with watery veg by dinner time. Whatever else was on the menu – rolypoly pudding, stew and dumplings, fried fish and mushy peas – the smell of boiled cabbage drifted in through open windows and hung like rising damp in the confined atmosphere of the school staff room. So familiar that you ceased to notice it.

The room was skirted by a ring of easy chairs. In the corner a heavy, ink-stained table was piled high with blue exercise books waiting to be marked, a box of coloured chalks and a bundle of rolled up maps and charts describing sheep farming in Australia and the demographic characteristics of Sub-Saharan Africa. The staff notice board was devoid of colour or contention. No announcements about union meetings or posters about conferences. No articles from the educational press about current trends and new developments. Simply a dog-eared timetable, transcribed laboriously by hand onto graph paper by the Deputy Headmistress, in different coloured inks. A list of mock exam marks and a duty rota. This week it was Alice's turn to supervise detentions and Frances Tate's opportunity to patrol the line of juniors dressed in green gym slips, striped ties and thick soled, laced up shoes, queuing for their dinner. Holding them suspended, like sprinters on the starting block, to establish silence and decorum, for slightly longer than was strictly necessary, as a point of principle. In the staff room at St Swithuns you would never guess that Mary Quant existed. Or the mini skirt. Or that astronauts were being launched in rockets into outer space.

It was period three on Monday morning and Alice had a free lesson. Time she usually spent selecting quotations for her O-Level class on William Shakespeare. Miss Tate was watching from the window as 4 Alpha trailed in desultory fashion towards the new science block.

'Jennifer Curtis has put on tons of weight', Tate observed. 'Breasts bursting out regardless of her buttons. It's usually this age that girls get blowsy don't you think?'

Alice had to assume she was the focus of Tate's remarks, since no one else was present. But she had a terrible habit of standing with her back to you when she was talking. Tossing comments at random, like autumn leaves, caught in the crossfire between wind and rain. Making reasonable communication difficult.

'Puppy fat, I expect.' Alice marked a number of speeches by Mark Antony with slips of yellow paper to illustrate the use of metaphor.

'Too fat for sprinting now.' Tate flicked ash in the general direction of the waste paper basket. And missed. 'Bolt should talk to the fourth year about their diet. Or make them do more press ups!' She adjusted her position at the window to get a better view of Stella Flint and Janet Parker who were bringing up the rear.

'Sauntering along as though tomorrow hasn't been invented. In a world of their own those two!'

Alice kept her attention glued to the task in hand.

'Do you know what I mean?' Tate turned away from the window.

Alice could feel her cheeks begin to burn. Tate had a way of making you feel uncomfortable. Probably because Alice never knew what she would say next. And because she didn't want to become the object of her interrogation and speculation. Tate drew the smoke from the cigarette into her lungs and out through her nose. Alice pretended not to hear.

'How are you settling in Alice? Not feeling lonely, I hope?' Tate stood facing her now, a wicked twinkle in her shrewd grey eyes. Alice looked up awkwardly.

'Sorry, I'm miles away. Were you speaking to me?' She breathed a sigh of relief as someone knocked lightly on the staff room door and Tate strode briskly across the floor to see who it might be.

'Why Mattie!' Tate said 'Shouldn't you be considering the decline of the British Empire?'

'I'm not in History at the moment Miss Tate.'

'I can see that, Mattie.'

'I wondered if I could have a word with Miss Morrison? About my homework?' The girl was tentative.

Frances Tate allowed her eyes to take in Mattie's awkward shift from foot to foot, the way the cuffs on her school shirt were now frayed along the edge. How the slender, nervous fingers which pushed back wayward curls from the frown across her forehead, had nails she'd bitten to the quick. Tate noticed Mattie's lightly freckled skin and the tell tale beads of sweat along her hairline. She smiled.

'Still searching for a meaning of life Mattie?' Tate enjoyed the slight frisson of discomfort she was able to provoke in girls. 'I'll see whether Miss Morrison can be dragged away from her lesson preparation to be bothered with you', she said. 'and don't eat your fingers whilst you're waiting for the verdict. It's almost dinner time.' She closed the door.

When Alice came to find Mattie in the lobby she too was blushing.

'I think you've got a fan', Frances Tate watched the colour rise as Alice fumbled with her books and papers. It was impossible to ignore the exchange with Mattie and unforgivable of Tate to now turn her delight in being disconcerting towards Alice. It made Alice feel much like a schoolgirl herself, who had no more power than Mattie to prevent herself from being deliberately unsettled.

'I'll see her in the English Room.' Alice dropped her copy of *Antony and Cleopatra* on the carpet. The slips of paper she had patiently placed between the pages fluttered free like stray petals from a trampled blossom.

'Nothing wrong, I hope?' Tate retrieved a strip of yellow paper with its reference to 'the serpent of old Nile'. She so enjoyed it when her hunches developed substance out of speculation.

Alice shook her head.

'Not that I'm aware of. You're Mattie's Form Mistress. I'm sure you'd know more than me about any problems she might be having.'

'I wasn't referring to Mattie.' Tate smiled, her voice suddenly persuasive. 'It's you I feel concerned about, Alice. You do know, don't you, that you can count on me – let's say – to understand about these things.'

By now Alice was completely scarlet.

'You've lost me, I'm afraid.' The staff room suddenly seemed vast and empty. The space between them much too close for comfort.

Alice stepped quickly to the door, still feeling flustered. Waiting nervously in the lobby, Mattie was feeling too self conscious to notice that Alice was also less than easy in her presence.

'I wanted to check with you about the Thomas Hardy homework.'

Mattie was now 17. Alice 23.

'Did you want me to discuss his attitudes to women. Or ... what?'

Mattie's ingenuity and capacity to sustain long sentences petered out. Sitting side by side in the English Room was the closest she had ever been to Alice in her life. Three more inches and Mattie could have brushed the soft full flesh of Alice's bare arm where it rested on the desk in front. She could feel her own skin prickle against the collar of her shirt. Smell the lemony scent of summer flowers she'd already come to associate with Alice Morrison.

'I wanted to find the answer to your question about women. Is there anything particular I could read to get me started?'

Alice jotted down a list of books. Taking refuge in the role of teacher.

'These would be useful. But what I'd really like would be to hear your own ideas. Once you've had the chance to think about the characters in Hardy's novels and read a few more of his poems.'

'Could I do English at university, Miss Morrison? I might do Politics or Sociology. I can't decide.'

'Why would you choose Politics or Sociology?' Alice noted how Mattie's hands moved in explanation as she talked, grew more relaxed. She liked physicality and movement in a person. She hated the tight, cautious way her own uncertain attitudes to touch seemed tied up and restrained. Frozen at the point of connection. When all she really wanted was to let go of inhibition.

'Because I want to change the world. Help people have a better life.'

'That's quite a big ambition', Alice was amused, 'and it might not be quite as easy as you think.' She was teasing. Mattie had extremely bright blue eyes. Like cornflowers, she thought, or forget-me-nots.

'I don't imagine, for a moment, that it will be easy.' Mattie's voice was speeding into gear. 'I can see how capitalism, for example, works against the interests of the people, in families like mine, in my street. How much easier it is for working men to take advantage of their wives and daughters, rather than confront the bosses. Are you a socialist Miss Morrison? I hope you are.'

By now Mattie had forgotten her initial shyness. What a question to ask a teacher! It wasn't usual to have such discussions in St Swithuns. Where politics were strictly out of bounds. And familiarity across the ranks was not officially encouraged.

'It's not a term I'd use about myself.' Alice struggled to be honest. 'I don't think about the world in labels and affiliations, Mattie. Perhaps I should. I don't like privilege or corruption. And I don't like the ways some kinds of men imagine they're superior to others.'

'Especially women', Mattie interrupted.

'Yes probably', Alice smiled. 'Perhaps I read too many poems. Too much philosophy. I place more emphasis on feelings and ideas than politics.'

Mattie nodded. It wasn't what she wanted Alice Morrison to say — that she wouldn't call herself a socialist. But she didn't seem the type to vote conservative or make lame excuses for the middle classes either. Even though she'd been to Oxford and grown up in the south of England.

'Should you be researching History in the library,

Mattie? It's very interesting to talk to you of course. But I wouldn't want to keep you from your lesson.' Alice retreated into more familiar territory. She was feeling confused and slightly panic-stricken. It wasn't easy to explain.

'God, yes!' Mattie jumped into action and headed for the door. She pulled the kind of face at Alice which she usually reserved for Joyce. Already intimate in a way that breached a subtle boundary. 'Thanks for the book list.' And she was gone.

'You took your time.' Joyce looked at her in total disbelief as Mattie piled into her chair, pretending to consult the faded *History of the British Empire* on the desk in front. Her head was full of poetry, clever words and big ideas. The smell of summer flowers on olive skin.

In the April of the lower sixth Joyce acquired a new boyfriend. She said it was because spring was in the air, and she was growing tired of Malcolm Smith, who she'd been seeing for the past two years. She met Phil in the Locarno Ballroom at a dance. He was 19 and doing 'an apprenticeship' in decorating. Which probably meant he worked with his father and was learning the trade whilst helping on the job. It also meant he got to use his father's van to run errands and pick up more supplies.

Increasingly he timed his visits to the warehouse to coincide with Joyce and Mattie coming out of school. Or over lunch. On pre-arranged occasions Joyce would bolt down her mince and onions, or steak and kidney pie, and rush along the driveway to sit in Phil's van for half an hour before Biology or English. Sometimes he'd turn up after school, lounging with calculated indifference by the lamp post near the gate, puffing on a Park Drive. Suzanne Haliday whispered her disdain. It was something about his paint splattered dungarees and tousled Beatle cut. But she was too afraid of Joyce to criticise directly.

Mattie did her best to be enthusiastic. But quite honestly, she'd rather have Joyce to herself. And be going home by 14 bus. Instead, as Joyce climbed into the front of the van beside Phil, Mattie had to scramble in the back, among the pots of paint and rolls of anaglypta. It was not a peak experience. But for a while, both she and Joyce tried to persuade themselves it was. Not a lot of girls had boyfriends with their own transport in the sixties. So sitting in the front of Phil's dad's van, in full view of those who rated such things, was an experience to be savoured. Joyce felt like a real woman. Not a schoolgirl. With a man. Not a spotty adolescent from King Edwards. She loved the envious and curious attention of her classmates, waiting by the bus stop, as the van sailed past them towards town. Stuck among the step ladders and assorted brushes in the back did not provide Mattie with the same amount of opportunity to acquire new status. It felt like squatting in the outside coal house in Ceylon Street, which her father had transformed into his tool shed. Something she only ever did in dire emergencies. When she was hiding from her mother or the brothers. The final resort she hadn't felt the need to contemplate for months.

It's true that Joyce could have ditched her altogether. It wasn't so unusual for the best of friends to come unstuck as soon as romance with the other sex appeared on the agenda. But Joyce was loyal to her mates and Mattie was the only one she had at school. After a week or so, however, the stakes got altered. As Joyce and

Mattie were stepping out along the drive, with the usual exhilaration of release, and the usual air of expectation about Phil and the van and Joyce's love life, they saw a second, grimy youth in overalls lounging by the lamp post. Joyce yanked her beret off her bouffant and stuffed it in her satchel as per usual. An act of reckless disobedience given they were still in spitting distance of the school. In eye shot of sanctimonious prefects and the kind of teachers that left like lemmings on the dot of four, as soon as the persistent ringing in the lobby announced the end of lessons for another day.

'This is Vic.' Phil directed his introductions towards Mattie with a smirk. 'He was just passing.'

The boy was smaller and thinner than Phil. In fact he was smaller and thinner than all of them. He looked embarrassed as he nodded at the girls. Phil said he'd sort him out a girlfriend. But it wasn't an arrangement Vic would have chosen to be conducted in this rather random way.

'Alright?' Vic said.

Joyce looked him up and down with little interest and planted a pert kiss on Phil's dusty cheek. Phil's arms flayed around her in a gesture of conceit and ownership. Little recognising the realities of his own brief existence in the general scheme of things. Mattie couldn't help but notice that Vic was wearing sandals. Colourless, round-toed, plastic sandals. With grey woollen socks.

'We used to be at school together', Vic said about himself and Phil as he helped Mattie climb into the back of the van. There seemed to be more paint and rolls of wallpaper than usual.

'Just been to the warehouse.' Phil watched them through his rear view mirror. 'You might need to snuggle up together on that bit of plank.' He winked at Joyce who turned to give Mattie an encouraging grin.

'I could get the bus if it's any trouble.' Mattie wished she'd had the foresight to object, before she let Vic climb aboard behind her, and slam the door.

'It isn't any trouble is it Phil?' Vic smelled like Mattie's elder brothers. A mix of sweat and aftershave. Old Spice, probably, or Brut. She knew, only too well, about the general shortcomings of men in relation to their personal hygiene. Doused in Brut, forgetting entirely about those quaint, old fashioned solutions to the stink of sweat. Called soap and water.

'Learn anything of interest?' Vic tried again.

Phil glanced into the mirror, hoping to see signs of progress in the back. But Mattie was not easily impressed. And whilst it wasn't Vic's intention to make fun, if Mattie could be bothered, she would have told him things about school that would have blown his mind. But he wasn't worth the effort. She took out a book and started reading, in the hopes that, by registering indifference, he'd soon lose interest. The van pulled up at the central bus station as usual. It wasn't easy to scramble out the back, clutching her satchel and her extra duffel bag, stumbling over tools and piles of decorating materials. Trying to keep her skirt in place and cling on to some semblance of sophistication. Vic's plastic sandals slapped against the pavement as he jumped down eagerly in a final effort to be appreciated. She took his outstretched hand ungraciously, just as Phil cracked one of his usual jokes, and Joyce screeched out the sort of laugh that could shatter crystal. And just as Alice Morrison was crossing to the bus stop opposite. She turned to see Mattie descending from the back of a painting and decorating wagon in the grip of a spotty youth who was holding onto her hand as though he'd won it in a raffle. Her heart skipped. She looked away. But not before Mattie caught the glimpse of what seemed like disapproval in her otherwise impervious expression.

'Oh fuck off Vic', Mattie said. 'Fuck off all of you.' She charged off in the opposite direction, leaving Joyce confused about the wisdom of trying to find Mattie a boyfriend, against her better judgement. Vic shook his head and climbed into the front seat next to Phil to contemplate the mysteries of women.

'She's not your type', Phil said. 'I wouldn't worry about it.'

'Then why did you say she was?'

'I thought you were feeling desperate.'

'Not that desperate.'

They sped off back to work in silence.

The year passed. Alice walked home each night to her first floor flat at 29 Acacia Avenue. She made herself a light meal for one, listened to the Archers or a concert on the wireless, prepared her lessons for the morning and, increasingly, it must be said, derived enormous pleasure from the satisfaction of a job well done.

At first the activity was innocent enough, and insubstantial. Alice re-ran the conversations and exchanges of the day, from the loneliness and quiet of her little room. To reflect back on her teaching, to think about the idiosyncrasies of colleagues, the moods and mysteries of children. If Mattie, for example, hadn't lasted till the sixth form to do A-levels, she would be out at work by now. Going steady, possibly engaged. By Alice's age, she would be married with children of her own to keep the circle turning. Generation after generation.

'I'm going to be a woman of the world', Mattie laughed. 'No barriers or frontiers. No Sunday lunch at one o'clock, slept off by idle men, whilst women clear away the dishes. No Saturdays around the television, watching cowboys killing Indians and stand up comics telling boring jokes about their mother-in-law.'

Alice saw a way to help her. She lent her books and added extra comments to her homework. She watched her face in class for signs of understanding or confusion, encouraging her to answer questions. To speak her ideas out loud with growing confidence. To forget about the jibes and jealousies of other girls.

Sometimes the atmosphere in English lessons felt quite tense. Mattie often seemed preoccupied. She spent a lot of time gazing out the window. She lived inside her head a lot, in ways she couldn't speak about to Joyce or to her family. Sometimes she tried to talk it through with Elvis, in the privacy of the upstairs room at home. He understood about these things. When Mattie thought she couldn't keep the feelings to herself much longer, he listened and she felt better. Maybe she should ask Miss Morrison for an opinion? But she never did.

Alice continued to prepare her lessons with single-mindedly dedication. Apart from school, she lived a fairly solitary existence with no one much to talk to. Overtures of friendship from Frances Tate felt positively lethal.

'I'm surprised you don't include Radclyffe Hall in your Famous Women Writers series. Tate was reading Alice's advert for the English Club, which met on Thursday evenings after school. Alice pretended not to hear.

Another time she tried more direct action.

'Pip and I are going to a place in Leeds on Saturday

night. Only an hour in the car but completely out of bounds.' Tate pulled her chair close to Alice in the staff room, so that she could talk without being overheard. 'Would you like to come? It might do you good to have some fun.'

Alice could guess the kind of place she meant. She had no idea who Pip might be, or how Alice fitted in with Tate's unspecific attitude to 'fun'.

'I'm going away this week-end', Alice lied. 'Perhaps some other time.'

'Would you like to come round for a bite to eat one night? We probably should stick together, don't you think?' Tate brushed Alice's sleeve briefly with her hand, as if by accident.

'Well . . . Yes, indeed. Thank you Frances. Marking's pretty vicious at the moment – what with mocks and everything. I . . . ummm . . .' Alice's excuses slithered into dust.

Meanwhile, she guessed that what she was feeling about Mattie was completely out of order.

'How are things Mattie?' Her attempts to be discreetly chummy were fraught with tension, in ways that made the slightest small talk seem excruciating.

'All right, thanks.' What could Mattie say that didn't fill the void with nothing? Joyce. The family. Elvis's new record. The daily journey on the 14 bus. Not much to offer here that would be of interest to Miss Morrison.

'What have you been up to then?' Alice's question fell like gravity between them. Death by conversation. No big ideas that she could yet articulate. No interesting foreign films or visits to the theatre. No life outside her imagination and the confines of her terrace bedroom. Even homework had its limitations. Mattie could ask Alice questions. But how could she discuss her insights and her theories about literature with someone who already knew everything there was to know about the subject? And how could Alice, who spoke about herself to no one, suddenly find intuition, solace, reciprocity in one who had to call her Miss and wear a faded beret with a silly badge, and a green striped tie?

Inside their heads both women formulated detailed conversations and debates. Interpreted each nuance. Each tortuous exchange. Asked questions about feelings and emotions. Shared secrets. Touched minds and reached out to connect. In practice, everything that wasn't being taught or learned, came out as fractured, awkward ricochets of language, shot against embarrassment and into gulfs of silence.

With mutual needs spectacularly unmet, and as the sexual tension grew between them, it wasn't easy to avoid recriminations.

'Are you concentrating on the question Mattie? Or are you swapping gossip there with Joyce?' Alice sounded like a teacher. But looked like a peevish lover.

Joyce couldn't stop the smile of recognition that spread across her face. Mattie blushed and looked away.

'I'm sure this lesson is very boring, compared to the details of your social life. But you have to do an exam in four weeks time, and no one – even you – can afford to waste their time.'

Joyce breathed a soft, low whistle. Unconsciously, it must be said. But registering the danger of explosion. Mattie banged her book shut and threw the pen she had been using on the desk. Her face was scarlet. The rest of the class watched the unfolding drama with a mixture of amusement and amazement.

'There's no need to put down your tools and go on strike.' Alice's attempt at levity and reconciliation was far from ept. Joyce wished she had the confidence to take control. To clear the room, send everybody out. Give Mattie and Miss Morrison a chance. But she was neither old enough nor brave enough to intervene.

'Sorry Miss Morrison.' She tried the next best thing, a cheeky grin. 'Don't lose your hair. We were talking about English. Honest.'

It was now a toss up which of them – Joyce or Alice Morrison – would get the flack from Mattie's anger first. Joyce slid down her chair in an effort to retreat. Suzanne Haliday was laughing in the corner. There would be hell to pay for this at break time.

Fortunately, for all concerned, the end of lesson bell sounded from the lobby, splitting the tension like an exclamation mark, a sudden shaft of sunlight puncturing a cloud. Alice returned to her desk at the front and Mattie headed for the door at breakneck speed.

'Will you be staying for the English Club tonight?' Alice's question scuttled after Mattie like an echo, its note of desperation charged to bring her back, to make amends. Without success. Mattie banged out through the door, along the corridor and off towards the gate. Tears of anger and humiliation spilling down her boiling cheeks.

The rest of the class left the room in silence. Suzanne Haliday was wearing the kind of smirk that made Joyce want to stick her stupid face into the toilet. She collected her books and papers slowly and fixed her focus on the task in hand.

'Just a moment, Joyce.' Alice's restless fingers on the button at her neck were white with agitation. 'I'm sorry about that. I clearly got it wrong.' Her voice sounded as though she might cry. 'Will you give Mattie my apologies? I didn't mean to imply that either of you are not committed to your studies.'

Joyce nodded and tried to shape her mouth into a reassuring smile. It turned out rather tight and unconvincing.

'See you tomorrow, Miss Morrison.' She closed the door quietly and sped off down the corridor in search of Mattie.

For four days Mattie stayed away from school. She couldn't sleep. She didn't know precisely what had happened. Or why she felt such great betrayal. Alice cancelled the English Club on Thursday night without an explanation. On Friday she taught badly and resorted to giving tests and silent reading to disgruntled juniors. By Wednesday she was visibly upset. And no longer able to conceal her agitation.

'Something wrong Alice?' Frances Tate watched Alice's distraction turn into obvious distress. She didn't know about the outburst in the English class. Or imagine that Mattie's non-appearance was anything but illness.

Alice should probably have avoided Tate and not colluded in her own capitulation. But her usual defences were blown to bits, and Tate was not the woman to ignore an opportunity.

'I'm worried about Mattie Reed', Alice said. 'About her absence. It may be something that I said.'

'How do you mean, something that you said?'

'I accused her of gossiping with Joyce in English. Implied she wasn't concentrating.'

Tate laughed.

'Oh dear, how terrible!'

Alice knew she must sound foolish but couldn't stop the flow of personal regret.

'Sometimes the girls seem very special to each other, don't they?' Tate continued. 'And when they get their heads together and start to giggle . . .' Tate watched the colour rise in Alice's cheeks. She didn't feel the need to spell out jealousy.

'I was rather tired. Irritated', Alice said. 'I don't want Mattie to miss this time at school, so close to her exams.'

'Don't worry about it Alice. She's probably got a cold or tonsillitis. Nothing in the slightest to do with your temporary absence of approval. If she isn't back by Friday I'll break the pattern of a lifetime and phone her up. Become a truly conscientious sixth form tutor. Will that set your mind at rest?'

Alice smiled weakly, thanking Tate. But knowing that she'd blown her cover. A disclosure which she'd rather not repeat, if she could help it. And one which she would certainly deny, if ever she was called to account.

By Wednesday evening, Friday seemed too long to wait for news of Mattie. Alice checked the phone book and convinced herself sufficiently about her personal disinterest to ring the number in Ceylon Street.

'I suppose that we've become a laughing stock.' Mattie spoke quietly into the telephone, conscious that the house was small and full of curiosity.

'A two-day wonder.' Alice preferred not to contemplate the obvious so long as she could still ignore it. 'I want you to come back to school tomorrow', Alice said. 'What does your mother have to say?'

'How can I tell my mother? She thinks it's overwork.'

'It probably is to do with feeling under pressure Mattie. To get the grades for university.'

'Is that what you think?'

'What should I think?'

'I don't know. You're the one who teaches about feelings, Miss Morrison.'

Mattie slammed down the receiver and shot upstairs to the safety of the sofa in her room. To turn up the volume on her Dancette. And play Elvis at full blast.

Seven

When Mattie returned to school on Monday neither she nor Alice made any reference to the phone call. Mattie was ashamed of herself and irritated with Alice for not having a better idea of 'what to do'. Alice seemed so thoughtful when it came to reading other women's writing about complicated feelings and emotions, but full of contradictory messages when it came to dealing with her own.

In truth Alice was confused. It was not personal preoccupation or perversity that stopped her sweeping Mattie off her feet. It was not the lack of opportunity. Or inertia. It was fear. When Mattie came back to school after the phone call Alice took refuge in her routines and set about preparing her revision classes with clipped efficiency. She issued notes and model answers like an automaton. She insisted on subjecting already overanxious insomniacs to timed essays in exam conditions. She made them recite quotes by heart that could be used as 'evidence and illustration'. She made no concessions, in her drive for academic excellence, to the competing tensions of the body and the mind, the pleasures of the flesh, the law of nature that guarantees a broken heart or shattered love life will make its predictable appearance at the most inconvenient moment in a girl's career.

In private she explained the sexual turbulence she was experiencing as the probable consequence of her psychology. The legacy of a confused, and for the most part, unhappy childhood. The horror of her brothers' fumbling and distasteful overtures to sex, worked out in ways that made her feel abused and dirty. The fact that sexual encounters in her Oxford days provided only further confirmation of her failure; of loneliness and longing.

Mattie was more impulsive. She was more likely to ignore the signs of danger and take risks. She felt like a woman, with strong emotions and sexual priorities – but with no experience, or repertoire of language to make much sense of why her body bumped so skittishly against her mind. At school she still came dressed in the identity of a child, in a uniform which had changed only slightly since the time the school was founded. Her face scrubbed, her brown laced shoes well polished, her thick beige stockings the only small concession made by regulations to her sixth form seniority. Each day she sat in dismal, creaking classrooms under glass, whilst teacher after teacher restricted their instructions to matters of the mind. She was among the first of her generation of working class girls to be allowed access to the ideas and institutions of men. She already knew so much about their history, their culture, their values and ideals. She could recite their mottoes and sing their songs. She already suspected that her independence and escape depended upon building a career that mirrored that of men. An honorary incumbent or a token woman. But what she couldn't quite work out, was how the exhortations of her teachers to be dedicated, concentrated, and as Joyce said, 'automated', in the pursuit of knowledge, fitted in with all the messy-round-the edges, and utterly confusing, compulsions and desires, that raced around the confines of her body, without regard to rational thinking or accumulating A-levels.

Alice was of little help in this respect. If she had reconciled the competing claims of her emotions, lusts and intellect, if she was, in any, well-worked-out, sense her own woman, she seemed reluctant or incapable of communicating the ingredients to others. Her over-riding fear of failure and rejection counselled caution. When Mattie thought of growing up, she wanted to be like Alice, but more decisive. Like Alice, only daring. Like Alice, with more determination.

The day after the A-levels were over, Mattie left school for a summer job in the laundry where her mother worked. She came to say goodbye, and a rather graceless thank you, given that Alice had not quite delivered the goods she would have chosen. She handed over a giant box of Cadbury's Milk Tray in an offhand kind of way, as if embarrassed by the kind of cliché she could read about in any teenage magazine. Played out less predictably, perhaps. But none the less consistent with the current iconography of romance. Across mountain ranges and through blizzards – 'and just because the lady loves . . .' The slightest suspicion of amusement or restraint in Alice's response would have caused Mattie to drop the box and run. Or take Joyce's advice and eat the bloody lot herself. She needn't have worried, though. Alice, for some sudden reason, let go her usual reserve. She stretched out her hand to brush Mattie's cheek, where it now burned red with probable embarrassment. Alice was startled by the softness of her skin, the kind of lightening that started from her fingers and swept through her body of its own accord. With nothing she could do to stop its force or energy. But which also caused her hand to tremble and her resolve to waiver.

'You are so beautiful', Alice heard herself speak to Mattie as though for the first time. 'I'll miss you when you're gone.'

Their eyes held onto each other as if, for that second anyway, their lives depended on it. Years later it was the memory which, for each of them, recorded the moment when it happened. The beginning of a journey that started long ago, the birth of a love affair, Alice's hand reaching towards Mattie's hair.

The moment passed. Alice could hear the noise of laughter in the distance as girls ran screaming through the shrubberies beyond the dining hall, drunk on cider, and in the familiar, crazy ritual of release. France Tate had obviously abandoned all attempts to stop their fun and was working through the lists of next year's girls to identify prospective prefects. And, as usual, failing to prevent her personal preferences from clouding her selection.

'Shall we write?' Alice looked unsure. 'Perhaps we

could be friends', she spoke tentatively, 'when you are no longer here?'

Mattie smiled and nodded. If Alice had been more experienced, she would possibly have detected the fleeting register of victory in Mattie's smile. But she was not. And Mattie had not yet worked out the best way to drive home her advantage. But it was a lesson she would come to learn. And one that Alice would always find it difficult to resist.

That evening Alice finally accepted Frances Tate's invitation to eat dinner with herself and Pip. She arrived with a bunch of flowers and a bottle of Bordeaux at the door of a modern bungalow on the edge of a small private estate. A neat garden announced a nondescript red brick box. One of a regimented row with netted windows and brown varnished doors. Standard roses and golden privet. Inside the boxes there lived bank clerks and public servants. Professional wives and newlyweds and widows. At number 17, a pair of stalwart spinsters – combining their resources. Alice rang the bell.

'Hello, I'm Pip.' The woman who answered the door wore a creased apron around a stocky body of indeterminate dimensions. Her hair was clipped short, gun metal grey. Her face crisscrossed like tissue paper with fine wrinkles. Slightly flushed. A face that laughed a lot and probably enjoyed a drink. In her hand she carried a large tumbler of gin.

Pip beamed and stood aside to let Alice through the door.

'Come in. Come in.' She studied her with practised familiarity. Like a proposition. An affirmation of connection. Another one of us – miscreant, outcast, sinner. Like Tate she was discrete at work. But now they were on home territory and the steady flow of alcohol had already begun to blow caution to the wind.

'I'm glad you could make it. Tate has told me all about you. Drop your coat over there.'

Alice handed over the wine and pink carnations and followed Pip into a bright, messy kitchen with neon strips of light and dusty corn dollies tacked onto pale yellow walls against white Formica shelves.

'Help yourself to ice and tonic.' Pip thrust a generous double gin towards Alice, despite her look of indecision. 'You can talk to me whilst I make dinner.'

A dog of small and snappy persuasion sniffed suspiciously around Alice's ankles.

'Don't mind Gordon. His bark is much worse than his bite. Rather like Tate!'

Pip laughed heartily at her joke, wiping the tears from her eyes on the back of her thick square hand, as she crushed numerous cloves of garlic into the onions cooking on the stove. Red and yellow peppers bled their sweetness onto the chopping board, got stripped and shredded with thoughtless competence, and tossed into the pan to bubble and collapse into the garlic. The board was bleached and scored with the multiple scars of sliced shallots, chopped chives and plump rump steaks smashed into submission.

'Can I help?' said Alice.

'Goodness No!' Pip straddled the kitchen like a speaker on a soap box, regaling her audience with rhetoric and accusations. Flourishing food in ways that transformed appetite into eating and eating into art. Lavish, obscene, excessive. Like a bacchanalian feast, behind nets, and beyond an otherwise quite commonplace façade.

Across the lawn Frances Tate was clearing weeds from the flower bed.

'Go and tell her you've come.' Pip was bossy. She pushed Gordon out of her way with a well angled shove against his scraggy ribs. Plum tomatoes split their skins and flooded tiny yellow seeds into the slippery spill of onion juice and peppers in the pan. 'She'll enjoy showing off the garden.'

Alice did as she was told, trying to adjust her composure before confronting Tate.

'Hello Frances', she said brightly. 'The garden's looking lovely.'

Tate lent on the wooden handle of her hoe. She had changed from her school clothes into baggy cords, a checked flannel shirt and thick ribbed pullover. Her brown hands were weathered and strong. Her eyes twinkled with the arrogance of someone who was used to getting her own way. She struck a match against the surface of the wall and offered Alice a Sobrane cigarette. Alice took it gratefully.

'I'll show you some of my handiwork.' Tate strode across the grass to where a splashing of water tumbled through a pile of rocks into a fair sized pond.

'Dug it out myself. Fetched the stones from Wharfedale. Planted the rockery and filled the pond with fish and frog spawn. Took me two weeks. I did it after school whilst Pip was playing wifey in the kitchen.'

'Really?' Alice said. 'Well it looks really professional.'

Tate nodded.

'I like to see a job well done. The satisfaction of honest-to-goodness physical labour after a day of prising Latin translations out of scatter brained schoolgirls.

Those trees over there will have to come down. They block the light. But I'll plant a hedge of copper beech instead and build a greenhouse round the back to bring on seeds and cuttings.'

Alice could see the attraction. The opposite to introspection.

'It must be very relaxing – gardening.'

'It's proper work', Tate corrected her. 'I don't suppose that woman sent me out a drink did she?'

Alice shook her head.

'Give her a shout will you Alice? Tell her to pour me a large scotch. I'll just put the tools away and then we can dedicate ourselves to getting sloshed.'

Frances Tate by-passed the kitchen without a second glance and launched herself into a chintzy armchair beside the fire place. Gordon jumped onto her knee and looked like he was digging in for the duration. Alice faltered. Wondering whether she should try again to offer Pip some help. But her head was buried in the nether regions of the oven, a skewer prodding at a breast of chicken. The sitting room was functional and modern. What they spoke of in the sixties as contemporary. At one end a teak wood table was already set for dinner. At the other, French windows opened onto a slabbed patio overlooking the garden. A picture of the royal family hung above the mantlepiece, the royal children still a mix of toddlers and teenagers wearing kilts. On the sideboard was a photograph of Pip and Tate, looking light and windswept, against a mountain side in Scotland. Dressed like serious walkers in draw string anoraks and canvas rucksacks. Their curly heads inclined together, laughing into the eye of the camera.

'Don't dawdle', Tate insisted. 'Come and tell me how you're going to manage now your little bird has flown.'

She watched Alice blush and shift her body in the chair, providing all the evidence she needed to confirm the accuracy of her suspicions.

'She's not so innocent as she looks – young Mattie. Did you persuade her to confess her passion for you Alice? Or are you waiting for the inevitable letter, now that she's left?' Tate was not going to be deterred. Or waste her breath on euphemism.

'It's like a volcano waiting to erupt, don't you find? The last year at school? So much emotion. And such intensity around exams. An important climax to a school career, I suppose. So much depending on the outcome. The girls get anxious. So do we.'

'I'm not talking about grades and jitters.' Frances took a hearty swig of scotch. 'I'm talking bout sex. The kind of thing that in my day we called "particular friendships". The urge girls get to kiss each other on the lips when they should be batting balls across a tennis court or conjugating verbs. The way that some of them can spot a gay girl on the staff at fifty paces. And then proceed to fall in love with her. Become obsessed. Watch her every move. Memorise her every word. Blush and bridle like a frisky colt when she's around. Fall into cruel moods of bleak despair in holidays or when she doesn't immediately approve the poem or the essay that was written just for her. I'm talking about "unnatural passions" Alice. The kind we know about too well. No need to be shy with me, you know. Not now you've met Pip.'

Alice looked uncomfortable.

'I don't know what you mean.' She sounded quite unconvincing.

'It's better that you know yourself, Alice. Whatever else you choose to say to others. Although discretion is usually the better part of valour.'

Frances Tate fingered a black Russian Sobrane into a small gold holder and drew the smoke into her lungs.

'We "women of the shadows" ', she laughed mischievously. 'Inverts and pseudo inverts. Nature's casualties.'

'All right!' Alice raised her voice with some emotion. 'I know I'm not like other women. But I'm not a casualty. My career is important to me – teaching girls. I would never, never do anything to jeopardise my job, or act improperly in a position of responsibility.'

'I know that.' Tate was serious. 'But it will not always be so easy. You are young and I am not. Teaching beautiful young women is heady stuff, Alice. So easy to become emotionally involved. So hard to separate conviction from commitment. Intellect from feelings. Emulation from adoration. And Mattie is one of us, don't you agree?'

'I don't know.' If Alice knew the way to leave she would have gathered up her coat and headed for the door. Instead of feeling trapped by Tate's interrogation.

'Dinner's ready', Pip shouted from the kitchen. 'Are you coming to carve this poor dead bird Frances? Or are you drunk already?'

Tate raised her eyes to heaven with the kind of long suffering sigh that Alice had frequently observed in the demeanour of her father.

'Coming dearest! I hope you haven't drowned the sauce in garlic as usual!' She winked at Alice. 'Pip's a first rate cook. I hope you're feeling peckish.'

At dinner Pip fussed around the table. Fetching and carrying plates and dishes. Unfolding napkins and refilling glasses. She piled a selection of vegetables onto Tate's plate and placed it in front of her.

'Help yourself, Alice We don't stand on ceremony here.' Pip pushed a dish of steaming celery towards Alice.

'Is it sweet?' Tate poked the white meat on her plate

suspiciously with her fork. 'If it's past its best the flavour will be bland.'

'It came from the butcher this morning. Why don't you try it before you start complaining? When do I ever give you chicken that isn't in peak condition and roasted to perfection?'

'You see where marriage gets you, Alice? What a crusty couple we've become.'

'You speak for yourself', Pip interrupted. 'My sunny temperament and tolerance are legendary. I could be driven to despair by your many misdemeanours, but I'm not. Pass Alice the wine and stop embarrassing our guest.'

Frances tucked into the chicken with relish.

'How do you manage on your own, Alice? Are you fond of cooking?' Pip's face was glowing from all her culinary exertions, and from the relative speed with which she downed the wine to keep in step with Tate.

'It's probably quite social – cooking.' Alice heard herself repeat the usual clichés. 'I don't do much of it, in fact.'

'Well, if you're feeling lonely, don't get rushed into anything you might regret. Women are much, much worse to keep in check than men.'

'How would you know?' Tate interrupted Pip as usual. 'What men do you know about?'

'I knew about my father and my brothers. At least they did the washing up occasionally!'

'Let's change the subject shall we? Alice will be extremely bored by our domestic squabbles. What Alice needs is the opportunity to meet some decent women.'

'Watch her!' Pip leaned across the table, laughing and pointing a stubby finger at Tate. 'No one would believe she's a respectable school mistress. She knows every bar and pick-up joint this side of Watford. Been thrown out of most of them. You can't take her anywhere any more!'

Alice began to feel like she was losing ground and wading into waters that were well out of her depth.

'We know a little place in Leeds', Tate persisted. 'You would like it, wouldn't she Pip? There's a dining area that does quite reasonable food. A professional crowd. The women behind the bar are quite discreet'.

'It isn't heavy', Pip confided. 'I've been in places with Tate where I was terrified and thought I'd never see the light of day again...'

'But lived to tell the tale.' Tate chuckled, pulling the cork out of another bottle. 'We'd keep an eye on you, Alice. Keep you out of mischief... unless you want the chance to run amok?'

She beamed at Alice with all the usual inhibitions and coded innuendo of the staff room long forgotten.

'Have you known each other for a while?' Alice grew in confidence with the help of wine and in the jet stream of Pip and Tate's high spirits.

'A lifetime', Frances groaned.

'Ten years, on and off.' Pip retained some small commitment to the truth.

'More off than on, of course.' Frances finished up the celery and sweet pepper sauce.

'There was a hiatus in the middle', Pip confided, 'when I went to Cardiff for a while.'

'Can't you tell she used to be a midwife?' Frances always managed to maintain a reasonable association with sobriety, despite the occasional slurring of a sentence here and there.

Alice, not surprisingly, grew increasingly confused.

'A hiatus has got nothing whatever to do with the medical profession', Pip said.

'But it was brought about by the intervention of a nurse!' Frances slapped the table in delight, enthralled by the cleverness of her own verbal ingenuity. Both she and Pip were now quite flushed and rising to their regular routine of banter and belligerence. Neither of them required much of a contribution from Alice to enliven the occasion, so long as she performed the role of audience.

'To put it bluntly, this woman decided to rope in someone else.' Pip's mouth tightened imperceptibly. 'A Ward Sister at the General. Supposed to be some kind of lodger.'

Tate winked at Alice.

'She was a lodger. At first. Not my fault that she fell hopelessly in love with me.'

'It was your fault she ended up in bed with you. And your mistake to think I'd simply grin and bear it!'

'But I loved you both', Tate protested. 'You know I can't stand uniform monogamy. It's not suited to my disposition.'

'Except when no one else but me will have you.'

'So what happened?' Alice interrupted. Anxious that the banter was becoming acrimonious.

'Pip buggered off to Cardiff and left us to it.' Frances spoke as if she felt abandoned.

'You old goat!' Pip grabbed the empty plates and dishes and stumbled them precariously from the dining table to the kitchen. 'You gave me no choice but to leave.' The door slammed shut behind her whilst Tate raised her eyebrows in a gesture of confused innocence.

'I'm sure you can appreciate my problem here.' It didn't suit Tate to pretend to simper. 'Pip is so possessive. And I have a profound distaste for jealousy.' She stretched a sun browned arm across the hand embroidered table cloth to touch Alice lightly on the sleeve. 'I'm sure you understand.' She tried to hold Alice's eyes in a kind of secretive collusion. But Alice was not the one to even recognise a proposition. She pulled her arm away quite fiercely as Pip elbowed her way back through the door, balancing an enormous sherry trifle and a jug of cream.

'Anyway, I came back. More's the pity. The nurse got fed up with the endless domesticity involved in looking after someone who is so relentlessly untidy. On top of night shifts. And too little sleep. And Tate got sick of living out of tins. Didn't you my darling?'

Frances poured herself a glass of wine, her mouth set into a sulky line of disaffection.

'Give Alice another drink as well dear. And mine could do with topping up.'

Frances did as she was told. With about as little grace as a disgruntled child.

Pip lobbed the sherry trifle into crystal dishes and directed them unsteadily around the table.

Alice focused her attention on the task in hand, winding her spoon into the excess of double cream and maraschino cherries, until it once again felt safe to raise her eyes above the richochet of allegations.

'So.' After a few moments of concentrated eating Tate seemed like she'd regained her equilibrium. And Pip was not the one to nurse her grievances for long. 'Nearly the summer, Alice. Planning to do anything exciting?'

'I thought about Italy.' Alice was relieved to take up refuge in more neutral territory.

'Umm...' Tate was clearly unimpressed. 'The problem with Italy, so far as I'm concerned, is the Italians. Quite uncivilised! Venice is filthy in August. And stinking hot...'

'Alice might like Italy', Pip intervened to cancel out another tipsy stream of consciousness. 'Just because you get irritable in sticky climates.'

Alice nodded gratefully.

'And what about you?'

'Probably be Brighton.' Tate slid her finger round the last remaining trace of double cream and sucked it thoughtfully. 'You always know where you are in Brighton.'

Pip smiled across at her through flushed and watery eyes of familiarity and resignation. As Alice made a move to leave, her private consternation still in tact, it seemed as though the status quo had been restored.

Eight

In the end it was Tommy that drove Mattie to the university. The proud owner of a two tone Anglia, an endorsed licence and no road tax – they made the journey by the back roads in the days when it was still possible to drive from Holderness to Leicester without any sight of motor way. Mattie packed two small suitcases and a box of books carefully into the boot and Tommy packed his tool kit. Just in case.

'Always wash the bath out *before* you use it', Mattie's mother couldn't contemplate communal living in 'halls of residence' without imagining disease. 'And don't talk to strange men.'

'Ring your mother once a week', her father said. 'She'll only natter herself if not. Don't get into trouble and mind your ps and qs.'

As the car pulled away from the kerb, Mattie's mother and father waved like automatons from the netted windows in the front room. Mattie's mother sighed and took her husband's arm. 'I'll put the kettle on', she said. 'Make a nice cup of tea.'

Mattie left, like swallows in September, without a backward glance. The broken ends of terrace and slabbed grey streets were, as usual, dull in the faded autumn light. You can shut out the sunlight with curtains. Warm the frosty mornings with a well laid fire. But it's the decay that creeps in imperceptibly and takes root in the bricks and timbers of a town. That, no one has the wherewithal to shift. Crumbling the brickwork, swelling and blistering the wood, cracking the paving stones and leaving trails of rough grey dust and mildew along the floor line of a 100 damp and dingy terraced houses. Built for railway workers and factory hands of the previous century. Still split to bursting with the urban poor. The ones whose poverty had displaced community and was waiting to be re-discovered by tense young men in green duffle coats. Carrying clip boards and speaking in the rhetoric of social deprivation.

As they left the edge of town, the grey black streets slid through the rear view mirror and into history. A place from which Mattie might occasionally draw reasons for her politics. But which she would rarely re-visit. And where she would seldom stay. Beyond the town the autumn fields were spiked with yellow stubble waiting to be burned. Silence snaked like a river through tumbled reeds. The skyline wide and flat against dark chocolate soil and occasional rows of green.

Tommy whistled as he went. Cocky in his car. Pushing 50 mph on the flat straight roads. Belching smoke from the decrepit exhaust system like an exuberant but asthmatic steam train. A day 'off sick' from Metal Box to take our Mattie to the university.

Leicester might have been a million miles away. It seemed so to Mattie who had rarely travelled further than Scarborough on a bus trip, or to the occasional week-end with her Auntie Jean in Halifax. As they approached the city centre the dismal terraced streets looked much the same as those she'd left behind. The same insidious decay. The same pinched faces of the poor. But here were mosques and temples and brightly painted shops. And window displays selling saris and bales of cloth in incandescent colours. And restaurants and aromatic spices she had never seen or smelled before. The grim streets jewelled with brightly dressed children, their dark eyes and blue black hair gleaming in the last light of an alien afternoon.

Mattie watched eagerly from the window as Tommy steered the Anglia through a maze of shops and building yards. And run down garages and factories making shoes and hosiery. Towards the brash and neutral city centre and the wide green park that flanked the university. It was an ordinary kind of place – called red brick – which the rich and famous chose only as a last resort. But which to Mattie seemed like Camelot. A wonderland in which to shift her life into the fast lane. Where anything was possible.

Mattie, of course, was never very rich, and only famous for five minutes at some point in the future. But the late sixties was an exciting moment to be a student – and seemed so at the time. A time that felt like she was making history. In student politics, in Civil Rights in the Women's Movement.

In 1967 Mattie was a socialist. Of the International variety. which meant she had to give out leaflets at factory gates. On her bike at half past five to catch the workers (male) as they were coming off the night shift. And argue with International Marxists about who amongst the proletariat or critical intelligentsia would first ignite the revolution. That's if they could make it to the barricades in time, after the pubs threw out. Many an evening was spent sitting in the corner, on the floor. In an upstairs room above the Engineers Arms, packed thick with student revolutionaries, smelling of smoke, stale sweat and spilt beer. Sipping Guinness from a half pint pot (she wasn't yet a feminist) and thinking how she would describe all this to Alice.

On a small raised platform, beneath a crumpled poster showing Lenin as an icon, the speakers for the night outlined the contemporary significance of Marx and Trotsky to the overthrow of Capital. Mattie usually took notes. Sometimes Carol Riley took the minutes. Announcements were made about future demonstrations. Help was solicited to produce news letters and print leaflets. The student leaders called each other comrade. In years to come they would become one major and several minor academics, a left wing Labour politician sliding inexorably towards the Centre Right, a journalist, a junkie and a stockbroker. Their celebrated groupie, Wild Madge Miller, whose electric energy lit up every late night party and every student sit-in that was ever organised, was still on the circuit 25 years later, going strong. Still playing mean guitar in student raves and venues south of Birmingham. Still high. Still struggling against convention. Otherwise the women were few in number, and rarely vocal, except when pressed to offer typing skills and answer telephones in dusty Union offices, religiously appropriated as temporary campaign headquarters.

Leaderlike politicos came dressed in donkey jackets or army surplus great coats. Their hair worn long, and if not always lank or greasy, at least deliberately dishevelled. They studied sociology. Or political philosophy and economics. Their current heroes Jean Paul Sartre and Che Guevara. Half concocted speeches on loosely folded paper and Zeroxed pamphlets stuck from their pockets like rounds of ammunition, with scribbled exclamation marks and thick black underlining of important truths. They rolled up joints to pass around in dedicated concentration and drank a lot of Guiness.

Politicos like these didn't live in halls of residence. They lived in flats. In which grease laid down upon the carpets and died like industrial effluence. Where fetid dishes waited to be noticed in reluctant sinks, until someone, secretly obsessed with hygiene, finally succumbed and washed them up. Girl friends came and went. To bring noisy love between damp, unlaundered sheets. To listen self consciously on the periphery of heated arguments about human capital and surplus value. To cook up mountains of spaghetti in tinned tomato sauce with garlic bread. And come back three days later to find the remnants still waiting to be trashed.

Mattie, on the other hand, lived next door to Carol Riley in a hall of residence. With thin walls, a brown and orange bed spread and matching curtains. 'A' Block. Number 46. The same number as the road that led from Holderness to Leicester.

'Well, that's a coincidence our Mattie.' Her mother put a lot of store by fate. And faith in proverbial wisdom like 'Never count your chickens', and 'Don't cross your bridges'. Most of which were negatives, influenced by resignation and the expectation of disaster. The need to 'keep your head down' and 'your nose clean'. Just in case.

Mattie liked her little room. It had a built in washbasin, a desk and wardrobe with a door that swung open every time she turned on the light. Home from home. But twice as nice. Elvis came to join her for a while but soon got rolled away in favour of the young Bob Dylan. Then Joan Baez. Then Leonard Cohen looking suicidal. Dusty Springfield made it to the wall above the bed because she reminded Mattie of her old friend Joyce. And of something else she couldn't quite articulate. Or put her finger on.

Carol Riley didn't look like Joyce. She was middle class. Her father worked in somewhere called Iran in something that had to do with oil. When she was in Iran her mother had got used to servants. So had Carol. Her room was a litter of discarded clothing, in a trail between the doorway and the washhand basin, leading to the bed. Discarded, like inhibitions by a jaded stripper, on her long day's journey towards night. Whenever there was screaming in the kitchen, it was usually because Carol Riley's nocturnal macaroni was still sticking to the bottom of a communal pan, or Carol Riley's dead French stick was growing mildew in the cupboard by the biscuits, waiting for someone to clean it up.

The only time she did anything domestic was when her boyfriend Kevin came across from Loughborough.

Carol washed his shirts and socks. And chose to iron them – the shirts – just at the moment when other women were failing desperately to find much true romance. Or feeling suicidal. At least Carol had a man. She carried his shirts like a banner to her study bedroom and hung his socks, like medals, on the washing line. Kevin had a clapped out Triumph Herald and a splash of acne. He was a post graduate engineer studying for a PhD. Which made him think himself superior to Carol (doing geography) and her friends like Mattie. Kevin had a view on everything, mostly ill-conceived, but which did not stem his stream of consciousness. Mattie already believed that engineers were generally illiterate and liked to catch him out on books he hadn't read. And words he couldn't quite pronounce correctly in his native geordie.

But, despite her attachment to Kevin, and despite her thoughtless but relentless certainty that someone, other than herself, would wash her dirty pans, and relegate discarded underwear to its appropriate drawer, Mattie took a shine to Carol Riley. Carol's Ma and Daddy voted Tory. In this sense she was not unlike the girls that Mattie had grown up with at St Swithuns. Except that Carol was in rebellion from her parents, brought about by 'post traumatic shock'. When she turned up from Iran at the beginning of her university career, she was sure that she was pregnant. The result of a one night stand with a junior diplomat in the British delegation. Mattie went with her to the Brook and got her checked out and reassured. And well supplied with pills.

'Get some for yourself whilst we're here', Carol said to Mattie.

'Alright.' Just to be in keeping with the times. But

she put them in her drawer unused and couldn't quite imagine why she'd bothered.

Under Mattie's influence, with gratitude and in life long solidarity, Carol came to view her parents and the junior diplomat as functionaries. The following week she joined the International Socialists. It took her rather longer to denounce Kevin. He was like going to church, she said, something you only had to do once a week, but which acted as a kind of buffer. A hedge against damnation. Mattie liked Carol because she had a wicked sense of humour. And because she was doing sex, and had a week-end boyfriend, she was much less preoccupied than the other women with getting laid and sorting out a husband.

'I would be married to the boy next door by now, if I'd have stayed at home', Mattie grumbled 'I haven't come as far as this to get landed with some other "boy next door" who just happens to live further afield.'

In this respect Saturday evenings were by far the worst. The earlier part of the day was spent in trying on clothes and shortening skirts. Followed by interminable queuing for the bathroom in an atmosphere of steamy desperation.

'Which band is it tonight?'
'Are they any good?'
'Does it matter!'
'Is Rick going?'
'Don't know. Is Pete?'
'He's sweet, Pete. Don't you think?'
'I don't like his nose. It's huge!'
'But he is sweet!'

Followed by orange pan stick, applied like airtex, to cover over spots. Hair ironed on a board till it stretched out straight and long over thin shoulders and angora sweaters. Plastic handbags packed with powder, blush and lipstick. Tampax in a plastic tube for privacy. A tooth brush and extra pair of knickers, in case of staying overnight, somewhere longed for but as yet unspecified. And off in little convoys, arm in arm. Eyes out on stalks and heady with anticipation. Like lambs to the proverbial slaughter. Down College Road towards the Students Union. Converging for the weekly cattle market, the pounding, airless heat and bittersweet excruciation of the Union dance.

By nine o'clock the rugby club was already shot to pieces in the bar. Their loud discordant voices and vulgar repertoire of songs establishing their elemental bonding with the boys, and general disregard for women. Those who were still left standing by 11 pm did their best to stumble round the dance floor, in search of some one daft enough, or desperate enough, to take them home to bed. And watch them vomit on the bathroom floor.

The women from College Hall sipped their bitter shandy. Stiff with nervous tension. They stood in huddles beside pillars, trying to pretend they liked the music. Trying not to sweep the floor with eyes like searchlights in the gloom. Waiting to be chosen. No one danced alone in 1967. No one except Wild Madge Miller expressed any initiative on her own behalf.

Some men made their decisions from a safe distance and then swooped. Others wandered round in packs to view the merchandise and weigh their chances. Women turned their anxious eyes away, suddenly intent on phoney conversations with each other. Pretending not to notice they were being rated. Standing with friends provided some security and helped to cultivate a thin bravado. But it could also be a problem, which placed women in competition with each other, to be judged according to their looks. Men usually approached in twos and threes, the bravest in the lead. Their selection already agreed among themselves, according to their preferences and aspirations. Inevitably more ambitious than you might expect, given their variety of imperfections. The women less discerning than you would have hoped. The mystique of manliness already well entrenched, with women well conditioned to feel desperate, and consequently grateful to be chosen. Fearful of the biggest shame of all – to be left standing on their own when the preliminary selections had been made. Waiting for the tune to change.

But the dancing, when it happened, was only the excuse. It helped provide the ritual and the context in which mating could begin. The chance to form initial impressions and to gauge the strength of possible attraction. Fast numbers indicated style and confidence. Slow numbers sanctioned physical engagement, relaying a preliminary sense of shape and smell and texture. It made Mattie feel instantaneously a-sexual. Although she felt the pressure to remain polite. And to look like she was going through the motions. When the music stopped, it marked a moment of decision. To stay or go? To hang in there for the imminent duration. Or take the risk of being picked on by someone more conducive. Back into the melting pot and on your marks beside the pillar.

As the night wore on and the temperature began to climb, preliminary skirmishes were gradually transformed into serial arrangements. Couples began to formulate and separate themselves from the groups in which they had first established their security. Around midnight the tempo changed. The music grew quieter and slower and sweating bodies stumbled round the floor as if indented to their trophies in some essentialist state of symbiosis. By now the first kiss had already taken place. Men's hands had moved tentatively to those female places which provided the necessary information they required about how much further they could hope to go. Women had allowed, or not allowed, their responses to be positive. It would take a little longer, perhaps the journey home, to raise in conversation the question of the pill.

The clutch of hopeful revellers, that earlier set out at 7.30, now dawdled back along the road in ones and twos. Either sadly, on their own after another night of failure, or wrapped around the object of the exercise. And holding to it like a limpet. Outside the College gates a queue of couples kissed and cuddled their commitment to another date, swapped scribbled names and numbers on the backs of hands in blue biro and swaggered off to bed with heads full of nonsense and romance. Those who were more reckless or persistent, or needing more immediate gratification, risked the danger and the consequences of the open window at the back, which served much the same function as a cat flap and was always known as such. Any women caught with boyfriends in their room beyond 11 pm, faced automatic condemnation, and immediate expulsion for their sins. Retribution which made former prefects and girl guides into liars and then hypocrites.

'Just cry', was the conventional wisdom.

'Swear to God it was the first time and the last.'

'Offer to clean the kitchen or take the Warden's poodle for a run.'

At 7.30 in the morning, prompt, the men who stayed the night had got to leave. Before the dawn patrol made its obligatory swoop and before the breakfast gong was sounded through the College. Breakfast on a Sunday morning was both the best of times for the successful and the worst of times for the faint-hearted. Across the cold toast and mounds of scrambled polystyrene the failures and the fortunes of the previous evening were carefully dissected. Gossip spread like black ink on a blotting pad. Reputations were ruined. Achievements were acknowledged. None of those who wandered home alone came down to breakfast, unless they were genetic masochists. Sunday morning breakfast was the big occasion for those who had passions to declare and new names to drop into the relentless conversation about men.

Just one such dance was quite enough for Mattie. She didn't end up on her own. She didn't miss her breakfast. And she didn't make precipitate use of the cat flap. But a wet and sloppy kiss outside the College gates, delivered uninvited on her mouth by one who thought that Trotsky was a make of foreign car, remained the low point of the winter term.

But it wasn't dancing at the Students Union which gave Mattie the feeling she was making history. Seeking sex through rituals happens everywhere. It was more to do with politics and agitation. About being against the racism expressed in the columns of the local paper and American imperialism in Vietnam. And lining up on demos with banners and loud hailers to protest about it. It was campaigning for changes in the law – the rights of women to have legal abortions. To let men over 21 sleep with other men, albeit surreptitiously. Women's Liberation, Civil Rights for Black people, peace and love – not war.

The corridor that led to the philosophy seminar room was long and narrow, with doors on either side and at regular intervals. It used to be part of a lunatic asylum, so rumour had it, before it got incorporated into the university. Mattie never doubted the story at the time. The odd behaviour of the philosophy professor simply added to its credence. Now, as Mattie swung along the corridor, in search of his room and her first tutorial, she could hear a chuckling followed by a bumping. And then a thumping and a chuckling again. Culminating in an even louder thud of something, or someone, landing heavily on the floor, as if from a great height. She turned the corner to find Professor Singleton running up the stairs with the folds of his black gown flapping like a crow. He was practising, one step higher every time, jumping down into the corridor below, his arms waving like wings.

'One more go', he shouted to Mattie, running up the stairs again to the seventh step.

She watched him in amazement.

'Batman', Professor Singleton launched himself into the void with black gown billowing round his ears. And down into the corridor with a resounding thud. 'Right', he said, 'I suppose you're going to tell me something I don't already know about Aristotle.'

In the seminar room it was 20 past 11.

'Simpleton's late as usual. We should write him a message on the board and go.'

'It'd be all the same if we actually wanted to be here.'

'I do want to be here', Mattie said, 'and this man's wasting my time.'

'He's coming. Look.'

Across the lawn in a flurry of black, carrying a moose's head mounted on a plaque, tripped Professor Singleton.

He hurried to the window and tapped disingenuously on the glass. The students looked at each other with hesitation, deciding who amongst them would be the first to crack. Singleton dropped the moose's head and hammered on the window, his bright eyes peering through round rimmed spectacles into the circle of students collected inside. Mattie pushed the sneck and raised the sash.

'Hold this young woman.' Singleton passed Mattie the moose's head and clambered in through the open window.

'Do I see a chair before me?' Professor Singleton deposited the moose's head on a table by the door and centred himself beside the blackboard. The chair he usually chose to sit on to orchestrate his seminar waited expectantly for him to sprawl himself upon it. The students looked bewildered.

'Your chair is there Professor Singleton. In its usual position.'

'Is it occupied or empty?' He searched the faces of his first year undergraduates.

'It's empty', Mattie said.

'How do you know that, young Lady? Can you prove it?'

'I can see it', Mattie said. 'I can see that it's empty.'

'And seeing is believing I suppose. But I can see that it is full.' Singleton placed himself in front of Mattie, watching her like a weasel. 'Full or empty, which of us is right?'

'It's empty.' The other students shouted their support.

'Ah.' Singleton swung round and watched them all intently. 'A vociferous majority. Almost a rabble. Taking sides against a lonely individual. Myself. who is equally convinced that what he sees is a chair that's full.'

'Full of shit', someone whispered through the rustle of nervous laughter.

'My point is serious, young man. Be so kind as to think a little more profoundly before passing superficial judgement. I want you to consider whether what is seen, automatically equates with what is true. Is a phenomenon more or less real because many people believe it to be so, rather than a singular dissenter? And what of the dissident perception? Do we take it less seriously because it contradicts the reality of the majority?'

'All versions of reality are equally important', Mattie ventured. 'It's just that some are more commonplace than others'.

'No hierarchy of perception or authority. I see. Then what of fascism? Or racial prejudice? All equally valid? Just different?'

'No racial prejudice and fascism are not valid they are based on distortions of the truth', Mattie said.

'And truth is absolute?' inquired Professor Singleton.

'Yes.' Mattie said.

'But "different versions of reality are equally important". Your words, young lady.'

Mattie needed time to think.

'Should this chair be allowed to vote?' Professor Singleton turned his attention to a young man sitting by the window.

'I don't know.'

'Its existence in this room, this university, this country will be affected by the requirements of the majority, expressed through democratic government. It could be sat upon by students. Or turned into firewood. The university in which it lives and has its being could be shut down. Surely it is entitled to participate in the decision making process which will affect its future?'

'But it's inanimate, Professor. It isn't human.'

'So! Are we to assume that rights are only to apply to the human species?' Singleton smiled benignly at the girl who spoke. 'How convenient for us. And how unfortunate for animals. For the environment. For property . . .'

'What's he going on about?' Carol Riley looked confused and wished she'd stuck to geography.

'I'm not sure', Mattie said. 'I don't know whether he's very clever or very mad.'

'Or both!'

'Write me 1500 words by next week on "the meaning of truth"'. Professor Singleton picked up the moose's head and climbed back onto the lawn via the open window.

When Mattie described the seminar to Alice later, in one of her frequent letters home, she'd come to a conclusion.

'We need to change the knowledge base of the entire curriculum. It's irrelevant. It's bourgeois. It's out of date. I'm going to tackle Simpleton about his teaching methods. This kind of self-indulgent lunacy has to become more useful and more accountable to students.'

By the following term debates about the nature of knowledge and the purposes of education had become the focus of student politics. Whilst members of the rugby club carried on regardless, and Saturday night dances continued to exercise the agony and the energy of Mattie's hall mates along the corridor in A Block, the politicos and would-be intellectuals had begun to take part in academic combat with their teachers. Lecturers who relied on reading monotonously from dog-eared typescripts were interrupted. Examinations were sabotaged and picketed. Exam papers were stolen and posted on notice boards to reveal the questions in advance.

Student files were broken into, to be checked for defamatory remarks that could be used to blacklist activists. Mostly what emerged was that lecturers and student advisers were rather slow to complete reports and rather lazy about their pastoral and professional responsibilities. But accusations about intended witch hunts remained the popular fiction of student paranoia. Some decided to hand in identical essays to different tutors, only to receive widely conflicting comments and totally different marks. All of which led to the disruption of faculty meetings and attempts to invade the senate. The tutors who were relatively young themselves, and keen to preserve their popularity with students, turned up to lend support at sit-ins and occupations. They could be seen drinking in the bar with student leaders and driving second year girls home to bed in open topped sports cars – in the days before sexual harassment was identified as anything other than expected perks. 'But don't you think it constitutes an abuse of power', Alice wrote to Mattie with some concern. She could imagine Mattie, full of passionate intensity, the likely target for some arrogant and licentious lecturer.

'It doesn't matter who you sleep with', Mattie wrote back at once. 'Staff student relationships have to become more equal. That's all part of the revolution. Personally, I don't fancy any of them. But I would sleep with them if I did.' She spoke with some bravado since, as yet, she still remained a virgin. Mostly her head was too full of politics and demonstrations, and waiting for the post to come from Alice, to waste much time on thinking through her non-existent sex life.

At the end of her first year Mattie was asked to leave College Hall by the Warden for writing seditious pamphlets about the authoritarian and intimidating nature of her leadership style. In a sprightly piece in the student newspaper entitled 'A Change of Climate' Mattie detailed what she imagined was the excellent argument for more democratic organisation of the College and a complete revision of the rules.

'I hope you will find yourself somewhere else to live in the coming year Mattie.' The Warden called to her a meeting in her office after Sunday lunch. 'I think you have over stayed your welcome in the Hall. Since I have no plans to act on your advice about organisational reform, you will doubtless feel more comfortable elsewhere.'

'Let's get a flat together.' Carol Riley was ecstatic. 'I'm sick of the cat flap and Latin graces before High Table. We've got much more important things to do than waste our energy on changing College Hall.'

It was true. The summer would soon be upon them and Mattie knew she had to do something conclusive about sex. She wrote regularly to Alice, who returned her letters within days, and who had begun to shift the awkward teacher-pupil relationship in which they'd started out, into an exchange of affection and ideas. It seemed more possible to be adventurous from the relative safety of the written word and from 200 miles away. Odd intimacies crept in beside carefully coded clues about her feelings and desires. Which could be read as simple overtures of friendship but which Mattie read and re-read as intimations of extravagance in the commitment of emotion. In response Mattie painted pictures of her emerging political priorities. Her shifting allegiances to new ideas, which she embraced with enthusiastic conviction. She seemed angry often, and impatient. Scathing about the frivolity of women in search of husbands. Impressed by men who argued with confidence and knowledge about social transformation. Disrespectful of convention and the usual constraints of orderly procedures. For a while she declared herself to be an anarchist.

'But does that take account of reason and responsible action in pursuit of change?' Alice queried Mattie's predilection for extremes. But by the next exchange she had returned to international solidarity of the socialist variety with left wing students from the Sorbonne, massing in the streets of Paris with the workers, and all intent on revolution.

In less didactic moments she pursued a line of literary flirtation. If her intention was to make Alice blush with pleasure and read tentative allusions to some kind of mutual sexual consummation of their growing friendship, she was totally successful. But it turned out to be Alice, rather than Mattie, who suggested the initiative which led them into sex.

At some point earlier in the summer term Alice had acquired a car. She had been searching the appropriate section of the *Exchange and Mart* for weeks but was being indecisive. It was Tate who drew her attention to a small insertion in the personal column of the *Yorkshire Post*.

'I have a nose for bargains', Tate proclaimed. 'Trust me!'

The advertisement was more considered than is usual, as though the 'single lady owner' was looking for a 'special relationship' to assume responsibility for a favourite friend, rather than an ordinary customer. Alice had to read it twice to work out who or what was being offered.

'Wanted. Someone with considerable tolerance and a sense of humour to take me out on little trips. I don't like to be rushed and tend to cough and splutter quite a lot on cold mornings. Although I smoke and drink considerably myself, I do not appreciate these qualities in others. Only apply if you like cats and have a clean driving licence.'

Alice rang the phone number, included almost as an afterthought, and arranged to visit on the following afternoon. The car in question was a Morris Minor, painted green, with red leather seats and a polished walnut dashboard. It gleamed in the driveway of a grey stone cottage, slabbed in Yorkshire stone, and hidden from the road by a bank of rhododendrons. Alice rang the bell. After several minute – in which she came to expect that the occupant was out – a grey haired woman in baggy linen shorts and tennis visor appeared round the corner of the cottage, accompanied by a furry, long haired persian, with a velvet collar.

'Come and have some tea', the woman said. 'I've spread the table cloth beneath the lilac tree. This is Jemima.' She pointed at the car. 'You can take a look at her when you've told me all about yourself.'

Alice could tell that she was being given a preliminary inspection to assess whether or not she would be allowed to contemplate the purchase. Her personal credentials were clearly more significant than the state of her bank account to Miss Manley-Hopkins.

'So, you're a schoolmistress', she watched Alice curiously with twinkling eyes. 'In what kind of school may I ask?'

Alice stated the name, type and general location.

'Not a private school for girls then? I suppose the area doesn't lend itself to boarding.'

Miss Manley-Hopkins had spent most of her life in the depths of Sussex, not so far from Roedean. And hadn't felt the need to contemplate the inevitability of state education.

'And do you intend to drive about the Dales? Jemima is particularly fond of Swaledale – although she sometimes objects to the very fiercest hills.'

'I'm not much of a mechanic', Alice volunteered. 'If she breaks down I . . .'

'Breaks down!' Miss Manley-Hopkins was horrified. 'Breaks down! She never breaks down. Jemima is the most reliable car you could ever wish to meet. But she is temperamental. She copes best when she's well topped up with oil and water. And quite responds to company. I often let Burford sit beside me.' Miss Manley-Hopkins nodded towards the cat who was lying on his back in the sunshine, with his paws hanging in mid air, as if he'd fallen asleep in the act of swotting flies.

'You seem very fond of your car', Alice said. 'I wonder why you want to sell her?'

Miss Manley-Hopkins tapped her chest. 'Heart trouble', she said. 'The doctor's written me off. I need to get everything in order whilst I can. Not allowed to drive, do you see? I simply want Jemima to be happy.'

How could Alice refuse?

'What price?' she asked tentatively, knowing that if she was to be chosen as her intended heir by Miss Manley-Hopkins, she would have great difficulty refusing the compliment.

'What do you say to £150? She's probably worth more but I would take £150.'

Alice nodded.

'If I could just take a look? Try a little drive?'

'You can look, of course.' Miss Manley-Hopkins seemed reluctant to concede a drive if Alice was going to be difficult. She led her to the car and opened the door at the driver's side. The leather upholstery was scuffed and faded from a lengthy life, the driver's seat in particular was well polished by Miss Manley-Hopkins considerably capacious bottom.

'Get in. Get in', she said. 'See how you fit'

The chassis creaked slightly, but with a comfortable release of tension. The dial on the dashboard showed that Jemima had travelled 80,000 miles. When Alice turned the key and eased her foot onto the accelerator, Jemima spluttered into life. And rattled with an enthusiastic commitment to some action.

'She does 30 miles to the gallon without fail. Her tires were new last year. She's a legend in her lifetime Miss Morrison. She will not let you down.'

It seemed that Alice had been approved. She nodded her agreement.

'I'll take her then', she said.

'Good. That's good. Now come and finish your tea whilst we sort out all the paperwork.' Miss Manley-Hopkins handed over the log book and the registration documents. Alice handed over a cheque from the Co-op Bank for £150.

Although the business was quickly done Alice still had the sense that she was being scrutinised by Miss Manley-Hopkins.

'I'm sorry', she smiled wistfully. 'You have a look about you that takes me back to Charleston in the thirties.

Your dark eyes, showing sadness. Your strong aquiline nose. Your olive skin.'

Alice could feel herself begin to blush. Miss Manley-Hopkins disappeared into the conservatory and returned carrying a battered felt hat.

'Will you wear this for a while? Let me see your face in profile.'

Alice did as she was told, amused by the old lady. Quite happy to indulge her in this unexpected game.

'Just as I thought.' Miss Manley-Hopkins peered at Alice with steely eyes. She patted Alice's knee with coy affection. 'You have the same sad eyes. The same mouth and colouring.'

Alice turned in curiosity.

'He always kept her on too tight a rein, you know. He said it was because her state of mind was usually precarious. I think he was afraid she'd run amok. Especially when Vita turned up.'

Alice was delighted.

'I love her writing, I always have. Did you know her well?'

'Not really. The odd house party, the occasional dinner. The poor dear soul. Too clever for her own good I'm afraid. She simply wanted to be ordinary, you know.'

Alice wrote to Mattie.

'It seems I am to be mistaken for Virginia Woolf. And with the same intimations of mortality, I have no doubt. Although personally, I have no wish to be ordinary. On the contrary. It's the fear of being ordinary that will lure me, in the end, with rocks in my pockets to the river, and pull me in. Anyway', she continued, 'now I have a car. Jemima. I'm thinking of taking her down to Dorset in the summer. Kick over the traces for a while. My mother's house is empty now that she's living in a nursing home.

You could come if you have nothing more exciting planned?'

Mattie swooped around the room with joy. A holiday! With Alice. How uncharacteristically forthcoming. How bold. How possibly opportune. She re-read the letter several times. Carrying it in the pocket of her jeans like a talisman. Feeling its warmth spread against her hip. Its careful understatement reaching towards passion. She found herself interpreting and re-interpreting each cautious, complicated overture. At once provocative and yet restrained.

Mattie did not reply at once in case Alice should imagine she was desperate. Although she began to compose a note of agreement in her mind almost at once. After three days she could contain herself no longer and committed her brief acceptance to a few lines on yellow notepaper. She postdated it for a further week and watched where the yellow envelope burnt a hole into the desk as it waited to be dropped into the letter box. Her parents weren't expecting her to come home she assured Alice. She had no money – or inclination – for foreign travel. She would be delighted to spend a week or so in Dorset if Alice was sure she could put up with her.

Alice had almost given up hope by the time Mattie's letter arrived. She did not expect an immediate reply, but, of course, she wanted one. She calculated that if Mattie should reply by return, then a letter would arrive on Tuesday. At great cost to her routines, she left the flat ten minutes later than usual, to coincide precisely with the moment when the postman's bicycle appeared at the corner of Acacia Avenue.

'Two letters this morning.' He handed them briskly from his bag. Alice smiled and stretched out her hand casually as she walked steadily on her way. Waiting till she was out of sight before examining the handwriting and postmark. One was from her brother. The other was a bill for electricity.

By the following Tuesday this daily ritual had assumed the obsession of a new routine. Derek, the postman, held her letters in his hand all ready, as he turned the corner of the avenue and tipped his hat in greeting. She was a fine looking woman, Miss Morrison and his job was boring for the most part. Increasingly he tried to extend the exchange of correspondence into a conversation.

'Looks like rain.' He paused as he passed over a large Manilla envelope and a post card from Geneva. Alice was, of course, oblivious to his pleasantries and interested in him only in so far as he might carry messages from Mattie. A week had gone by in which there was still no word and it was only a fortnight until the end of term. Alice would give her until the week-end at the latest. If there was no reply by then, she would drive the bloody car to Dorset by herself, and be done with it.

On Saturday the post came later. Alice watched from the window as Derek wheeled his bicycle along the pavement and rested it beside the lamp post outside number 33. His hands were full of letters. She watched him ring the doorbell at number 31 and hand over two small parcels and a pile of birthday cards. She watched as an old man wearing red carpet slippers gathered up the gifts and good wishes to his thin chest. Alice tried to steal herself against disappointment. Mattie was still only a girl after all. Probably fornicating with some long haired revolutionary by now. That, or pregnant, like others of her godforsaken kind. She heard the rattle of the letter box and watched Derek linger with his finger on the bell. There was no letter on the mat. The dark outline of his uniform rippled through the frosted door glass. He was smiling as she pulled it open.

'Could this be what you're waiting for?' he beamed. In his hand was a yellow envelope with neat black writing and an orange stamp.

'Quite possibly.' Alice tried to be as nonchalant as it was possible to be in a blue candlewick dressing gown and anxious smile.

'Bit better weather', he volunteered. 'I'll be through by twelve if you feel like a stroll by the canal?'

The letter was burning in her hand, her mind distracted by the urge to rip it open.

'What? Today? Oh sorry. No I can't. Thank you for your trouble.'

Derek shook his head as he collected his bicycle from the lamp post and adjusted his sack of letters.

'Some women', he reflected philosophically, 'don't know when they're well off!'

Alice's heart was thumping. The message from Mattie was to say she'd come. Alice spent the days until the end of term smiling the kind of smile it was hard to wipe from her face – despite exhaustion and the usual dreary meetings.

'If I didn't know you better', Tate whispered in her ear during Morning Prayers, 'I'd swear you were up to no good. I hope you'll let me know if anything should happen in the relationship department.'

Alice merely smiled, her voice rising in complicity as the final salutation of the school year rang out across the playground and the tennis courts in a spirited crescendo of approval: 'there's no discouragement, shall make him once relent, his first, avowed intent to be a pilgrim'.

The rest, of course, can be consigned to history. When Alice thought about it later – which she did occasionally – she could remember almost every detail. These days she tried to push it from her mind. Mattie had taken countless lovers since then, with various degrees of seriousness and significance. One of her usual gambits was, 'You always remember the first time'. At which point she frequently became misty eyed and focused somewhere in the middle distance. Stitching her heart into its usual prominence on her upper sleeve. The routine served its purpose for a while. The cultivation of romance. Irresistible when consummated by a past mistress of the art, in search of grand passion. But not so convincing once the novelty had subsided. Or Mattie, becoming quickly bored, had transferred her intensity to someone else. Leaving casualties behind her like debris in a sudden storm. As though a hurricane was passing through.

The first time, though, was something special. They arrived in Dorset to one of the hottest summers in living memory. Driving through the Cotswolds, Berkshire and then the New Forest towards the site of Alice's abandoned childhood. Her mother's house smaller and less gloomy than she remembered. The attic bedrooms, with blackened iron fireplaces and natural beams, now feeling snug and quaint, rather than remote. They piled their belongings into separate rooms, arranged on either side of a steep narrow stair, leading to a small landing and tiny bathroom with porcelain basin and Edwardian bath. The attic windows, thrown open to the heat, looked out onto rolling countryside the colour of smudged ochre. By evening the tattered sunlight stretched a veil of pink along the horizon until above their heads a small and nimble moon raced across the darkening sky.

Each evening they talked late into the night. Sometimes in the kitchen after a meal of fresh local crab and mackerel. Washed down with sweet dark beer, brought home in flagons from the brewery in the village. Sometimes, after a day of wandering through dusty fields of poppies and wild orchids, or tracking the ledges along chalk and limestone cliffs to find the caves and hideaways of Alice's remembering, they came home tired and polished by the sun into a bright healthy glow. Even Mattie. Her fair skin turning golden under freckles. Her hair worn loosely in a twist of ribbon, bleaching into streaks like ripening corn.

'Let's take the supper into the other room', Alice would say. 'The chairs are more comfy in there.'

She would pile a tray with bread and pickled fish and cheese. Some apples maybe, or a bowl of cherries. They ate quickly and full of hunger, downing the beer from pewter pots that once belonged to Alice's father.

'I used to pretend I was a pirate', Alice said, 'or a highwayman. I seemed to spend most of my childhood wishing I was a boy.'

'Why?' Mattie laughed. 'Boys are so uncouth. My brothers are like morons. The men at university might occasionally be interesting. But I wouldn't like to be one'.

'Confusion.' Alice conceded with a small sigh. 'I thought for ages that I was trapped inside the wrong body. That God had made a major blunder during a lapse of concentration.'

'And now you know it isn't true?' Mattie was amused.

'Probably', Alice faltered. 'But I still don't feel convinced that I'll turn out like Mrs Average – with 2.4 children and a husband in accounts.'

'Or Frances Tate, I hope.' Mattie buried her nose into the pewter tankard to hide a smile.

'She's not so bad.' Alice had begun to wonder whether Frances Tate or Pip might be the only other possibility.

'Better start practising with a pipe and Brylcream then', Mattie grinned. 'Unless you prefer the role of little wife.'

'I'm done for.' Alice changed the subject. She was exhausted after days of walking. 'What about tomorrow? Do you want to spend it doing nothing for a while?'

'I'd like to walk along the cliffs beyond Lyme Regis', Mattie said. 'And look for ammonites in Fossil Bay. We could take a picnic and lie on the beach if you're feeling tired.'

Alice smiled.

'Sounds more adventurous.' She kissed Mattie lightly on the cheek. Withdrawing awkwardly as Mattie tried to hold her longer in a tentative embrace. It was too late. Alice was by the door and standing in the shadow of the hallway. 'Sleep well', she said. 'I'll wake you in the morning if you haven't surfaced.'

Mattie watched as Alice retreated into obvious confusion. Conscious that the tingle spreading through her burning skin could only partly be explained by an earlier seduction from the sun.

Next day they left the noise of children playing on the beach behind them and set off along the cliffs, choosing a pathway that became increasingly unsure and broken by collapse into the sea. Occasional boats bobbed on the horizon, marking the only distinction between sea and sky whilst another cloudless day was laid to waste beneath the scorching license of the sun. At Fossil Beach it was possible – with care – to slide the scree and stones from ledge to ledge until they hit the sand. A journey which very few attempted. And which left the bay deserted. The fossils lay abandoned like discarded jewels, making the search for better specimens endlessly obsessive.

'We can't take the whole beach', Alice said. 'We have to climb the cliffs again. And find our way back along the track.'

'Maybe we should stop looking then.' But Mattie was reluctant. 'I want to find the one that's perfect. Without any cracks or flaws. Perhaps it isn't possible.'

'Hundreds of thousands of years is a long time to survive without getting chipped', Alice laughed. 'Especially when the elements are inconsiderate. Let's eat. We can try again before we go. When we've made some space to carry them home in the rucksack.'

'Shade, I need shade.' Mattie looked in vain along the beach. By now bleached and bright beneath the noon day sun.

'There's a cave, if I remember right, where...'

'Where you used to play at pirates! Can you remember where? Maybe you left a rug behind that we could lie on.'

Alice unpacked the picnic like a child. Remembering the secretive delight she used to get from eating out of doors. Food she'd stolen from the kitchen when the others were asleep. Now even more exciting because she wasn't on her own.

'I used to take jam sandwiches made with marg and white sliced bread, and a bottle of water, to the mud hills', Mattie said. 'A place like no man's land. With slabs of concrete and trenches overgrown with grass and weeds. A bomb fell there in the war, according to my father. When I was nine it was the last stretch of open space in the top street not reclaimed for houses.'

Alice poured them each a cup of wine and pressed crumbling yellow cheese into crusty rolls with slices of cucumber and pickled gherkins. They ate and drank until the sun moved out of sight behind the jagged summit of the cliff, casting a lengthening shadow along the entrance to the cave. Across the beach the tide spread in across the shingle, shuffling and scrunching the mix of tiny stones and shells into new arrangements and connections with the shore. Lapping at the stillness like a muffled roar.

Mattie lay back against the sand, her eyes closed against the surfeit of fresh air, her body relaxed by sun and wine. Alice watched as the creeping tide began to melt each ragged line of surf into oblivion. Only to be replaced and buried in its turn by the retreating wave. She poured herself another cup of wine and turned her attention to where Mattie lay along the edge of sleep. Her tousled hair across her face, her skin glistening from the sun. Alice reached down to brush a twist of yellow curl from Mattie's cheek. It was a familiar gesture, showing the tenderness she'd built on years of caution. As Alice's fingers lightly touched her skin, Mattie opened her eyes drowsily. They smiled. For once Alice didn't look away. Although she blushed. Her face now just a breath or two above Mattie's lips. Mattie reached her hand to wipe the line of sweat from Alice's brow, to trace curious fingers down the contours of her cheek, to stroke the yet unspoken question on her lips. She could feel her body tremble. Alice kissed the tips of Mattie's fingers one by one. Taking them between her teeth in turn, to taste the mix of salt and heat, allowing her tongue to explore the smooth flesh against the sharper edge of nail. She felt like sucking long and deep. Just as she had watched the surf consume the shells and pebbles on the beach. Mattie raised her other arm and drew Alice down to lie beside her on the sand, until their lips were kissing and their eyes were holding each new shift into desire.

'Are you an expert?' Mattie teased.

'My first time with a woman', Alice said. 'But I've wanted to be like this with you for longer than you can possibly imagine.'

Mattie's skin was damp beneath her shirt. Her small breasts flattened under Alice's strong weight. Mattie pushed her hands into the back of Alice's shorts, feeling her bottom tighten and then relax into the grip of Mattie's fingers. Already her cunt began to ache and moisten against the ridge of bone that marked a line of slender hip.

'I love you', Alice said. 'For what it's worth.'

'Such a surprise!' Mattie grinned. 'But I thought you'd never get around to saying it. Does this mean we can climb the narrow stairway to the same small room? And go to bed as soon as we get in? I've had enough of midnight conversations.

Alice rolled over on her back and laughed. 'I was never so shy about taking men to bed – in my previous, inauspicious, and quite limited, experience I was quite determined and quite assertive by present standards.'

'So what happened?' Mattie couldn't bear to think of Alice making love with anyone but her.

'Not much. The earth stayed remarkably immobile and I remained considerably intact. A technical submission on the second try, I think you'd say. But not without great effort and not serious enough to encourage repetition.'

'I don't want to know', Mattie said. 'I want you to think of me as your first and most important lover. The one who steals your heart.'

'The perfect specimen.' Alice weighs the chances

against her inclination towards melancholy. Discarded like a jewel on the beach and old as time. 'You are already.' She smiles. 'Let's find a more salubrious place to finish what we've now begun.'

As soon as they got home they went upstairs and made love for hours, until they fell asleep exhausted in Alice's feather bed below the eaves. For Alice it was her confirmation. At last she could imagine the future with a sense of purpose and permanent commitment. The subsequent recriminations and feelings of betrayal not coming through until much later, when Mattie had grown tired of Alice and of England, and booked herself a one way ticket to the States. For Mattie it was lust and politics and passion. The blueprint for a life of lesbian sex and personal freedom. Begun this day in Dorset in the sun. The fundamental contradictions broached between them – 25 years on, still rumbling unresolved.

Part Three

Nine

Viv Williams hurries out of the Council Chamber in the Town Hall, along St Aldgates to the River Pub, and orders a long, cool pint of lager. It's the end of the summer. Late tourists wearing Bermuda shorts with deck shoes are still crowding out the tables on the tow path. The swans, self dedicated and demanding. Expecting to be photographed, fed, allowed to sail the waterways untroubled by the smack of punts in unprofessional hands.

She finds her favourite corner on the first floor, iron balcony that overhangs the landing stage. Tied along the bank, a clutter of small boats and barges creak in the ruffled shallows where the mellow breeze moves among them without contention. Lost in the distance in a layer of pink and yellow haze, the spikes of towers and steeples prick the faded sky beyond the water meadows, where cows and horses stand in stillness like statues in an eighteenth century landscape. The air is sticky. The business of the meeting in Viv's head still blocking out the general atmosphere of relaxation.

Last summer there were riots on the other side of Oxford. The sprawling big estates physically dissected from the tourist mecca by the urban ring road. And by the collapse of Cowley and 30,000 jobs involved in making cars. Now, despite the university, despite the dons and scholarship, despite the tourists, despite the most powerful academic lobby in the world, more people live in poverty here than Oldham. Communities increasingly in crisis. Now breaking down and stealing from each other.

This is why Viv has joined the Labour party. Become a local councillor. To argue about cuts in council housing, cuts in education, cuts in social services. The ritual dances of democracy. Not that Viv knows what it's like to live, year after year, on next to nothing. Not any longer. She is one of the lucky ones. That managed to climb out from under. Or at least, Bill did. And she came with him. As you do in such arrangements. For just so long as no one rocks the boat. Or forgets which side their bread is buttered.

Viv calls Bill a champagne socialist. He was once a works convenor in an engineering factory in the midlands. He came to Oxford in the late seventies on a union scholarship, to take a place at Ruskin College.

Viv can't quite decide the point at which he changed.

At first his struggle to succeed in education and then his passion to make money, all seemed the kind of project which, as his wife, she should support. She took a course in book keeping and computing at night school and became his unpaid secretary and accountant. Tax deductible at source. In between the move to Oxford, the administration, and the company accounts she delivered three children, Clancy and the twins, and for a while believed Bill when he said that working from home would fit in well with her domestic responsibilities. Meanwhile Bill made the most of the promiscuous property bonanza in the eighties before shifting into contract engineering when the bubble burst. They moved house three times in five years as Bill's investments grew, each time to a bigger place in a better neighbourhood. Viv didn't need to get a job. Bill liked to think he was a good provider. When Clancy started playing truant from the local comprehensive, Bill said he'd pay to send her to a private school, to make sure she didn't waste her opportunities.

Many women would not survive this kind of life. Would not lift themselves out of their subordination. But Viv is not among them. In time she looked around for people with the same ideals and joined the Labour party, as Bill moved his office to the factory on the industrial estate and employed a full time secretary and three part time assistants to put his business on a proper footing.

That was a few years ago. Viv is now a councillor. A member of the Women's Committee. A confident speaker with an interest in education matters and the environment. She's a member of Amnesty. And the Campaign to close down Campsfield – a refugee detention centre that blights the Oxford conscience like a cancer. She doesn't see that much of Bill. Sometimes at breakfast. Sometimes asleep in front of the television after business meetings keep him late at work. She doesn't know exactly who he sees or what he makes these days. She isn't really interested. The money's in the bank. She assumes the source is legal. Twenty years is a long time to keep listening to the same man, especially for a passionate woman. Like most men, Bill doesn't realise the point at which he begins to lose the woman he thinks it is enough to call his wife.

Across the balcony a man gets up to leave. Viv notices him because she feels he has been watching her. He is not handsome. Rather gaunt, in fact. Most men are less than interesting these days. Usually they want something for nothing. Love without commitment. Safety without tedium. He leaves without a further glance in Viv's direction as she returns her attention to the river and the argument inside her head about detaining refugees like criminals.

'Could I join you for a minute?' Steven Rowntree waits politely by an empty chair. 'Or are you expecting someone?'

Viv recognises the man who teaches Clancy music. She smiles. 'Mr Rowntree isn't it? Sorry, I was miles away.'

'We thought you might want to be alone but...'

Viv looks around.

'My friend, I mean. He's gone now' Steven says. 'I just wanted to say how pleased I am that Clancy did so well in music. She worked hard, you know.'

'I'm very glad to hear it,' Viv laughs. 'I don't ever see much evidence of it at home.'

'She'll be all right, Mrs Williams. I can just see her, in a few years time, on some stage somewhere. Doing something in performing arts.'

'Well thank you for your confidence. She's always very

enthusiastic about your lessons. It's the others she can't abide.'

Steven sits down and leans across the table with a slight air of conspiracy.

'This is strictly off the record, you understand.'

Viv nods.

'Miss Morrison would not approve, I'm sure, of speaking to parents "out of turn".'

'I think that Alice knows me well enough to know I can be trusted', Viv reassures him. 'We get on rather well as friends away from Henley Manor.'

'I know you're on the council', Steven says. 'Probably we share some of the same political views about education . . .'

'The council doesn't have any jurisdiction over Henley Manor, more's the pity. A private school and all that . . '

'I know. I know that.' Steven's voice is slightly agitated. 'But a couple of the governors are local councillors. I think their influence is quite pernicious. Especially since the ones I'm thinking of have quite close links with some of the staff.'

'What kind of links?' Viv is suitably intrigued.

'Political links obviously. But also religious links.'

'I see. And how does this come up? In school I mean.'

'Well, it comes up in the staff room quite a bit. I'd say the attitudes are generally right wing. You know, they see declining moral standards and increasing promiscuity everywhere. No one wants to teach sex education – and in some respects, you could worry about the kind of values that would come across if they did.'

'I suppose it's hard for you to challenge all of that – being one of the few men on the staff.'

Viv remembers seeing him at open evening. Surrounded by pupils. Visibly aloof from others of his colleagues.

'The only man', Steven looks away. 'But it's not only sex. That's just one example. I mean politics and social conscience. About the way discrimination operates...'

Viv nods. 'But that's the Thatcher legacy...'

'I know. It doesn't exactly make you feel safe.'

'Safe? That's a rather odd way to put it. What do you mean?'

'Well, I mean it doesn't feel safe to be different. It feels like there's a three line whip on traditional family values and backlash ideology.'

'But Alice Morrison isn't like that. Surely her middle name is liberal. She's one of the most non-judgemental women I've ever met.'

'That's part of the problem', Steven says. 'She doesn't think badly of anyone. She gives everyone the benefit of the doubt. She's quite strict, of course. Because she wants her girls to do well. And she doesn't like to think they'll be distracted from their studies by "teenage fads and fancies" as she calls them. So she tries to keep their noses to the grindstone. But also, she doesn't really know what's going on. She doesn't sit in the staff room when the bigots are having a field day. She doesn't hear the odd crack that gets made about her when she's well out of earshot.'

'What kind of crack?' Viv begins to feel incensed on Alice's behalf.

'Well, you know. I'm sure you can imagine. She's not exactly happily married with 2.4 children is she?'

'No. But she makes the school her life.'

Steven shrugs his shoulders. 'You can never win in that respect. You're buggered if you do and you're buggered if you don't.'

'Why are you telling me all of this Mr Rowntree?'

'Please, call me Steven. I don't know really. I wanted to get a few things off my chest, to be honest. Start making a few allies in case anything blows up. Parents help to pay the wages after all.'

Viv nods. She understands the principle of forming networks.

'All right. I understand. I'll do some investigating of my own. Ask a few questions here and there. Not all the parents will be Tory hacks. Some of them might be sending their daughters to a girls school for feminist reasons. And though my old man's a business man, he'd have apoplexy if he thought there was any kind of fundamentalism at work in Henley Manor.'

'Thank you for talking to me, Mrs Williams. And I'll keep you posted, if I may?'

Steven swings his rucksack across his shoulders. Viv watches him disentangle his bike from the fence below and head off along the tow path towards the water meadows. Clancy likes him. But that's not necessarily a good recommendation.

When Viv gets home the house is like a squat. She is used to turning a blind eye to domestic chaos since her principles don't allow her to employ a cleaner and no one else is offering to behave like the responsible members of a collective and do their share. Every three weeks or so she has a blitz and sweeps and polishes through the house like a wild tornado. She closes the door on Clancy's room and the twin's bedroom. She reckons they're old enough to decide for themselves to live in filth if they want to, but she continues to wage a losing battle for the stairs and landings, the bathroom and the sitting room, the kitchen or the engine room as Bill likes to call it.

Bill floats above the chaos like a visitor from outer space. Occasionally he flings a dirty shirt at Viv when he can't find what he needs for some important meeting. These days she flings it back.

He arranges for the laundry van to call and adds the bill to his expense account.

Tonight a pile of football boots, muddy kit and shin pads are blocking the hallway, dropped where they landed when the twins came home defeated.

'Five nil', Boyd grumbles. 'They had an ace striker. We was wiped.'

'The football gear goes in the shed. The dirty clothes go in the washing basket. You *were* wiped.' Viv doesn't want to seem unmoved by their tragedy.

'It's Philip's turn', Boyd says. 'He never puts his stuff away.'

'I do.'

'You don't.'

'All right. All right. Don't argue. Boyd can put the stuff in the shed. Philip can put the clothes in the basket. Where's Clancy?'

'Out.'

Viv looks at her watch. It's ten o'clock.

'Where is she? I thought she was supposed to be baby sitting you two.'

'We don't need baby sitting. Anyway, Dad was around.'

'*Was* around?'

'Some woman rang. He spoke for hours and hours and then he said he was just popping out.'

Viv nods. 'I see. And when you've cleared up that mess, you can go and wash your faces and brush your teeth for bed.'

'Aw Mum! It's only ten o'clock!'

'Then you're half an hour late already! Hurry up now, I'm tired and I want you in bed in ten minutes. I'll come up and say good night at ten past ten.'

Viv begins to clear away the tea things and load the dishwasher. Clancy's underwear is spilling from the washing machine which is turned off but not unpacked. Viv piles the assortment of grey and muddy coloured knickers into the spin drier.

'Close your eyes.' Suddenly Clancy's voice is behind the kitchen door.

Viv laughs. 'What is it now? Don't tell me. You're wearing the new dress I bought in the vain attempt to improve your image.'

'Good try, Mother. But you're wrong. Have you closed your eyes? I've got a surprise for you.'

Viv closes her eyes and turns towards the door as Clancy leaps into the kitchen taking up what seems like almost all the space.

'Bloody hell, Clancy! What's happened to your hair?' Viv is not delighted.

'It's shaved', Clancy beams, 'do you like it?'

'I can see it's shaved. You look like a coconut.'

'Aw Mum. You've got absolutely no taste. This is cool. Everybody's . . .'

'I'm sure everybody isn't Clancy. And even if they are – becoming a clone is not a recommendation. What about school tomorrow. I don't suppose you've considered the small matter of school uniform?'

'Hair isn't uniform, Mother. It's identity. This hairstyle is part of my identity.'

'Tell that to Miss Morrison.'

'Oh Miss M won't mind. She's a sweetie under all that tweed and terrorising.'

'What about the others? Mrs Maudling and Mrs Barker, for example?'

'They won't like it, of course. They'd prefer an alice band and kirby grips. But they're dead. They can't say anything anyway. I'm in the upper sixth for God's sake.'

Viv sighs. Of course it's all too late to make a fuss. The deed is now well and truly done.

'Well, on your head be it, Clancy. I shan't be there to defend you.'

'Don't you like it just a little bit?' Clancy wheedles. 'Just a teeny weeny little bit?'

'I can see why you like it, kiddo, and that's what matters. I dare say it'll grow on me. It'll have to.'

Clancy gives her a hug. 'You're a funny old stick, Mum.'

'I saw Mr Rowntree tonight in the pub. He was pleased about your music result.'

'Oh Steven, yes. He'll like my hair. Was Miss Armitage with him?'

'No. Why should she be? It was out of hours, you know. I expect he has another life besides Miss Armitage.'

'Just wondered. They're friends, that's all. But then, he is supposed to be married.'

'Talking of which – your father won't approve.'

Clancy shrugs. 'I know. It'll be the final straw.'

She hugs Viv one more time.

'I'm off to bed now Mum. Got to get my beauty sleep.'

Viv falls asleep in the large double bed that she and Bill have never quite vacated, although its function, other than for sleeping, is now largely symbolic. His book is on the bedside table. His striped pyjama trousers bundled under the duvet on the left hand side.

Downstairs, Bill turns his key quietly in the lock and switches on the light to avoid the twins' roller boots and Clancy's rucksack, dropped like natural hazards in an obstacle race. He takes the treads two at a time. Softly. So as not to wake the sleeping house.

Viv stirs. As she always does. She hears Bill pass by the bedroom door on his way to the bathroom. Followed by the hiss of steam as the shower washes the smell of sex from his body. Viv turns her back from the space he will soon inhabit, with breath still inside him from another woman. As Bill slips in beside the rigid angle of her spine he murmurs a fragment of appeasement.

'You O.K. Love?' His hand reaching to brush the tight defences of her shoulder.

Many nights she pretends to be asleep until she hears the sequence of his breathing change. Until the density of sleep removes the moment of anticipation. The shadow of his guilt. But now, her voice is quite controlled. Her eyes wide open in the blackened room.

'Is there someone else?'

Viv waits for the silence to explode.

Bill folds his body round her back, his hand reaching to caress her inner thighs. Resorting to the reassurance of familiar movements and the gut reactions of a coward. He lies.

'Of course there isn't.'

His hands turn her body towards his and Viv softens into acquiescence, wanting to believe him. She smells the talcum Clancy bought for Christmas. Worn like a veneer. The trappings of his disguise.

Next morning the calculated distance grown between them quickly reasserts itself. Viv gets the boys bustled into breakfast and Bill makes phone calls to confirm his meetings for the day. 'In Birmingham by two. And then dinner back in Oxford. I'll call in for the papers on the way. No she isn't coming. Tell Peter wives aren't obligatory tonight.' Bill laughs as the woman's voice on the phone line reprimands his sexism. Viv learns more about Bill's whereabouts this way than any direct information called domestic communication.

Clancy is lying low until he's gone. Viv times her bath to let the noise of gushing water obliterate perfunctory farewells.

'Can we go swimming tonight?' Boyd watches as his father puts his briefcase by the door. 'You said we could last night!'

'Probably not tonight. I might be late. Will Saturday or Sunday do?'

'I want to go tonight.' Philip overloads his bowl with Cheerios. 'Saturday's forever.'

'Ask Clancy', Bill says, 'or your mother. They could take you.'

'You never take us swimming any more.' Boyd angles the remote control towards the television and turns it on full blast.

Bill shouts goodbye to Viv upstairs and steps up his retreat. He throws a fiver at the boys and makes his usual escape with his usual feelings of relief and guilt.

It seems forever since Viv has spent any time with Alice. Summer has been and gone and it's the beginning of October. Clancy has been back at school three weeks.

The phone rings in Alice's study for several minutes before her soft, slightly husky voice says 'Alice Morrison'.

'Alice, it's Viv. I'm ringing to apologise about my dreadful daughter'

'Clancy? Why? What's she done now that I should know about?'

'She's grown a skin head. Don't tell me you haven't noticed. She looks terrible.'

'Oh that, yes.' Alice laughs. 'I don't think it's going down too well with Hilda. But then, I always think that Hilda has a rather eccentric attitude to hair herself. Something short of vaudeville.'

'So there's been no serious complaint? Well that's a relief.'

'Not from me anyway. How are you Viv? It seems ages since I've seen you.'

'I know. It's been a long hot summer. We went away for a while. Bill is up to no good with some floozy from God knows where. The house is like a tip and I'm probably going to get myself arrested at the Campsfield demonstration on Saturday.'

'You should take your life more seriously', Alice laughs. 'I've missed you. Did you enrol for the new term of horticulture?'

'I did indeed. And where were you? I only keep up the pretence of being interested in growing things for the sake of seeing you afterwards in the pub. Have you given up? I know you can scarcely remember to water pot plants let alone consider the likely causes of disease in roses.'

'Well actually, I'm renting an allotment with Jack in St Ebbes. Behind the railway station. Beside the canal. I'm waiting till he's cleared out all the nettles before I show much interest.'

'With Jack? Is that the man from the Bodleian? I

thought he liked to lock himself in at night and go to sleep curled round a pile of documents.'

'What do you mean?' Alice is genuinely confused.

'Oh never mind. When can I come and see you? Or are you very busy?'

Alice takes a deep breath. Viv registers the pause.

'Well actually, I've got a friend staying with me. She used to be a pupil of mine, years ago. Back in the dark ages.' Alice tries to keep the information accurate. 'She's having a bit of a rough time. So I've said she can come and stay for a while to recuperate.'

'Oh, that will be nice', Viv says. 'Or will it? How rough a time? You're still allowed out to play in the evenings, I hope.'

'Yes, yes. Of course', Alice laughs. 'She's not a child for goodness sake. And I'm not her mother.' Alice forgets for a moment that she isn't talking to Orlando.

'I'm very glad to hear it Alice. So what about next Thursday evening in the Café Can Can? Before the jet set arrive and they turn the music up. Bill's on kitchen duty – if he's not philandering.'

Viv always makes a joke about Bill's alleged affairs. Alice isn't sure whether she minds or not. She doesn't know how to ask Viv about being married to Bill. When they get together for a drink there are always much more interesting things to talk about. She quite forgets that Bill exists. And for a while, so too does Viv.

Mattie is sitting quietly beside the fire. Motes of dust are caught in the still, yellow light.

'What's happened this time?' Alice asks.

Mattie's life is punctuated with emotional disasters.

Some of them involving Alice. Others entirely self induced. She regards each as a learning experience from which she usually learns nothing. Or at least nothing she is able to apply in future incidents and episodes. She thinks that suffering intensifies experience. Habitually careering between high and low, she is scathing of the mediocre. But she also has resilience, based on a strong commitment to her own preservation. Her life is littered with discarded remnants of the big ideas and grand passions which did not measure up to her expectations. She gives up easily and moves on quickly.

Alice puts a tray of coffee and some brandy on the low oak table. Her home is as you might expect. Dusty and dishevelled. Piles of books are heaped against the wall where a bookcase, bleeding books, has long run out of space. Along the window ledge a straggle of plants search desperately for light, and pine for lack of water. Some have categorically refused to grow until they are reassured of larger pots, fresh compost and a shot or two of liquid nitrates. Around the faded walls a clutch of old photographs and lithographs record the preoccupations and assignations of Bloomsbury in the twenties. And Alice's affection for her literary heroines, Virginia Woolf, Katherine Mansfield and Rebecca West. Her tastes have barely registered the cultural shift to post-modernity.

Alongside dust, the cottage is cluttered with the souvenirs and useful snippets which Alice cannot bring herself to throw away. A record of her life which she heaps around her like collateral. Preserving memories and continuity as distinct from capital. Mattie has forgotten quite how infuriating she finds Alice's obsession with the past. Her retreat into an inner life of intellect and imagination. Her near total oblivion when it comes to tidiness and order.

'How can you bear to live in such a muddle?' she used to shout at Alice in exasperation on the occasions they had tried to live together. Since when Alice has become even more committed to her hoarding instincts.

'Tell me what's the matter', Alice tries again.

'A little local difficulty'. Mattie resorts to her usual tactics of evasion. 'I need a change of climate I expect.'

'You need a change of personality, I suspect. Come on, Mattie. This is me you're talking to. Not some unperceptive groupie who can't see further than her own nose.'

Orlando pads silently across the carpet, nursing her irritation like a gathering storm. She stops to polish her claws on the side of the sofa and waits for Alice to shout at her to stop. It is one of their familiar rituals. Alice keeps shouting. Orlando keeps scratching. The spill of foam and broken threads revealing wood measures the momentum of Orlando's excavation. She jumps onto the cushion and watches Mattie through narrow yellow slits, grown cynical from previous experience.

'Intimations of mortality.' Mattie tries again, with increasing honesty but continuing obscurity. Always so good with words but still keeping things vague.

'You begin to feel your age?'

Mattie's hair is slashed and cropped around her ears with no pretense at style. Into some kind of mutilation that seems a stark corruption of her former self.

Alice sips her brandy. On the last occasion she saw Mattie she was 37 or 38 and ostentatiously a woman in her prime. Extrovert, gregarious, radiant. She was still being courted as a leading feminist dissident. Who could be relied upon by the media to deliver snappy and perceptive sound bites on radio news programmes and a well practised mixture of polemic and analysis on TV documentaries. One of the remaining few who hadn't yet sidled into personal solutions and psychotherapy as internal ructions in the Women's Movement and the Thatcher revolution began to take its toll.

'I feel tired', Mattie says. 'Fighting the same battles over and over. Like the last 20 years haven't happened.'

'At work, do you mean?'

'Feminism, equal opportunities, no longer necessary, they say. Either that, or a dangerous subversion. Trying to preserve some sense of education being about critical thinking feels like the final death gasps of a dinosaur. Students packed into lecture halls from floor to ceiling and counted out as customers. Racing around in ever fragmenting circles, accumulating learning credits like Green Shield stamps, collecting spurious qualifications that end up nowhere. So long as they keep consuming, we get the funding and we have our meal ticket. Even better if they come from overseas. However fascist or dubious the regime, it matters not, so long as there are bums on seats with the requisite amounts of dosh'.

'The expansion in Higher Education', Alice nods.

'Market economics.' Mattie heaves her shoulders in a lengthy sigh.

'Not good for women's writing?' Alice asks.

'Not bloody good for anything', Mattie says. 'Women's Studies gets replaced as Gender Studies and suddenly there's loads of men researching masculinity as though patriarchy hasn't been invented.'

'I see.' Alice refills her glass. 'Do you want another drink, Mattie?'

'Why not! It all helps to close down the remaining brain cells. Once I'm comatose I might not be so dissatisfied.'

'Maybe you need a sabbatical?'

To be honest Alice thinks that Mattie has already

done quiet well out of Fulbright Fellowships and study leave to write her books. Alice has never known the luxury of time out. She doesn't now expect it, and has long since given up imagining what she'd do with it any way. The definitive analysis on Virginia Woolf that was stillborn at 20 is still buried at the bottom of the captain's trunk in Alice's bedroom. Not for half a lifetime has it seen the light of day. Since when Alice has put her energies into persuading others into print. Like an unpaid agent or a full time waitress at their banquet of life.

'I need some quality time in which to write.' Mattie is rising to her theme. 'You can't seriously produce your best in odd moments snatched between tutorials. Or when your head is full of inter-departmental squabbling. How any one in academia ever writes anything creative, I can't imagine.'

'You should try school teaching.' Alice is merely underlining the obvious. Mattie, if she's listening, doesn't hear.

'It's all right for the men, of course. They have their wives to take the strain. Keep the children out of sight. Maybe I should get a wife.' She laughs perfunctorily at the stale old joke.

'You haven't got any children.' Alice is a stickler for historical accuracy. 'But I thought you had a wife?'

Orlando blinks in expectation. Watching from the side line as the exchange swings back and forth like tennis on the Centre Court. Waiting for the killer serve. The immaculate recovery.

'Yes, well. I don't think I ever thought of Jess in quite that way.'

Only me. Alice keeps her observation to herself. No need to start the visit with recriminations.

'Although I did begin to feel more like her bloody

mother.' Mattie looks across the room at nothing in particular.

'How do you mean?' Alice could now be earning forty-five pounds an hour if she was sitting in a Lloyd Loom chair and going by the name of Meredith.

'A bag to punch against. Someone to accuse of spying, restraining, not understanding – whatever it takes to be rebellious.'

'How old is Jess? You talk about her like a stroppy adolescent.'

'27 going on 15. She behaves like a teenage crisis of identity most of the time.'

Alice is surprised. Mattie, the archetypal 'angry young woman' now sounding like the voice of middle England. Forty-something going on retirement. Alice is used to adolescents. She finds them increasingly mature these days. And wise beyond their years. Something of the success of the Women's Movement has made the girls she comes across more independent minded than ever she, or even Mattie, was at their age.

'What form does this crisis of identity take.' Alice can see that Mattie is trying hard to keep control.

'Oh. Every sexual fad and fleeting fashion going. Believing style is sexy. And that sex replaces politics. It's the flip side of the Thatcher generation, Alice. All they know about is being "in your face" and having fun. As though thinking is a dirty word. And sex is liberation.'

'No one likes to be accused of being out of style.' Alice is speaking from experience. She remembers Tate's response to meeting up with Mattie a few years after leaving school. 'Political lesbian, my arse! I expect she thinks she's invented being queer. No doubt we'll be getting lectures next on where we're going wrong and how to do it properly.'

Alice can remember feeling much the same herself when Mattie said she had to practise multiple relationships. And let go of jealousy. Suppress the urge to share her life exclusively with Mattie.

But Mattie has forgotten that her vanguard days were based on relegating others to the history books. And to the sleazy underworld of butch and femme.

'I feel old hat. As if it's somehow boring to believe in politics. As if feminism means being serious and grim. As if dressing up in drag or bondage gear is the only true expression of resistance.'

'I can see that there might be a new generation gap emerging', Alice says. 'And that it could make for lots of personal introspection. But surely Jess respects your long experience and the risks you've taken on behalf of lesbians?' Alice still says the word with difficulty.

'She says it was a different planet.'

'Sounds like a Joyce remark.'

'Who?'

'Joyce Brown. Your best friend at school. Both of you relied on being rather churlish and ill-tempered when you were feeling got at.'

Mattie's memories of being young and working class are now largely academic. She revisits her past periodically with the kind of sanitised nostalgia in which the lessons she has learned are that you can 'rise above adversity' and escape from 'the poverty of limited horizons' by political awareness and determination. Having acquired the necessary cultural capital along the way she has severed her connections with much contemporary understanding of what it means to be part of the lower orders. She fails to see how virtually invisible have her origins become. And how Jess might experience this as arrogance or intimidation.

'I'd forgotten about Joyce', Mattie says. 'We were so busy defending ourselves against the snobbery of the others – the taunt of being "slags" – we lived up to the reputation with a vengeance.'

'Or, in your case, swot', Alice laughs. 'Joyce became the good time girl with mounds of bleached hair and eye liner. You became the only girl that year to get three As at A-level.'

'And much good did it do me.' Mattie is feeling sorry for herself. 'Anyway, all of that happened in another lifetime. It's living in the here and now that I have to deal with.'

'Another planet?' Alice says. 'So maybe your friend is right?'

'Look, I'm sick of talking about Jess – if that's all right with you. I've already wasted too much energy in her direction.'

(In days that began on summer mornings with making love and eating passion fruit and toasted croissants in the sunshine. And ended up in rows and recriminations about class and power. 'What's this?' Jess would say as she sniffed the warm sharp spill of juice and seeds disdainfully. Watching sceptically whilst Mattie stuck her tongue into the crinkled skin and sucked the luscious fruit into her mouth. 'I think I'll stick to Cornflakes!').

'Tell me something exciting, something positive. Tell me something about you', Mattie now asks Alice.

She speaks with the kind of inflection that registers exhaustion and pre-empts any thing but the most cursory response to her invitation, Her eyes have already glazed in anticipation of a lengthy reply. Alice could feel quite worried about the note of warning in the Governor's Report, waiting on her desk at school, about declining standards and the onus on the staff to be supporting Christian morality in a degenerate climate. But this is something she will need to face tomorrow. It isn't something she can share with Mattie. She begins to stack the tray with empty cups and glasses and retreats into arrangements about sleeping and hot water bottles.

Alice has put anenomies on the table by the bed in the spare room and a squat, translucent candle fills the dim light with the scent of musk and lavender. Mattie pulls the covers round her ears like a child, afraid that the darkness will bring back dreams of danger and distress. Not safe enough to sleep. But she is also exhausted – by a bitter year of breaking down and coming loose from the edges of her life. That once had fixed meanings. And made sense of her reality. In the next room Alice is playing Brahms.

Orlando on the cushion yawns precociously and sees no reason to modify her initial feelings of antagonism. She hears the bolt being drawn across the cottage door and the light click off in the kitchen. Followed by Alice's footsteps in the hall.

'Time for bed old girl.' Orlando pounds the duvet with her paws into a suitable and familiar nest, deciding for the moment to let discretion be the better part of valour.

In the night the dream comes back. It is getting dark and a cold wind is slicing round the corners of the street. Gradually the traffic dies and only transitory pedestrians step briskly on their way. Mattie is walking home from work in London. She is naked. For some reason she cannot find the tube. The busses pass her by unnoticed, packed with groups of revellers holding on to ribbons and balloons. En route to some kind of celebration. Some are wearing sequined frocks in frothy, garish shades of pink and lilac, false eyelashes and bright red lips. Some dressed in suits like mannequins from Harvey Nichols. Neat, tight-arsed, pinstriped. Carrying a flag. The buses do not stop.

She is feeling chilly with no clothes, her swaying breasts grown loose against her skin. A blue vein breaking by her knee, the muscles in her thigh revealing fat. What is happening to her body now. Each morning she feels as though her face will drop away. She needs to check the mirror several times to make quite sure the eyes, the pointed nose, the lips are still in their appointed place. That she can recognise herself enough to start the day. On mornings when she hasn't slept, or wakes with the taste of last night's whisky on her breath, her face is slipping in the glass. Sometimes she has to cancel her engagements. But now her body is joining in the general decline. The process of disintegration. She is feeling ugly and on the street without defences.

Not that people notice. The buses come and go. The pedestrians on their diverse routes to families and friends dip their heads into the wind and hurry by in silence. Across the road a drunk is stumbling in a crooked line towards the church. His face is buried in a mass of beard. His stomach bulging from the rope that ties his trousers into place. He is carrying a pile of manuscripts. Old books, legal documents and music scores. Turning yellow at the edge and stacked meticulously into a form of random logic. The drunk stops outside the church. Throws up his head towards the sky until his eyes can see the tower. And howls. Lonely, she imagines, like a wild coyote in the desert. The kind her father loved to watch on television whenever the lace cover got removed on Sunday nights. She passes by unnoticed.

She moves across the silent river with her back towards the city and out towards the suburbs. The journey she is walking passes several milestones in her life, reproduced as though in murals on the walls of offices and foreign restaurants. Her graduation picture on the mantlepiece at home. The first time, three years later, that she walked away from Alice in defiance, and caught an aeroplane to California. The golden, rolling hills of California. The angry episode in Moscow, more than a decade further on, when Natalia's husband dragged her screaming out of Mattie's arms, towards a block of glass and concrete flats in which he wanted her to live. Natalia, the Russian dancer, who stole Mattie's heart from Alice for a song. The performance that unleashed a major trauma. And ghosts from the past. The diamonds and the rust.

At long last, she recognises the street in which she lives. By now she is very cold and it is very dark. The street is black except for the apartment which she shares with Jess. Each window is ablaze with light. The curtains open to the night. Revealing laughter, music, revelry. The garish swirl of pink and lilac tulle, the painted faces of the mannequins, distorted in the candlelight beyond the streamers and the glass.

She hammers on the door but no one comes. The bolt is set with resolution in the lock. She steps back into the garden and looks up to where the music pulses through the windows. The faces looking out are those of strangers in her house. Somewhere deep inside her heart she wants to howl her sadness to the skies. Until Jess comes down to let her in.

But the dream fades. The sound of gentle knocking

on the door is followed by the pad of furry feet across the floor boards to the cushion on the rocking chair.

'Are you awake?' Alice is dressed for anonymity and reputation. 'I'm off to work', she says decisively. 'There's orange juice, and tea or coffee in the kitchen. And anything else that takes your fancy.'

Mattie tries a smile of gratitude. But fails to shift the look of panic in her eyes.

Time passes. Alice continues with the business of her job. Each day a set of routine decisions to be made. A pile of references to write. Accounts to check. New staff to interview. She wanders through the corridors of her domain like a familiar tune that people hum when their thoughts are usefully preoccupied and grounded in security. She is not the kind of Head to be aloof. At least not where the pupils are concerned. She likes to be about the place – asking questions, watching progress, learning names. Establishing an atmosphere of serious intent. 'Too little time to squander, girls – a complicated world to understand.' Alice explains to the first years at Morning Meeting why *Ad Lucem* has been chosen as the school motto. 'Now is the time to build your dreams, hone your mind, feed your talents, establish your ambitions . . .'

'Pick your nose', Clancy mutters underneath her breath.

The staff have also heard it all before. Theirs is a more instrumental attitude to education. Good grades at A-level establish a good reputation. A good reputation attracts ambitious parents. Ambitious parents enrol well motivated pupils. (On the whole). Well motivated pupils are the easiest to teach. It means you can then expect a private life that isn't dominated by exhaustion and mental stress. Not like the kind of collapse you read about in state schools, where teachers are more likely to get mugged than find job satisfaction. The world outside the window is a world to be avoided, if you can. So long as privilege can be preserved.

'I suppose they all vote tory', Mattie says. 'When are you ever going to put your money where your mouth is? If education is so important, and the world so complicated, why restrict your efforts to the favoured few?'

It's an old argument. Mattie the champion of comprehensive schools and state education. Alice only ever easy in a situation she can, at least, control. In which she knows the routines and the rituals. In which she's learned the ways to keep her secrets safe, and can rely on rules of interaction that separate the private and the public sphere.

'I don't think about school teaching in terms of class and privileged minorities', Alice says. 'What I care about is educating girls and providing springboards for greater choice and independence.'

'A room of one's own and £500 a year to live on! Virginia didn't always get it right, you know. How would it be if they knew the real truth about your life? Could the centre hold? Would the information be quite irrelevant in this day and age, or a serious scandal?'

Alice shakes her head.

'There is very little to know', she says, 'that could possibly create a scandal. Unless solitude and spinsterhood and living with Orlando have suddenly become subversive.'

Whilst Alice is at work, Mattie sets about recovery. She isn't very good at solitude. Despite her ostentatious defence of personal freedom, self-reliance and symbolic space. She watches for the post. She paces up and down. She makes telephone calls to Meredith in London, her office at the university, a woman in America about a seminar. Orlando notices the shift in mood from a suffering, deserted has-been, designed to capture Alice's attention and compassion, to a somewhat assertive, self-absorbed, opportunist as Mattie begins to benefit from the solid comfort of Alice's cottage, the fullness of her fridge, the quality of her wine rack and the familiar feelings of being indulged despite her frequent bouts of bad behaviour. Just like coming home. Orlando misses very little as she keeps an eye on Alice's well being. She would like to alert Alice to the phone calls to America. But she knows that Alice won't take her warnings seriously at first. She'll say, 'It's good that Mattie's thinking about work again. It means she's getting better.'

It will be quite another matter when the bills arrive.

On Thursday, as arranged, Alice keeps her date with Viv at the Café Can Can.

'So who is Mattie, did you say?' Viv pours two glasses of Chardonnay bottled in Victoria beside the Murray River.

'An old friend. A former pupil. Light years ago.'

'You kept in touch?'

'Ummm.' Alice sips her wine.

'Will she be staying long?'

Alice is usually more talkative.

'Not sure. It depends.'

Viv nods. Another question will seem like an interrogation. She waits.

'Clancy looks more settled this term.' Alice changes tack. 'Has she given up the idea of taking a year out?'

'No. But I've said that if she does, she has to get a job. Or fix up something serious in Africa. I can't stand the prospect of her dossing around the house – picking fights with Bill.'

'What does she say?'

'She says she wants to "find herself", "discover who she is". I say "Clancy Williams?" She says the trouble with me is that I have no spontaneity. She could be right.'

'So what do you think she'll do?' Alice looks concerned.

'Quite honestly, I hope she gets her A-levels and goes to College. Although she hasn't got a clue what subject to do. One minute it's anthropology. Then archaeology. Last week it was philosophy.'

'I wouldn't have thought she would be interested in such things. Isn't she at her best when she's on the stage?'

'Life's a stage so far as Clancy is concerned. Unfortunately the script usually comes courtesy of *Neighbours*.'

Alice smiles.

'I tell them in my English class not to waste their time on trivia. But I can see, as I say it, the glazing of the eye, the humouring little nods to shut me up', she says.

'Bill gets very angry. Especially about the money. But being reminded that she should be grateful or cost-effective is just the argument she needs to do the opposite.'

'She's a lovely girl, Viv. Her own person, I expect.'

'I know. And Bill is a fine one to talk about responsibility. He only ever does precisely what he wants. He calls it enterprise.'

'Did you say he was seeing someone?'

'Again. Yes. I don't know who. He lies of course.'

'Do you mind?'

'I don't like to be taken for granted or taken for a fool. But I don't long for candlelit dinners *a deux* or any more fucking than is absolutely necessary.'

Alice doesn't think she can make any comment about men. Although she has some experience of feeling sexually betrayed. Mattie was never one to place fidelity very high on her list of priorities.

'It doesn't feel very good to be lied to. In any circumstances.' Alice pats Viv's hand in a brisk, uncharacteristic gesture of affection.

Viv laughs a little nervously.

'Oh well. Enough of this. What's the gossip from the staff room? How many "born again" Christians have you signed up now?'

'What do you mean?'

'Fundamentalists. The moral majority. Steven Rowntree says the place is stiff with moral outrage.'

'Oh Steven! He's very headstrong. Most teachers seem completely staid compared to Steven. It doesn't mean they're automatic bigots.'

'Would you notice?'

'Well I think I know a bigot when I meet one!'

The waiter brings monk fish chargrilled with thyme and saffron, some boiled potatoes and a light green salad.

'He says you don't spend much time in the staffroom – socially.'

'We're not a collective, Viv. I know you have enthusiasms about communal working. But I am paid to be the boss. And that means keeping a proper distance. Anyway – I don't expect to have much in common socially with hearty Oxford wives obsessed with family preoccupations.'

Viv looks away.

'Is that how you think about me? An Oxford wife with family preoccupations?'

'No. No, of course not. I completely forget that you are married most of the time. And I don't have to be nice to Bill or polite about him do I? I'm sorry if it came out harshly. Been living on my own too long. I can't stand couples, I expect.

'Neither can I.' Viv looks distracted. 'If it wasn't for the kids and the collateral I would prefer a different kind of lifestyle.'

'Time out?'

'Yes. But not just for a year to do something serious in Africa.' She smiles.

Alice pours another glass of wine.

'Your fish is getting cold', she says.

When Alice arrives at school a few days later, there's a feeling in the air she can't quite put her finger on. The familiar straggle of junior girls outside the gate go silent as Alice crosses over the road and heads towards the drive. She smiles as usual and stops to have a word.

'All ready for the hockey trials?' She notices the junior eleven captain and the centre forward huddled in conspiracy.

'I expect so', Nicola replies.

Alice waits. The silence festers.

'Well, we're counting on you to pack the forward line at least.' Alice moves on sensing trouble.

Stubbs is leaning on his shovel. He could be sulking or resting. Alice tries a breezy greeting.

'The trees are looking wonderful. I love the moment

when they turn to crimson before the leaves begin to fall.'

'They're falling all too fast Miss Morrison which means it'll be a hard winter.' Stubbs is rarely optimistic.

'Good job we're rather sheltered here', Alice says. 'We always seem to miss the worst of the weather.'

'You can't count on it Miss Morrison. Not since the Russians started with the nuclear bombs.'

Alice knows that Stubbs' analysis lacks a certain logic. Not to mention accuracy. But she is only paid to teach adolescent girls, not jobbing gardeners. She smiles tactfully.

'Well you're making a good job of clearing that border. I do appreciate how beautifully you keep the grounds.' She begins to move away.

'There's been some damage done.' Stubbs calls her back. 'To my tool shed.'

'What kind of damage?' Alice turns to look at him.

'You'll hear about it soon enough.' Stubbs actually enjoys the anticipation of disaster. 'But you'll need to sort it out, good and proper Miss Morrison, if you don't want more trouble on your hands.'

'Thank you for your advice.' Alice climbs the steps towards the front door of the old house where her study and the school offices are situated.

Three girls are sitting on the hardback chairs outside her room. In the no man's land where punishments and detentions are meted out in response to misdemeanours. One of them is Clancy Williams. They all avert their eyes as Alice comes towards them. The same old trick she used herself as a child. If you don't appear to see, you can't in turn be seen. It doesn't work of course and the atmosphere is palpable.

'Good morning', Alice says briskly, preferring to be

briefed by Hilda before she launches in. The three girls mutter an inaudible response.

Alice calls for her usual pot of strong black coffee and turns her attention to the pile of post placed on her desk. Yesterday's letters are still waiting to be signed and the end of the year report from the governors, now bound and set in stone, is positioned centre stage for maximum effect. Alice moves it to one side for later. She hates the way the governing body now makes her feel like the manager of her local supermarket where sales – and therefore profit – are in decline. She despises the creeping decimation of their words into a kind of business speak that so offends her literary imagination and love of language. She hates the way more money is now spent each week on the National Lottery than on books or bread. But that's another story.

Hilda bustles in. Full of grievance and offence. She bangs the tray of coffee on the table and takes up her position facing Alice for maximum effect.

'Drugs', she says.

Alice blinks, 'Drugs?'

'Drugs on the school premises', Hilda spells it out in simple, direct speech.

Alice pours herself a cup of coffee. 'Will you join me, just for once?' she asks Hilda.

'Thank you, yes.' Hilda sits her body on the chair beside the table.

Alice waits expectantly. She respects Hilda's residual taste for the dramatic, cultivated in a previous career as a theatre landlady.

'Stubbs caught them red-handed in the tool shed.' Hilda says. 'Clancy Williams and her cronies. I knew that girl was trouble, the first time I clapped eyes on her.'

Alice knows what she means.

'She isn't attracted to conformity that's for sure. But drugs? What kind of drugs for goodness sake?'

'Dope they call it don't they? Cannabis. Marihuana. The stuff you put in joints and smoke.'

'Is that right?' Alice doesn't feel too clear about the details 'So were they smoking this dope when Stubbs found them?'

'Yes. Passing it around from one to the other. And giggling', Hilda adds with emphasis.

'Giggling?'

'Like they were drunk', Hilda says.

'Or drugged?' Alice is a stickler for linguistic accuracy.

'I think you call it "stoned", Miss Morrison. Sounds like we could use some staff development round here', she adds as an afterthought.

Alice in her ignorance is the first to agree.

'Would you be so kind Hilda as to ask Miss Streatham in the library if she has any books on the subject. And if not, could she please acquire some?'

'Steven Rowntree and Wendy Armitage will know', Hilda pronounces their names with the kind of disdain that immediately implicates them as potential pushers.

'Good. That's good. I'm glad we have resources on the staff. Could you please tell Clancy and her friends that I'd like to see them here at 12.15? I need some time to think this one through. I assume that what they were doing is against the law?'

'Of course it is,' says Hilda impatiently. 'Why do you think I'm making such a fuss? You must be about the only person in the entire universe who could ask such a question in this day and age!' She bustles to the door. 'You've got a soft heart, Miss Morrison, underneath all that intellect and academic excellence. But this is not the time to let it show. What we need now is leadership and moral authority.' She leaves in a flurry of self importance to track down further information.

Ten

Alice prides herself on keeping her emotions under control. She knows from past experience that if the flood gates were to open, she could easily drown. 'A safe pair of hands' is how she was described when she got this job. Not the kind of accolade that would have appealed to Mattie. But Alice has learned the wisdom of a moderate disposition. If only as a shield to keep her from extremes. She is under no illusion, however, that the challenge to her credibility brought about by drugs on the school premises is a development she must take seriously. An occasion when she must be seen to act decisively.

'The reputation of the school, my authority, all that I've worked for since I came here is what's at stake.' Alice is angry with Viv. Angry for having a daughter who smokes dope. Angry because Viv is her friend. Angry with herself for mixing friendship and professional responsibility. 'She'll have to go Viv. I can't afford a scandal. I must be seen to take decisive action.'

'Let me talk to her', Viv says. 'I'll soon put a stop to all of this. She's daft, Alice. Thoughtless. She isn't a bad girl.' She sits down on the chair beside the telephone.

'I know.' Alice has to agree. 'But she's old enough to know better. Now she'll have to face the consequences of what she's done. She must know that she's left me with very little choice. Otherwise I'll look like a total libertarian. I can't think of anything that would be worse. Unless of course I caught her doing sex in the potting shed with the boy on youth training. That would be worse.'

'She's probably doing sex as well. All of them are.'

Alice cringes. She'd still rather believe in the excitement of English Literature or French or Physics helping to keep her girls out of harm's way until they're old enough to make considered choices.

'Are they?' she says in a dull voice.

'Alice, most teenagers these days are preoccupied with getting drunk, getting laid and watching smutty videos on a Saturday night when they're supposed to be babysitting. English Literature doesn't have a lot to recommend it by comparison.'

Alice wonders why she spends her life believing that it does.

'And all of which are probably more disastrous to the mind and body than smoking dope in broad daylight with a couple of school chums.'

'But that's not the point', Alice says. 'Not if I am to believe Hilda who says it's a police matter and requires immediate expulsion.'

'That woman should carry a government health warning for her mouth', Viv explodes. 'Look, I know its difficult. I'm not asking you to excuse Clancy or to condone what she's done. Suspend her for a while. Set her loads of extra homework. Let me lay it on the line at home. I won't leave her in any doubt that she's in total deep shit. But to call in the police! To expel her now! Just when she's doing her A-levels. It's out of all proportion.

'It's against the law. What if she's dealing? Can you imagine the kind of field day the press will have about all of this? She could get hooked. She could start taking something worse. She could do serious damage to her health. Don't you worry about where it all will end?'

'I know. But she won't. Do you think I think this doesn't matter? Just give me chance to talk to her, Alice. I promise you I'll put a stop to it. Don't ruin her life by making her some kind of sacrificial lamb.'

'She should have thought about that before. She's not a child.'

'Alice we are all children sometimes. I'm sure you've done things you regret. I certainly have. And I was older than Clancy at the time.'

Viv can feel Alice soften at the other end of the telephone.

'What about the other parents?' she says, 'I haven't rung them yet. I don't expect the Montagues will be too pleased.'

'Well I hope they don't blame Clancy.' Viv imagines they will. She knows that Sophie Montague is a wimp who trails around behind Clancy like her shadow. Certain to do anything Clancy dreams up to be the latest measure of her loyalty. 'You can't hold Clancy responsible for the others. They're all the same age. With the same degree or absence of intelligence.'

'Far be it from me to exaggerate Clancy's leadership potential.' Alice is being won round by Viv's fierce defence of her daughter. 'But they will have to be told. And they won't be too delighted.'

'But they won't want you to invoke the kind of reprisals you have in mind', Viv says. 'More like a ritual lashing if I know anything about Albert Montague! What if you get us all together? Do a heavy number on us too. I promise to be "totally distressed of Tunbridge Wells". I'll plead with the other parents to take punitive action on the home front. You can threaten anything you like short of expulsion and the police.'

'It isn't funny Viv.' Alice wishes she could dislike Viv. It would help to clarify things. 'I need some more time to think about it. In the meantime I'll write you an official letter I'll tell the girls I'm making contact with their parents and instruct them to say nothing to anyone – friend or foe – until I see them again. I think you should be available to come into school as soon as possible – certainly by Wednesday at the latest.'

'Good. Thank you Alice. You won't regret this.'

'Will Bill be able to drop everything and come at such short notice?' Alice turns the pages of her diary to identify a time tomorrow or the next day. She registers the sudden silence.

'Does Bill have to know?' Viv weighs the consequences of what this means. She knows he'll go ballistic on the home front. Clancy might well prefer the police to put her into prison for a month.

'Look, I'm writing to you both', Alice says. 'I have to. If you open the letter and choose to come on your own without telling Bill – that's your decision. I shall assume he knows but I shan't insist on seeing him.'

'Thanks, Alice. Like I say, you won't regret this.'

As Alice replaces the telephone receiver she hopes that Viv is right.

'I am making you some supper.' Mattie is looking perky. 'I thought you might like oysters and a bottle of champagne.' She kisses Alice on the cheek.

Orlando stretches her back and contemplates the distance to the dining room in anticipation of an evening of excess.

'Oysters! In Oxford in October!' Alice remembers the speed of Mattie's conversion to the pleasures of the good life but even she has lost track of the lengths to which Mattie is now prepared to go to compensate for earlier deprivations.

'The covered market', Mattie laughs. 'You can buy everything exotic in the covered market. The traders are used to cultivating the visceral cravings of junior recruits to the ruling class and indulging the whims of College Master's dinner guests at High Table.'

'Are they French?' Alice inspects the score of complicated crusted shells piled high in the plastic bucket waiting to be shucked.

'Scottish.' Mattie is in her element. 'Fresh from the crystal waters of the Highlands. Blocked in ice and flown in this morning. Wouldn't you just die without a regular supply of oysters?'

Alice looks quizzical. How could she possibly begin to disagree.

'Might you want time to take a bath? To change?'

Mattie has the sense that oysters and champagne by candlelight would be better suited to something more elegant or more casual in the clothes department than Alice's tweed skirt and cashmere cardigan. She would prefer a tailored cotton shirt or something soft in deep blue silk. Trousers cut with style – in wool or linen. Preferably without flares or an elasticated waistband. But she will wait indefinitely for Alice to change the habits of a lifetime.

'Ummm. You could be right. I am feeling pretty grubby after three hours teaching on top of drug busting the upper sixth.'

Mattie is adjusting the volume control on the stereo. So that Callas singing Carmen rather drowns the impact of Alice's final sentence.

'I'll give you half an hour', she beams. 'Would you like a glass of bubbly whilst you're soaking? A dish of olives?'

Alice nods. She'd like a glass of champagne and a dish of olives immensely. She waits patiently to collect her supplies, anxious to pre-empt a visitation from Mattie in the bathroom when she is naked. The old familiarities of domestic life are sweet enough to be remembered, but too long ago to be resumed without special invitation. She is not feeling in good enough shape to be scrutinised by Mattie's incautious curiosity. Let alone collude in moments of unexpected intimacy.

But if Mattie is considering seduction, it doesn't show. Her inclinations are rarely premeditated. She prefers to act on impulse. She never closes her mind to possibilities. And never lets the big questions of morality or responsibility prevent her from doing what she wants. As the spirit moves her, so to speak. Although she has been feeling generally a-sexual in recent months. As though some tap has been turned off. Almost as quickly as it was once turned on. She blames Jess. She could blame an early menopause. Except she doesn't like to give too much significance to hormones, having spent a lifetime discounting arguments about biology and women's nature. She doesn't rule out sex at some time in the future. Sooner rather than later if she has the choice. But not particularly with Alice. Alice knows too much to fit the bill. Too much about Mattie's limitations. The kind of information you keep from prospective lovers when what you want is their infatuation and the buzz that comes from then pretending to be taken by surprise.

Alice clutches her champagne and balances her dish of olives on the soap stand. The bathroom door, which usually she leaves ajar when Orlando is her sole companion, and who is fond of strolling in and out to chivvy her along, she now closes quite decisively. Without the benefit of a lock she hopes that Mattie has no reason to intrude. The sound of Callas drifting through the cracks helps to melt her body down to spirit in the steamy bubbles.

Mattie is lighting the candles as Alice returns, wearing a pair of faded jeans and a red tartan shirt. Mattie wonders if Alice has bought anything remotely sexy or carefully understated in the last 20 years. But she refrains from making any comment.

'Are you feeling better?' Alice pours herself a second drink.

'Today is a good day', Mattie says. 'The depression comes and goes like a huge black cloud. But today the sky is wide and clear and I've done some work.'

'Some university work or some writing?'

'The beginnings of a poem. Nearly the first draft.'

'That's good.'

'It usually takes a week or so to get it right. Various reworking. Until I've got the proper blend of simplicity and depth. This one could be another false start, of course. But it seems a possibility.'

Alice is always surprised that the introspection and intensity which Mattie must deploy to produce good poetry isn't nearly so apparent in her everyday dealings with the world. Mattie explains writing poetry as a job.

'Its a craft, Alice. You can learn it and perfect it. I've had some good teachers in my time.' She smiles.

'But don't the ideas come from somewhere deep inside? Don't you prise them out of your subconscious, like oysters from a shell, with some degree of pain?' Alice has read *The Fruits of Love* – a collection Mattie wrote in her middle thirties – which Alice thinks reveals an enormous capacity for passion, if tightly controlled.

Mattie laughs.

'All life is pain, Alice. Don't you know that? But in every human tragedy there lies the potential for a poem. The secret is to avoid sentiment. To regard experience as substance to be recorded. It needs to be given colour, texture, depth. A context. Subtlety. Layers of significance, like an onion. It might become a metaphor for something else. But once you see it in this way, like an artifact which language, used with flair and precision, can fashion into shape – the poet becomes more like an engineer than a repository for experience.'

'But the feelings which your poems undoubtedly unleash in others? Surely you take some moral responsibility for helping to make emotional connections?'

'I'm not a theologian or a psycho therapist.' Mattie moves to deflect the gentle note of criticism in Alice's question. 'People must take responsibility for their own emotional responses.' This is the usual door that Mattie closes as she reaches for her suitcase. Leaving chaos in her wake. 'Are you going to try these oysters?'

She places the dish of glistening, slippery molluscs in their shiny, pearlised shells, in the centre of the table. Their soft, pale bodies still clinging to the blob of sinew that once fixed them to their shelter. She takes a lemon and sprinks the juice with generous excess.

'Try one.' Mattie helps herself as Alice contemplates the tiny, elemental folds of flesh.

She pulls each oyster from its shell and holds in her mouth for a moment before it slides into her throat. Lingering with a touch of salt and sea and sharpness on her tongue. Like sex.

'They always make me think of Sydney Harbour in the moonlight. So beautiful but I couldn't live in Australia.' Mattie is reliving her travels. 'It would seem like profiteering from conquest. I would feel implicated in the genocide.'

'You are implicated in the genocide', Alice says. 'We all are. You don't need to live in the colonies to be associated with our imperial past. You can see the consequences every day on the streets of London and Oxford.'

'Yes. But this is different. This is racism born out of post-imperialism. At least we're not taking over someone else's land.'

'We've taken over plenty in our time. Still, we like to call ourselves the motherland, but when it comes down to it, we don't really want to share our space with anyone who isn't completely British, born and bred. And that means white.'

'I know this Alice. I do know all this.' Mattie chews a

second oyster. 'I thought you were the one who couldn't bear to discuss politics!'

'It isn't about politics is it? It's got to do with natural justice. What I can't bear to contemplate is how racist we are.'

'How was school today?' Mattie knows this argument inside out and finds it boring.

'Oh it was all right. A fairly typical "day-in-the-life" at the petit bourgeois sausage factory – that is, until Clancy Williams and her girlfriends took it into their heads to smoke dope.'

Orlando opens her eyes expectantly and fixes them on Mattie. She can remember when dope meant you were one sandwich short of a picnic. Threepence off the shilling. Dim.

Mattie stops eating and looks intrigued.

'Did they now! But not so unusual I suppose?'

'Well, pretty unusual for Henley Manor. This is the first time we've caught anyone in the act, so to speak.'

'Then Henley Manor must be the truly unique establishment you boast about in your prospectus. Half the kids in the country are doing drugs of some description. In London you can see it in the streets and smell it on the Tube.'

Alice wonders how, until today, and now that she has talked to Hilda, Viv and Mattie, what appears to be common knowledge has managed so completely to pass her by.

'So you can't arrest and expel anyone then, not if half the school population is involved?'

'Of course not.' Mattie fingers another oyster from its shell. 'Simply at the level of police administration – the entire system would collapse under the additional strain. There'd be even more rootless kids pacing the streets looking for trouble. Most of the time the police and teachers turn a blind eye. Unless there's a chance of catching the dealers.'

'It's a terrible indictment on the absence of constructive alternatives.' Alice shakes her head.

'It is when the kids are poor or black or on the run from family rows. You'd think middle class kids would have more to lose. But they also have more to spend.'

Alice nods. 'They don't have the same reasons to be depressed or alienated. Not really.'

'Oh I wouldn't say that', Mattie disagrees. 'All kinds of parents can let you down miserably. Be feckless. Be domineering. Whatever their class. Not that smoking dope is a measure of insecurity or damage. Mostly it's a fashion. Like designer trainers or the latest rock band. It's pretty harmless, I would say. It just happens to be illegal in the ways that loud music and tobacco aren't.'

'Knowing Clancy – she'd do it out of curiosity. As another gesture of rebellion.' Alice can see this is a possibility. 'I shouldn't really hold it against her.'

'She's probably got a pair of snotty parents who are pushing her to achieve, or conform to a range of values she can't stomach.' Mattie is an instant expert. Already on the side of a junior rebel.

'Actually her mother isn't at all like that', Alice says. 'She's a Labour councillor. On the Women's Committee. Someone you'd approve of. Her father might be a bit of a tyrant. But so far as I know Clancy gets on very well with Viv.'

'Viv?' Mattie notes a hint of conviction in Alice's quickening defence of Clancy's mother. 'Is she a friend of yours' then?'

'Well, we do spend a bit of time together. We share an interest in horticulture and opera.'

Mattie's eyes stray to the limp-leafed geraniums and pot-bound spider plants on the dusty window sill. 'I see. You wouldn't want to be expelling her daughter then, I expect.'

'I might have to do it just because she is my friend. I wouldn't want it said that I have favourites. I must be seen to be professional.'

'Well of course! Does this woman know what a stickler you are for propriety? Tell me about her. Why would I like her? Is she a dyke? You say she has a husband?'

'She isn't a lesbian.' Alice cannot bring herself to use the term she still associates with abuse. 'Her husband is a local businessman. Self-made, I think. A bit of a bully, by all accounts. But he always seems quite pleasant to me when he turns up to parent's evenings and other school functions.'

'One more woman trapped in a loveless marriage! The world is full of them.' Mattie knows the type.

'I don't think Viv is the type to be trapped', Alice says. 'She's very extrovert. As you will see. I asked her round for supper next week. She said she'd like to meet you.'

Mattie pulls a face. 'I'm not up to being sociable with strangers, Alice. I don't mean to be churlish about your friends. Maybe you should have dinner on your own? Count me out.'

'Whatever you like.' Alice lets the last of the oysters slip between her tongue and the bubbles of champagne break against her lips. It will be easier for Alice to keep the different departments of her life quite separate. She hasn't said much to Viv about her past – or where Mattie fits into the complicated tragedy of loss she associates with sex and passion. It will be easier to avoid the inevitable embarrassment to herself which an evening spent together with them both could well occasion.

'Is she interested in you – sexually?' Mattie assumes that sex is always at the root of female friendship. However well disguised. Or overlaid with other things – like an alleged affiliation to hetero-reality.

Alice laughs, a little nervously.

'Of course not. She's married. She's a mother of three. She looks like she buys all her clothes from Laura Ashley.'

'So!' Mattie has no time for meaningless stereotypes. 'We're not talking about the tyranny of genetics here. Or biological inversion! Surely you don't still believe in all that crap!'

'No. Of course not. I just mean she's very, very straight. That's all. She likes me as a friend. I don't have the kind of body or capacity for seduction that confuses heterosexual women, Mattie. Or any women for that matter. I was never one to push my sexuality. Unlike you. Now I think it's no longer very relevant.' Alice begins to clear away the plates and dishes. This is not the discussion she has any wish to get involved in.

Nor Mattie either. Given her most recent feelings of failure and depression. Her appetite is somewhat subdued. Though not completely satisfied.

'Sorry Alice. I didn't mean to be intrusive. Let's call a truce, shall we? I'll be sweet and civil to your friend, if you like. Or stay well out of sight, if that feels easier. Maybe I should be going back to London anyway. I don't want you to feel embarrassed by having me here. Or irritated.' Mattie retreats into the beleaguered state of injured innocence she usually resorts to in her relationship with Alice. The kind of manipulation that makes Alice feel like her mother. But which it has taken her many years to recognise and to resist.

'You are welcome to stay for as long as it takes you

to feel better', she says mechanically. 'Just so long as you take my life seriously too.'

Across the other side of Oxford, in a terraced house beside the river, Hilda is contemplating the developments of the day and speculating on the reasons why Alice Morrison should have spent a considerable amount of time on the telephone – but not in conversation with the Oxfordshire Constabulary or the Henley Manor Chair of Governors.

'Set the table will you Clancy?'

Clancy moves like a zombie between the kitchen and the dining room, carrying cutlery and dishes. Usually she complains about the sudden disappearance of the twins whenever there are domestic chores to be done. 'You shouldn't let them get away with it', she tells her mother. 'I thought you believed in fighting sexism!'

It is the evening after the showdown with the parents and Miss Morrison at school. Clancy is feeling shell-shocked, guilt ridden, relieved that all it has amounted to so far is an array of serious faces, extra homework and a cut in her allowance, rather than immediate expulsion and the police. For all she believes that school is like a prison, and most of the girls are either snobs or swots, she quite likes music and drama lessons. She certainly doesn't want to work in Woolworths as an alternative, or be consigned to YTS. Tonight she is setting the table without resistance. Conscious that her mother is at the boundary of her tolerance.

As usual, the phone keeps ringing. The nightly internet of teenagers, fixing up the details of their social life, checking times and locations. Lining up lifts and allegiances. Planning the modern day equivalent of the Normandy landings or the liberation of Paris. Occasionally she carries the phone into the spare room and shuts the door for reasons of privacy. Bill often does the same. But for some reason it makes him angry to observe the white plastic cord trailing through the hallway and disappearing underneath a well closed door. His own motives for creating solitude in such circumstances no doubt adding to his suspicions about Clancy.

Tonight Bill beats her to it.

'Hello.' He repeats his name.

Clancy hovers expectantly, her hands full of serviettes and glasses.

'Yes she is in. Who's that calling?'

Clancy hates to feel she's under surveillance by her father.

'Gary? Do I know you Gary? You're not the boy with the shaved head and the blue Mohican?'

Clancy groans.

'Next door but one. I see I suppose it would be too much to expect that you might walk the 50 yards involved and save your father the cost of this phone call?'

The boy replies.

'Well no, of course not. Not if it's just starting. You couldn't possibly miss the latest episode of *Neighbours*!' Bill passes Clancy the phone, which she quickly takes into the spare room, closing the door noisily behind her.

At supper the twins are in boisterous mood, intent on flicking mashed potato at each other when they think that Viv and Bill aren't looking. Viv is feeling harassed. Clancy is lost in an altogether different hemisphere, chewing through her vegetarian lasagna with about as little enthusiasm as if it was made of straw. Bill is detailing the small eventualities of his day. 'Expanding the Board', 'Peters visiting from Chicago', 'winning the order against tough competition', 'a damp patch in the cellar', 'what Colin thinks about Oxford's chances in the match against Oldham'. Occasionally he turns a disapproving eye towards the boys when he senses that their game is getting out of hand. But mostly he has his sights set on Viv's attention. She nods mechanically behind glazed eyes. Providing the minimal cues and occasional murmurs of agreement that serve to simulate conversation.

'If you don't stop making such an appalling mess with your dinner Boyd, I shall feed it – and you – to the cats!' She is losing patience.

Philip explodes in giggles. 'Ow Mum! Boyd kicked me with his football boot under the table!'

'You liar! You always tell great big whopping lies!' Boyd appeals to the judgement and intervention of his parents whilst Clancy continues chewing her lasagne.

'If you have finished, you can get down quietly', Viv says to the twins.

'Yippee!' They jump down from their seats and rush towards the door.

'Just a minute!' Viv wonders how she retains the energy to insist upon a semblance of civilised decorum. 'Come back and clear your plates and glasses if you please. And don't pile them into the dishwasher without scraping off the dead food. It's not a magic dustbin.'

Bill keeps talking. 'The cost of software to upgrade the office system', 'a conference to attend in Venice' (slipped in amidst a weighty inventory of boring information, which at some later date will assume much more significance than Viv currently imagines – providing the excuse that Bill will need to be officially absent without leave), 'what Labour needs to do to look like a party of government'.

Clancy puts her knife and fork together on the plate and looks at Viv.

'Can I go out for a bit? Not for long!'

Viv sighs. 'How long? Where?'

'Oh just into town. I said I'd meet a couple of friends. I could be back by ten.'

'I want you back by 8.30 at the latest.' Viv gives Clancy the kind of look that says 'Or else!' 'I think a few early nights won't go amiss.'

Clancy is unimpressed but knows when she is pushing her luck.

'Thanks Mum!' Clancy beams at Viv. 'And thanks for sorting things out today.' She scurries her plate and water glass into the kitchen before Viv changes her mind or Bill catches up with what's happening.

Viv begins to clear the table.

'What's she talking about? Is there anything wrong with Clancy?' Bill has given up hoping that Viv will ask him anything of any significance about his day at work.

'How do you mean?' Viv is evasive.

'She seems very secretive, that girl. She'd rather spit blood than tell you where she's going, who with, or for what purpose. I hope she isn't up to mischief!'

'You don't talk to her enough.' Viv avoids the implication of his criticism.

'She's never in. Supper time feels like Piccadilly Station in the rush hour. How many different phone calls can she make in half an hour and how quickly can she be out the door before we realise she's gone. Who's Gary?'

'A friend. A nice boy. You know his father. He leaves his driveway just before you do every morning. Sometimes he waits to let you pull out first.'

'Oh. The guy with the Golf. I can never understand the attraction of German cars. Like tanks most of them.'

Viv assumes Bill's fleeting parental concern about his daughter is now extinguished.

'I don't like to think she's up to something and not telling me about it.' Bill folds his napkin. 'Does she speak to you about her friends and where she goes to?'

'She is seventeen, you know. It isn't so unusual for young people to expect some kind of social life which doesn't include their parents and their younger brothers.'

'I don't want to be included', Bill says. 'I'm not stupid, you know. Why do you talk to me as though I'm stupid? Like another one of your children?'

Viv refrains from saying it's because that's how he makes her feel sometimes. Like she's dealing with another kid – who clamours for her attention – and never sees for himself what needs to be done without being organised. In the end she accepts most things at home are down to her.

'No one likes to be deceived', Viv says. 'Or to feel that silence is a substitute for honesty.'

'That's what I mean', Bill says. 'Suspicion is a damaging condition.'

'Leading a double life – if only as a fantasy – is not the prerogative of those who are too young to know any better'. Viv wishes she could be more explicit. Call him hypocrite and wanker. 'People in glass houses . . . and all that.' She heads off into the kitchen with the remains of supper. Bill pours himself a double whisky and switches on the television.

It is possible to get to Alice's cottage by following the

cycle track that cuts across the water meadows and then dips in and out of snickets to the city outskirts – without too much attention to major roads. Everyone rides a bike in Oxford. Some have smart, lightweight racers. Others, high-tech collapsible models that can fold into the back of a car. The young man at the estate agent has one of these. He's called Damien and always seems to Viv to be far too upper class to be working in 'property negotiation' (his term). She imagines that even the aristocracy have to set their sights a little lower these days to earn a common crust. The stalwart spinsterhood of Oxford can be observed on plucky Sturminsters and faithful Raleighs. Serious bicycles, built for life by dedicated craftsmen in the small scale workshops of the Midlands, before global markets invented new technologies to turn out bicycles like Benetton sweaters and mobile phones. Antiquities, still painted maroon or olive green or black. With shiny mudguards, round chrome handlebars and mechanical bells you have to oil from time to time. A simple connection of gears, joined by steel wire to the chain, acknowledges that, even in a town like Oxford, inclinations in the geography can throw up long low hills that require a little extra recognition. Especially among women of a certain age. The ones who still, unmoved by what is fashionable, fix large wicker baskets to their handlebars for carrying manuscripts, their groceries, small, bright-eyed terriers with names like Meg or Annie. Their grey hair flowing in the jet stream beneath woolly hats and faded berets. Dressed, if not quite at Oxfam, most usually in the style of 20 years previously. For comfort, ease of movement and every eventuality.

Viv rides a mountain bike that once belonged to Clancy. It hasn't seen a lot of mountains but its broad wheels and strong frame can zip across the water meadows and through the snickets with a degree of certainty and confidence that suits Viv's tendency towards resolution. The trees are now completely bare and stand against the blue-black night like sticks of splintered bone. The early evening air still feels mild for November. Across the river, a low custard moon hangs precariously in what is otherwise an empty sky.

She turns into Alice's lane at about seven. The lights from the cottage windows suggest sanity, security, a cosy bolt hole in a stressful city. Alice is wearing a baggy, brown cardigan that looks hand knitted. But not by Alice. She is far too intellectual for quiet evenings crafting sweaters. It's probably a present to herself from some charitable event which has now become a constant comfort as the nights draw in. She has a lovely face. Viv always notices the deep furrows in her forehead that suggest a serious disposition, her dark skin and gentle grey eyes that twinkle with curiosity and amusement before her mouth takes up the urgency to smile. Her hair has gone the colour of iron but is tangled now with streaks of white amidst the grey. Curly of its own free will and used to being continually run through with strong determined fingers. A gesture Alice makes a lot but without any intention to effect adjustments.

'Come in. Come in', she says warmly. 'Do you want to leave your bicycle inside the porch?'

Viv is glowing from the exercise. Her cheeks rosy like candlelight. Her body quick and agile. In its prime.

She settles into one of the leather armchairs by the fire. A pile of books and papers have been hastily removed from the coffee table to make space for drinks and nuts. They rest tentatively by the book case, spilling words and information – a few significant ideas – into the general clutter of the sitting room. Alice brings gin and tonic in heavy, crystal tumblers that once lived in her mother's house in Dorset. Now antiques, like most of Alice's favourite possessions. She finds it hard to clear the decks of almost everything. But she makes new purchases of anything but books and music only rarely. The post-modern lust for shopping-as-performance remains an unknown quantity.

Orlando is feeling gregarious. She can hear the blurred sounds of amiable discussion through the crack in the sitting room door. She senses the kind of intimacy from which she does not like to be excluded. She tries mewing to make her presence felt, pushing the door with her head although the sneck is firmly in the lock. She scratches a little around the base, clawing up the threads of carpet she has already dislodged from their gripper on many a previous occasion. Orlando is smart enough to know that she can't shift a well shut door but she expects the combination of persistent mewing and scratching will be sufficient to provoke some action. When all else fails, she stands high on her back legs and rattles the handle with her paws, until human tolerance can stand the commotion no longer. Sometimes she gets speedily dispatched into the garden for her troubles. It is always a risk, rattling the handle. The dice not always falling in Orlando's favour. Tonight she is in luck. It is Viv who becomes persuaded by the histrionics and opens the door to let her in. Orlando skips past her to her cushion in the corner without a second glance. She is not a cat to give out gratitude too readily. She expects the humans in her life to allow her space and some respect. She's not a sycophantic kind of cat. She is fond of being stroked and being tickled underneath her chin but only when she's in the mood. Orlando always decides the moment, chooses her caresser with discrimination and initiates the intimacy. Mattie calls her Topcat in this respect but Alice misses the point.

Viv and Alice are discussing Mattie who is skulking in her bedroom, deciding whether or not to be sociable.

'... when she was at school.' Alice is filling in the details about when and where they met. 'After Leicester University, and a bit of a false start in teaching, she went to the States for a while – when everything was very radical. We kept in touch of course and met from time to time when she was passing through.' (In fact Alice wrote to Mattie in the States almost every week. Sometimes she got replies. Sometimes a flurry of enigmatic postcards. Suggesting passion. Alluding to affairs.) Alice makes it sound like *Brief Encounter* in a station buffet. 'She came back to England in the late seventies and got her present teaching job in London at the university. Her first book of poems was published about that time which made her quite a celebrity on the Arts scene. She did readings and signed autographs. I used to go and listen when she was in town. I was rather proud of her. Sometimes she'd come and stay for a while. Usually with some girl or other in tow. I didn't much mind. I got used to it.'

'Didn't you mind really?' Viv looks sceptical. Orlando opens a curious eye to check out Alice's response more accurately.

Alice has grown used to denying any feelings she might have known about jealousy or regret. It helps to keep her distanced from what seems like a lifetime of failure to live up to Mattie's exacting standards about open relationships and sex. There was no use minding. Mattie made a principle out of sleeping around. And always sounded very plausible. Her ethics were elastic – and capable of being stretched to include any amount of righteous justification for her shifting inclinations. On the various and frequent occasions when Alice behaved like most normal individuals in love – and expressed distress, a fair degree of pain, a failure to respond as positively as Mattie expected to her latest adultery – the suitcases would make their reappearance in the hallway and in a flurry of reproach she would be gone.

'Sounds like a woman who has trouble with relationships.' Viv sips her drink thoughtfully. Alice now knows that she is probably quite right. But has spent a lot of time feeling she should be persuaded by the passion of Mattie's invective. Should agree with Mattie's conviction about the perils of monogamy, although difficult to live with, as being essentially convincing. Alice certainly hasn't sought out 'matrimony' herself, or liked the way in which she observed Pip and Tate, for example, finish off each other's sentences. And occasionally appear in matching jackets or identical pairs of polished Oxford brogues. But as to imagining Mattie in flagrante with her latest lover – at the same time as she was sharing Alice's bed and wanting to make love a lot, in the general state of heightened lust that always seemed to coincide with her most recent discovery of a new romance – was more, in practice, than Alice could endure. It didn't help to be defined as hopelessly deficient either. Making Alice think for many years that it was she who had the problem.

'I'm rather old fashioned about these things', she now says to Viv with surprising frankness, and with the courage from a second gin. 'I never wanted anyone but Mattie at the time. At 23 I was already too old to change my ways in that respect.'

'Do you still want her?' Orlando can sense the merest quiver of tension in Viv's simple question. Alice is far too preoccupied with considering what would be an honest answer to be aware of any discomfort.

'I'm too old for any of it really', she says. 'And now she needs my help. She's full of woe as you will see if she decides to join us. I don't know what to do about it. Except let her be. Give her some space to come through.'

'When was the last time you saw her?'

Orlando has decided to vacate her cushion in the corner and take up refuge on Viv's lap. To feel more central to the action. She tests her claws against the cord of Viv's Laura Ashley jeans and fidgets for a while before she curls into a comfortable furry ball.

'There was a period in the early eighties, before I came to work at Henley Manor, when we lived together for a while.' Viv is curious. Alice is not used to speaking much about these things. 'No. That's not strictly true. We shared a flat in London. Well, it was my flat actually. Mattie decided to move in. I don't remember there being much of a discussion. She kept her favourite books and music and her clothes in the second bedroom and slept with me. In between stints under canvas at Greenham, getting arrested for obstruction and completing a second book of poetry.'

'There was quite a lot about those years that passed by me', Viv says. 'The politics of feminism. I don't know where I was when all of that was happening. Moving house a lot and looking after Clancy, I suppose. Trying to be a proper wife. Banged up with a man who once wanted to be a Labour MP but who was quickly getting seduced by the chance to make a million in the enterprise culture.'

'Did you love him?' Alice feels less and less inhibited now that both of them are talking personally.

'What's love got to do with it?' Viv smiles 'I had three

kids, no job to speak of, nil amount of personal equity. In August we had been together 20 years.'

Alice can't imagine anything but economic independence. Whatever else has happened in her life – the times when she has had very little emotional control – she has always been able to support herself financially. Made a point of it – if only to prove something beyond question to her father and her brothers. Her heart might not always have retained a mind of its own in the autonomy department, but she has never been one to stick around for reasons of material considerations.

'Did you leave Mattie then?'

'No one leaves Mattie. Not until recently anyway. It seems her latest lover has defied the patterns of a lifetime. But I know of no one else who's lasted long enough to do the ditching. She left me for a Russian ballerina. Sounds a bit unlikely, I dare say. The Russian ballerina bit, I mean. Not that she should leave me.'

'They met at some Arts Council shindig when Mattie was reading from her latest book of poems and Natalia was touring with the Bolshoi. Mattie brought her to the flat, of course. As a friend at first. But it wasn't long before they fell in love. She was very beautiful, as I remember. Quite extravagant. And full of dark moods and superstitions. With the kind of energy and brilliance which made my Englishness seem limp and pallid by comparison. "I'm in heaven and hell", she would say, as she tried to wrestle with her passion for Mattie and her conscience about the child and husband she had left in Moscow. I was not the best person to advise her. Or to reassure the Minder who came to find her – dressed like a caricature from John le Carre. He imagined a man was at the root of her increasingly volatile behaviour and sent her back to Moscow in disgrace. She made the kind of commotion at the airport which reached the national press – needing to be frog marched onto the aeroplane after a noisy episode of public weeping and distress.

'Mattie left soon after on an Aeroflot flight to Moscow, involved in some spurious lecture tour she had cooked up with the British Council. She reserved the right, as always, to pursue her own happiness, at whatever cost to me – and in the end, no doubt, to Natalia also. I lost touch with her after that, except for the occasional Christmas card. Until she contacted me again the other week.'

Alice is looking quite tired now, as she is speaking. If Viv is going to reach out and take her hand, this is the moment. But she is pinned beneath Orlando's resistant body, heavy in her lap, as if in warning. Whilst Alice seems quite lost within her memories, tied down in complicated feelings of her own, Viv lets the moment pass.

Neither hears the door swing gently on its hinges, until the familiar creak of unpolished wood pushes against the rise of carpet, where it sticks, on cue as usual, and Alice comments, for the hundredth time, that she must get someone to fix it. Mattie is not usually anxious about coming into rooms or meeting up with women she doesn't already know. In fact she's made a few flamboyant entrances in her time – with interesting effect. But her confidence of late has hit a low and dropped away like leaves in autumn. Making her feel exposed and mutilated. (Such times as these were when she got into the worst of rows with Jess. Her anxiety disguised as rage to minimise the fear of showing weakness and revealing vulnerabilities. An avalanche of rage which Jess was both too self-absorbed and too pissed off to try to understand. Seeking to escape – with mind and body still intact – she did what almost anyone else would do in similar circumstances. She left. With little more to do. And no ceremony.)

Now Mattie takes a deep breath, forces her face into a smile and enters the sitting room. Whatever it is that Viv is expecting from Alice's somewhat brief, but significant, description (the authorised version – which leaves out the occasional flying teapot hurled against the wall in temper, the sudden flash of anger which left Alice feeling stunned for lonely hours whilst Mattie, her anger exorcised, drifted like a baby into sleep, in the adjacent room), whatever it is, it isn't a woman who is quite so small. A woman with anxious eyes, wearing a smudge of green eye shadow and pale pink lipstick. A woman whose expensive shirt is fitting her more loosely than it should. Whose hair needs taking into hand by an experienced stylist. Alice moves quickly to her side. Like a protective hen.

'Mattie! I'm glad you're feeling well enough to join us. This is my friend Viv.'

Mattie – her feelings of depression calmed with happy pills – rises to the moment like the consummate actress she has become.

'Really Alice! Anyone would think I'm on my last legs!' She smiles engagingly at Viv as she reaches for her outstretched hand. 'How nice', she says. 'I've heard so much about you. Alice seems to have such few friends.'

Orlando feels the stakes increase. Suspects that Mattie will soon find the way to take control. Soon be dominating the discussion. As usual.

'Can I have a drink Alice? I can see I've got some catching up to do.'

'Some juice?' Alice doesn't want to draw attention to the mix of alcohol and anti-depressants.

'Don't be tedious Alice. I can see that you too aren't

opposed to knocking back the hard stuff!' She fixes her attention on Viv with such directness that Viv smiles nervously and looks away. 'So. What's the Oxford Labour party doing for women?' Mattie takes her drink from Alice without deflecting her attention from Viv's sudden shyness.

Viv is well used to social occasions and is not easily ruffled. Her political engagements and responsibilities, as the frequently reluctant hostess to dinner colleagues of her husband, have given her years of practice. But Mattie's sudden presence in the room is palpable – despite, and perhaps in contrast to – her look of frailty. For some reason Viv finds it difficult to think of very much activity that she can speak about with confidence.

Alice busies herself fetching more drinks and plates of savouries which she has prepared in an effort to persuade Mattie into more serious eating. A veritable feast, which must have taken considerable trouble – in between getting home from work and waiting for Viv to arrive. Mattie fingers the delicacies a little grudgingly.

'You'd make someone a lovely wife, Alice.' She is still smiling at Viv.

'Try this!' Alice ignores the taunt. 'You like asparagus as I recall.'

'I hope it's French. That Spanish stuff is so tasteless don't you think?'

Orlando imagines Mattie as a child, packed around the kitchen table in her terraced house. Two parents and a bunch of brothers competing for the space and a second helping of bread and butter pudding on a Friday evening. Orlando tries to be persuaded that an increasingly discerning palate reflects some kind of victory for the erstwhile proletariat in its struggle for political advance.

'Are you writing at the moment?' Viv tries to think about the kind of questions you should ask a poet.

'On and off.' Mattie is vague. 'I'm waiting for some inspiration. So many feelings of defeat around, don't you find? The legacy of years of political despair.'

'I don't think the Tory party are in despair', Viv says. 'They're much too self-satisfied for that. Bill says this is just the lull before the storm.' Viv can't imagine why she is referring to her husband. She doesn't usually. She couldn't care less what he thinks about anything. Least of all the political situation.

'Doesn't he object to you consorting with lesbians? Men usually do.' Mattie's note of playful innocence fools neither Alice nor Orlando.

'Have another drink, Viv. Boot the cat out of your way if she's irritating you.' Alice tries in vain to shift the conversation. Orlando, refusing to become a cheap distraction, sinks her claws still further into Viv's cream corded jeans. Viv assumes, inaccurately, that Mattie's question is a test of her credentials.

'He wouldn't even notice.' Viv isn't sure whether this is the right answer. She doesn't mean to imply that Bill is enlightened. Simply that this attention is always somewhere else.

'I've been trying to persuade Alice for years that she should come out. Don't you think she'd feel much better if she did?'

Viv looks at Alice nervously, who has by now relapsed into silence.

'I don't know', she answers briefly. 'I suppose it must depend on how Alice feels about it, surely? I don't think I'm best qualified to give advice.'

'Not within your area of expertise?' Mattie smiles. 'I

see. I always tend to think that close women friends of dykes have some personal interest in our direction.'

Viv imagines that her cheeks are burning. She wouldn't choose to put it quite so bluntly.

'I'm not a bigot if that's what you mean.'

Mattie assures her, most sincerely, that the thought has never crossed her mind.

'You've never understood about my job.' Alice feels her hackles rise to the old familiar bait. 'It's no doubt much easier to be open when you're teaching adults in a university. With an international reputation as a poet to lend additional credibility. But being a headmistress in a private school for girls is not the place to speak honestly about what most people still regard as deviance.'

'Not any longer Alice! This is the 1990s for goodness sake! I think you make your job into an excuse. You always have.'

'An excuse for what? I do my job to the very best of my ability. Its been the one area of my life which has given me the greatest pleasure and pride. I do it well because I'm a good professional. My sexuality is totally irrelevant. It's also increasingly academic. As you well know.'

Mattie is predictably dismissive. She knows the argument too well and has had it on several occasions in the past with Alice, without coming to any common understanding. She thinks it smacks of moral cowardice. Not to mention internalised oppression.

'What do you say Viv? You're a typical parent with a daughter in a private school. Would you move her somewhere else if the sordid truth got out?'

'Clancy is quite capable of getting *herself* expelled whether Alice is a lesbian or not. I'd say Alice is an excellent headmistress. What she does, or in her case,

doesn't do in bed, is no one else's business but her own.'
She remembers the conversation by the river with Steven
Rowntree. 'But I've no doubt some of the staff and governors would see it very differently. Not to mention stuffy
parents. Albert Montague would probably go hairless.'

'But not Bill?' Mattie is relentless.

'Bill wouldn't understand. He probably wouldn't like
it.'

'Then you're wasting your energies, Alice. Working
with the kind of people, and servicing the kind of bigots,
who – if the truth were known – would have your guts
for garters. You should go and work where you can be
yourself. Where your sexuality doesn't matter.'

'My sexuality doesn't matter, Mattie.'

But Mattie was rising to her theme. 'I'm sure she
doesn't fool anyone does she Viv? Come on, tell me. You
must have known as soon as you saw her that she was
a lesbian. It's pretty obvious, I would say.'

Viv is feeling embarrassed. She feels she should be
more *au fait* with these kinds of issues. Mattie is challenging all her liberal platitudes. Partly preoccupied with
her own performance she doesn't see the extent to which
Alice is becoming increasingly uncomfortable. Or
imagine that Mattie's onslaught might well be viewed as
rather cruel.

'How did she tell you, Viv? Come on, I'm intrigued to
know. I always feel amused to hear about Alice's coming
out stories.' She smiles mischievously.

Alice continues to look uneasy.

'I don't remember to be honest. A while ago. In the
Café Can Can, I expect.'

In fact Viv can remember very well. Every detail of
the conversation. Even what she was wearing. The way
her heart began to quicken, as though her pulse rate

speeded up a notch or two. How suddenly she seemed to lose her appetite. How much she wanted to reach across the table and place her hand against Alice's cheek.

'Did she tell you the story about the boy in the box? The same excuse she shared with Daphne Du Maurier?' Mattie glances at Alice. She knows that she is treading on sacred ground in hob nail boots. Orlando groans inwardly. A rather human response in cats.

'The boy in the box?' Viv is unprepared for the precision of Mattie's taunts and quite innocent about their likely consequences.

'Why don't you tell her Alice? Don't be such a prude! It's such a good story.' She waits expectantly for Alice to begin.

'It was all a very long time ago', Alice says. 'As you well know. I don't think Viv is the slightest bit interested.'

'She is, aren't you Viv?' Mattie is nothing if not relentless. 'I'm sure she's dying to hear about "your abnormality". Women who are curious about lesbian sex are always fascinated by the lengths that some women go to in search of biological explanations. She might not be too familiar with those interesting theories about inversion, about being a prisoner in the wrong gender.'

'Viv isn't doing research Mattie. Don't you think all this is rather tasteless in the circumstances? Why don't I get the coffee whilst you and Viv talk some more about the Council. Or the Campsfield Campaign. I am sure she's much more concerned about political prisoners.'

'Alice doesn't like to be reminded that she once used to think of herself as a boy in the wrong body. A boy that had to be kept locked way in a box. Who when he got out, encouraged her to behave like a man, with "impure thoughts".' Mattie laughs at Alice's expense. 'She still thinks he might escape, I'm sure. Put her precious career and reputation in jeopardy.'

Alice bangs the door as she goes to fetch the coffee. Being put on the spot in public by Mattie is an experience that has always upset her. Pushing her into corners and reducing her to silence. Making her feel awkward and ugly. Some kind of hypocrite or cripple. Another word she doesn't like. She clearly hasn't got any better at deflecting Mattie's cruelty or dealing with the masochistic feelings that get mixed up in her failure to respond with dignity. Now Viv has become privy to a public dose of private humiliation – which makes Alice want her to go away at once and stay away until after Mattie has been persuaded to leave town.

Back in the sitting room the atmosphere is already lighter. Viv and Mattie talk about Amnesty, Clancy and the drugs bust, whether Joanna Trollope's novels should be turned into television dramas. They both agree on almost everything. Including the tedious mediocrity of the dialogue invented by Trollope to stupefy middle England.

Alice returns to find the discussion about music. Orlando has slunk back to her cushion in the corner and turned her back on the proceedings.

'There's a recital in the Sheldonian on Tuesday evening, Alice. Viv is suggesting that we go. I'd like to, would you?'

'I've got a meeting', Alice lies. 'Perhaps some other time.' She pours the coffee.

'You wouldn't mind, then, if Viv and I went without you, would you Alice? It seems too good an opportunity to miss when I'm here with so much free time on my hands.'

Viv checks with Alice nervously. This is not at all the scenario she had in mind. But she can see it would look churlish to pull out now that Mattie is so keen.

'Maybe you could come and join us later, Alice', she says. 'After your meeting has finished. What about a nightcap at the Café Can Can?'

'I'm not sure when I'll be through, thank you all the same. It's probably best you make your own arrangements with Mattie. I'll catch up with you some other time.'

'Well, that's settled then!' Mattie is looking more animated than she has done for weeks. There is nothing like a potential conquest to refresh the spirits. And nothing quite like teasing Alice. She always crumples so completely.

'It's a good job one of us could manage to be entertaining', Mattie says when Viv has gone and Alice is stacking supper dishes in the kitchen. 'You don't get any better at socialising do you? It's a wonder your friend doesn't find you quite depressing when you're in one of your boring moods.' She picks up her cup of cocoa and slips quickly into the bedroom before Alice can reply.

Orlando knows that Alice doesn't like to face the awful truth as she watches her intently from her perch beside the microwave, but Mattie is a bitch. She always was. And she always will be.

Eleven

'Mrs Williams has phoned three times.'
Hilda's mouth is scratched into a short sharp line beneath a flat nose. She bangs the coffee pot down with a degree of grace that causes a glob of black liquid to shoot out of the spout and splatter the table in Alice's study. Alice takes a man-sized tissue from the drawer and dabs perfunctorily in the direction of the creeping coffee stain.
'Did she leave a message?'
Alice has no real desire to speak to Viv after Mattie's virtuoso performance the previous evening. She wants neither pity nor applause. Simply to be left in peace.

'Nothing.' Hilda has her own views about Viv's reluctance to give her reasons for ringing. 'I've only been your secretary for eight years. I suppose it's too much to expect that I might actually be able to remember messages and pass them on correctly.' Hilda quite enjoys the role of prima donna. It's one she has perfected over time with elaborate recourse to pregnant pauses and dramatic exits.

'It's probably not important.' Alice opts for evasion. 'No doubt she'll try again.'

Hilda sighs. Personally she believes that three unspecified intrusions from the same persistent source so early in the day is a provocation. Not that she would ever dream of saying so directly. She collects a folder from the desk and leaves the room, raising her eyebrows to a revengeful God, who sanctions her suspicions with a troubled silence.

Alice retreats to the window seat with her cup of coffee and looks across the leaf strewn lawns towards the river. November is running in chill after the warmest October on record. Since 1795 or thereabouts, the pundits say. Against the grey stone wall a splash of yellow roses continue to defy the changing season. And in the distance, beyond a thin stretch of low slung mist, ducks on the Isis chivvy unexpected chicks into the shallows. Alice, if she knew of their existence, would worry for their safety once the icy slash of winter begins to whip its ruthless way along the water line.

There was no sound from Mattie's room when Alice set out for work. Usually she leaves a tray of toast and coffee, but not today. Mattie can be dead for all she cares. There is a limit to her tolerance.

In the bleak night when Alice cannot sleep, a shadow moves across the moon, reviving old excuses, airing contradictions, bleeding pain. Expendable in darkness, tears spill along the creases of her cheeks. As though from somewhere long ago. Seeping through the cracks in her defences, where previous denials have worn a little thin.

In the morning Mattie hides beneath the duvet like a child. The adrenalin that helped to fuel last night's cabaret is now distilled in air. Her brows drawn tight against the dull pain of a sleepless night and too much alcohol. She waits until the radio is turned off and the cottage door slams shut before making her appearance. Orlando's disapproval disappears into the sitting room as Mattie comes in search of company and coffee in the kitchen.

In London it is never quiet. Always the sharp shriek of brakes, the dull routine of traffic in the streets. Here the sound of silence is extreme. Locked inside the leaded windows. Unbroken by the ticking of a clock. The telephone, patiently attending to its function, waits for the calls that rarely come.

Mattie places a small scrap of paper beside her cup and studies the forwarding address for further clues. She imagines Jess moving through a house she doesn't know, wearing clothes she's never seen. Making up a mind that's slipped the clutches of her former influence. Shifting residual feelings into memories of the past: the usual repository for old adversaries and ex-lovers. She dials the number scribbled beside details of a house, a street, a part of London Mattie doesn't know. It rings anonymously for long enough to start an answerphone. A swift, mechanical response that dutifully provides a disembodied message, 'Susie and Jess are all tied up at present', followed by peals of laughter. 'If you'd like to leave a message, please speak after the tone.' Mattie counts the pips that indicate the calls. Twelve before the bleep. There is nothing she can say to such a busy couple so clearly in demand. She replaces the receiver and throws the scrap of paper in the bin.

She tries again. This time a number she has learned by heart. Three rings and another disappointment for one who longs for human interaction. Meredith is deliberately illusive. She likes to guard her privacy from those who think that therapy means any time you need some help. At least her message is encouraging. 'Thank you so much for taking time to call. Meredith is working at the moment but will get back to you as soon as she is free. Please leave your name and number and stay well in your life.'

Mattie leaves her details and replaces the receiver. It's still only ten o'clock, and another empty, silent day snakes into the future without much point or purpose. She takes her coffee back to bed and pulls the duvet round her head.

Viv is washing the kitchen floor and pushing the vacuum through the pile of debris that invades the lounge and upper landing. She takes a stack of manilla envelopes from the bureau in the hall which indicate that bills are overdue. She signs her name with flourish on a clutch of cheques that never bounce, beneath the title Mr W. and Mrs V. Williams, a neat reminder of her easy access to communal assets. She checks her watch, its 11.15. Viv contemplates a further call to Alice to thank her for the pleasure of her company. But decides against another rude encounter with the dragon on the switchboard. Viv can only imagine that Hilda's secretarial skills must somehow compensate for making telephone enquiries seem like deliberate intrusions on her time. She decides to wait until the evening.

On Tuesday Bill gets home from work at half past six. The boys are playing on the stairs, a complicated game of cops and robbers that threatens to deteriorate into the usual tantrums, irritated adults and recriminations. A trail of white telephone cord twisting through the hallway and disappearing underneath the study door, suggests that Clancy is in lengthy conference with her cronies, at Bill's expense. He has forgotten that Viv is going out. After a busy day, a rather successful day in fact, Bill arrives home with a bottle of chilled white wine and a bunch of roses. Not the most original of gestures, but romantic none the less, after so many years of mutual inconvenience. The remains of chips and pizza on the kitchen table indicate a children's tea. He begins to clear a space, intending candles, conversation and a celebration.

But Viv is at the mirror, being indecisive. She settles for a woollen suit that is stark and elegant and didn't come from Laura Ashley.

'The concert at the Sheldonian', she says to Bill by way of explanation. 'I told you last week about the tickets.'

'Did you? I don't remember.' He passes over the roses with the optimism of a small boy who still hopes to get his way.

'They're beautiful', she smiles. 'Can you see that Boyd and Philip have a bath and Clancy does her homework before she disappears? I shouldn't be too late. About 11, I expect.'

'Who's the lucky man?' Bill's quip is delivered with a smile but issued in a moment of uncertainty. 'You look stunning that's all. I can't believe it's only Alice Morrison that brings you out in all your finest clothes.'

For some reason, best known to herself, Viv fails to

correct his wrong impression. She checks the mirror one more time.

'Perhaps I'm rather over dressed. It's only a local concert after all. Hardly the London Philharmonic.'

'You look terrific, Mum.' Clancy is wearing psychedelic leggings and a leather jacket breeding zips. 'I hope you have a brilliant time. I expect Miss M. will tip up in all the same old stuff she wears to school. You'll look like chalk and cheese.'

'Alice Morrison is a sweetie, Clancy. And she's been very good to you.'

'I know. I know. But she needs to get a life!'

'And you're an expert on such things I suppose.'

Clancy grins. 'Well . . . all that English literature . . . I mean. Really!'

'Which reminds me – don't forget your homework. And if you go out later, I want you back by 10'.

Clancy agrees without complaint, much to Bill's surprise. They stand together waving at the door as Viv's car disappears into the road.

'You and mum should go to a concert. You never seem to go out with each other any more. I'll sit on the babies for a tenner.'

'I'll sit on Philip for a tenner', Boyd shouts from the hallway. 'I don't need Clancy to look after me.'

'What if you all look after each other for nothing. Now that would be a novelty. You could do it in the name of brotherly and sisterly affection.' Bill risks a homily devoid of meaning in a household such as his. 'Perhaps I should change your names. To "I want", "Can I have?" and "Will you buy me?"' Boyd and Philip pull a face and Clancy disappears upstairs muttering incoherent liturgies about labour power and surplus value. It takes

Bill some time to realise that his daughter has become a Marxist.

'I thought you had a meeting?'

Alice is stuck into her marking by the fire. It seems as though she's been scribbling in red ink over potted versions of *Persuasion* for the best part of 30 years. She must have read the book on more occasions than Jane Austen. By now she knows the celebrated quotes by heart. Quite stripped of their significance.

'It was re-arranged.' Alice replies without looking up. She has a vague sense of silk and *Tendre Poison*. Though she's not one to set much store by perfume and appearance.

'That's a pity', Mattie says. 'You could have come with us after all. Do you want to take my ticket? I'm sure Viv would much rather go with you. I think I was bit of an afterthought.'

Mattie is not entirely serious. A calculated offer of self sacrifice. A suggestion of intrigue. But she has dressed for the occasion in a black silk trouser suit she bought in Florence, with a small cluster of rhinestones on the left lapel. A hint of perfume and a touch of lipstick. Alice notices the transformation.

'You're looking better', she says. 'Not so washed out.' She might have said, 'You look extravagant and beautiful. Are you planning a seduction?' But Alice has forgotten how to speak of sex. And she does not want to start again the torture of imagining. She has wasted many lonely years obsessed with thoughts of Mattie and her many lovers. Mattie being charming and flirtatious. Her latest conquest giddy with anticipation. Eyes holding onto eyes in special corners of secluded restaurants. Tips of fingers touching with intent across white, linen table cloths. Waiters moving discreetly through shadows that gather in a blur of candlelight and music, attending to the set, creating the occasion in which to entertain desire.

Mattie smiles. 'Do you want my ticket? Seriously. I'm not desperate to hear Rossini.'

Alice switches her attention to the characters and plot of *Persuasion*.

'You'll be late. Viv is always on time and she doesn't like to be kept waiting.'

Mattie moves quickly through the hall without a backward glance. Alice does her best to concentrate on half-baked theories of suspense and irony. But she is bored with marking essays. And bored with a life in which the narrowness of what is possible seems increasingly confined to this. She pours herself a large whisky and heaps another log onto the fire.

At eight o'clock the telephone in the study splits the silence of the cold, black night.

'Alice, are you there? And why have you deserted me?' The light, teasing voice on the other end of the phone is Jack. An old friend of Alice's from her student days. And now the co-owner of their allotment in St Ebbes.

Alice laughs. 'I was rather waiting for you to clear out the nettle and the rocks before I put in my appearance. Isn't it the wrong time of the year to do much in the garden besides digging and clearing out?'

'But digging is always much better with a friend', Jack insists. 'I thought this was to be a true partnership. Equal effort. Equal rewards.'

'You're quite right', Alice says. 'And I'm sorry. I've been a bit distracted recently.'

'Have you?' He waits. 'Nothing serious, I hope?'

'Unsettled, I suppose. I'm too old for trouble Jack. And out of practice, in a way.'

'What are you doing now?'

Unlike Alice, Jack never left Oxford when he finished his degree. He did postgraduate work for a while and then got a junior fellowship at Keble. Now he's one of the senior librarians in the Bodleian. Teaching required too much personal projection for Jack's inclination. He much prefers to organise books and classify manuscripts. And to grow vegetables in his leisure time.

'I'm getting slightly sloshed, if you want to know the truth.'

'Not on your own, I hope?'

Alice bumped into Jack again when she returned to Oxford. He was standing on the path beside the river, in much the same spot where they once walked together in the moonlight holding hands. The year she thought of suicide.

'Do you want some company? I could bring the plans round for the allotment. I need your advice about the shed. Do we pull it down and start again? Or try to mend the roof?'

Alice is unused to spontaneity. She likes to know in advance about arrangements. She doesn't like to change direction in mid stream.

'Well...'

'I don't want to intrude, of course.' Jack is always tentative. 'But if you feel like it... I wouldn't mind a chat myself.'

Alice agrees. 'Well, come over if you like. I'll open a bottle of wine and you can keep me company.' Jack isn't up to Scotch so far as she can tell.

They talk about mortality. And how it's preferable to live alone – to some extent.

'But getting your genes into the next generation. That's what it's all about', Jack says. 'A stake in posterity.'

'It's too late for me then.' Alice shakes her head. 'Bit too late to start thinking about children. My own, that is. I might leave a few suggestions in the heads of someone else's. But that's debatable.'

'Don't you think it concentrates the mind to know there's no one else but us?' Jack, like Alice, has never married, and, if what he says is true, he hasn't fathered any children either.

'All my life I've felt alone', Alice says. 'It won't be any worse when I'm dead, I expect.'

'You've had relationships, though. "Significant others" as the psychiatrists say.'

'One relationship to be precise. Which lasted longer in my life than it deserved.' Alice watches Jack in the firelight. His long thin body lounging in the chair. She remembers the time they tried, without much success, to do something about sex. Love, a relationship, posterity were not the issues then. She needed to know if she was sexual. To see whether she was normal.

'I'm sure you've had relationships?' Alice says.

Jack looks away.

'I've had sex,' he says. 'Sometimes good sex. Lived a little dangerously for a specialist librarian. But love? A relationship? Family? I'm not so sure I've ever felt part of a family. Even a pretend one.' He smiles sadly.

'Do you want a child?' Alice asks. 'I'm sure it's not too late if...'

'I don't want a child. how could I suddenly start with children now? It's more... the others.'

'The others?' Alice is not quite sure where this is leading.

'Well, others have children. Other men. Maybe they had them early. Before they decided they were gay, for example.'

Alice nods and waits for him to finish.

'Then, it's quite a wrench. If you have to think about your children.'

'Do you mean making the choice between a lover and your children?'

Jack nods. 'Yes, that's what I mean. And it isn't easy.'

Alice thinks of Viv and Mattie. Mattie wouldn't start anything when there are children involved. Would she?

'Do you have a lover who has children Jack?'

For some reason Alice has always imagined that the neat and modest bachelor flat, above the office in the Square where Jack lives, reflects a similar kind of solitary existence to her own. She remembers his confusion about sex in the past and has always assumed, till now, that he has chosen to put his energies into other things. Their conversations over dinner, his attachment to his garden, all the talk of books and music – none of it has ever got to do with sex.

'I think I am in love.' Jack buries his head in his hands. His pale fair hair, still long around his collar, falls in disarray across his face. He is a little drunk. He has the urge to tell her more.

'But your love isn't making you feel happy?' she asks him gently.

'I don't know if it's mutual. It could be. But he's younger than me. He has a wife and child.' Jack looks distraught. 'What do you think Alice? Is it possible?'

'I don't know him. I don't know the situation. Does

he want to stay married? What about his wife? I can't imagine that she knows he's gay.'

'He's very confused. Sometimes he wants to leave. Sometimes he wants to stay. He's got a lot to lose.'

'Of course. That's usually the thing that keeps us all in line.'

'You might know him actually', Jack looks away. And then corrects himself. 'I mean, you might have seen me with him.'

Alice doubts it. She waits for him to say. The silence stretches through the shadowed room. Until the moment passes.

'Look, I'm sorry Alice. I came to cheer you up. Not to be so selfish. Just talking bout myself all night. You're a good listener.' His voice is slightly slurred.

'You need a taxi, Jack.' Alice wants him to be gone before Mattie gets back. This is not the time to explain about Mattie. Or explain about Jack. 'You shouldn't drive like this. I would let you stay in the spare room but . . .'

'No. Don't worry about me, Alice. I need to get home. I do.'

Jack kisses her lightly on the cheek before climbing into the taxi. As it gathers speed along the lane Viv's car drops Mattie at the cottage gate. Mattie is smiling. As Viv pulls back into the night her heart is beating faster than is usual. When she gets home there is a note from Bill beside the roses, wilting where she left them on the kitchen table. 'Back soon. Just needed to see a man about a deal.' Viv cuts the prickled stems and plunges them in water from the kettle. It's quite a drastic remedy, she thinks – being up to your neck in hot water – in the interests of revival.

Twelve

Stubbs and his tool shed have become something of a joke among the girls at Henley Manor. 'Something nasty in the woodshed.' It's probably the mark of a private school education that a younger generation can still recognise a literary reference when they hear it – however misplaced. Alice Morrison always likes to read Stella Gibbons' comic classic to the third form but she gets cold comfort from its contemporary association. Her suspicions are not easily aroused. She is used to adolescent girls giggling in groups. It's usually best to overlook the substance of their preoccupations. More often than not it's got to do with sex in some disguise or other. And Alice likes to treat the subject with the lack of significance it deserves. But Hilda is not the one to let an opportunity escape.

'That shed has become a symbol of moral turpitude.' Hilda makes her announcement in the staff room at morning break. 'Girls are loitering in the shrubbery during free periods – when they should be doing private study in the library.'

'I haven't noticed much difference.' Wendy Armitage thinks Hilda is a harmless busybody. 'It's far too cold, for one thing.'

'You don't have a window that overlooks the nursery garden.' Hilda is as sure as eggs are eggs that drugs are still being dealt in Stubbs' tool shed.

'I've heard several pointed references to grass and weed.' Mrs Maudling, the Biology Mistress, is not a favourite with the girls. Her mouth rarely deviates from its downward droop of dissatisfaction. Dissatisfaction with her job. Her husband. Her three bedroomed, neo-Georgian town house built on reclaimed land.

Steven Rowntree wants to enquire about Mr Maudling who dresses up in Civil War uniform most weekends and re-enacts the Battle of Marston Moor. And her three thin-faced little girls who have followed each other in silence through the school. Instead he tries to explain how, in a place like this, in which very little happens that is out of the ordinary, speculation spreads like poison ivy.

'Puns', he says. 'They're simply exercising their satirical intelligence.'

'Well I think the police should be informed. Those girls should be expelled.' Hilda is not easily distracted from the purpose of her pronouncement. It comes from an evangelical upbringing in which shades of grey go unrecognised between polarities of black and white. 'It's not surprising we've become a laughing stock. Now they know they can get away with murder.'

'Who knows, for goodness sake?' Wendy Armitage is becoming irritated. 'Henley Manor is hardly the front line of the blackboard jungle.'

'You might prefer the atmosphere of Digwood Comprehensive, Miss Armitage. Perhaps you would like it better there. Personally, I think our parents expect something a little more refined and respectable for their daughters. They certainly don't pay good money to have them mixing with dopeheads and dropouts!'

Mrs Maudling has to agree.

'Dropouts?' Steven interrupts. 'I thought your complaint was that they haven't dropped out! I thought you wanted them forcibly removed!'

'You know what I mean, Mr Rowntree. It's a question of values and maintaining standards. There's no place for wishy-washy attitudes at Henley Manor. We have to set the girls a good example.'

'If we can help them reach maturity with their eyes and ears open to the possibility of LIFE, Hilda . . .' his voice rises to its theme, '. . . in all its different, glorious, complicated, messy forms – don't you think that is so much better than a narrow-minded, punitive distrust of anyone or anything that breaks the mould?'

The bell in the lobby puts a stop to the discussion as Steven grabs his briefcase and a pile of books. But Hilda can't resist a parting shot.

'You might think that, Mr Rowntree. But you won't find many others on the staff who agree with you. I'd be very surprised if this doesn't come up again on Governor's Day.'

'Why should it? Have you seen the agenda?' Steven

can't bear the prospect of a bunch of Tory business men and local dignitaries having the chance to air their prejudice in public. In a way that could still lead to expulsions and police investigations.

'I'm the one who draws it up.' Hilda smiles smugly. 'With the agreement of Miss Morrison, of course. She always checks it through to make sure I haven't left anything out.'

'Alice Morrison won't want the Governors to dwell on this. Otherwise she would have taken a much tougher line herself. Anyway, it's none of their business.'

'It is if it brings the school into disrepute, Mr Rowntree. Which being soft on drugs is bound to do.'

At this point Steven decides discretion is the better part of valour. Wendy is quite wrong to imagine that Hilda is a harmless busybody. She clearly believes the school is on the brink of moral anarchy and needs a higher authority to step in and take control. Now is probably as good a time as any to call up Mrs Williams. Before such things as these get out of hand.

On Friday after school Hilda generally treats herself to tea in Burridges, the café in the square. In the summer you can sit outside beside plastic tables under striped umbrellas. Become part of the ambience which tourists like to catch on camera for their folks back home in Arkansas and Buffalo. At one with the pigeons on the cobbles, fully breasted and well fed on walnut and sultana scones and crumbs of carrot cake.

Hilda makes for an empty table on the inside, by the window, and orders cheesecake and a pot of Earl Grey tea. She keeps a look out for Marion, her friend from church, who usually joins her for a cup of coffee before making her weekly expedition to the hairdresser. They talk about who said what at work. And whether God would approve of some of the organisations Marion gets sent to by the temping agency she works for.

'Some very dicey places, I would say. Like the photographers the other week. All those sleazy pictures on the walls. Pretending to be art.'

'What kind of pictures?' Hilda is quick to anticipate obscenity, but she does know, from mixing with theatricals, that art can be confusing to the uninitiated.

'Well, close-ups of what looked to me like bits of bodies on a plate.'

'Dismembered bodies?' Hilda lifts a large chunk of cheesecake into her incredulous mouth and licks her fingers noisily. She thinks of newspapers she has read. Full of gruesome details about serial killers and psychopaths. No woman is safe these days. She edges closer to Marion with a self-conscious shudder of solidarity.

'Still life, the photographer called them. A kind of collage. But I have my doubts.' Marion polishes off her wedge of 'death by chocolate' and orders a second helping. 'Anyway, there's nothing much to cause offence at the Bod. A change is as good as a rest is what my husband always says.'

Hilda yawns. It's been a long week at school with more than its fair share of aggravation.

'I'll be glad to get home tonight', she says.

Outside the light is fading. The occasional drunk is stumbling past the window with a six-pack and a bed roll. Deciding on a doorway for the immediate duration. A better option than the Night Shelter, full of New Age Travellers with mangy dogs and shaven heads, and other crazy people. Oxford is a mecca for the homeless. Rich pickings from the tourists and liberal academics with guilty consciences to contradict. Hilda shakes her head in disapproval. She'd throw them all in prison if she was on the council. Forget compassion. Hilda's is an angry God. Preoccupied with sin and retribution.

'Do you know that man?' Marion points through the window to Steven Rowntree. With one hand he is balancing his bicycle, with the other a bunch of yellow chrysanthemums. He is struggling with his shopping to retrieve spare change from his trouser pocket for the drunk who is standing in his path with outstretched hands. 'He comes into the library a lot. I've heard him mention Henley Manor.'

Hilda pushes an absent minded finger round her plate to trawl the last few crumbs of cheesecake.

'I do. He's the resident left-wing loony, for our sins. And up to no good with one of the new members of staff. A silly young woman who thinks the sun shines out of his earhole.' Hilda imagines that Miss Armitage has little backbone. She's gullible. Not deliberately devious but easily influenced. 'I don't think the example set to girls by fornicators on the staff is one we should tolerate. But Alice Morrison is weak as water when it comes to managing the troublemakers.'

'I doubt he's fornicating with your Miss Armitage.' Marion wipes a smudge of chocolate cream from her lower chin. 'Not if Mr Greyling has got anything to do with it.'

'Mr Greyling?' Hilda is intrigued.

Marion enjoys the moment of suspense and makes the most of it. 'I've noticed him more than once. As soon as he comes into the library he makes a beeline for Mr Greyling. I see them whispering together in Mr Greyling's corner by the window. Where Mr Greyling has his desk. You don't often see Mr Greyling looking pleased with himself. He's not one to let his feelings show. Your Mr Rowntree is very often staring straight into his eyes. It's the fact they're both men that makes me think there's something fishy going on between them.'

'What kind of fishy?' Hilda is oblivious to the waitress wiping a greasy cloth across the streaked Formica of the table, trying to drop a none too subtle hint about the imminence of closing time. She grabs Marion's plate before Marion can waste any more time licking up the last remaining splodge of monosodium glutamate.

'Well, you know what they say about bachelor librarians.' Marion's mouth forms into the smallest of smiles. 'Not that I've ever met a proper homo-sex-ual.' She pronounces the word with careful attention to each licentious syllable and with a fetish for the unexpected.

Hilda's eyes widen and then narrow as her brain catches up with the import of Marion's revelation. Hilda has. In Brighton, where she used to keep a boarding house for entertainers. Before she saw the light and gave herself to Jesus. Her mouth creases into a self-satisfied sneer.

'Well, well, well. And would you say that Mr Rowntree is like that too... from what you've seen of them together?'

Marion shrugs her shoulders. 'I'm not the one to draw conclusions. But usually it takes two to tango, as my mother would say.'

'Then it's a mortal sin.' Hilda fastens up her anorak and fishes in her pocket for her Fair Isle gloves. 'St Paul's letter to the Romans says it all. The practice of sodomy is an abomination. And him a teacher – with access to young minds.'

'Young female minds.' Marion gathers up her wicker

basket and plastic carrier bag. 'Led astray by an agent of the Devil.'

'Those poor children!' Suddenly it all adds up too clearly in Hilda's mind. 'Learning about music from a sodomite! And in the staff room – we use the same coffee cups. The self-same cloakroom.'

Marion checks the price of chocolate cake against the menu and counts out £3.75 as her contribution to the bill.

'And do you know what's worse? He's married, if I'm not mistaken. With a child of his own to be responsible for. And silly little Miss Armitage – pinning all her hopes on his affection. And do you know what's worst of all? Miss Morrison thinks he's wonderful! No wonder she overlooks the fact he's supplying half the upper sixth with illegal substances.' Hilda is anxious to get going. 'But not for much longer. I'll soon put a stop to Steven Rowntree and his little games. Thank you, Marion for this information. If there's anything I can do for you – just let me know.'

'Don't mention it', Marion fakes another small smile before setting off towards the hairdressers.

'Will you be at church on Sunday Marion? I'll save you a seat.'

'I never miss', says Marion. 'The vicar is such a nice young man, I always think.'

On Monday morning Steven tries Viv Williams at both the Council Offices and at home. But without success. It is already too late. The note written on cheap lined paper, in thick black capitals, is already folded into a manilla envelope and waiting with the morning mail to be opened by Alice Morrison. Postmarked Aylesbury. Dated Saturday, at four o'clock.

Alice is late for once. A broken filling over the weekend has meant an emergency visit to the dentist on Monday. The dentist is a woman who views teeth in the same way as some people view bricks and mortar. As fixed assets. She keeps her waiting for long enough to emphasise the disadvantages of holding on tenaciously to cheap treatment from the NHS. Alice knows that if she was prepared to pay the private rate she could jump the queue of elderly pensioners, young women with fractious children and a crazy man, who spends most of the time buttoning and unbuttoning his jacket with obsessive precision. If her parents were to take the same view, she would be out of a job. But teeth seem more fundamental, somehow. When it comes to principles. Alice ponders this on the way to school until thoughts of Mattie take over her mind and she relives the night before.

On Sunday after dinner there is an atmosphere of *déjà vu*. Of times past which she can still remember as the kind of loss that even favourite music cannot heal. Lost moments of domestic intimacy. Of meals cooked together and washed away in the warm intensity of quiet conversation and a glass or two of claret. When they were together at first Alice used to read aloud to Mattie in such moods. Tennyson. Wordsworth. Keats. Alice was fond of the Romantics. She could recite by heart *The Lady of Shallot* and *The Eve of St Agnes*. Mattie humoured Alice on such occasions. But there was also something about the poems that reminded her of school. And draughty classrooms, in which the pulse of passion rushing through her veins seemed dangerously subversive beneath her starched white shirt, her knitted cardigan, her navy blue pleated skirt. Still young enough, and far too gauche, to contemplate the possibilities of leaving home and escaping Holderness for good. Classrooms in which the flicker of the future was still much fainter than a vapour.

Half a lifetime down the line, Alice is anaesthetising her broken filling with a double brandy, and letting Mattie play at being thoughtful and considerate. She allows the fire to be heaped too high and Schubert's Quartet in D to slice through her heart strings like a razor through scar tissue. It is Mattie's turn to read. She reads some letters from Virginia Woolf to Vita Sackville West, and to her sister, Vanessa Bell. And a story by Katherine Mansfield about a desperate kind of coupling, in a dreary kind of city, in a seedy small hotel, which shows how youth is all too quickly gone. Then Mattie reads some of her own poems. She chooses ones about love because her mood is turning mellow. It seems forever since she's stretched herself beside a woman's body, in search of some salvation, ineffable and undefined.

Alice watches her with tenderness. The tenderness she always feels when Mattie concedes some recognition of vulnerability. When she isn't posturing or performing particularly, but allowing her preference for intensity to slip free from its usual restraint.

'Did you ever read to Jess?' It seems possible again to risk a little intimacy. As if she might be offered truth – beyond disclaimers and beyond anger.

Mattie smiles. 'I don't do the same things with different women, you know. I only ever think of reading like this with you.'

Alice nods. She is in the mood to be persuaded. She knows that Mattie, in the past, was not averse to making love with different women in Alice's bed. Which, at the time, seemed to reflect a certain absence of originality. Not to mention loyalty.

'Sometimes I read aloud to myself', Mattie confides. 'Is that pathetic?'

'Does it feel pathetic?'

'Not really. Sometimes the words are pleading to be heard. And often they're more powerful when they're spoken out loud. Anyway, I like the sound of my own voice. An occupational characteristic, I suppose. I've never read to Jess. She used to say I made her feel stupid. As though she had nothing to contribute of any value.'

'You can be quite daunting when you're in full flight. It would take a brave woman to contradict. .'

'But she was never quiet with her friends. And she is very bright. Either way, there's no excuse. I'm not a monster.'

'But what was missing was equality', Alice says. 'It's very difficult to make bridges across different life experiences, don't you think? You used to be shy with me at first. Though not for long.' She speaks without a trace of irony.

'But our differences have never been about inequalities. More complementary, I would say.'

'Yin and Yang!'

Mattie pulls a face. 'That's bullshit. I'm not into dualisms and polarities.'

'How could you be? You were "post-modern" in your predilections before the fashion was invented!'

Mattie laughs. 'I never thought of it like that. It's just I've always wanted to be my own person. Be free to come and go as I please. To be untethered. I'm not afraid of changes.'

'Aren't you? I thought all this distress was because of change. And being unsure about the future.'

Mattie thinks for a moment. 'It does seem to be, doesn't it? Maybe I'm in collision with, what Meredith likes to call, my "other self".'

'A bit like Freud?'

'A bit like psycho babble. Probably the truth about "the self" is what people always go to therapists to discover. She says I give up space to a bunch of fairly disparate contenders.'

'Is that the kind of insight which costs £45.00 an hour?' Alice is amazed. 'Aren't we all a mix of patterns and contradictions? They used to call them humours in the Middle Ages.'

'But this is more "serious". She gives out homework. Once I had to write about a conversation between my public and my private selves – to show who else I am, besides the person who does my job.' Mattie knows this must sound incredibly banal, but there have been moments in the recent past when she has felt sufficiently desperate to clutch at some of the more plausible of Meredith's suggestions.

'How did you set about it?' Alice can't imagine allowing herself to be so exposed.

'I wrote about a meeting between "Ms Women's Liberation" and "Miss Lonely Heart". I decided to invite them both to tea, but about half a dozen other variations on the theme turned up as well. It was quite a spectacle!'

'My goodness', Alice laughs. 'Did you have enough cucumber sandwiches and Lapsang Souchong to go round?'

'Only some of them liked cucumber sandwiches', Mattie says. 'Not everyone was vegetarian. And "Ms Why am I such a failure?" was intent on stuffing herself with

Rum and Raisin ice cream and being generally disgusting.'

Alice takes Mattie's hand. 'Oh Mattie. How can you talk about yourself like this? You're clever. Beautiful. A wonderful poet. The kind of woman that makes a difference in the world.' Mattie's eyes cloud up with tears.

'I'm a shit, Alice. And now I'm getting back some of my own medicine. I expect it serves me right. I haven't exactly played fair, have I? Not with people. Not relationships. Not jobs, even. No wonder I have no roots. My mother doesn't know me. Jess doesn't want me. I've got nowhere to go back to. No reason to stay. No blueprint for the future. Only self preservation and survival.'

Alice strokes her hand gently. 'I suppose what I'm learning about myself these days is that I can – not without pain – go along with the changes that come my way. It no longer seems so necessary to press things into the shape they "ought" to be. But I'm not so rash as to believe I still wouldn't try – given the right circumstances.'

'Like love?'

'I haven't been in love very often. I'm not even certain what it means. Not really.'

'Did you love me?' Mattie is seeking reassurance.

'I used to love you. I thought I always would. Now, I'm not so sure.'

'I wouldn't blame you for a minute.' Mattie says.

But Alice isn't into recriminations.

'Love and negotiations, they're sometimes mistaken for the same thing. These days I understand the differences a little better.'

'Its hard to ask for things which might be refused', Mattie says. She looks unsure. 'But could we go to bed?

For old time's sake? Just to lie in each others arms for a while? To be close again.'

Alice isn't shocked. Or noticeably distressed She has known this moment would come. It always does. At different times. In some disguise or other. Once she lets her feelings retreat from the safety of her head, into the openness of her heart, she can only bow to the inevitable. In the presence of Mattie.

She nods. 'I'd like to. I'd like to make love. Find some confirmation that I exist.'

Later, in each other's arms, beneath sheets that smell of lavender and starch, the evening gathers to a close. They do some serious and lengthy kissing, that melts their breath like snowflakes on the river. They lie along each other's bones, and breasts and bellies like a thick blanket of snow. Measuring and taking shape. The substance of their flesh a distant memory, now curiously familiar. On top of Alice, excited suddenly, and strong, Mattie's soft breasts press down and sink into her body like a stone. Across the room the light has faded to a shadow in the silence, waiting for the sound of coming to split the darkness like a star.

Viv hears the telephone ringing in the hallway, but chooses to ignore it. The answerphone is switched on and she is preoccupied with minutes of meetings and campaign flyers for another Campsfield demonstration. Mattie has agreed to join the organising group. She has a lot of experience of demonstrations. She knows what to do when the police move in.

If she is being honest, Viv has to admit that Mattie is disturbing her. She's beautiful in a ravaged kind of way. But other women she knows are more so. More conventionally attractive. Not that Viv notices such things. At least, she didn't use to. She doesn't fancy women, for example. These days she rarely fancies men. Bill is so predictable when it comes to sex. He has his routine. She has hers. Increasingly it feels like mutual guilt. His – because he knows he is unfaithful. Hers – because she doesn't really care.

Mattie bears no resemblance to a man. But Viv has the sense of being sexually assessed whenever Mattie looks her up and down. Not like women do – to check who's thinner, smarter, younger when you get to 40. But rather, with a mixture of enquiry and bravado. To see what's possible. To flirt. To disconcert. Viv finds it difficult to meet her eyes. But knows the fact she looks away, and even blushes like a stupid schoolgirl, supplies Mattie with the kind of details she requires for potential conquest.

The feelings take her by surprise. She's Alice's old friend. Her one-time lover, the one who caused her lots of pain. Viv is not exactly looking for romance. She is far too sensible to put herself in situations she can't handle. But last week she found herself in the Bodleian, looking up a list of Mattie's publications – just out of interest. Not only books of poetry, but articles and published papers in Women's Studies Journals. About biography and lesbian identity, mostly. Quite a long list, in fact. Some with further references to research.

Wife. Mother. Socialist. Pacifist. Is this how Viv would talk about her identity? It doesn't give much scope for passion or sexuality. Do women talk about heterosexual identity in quite the same way? Probably not. It's not a political statement for a start. You don't burst into rooms crowded with people to announce that you're heterosexual. They'd say, 'So what?' 'So are we!' 'Isn't everyone?' But now, of course, she can see that everyone is not. Alice isn't. Mattie isn't. The woman on reception at the council offices isn't. But Viv is. At least she thinks she is. At the last count. But then, why does she find herself flirting – just a little, in a harmless kind of way – with Alice? And getting rather flustered when Mattie touches her arm for a moment longer than is necessary or makes jokes about Bill in a way that suggests he must be grey and boring?

'We have an open marriage.' She hears herself repeat the tired old cliché, which is also, strictly speaking, not quite accurate. She has never had an extra marital affair. Bill has stopped counting. Mostly she doesn't know their names. He usually gives up at the moment when he thinks Viv might find out. Or cause a scene. Mattie raised her eyebrows in amusement and disbelief. 'Is this suburban wife swapping? Multiple relationships? Or adultery? When did you last exercise your equal rights to do the same?'

'Oh I'm really not interested.' Viv pretends sophistication. 'But he wouldn't mind – so long as nothing changed too much at home.'

'Would you tell him then?' Mattie knows the way straight couples operate. On silence and deceit.

'Probably not. It wouldn't be any of his business. We do lots of things separately. It wouldn't be a problem to Bill. Just a diversion.'

'So, it would be better if he didn't want to know?' Mattie looks quizzical.

Viv looks away. 'Anyway, it's all rather academic. I'm not looking for another man.'

'That would be the least of his worries, I expect.'

Mattie laughs. 'It's women that provide the real threat to men's position in a marriage.'

'Surely women lovers are more like friends?' Viv rises to the bait. 'With stronger spiritual and emotional connections? It's not the same sort of relationship is it?'

'Oh you mean – someone to do the shopping with and share the odd cosy insight about women's creativity and greater sensitivity to feelings? A minimum of below the belt contact? Actually women can be bitches, Viv. Possessive. Jealous. Arrogant. Demanding. Sex and passion are usually the focus of the relationship – especially at first. With all the intensity and desire and heartache you might expect in any socially subversive obsession.'

Viv has the sense she's being tested. Reprimanded almost, for her ignorance.

'I'm sorry', she says. 'Of course you're the expert. How could I know? I'm not a lesbian.'

'So you always say. And with such conviction.' Mattie laughs again.

Viv tries to return her attention to the work at hand. She decides to phone up Mattie. But not before she has done a little more reading. She wants to talk some more about this. But she doesn't want another lecture. And she wants to be certain she can recognise a proposition when she gets it. To be sure she doesn't appear quite so naïve as Mattie obviously imagines.

Alice arrives at school by 11.15.

'Any news?' she says to Hilda. 'I'm trying to smile but my mouth is still numb.' She notices that Hilda isn't trying to smile.

'Not so far as I know.' Hilda clicks on 'print' and waits for a letter to the Examination Board to emerge from the intricacies of her laser jet. 'I've got some letters for you to sign and Miss Goodison wants a word about the geography field trip.'

Alice fingers her frozen face absentmindedly and wonders whether Hilda can be persuaded to make some coffee. She isn't offering.

'I think my tooth would get back to normal sooner with a little liquid refreshment, Hilda. Would you mind?'

Hilda clicks ostentatiously on 'save' and disappears into the adjoining cubby hole which houses Alice's supply of Columbian coffee beans and her automatic grinder.

'Nice and strong', Alice urges, without much conviction. Hilda is clearly in a mood.

Outside the sky is grey and sombre. Rain is forecast for the late afternoon. But already the clouds are gathering in the west and moving in with obvious intent. Alice shuffles through the letters on her desk. Government circulars. Conference details. Requests for school prospectuses. Bills. She makes a note to contact the accountant before Governors' Day. The letters from parents she puts to one side, to consider more fully when she's drunk her coffee.

Which leaves only the manilla envelope, addressed in block capitals to ALICE MORRISON, HEADMISTRESS. She isn't curious about its character or origins, until the folded note inside causes her pulse to jump a beat or two.

A MEMBER OF THE HENLEY MANOR STAFF IS A PERVERT. THIS IS AN OUTRAGE AND A SCANDAL WHICH PARENTS AND GOVERNORS OUGHT TO KNOW ABOUT.

The note confirms Alice's oldest and most recurring

nightmare. The prospect of exposure. Followed by investigation, dismissal, humiliation and disgrace.

THIS IS YOUR LAST CHANCE. IF YOU DON'T TAKE SOME ACTION AGAINST WHAT IS GOING ON – OTHERS WILL.

Alice lets the letter drop on to the desk in front of her. Her hand is shaking. Her heart is racing like a thoroughbred. It takes all her courage to pick it up again and read the final sentence.

STEVEN ROWNTREE MUST BE INSTANTLY DISMISSED.

At least the allegation is not directed at her. But after a night spent in Mattie's arms she knows she wouldn't have a leg to stand on if it were. Mattie will have to go. She must be told. Alice can't contemplate another bout of secrecy and dread. The fear of being discovered.

The phone to the left of her desk rings. Alice lifts the receiver and waits for Hilda to relay some information.

'Can you see Miss Goodison now or should she wait til four o'clock?'

'Can you ask her to leave it until tomorrow, Hilda?' And then, by way of explanation, 'I'm feeling rather dizzy from the anaesthetic. This wouldn't be a good time to engage my sympathies if its money she's after.' Alice replaces the receiver and gets up from her desk.

Steven Rowntree? What kind of pervert? And who would think of choosing this way to denounce him? Obviously someone who expects her to take some action. And quick. She can't imagine who or how. She paces to and fro across the carpet. Well worn – but not by the urgency of making decisions like this. She is trying to work out likely options.

One. Ignore the letter altogether. Assume that it's a hoax.

Two. Inform the police and hope they don't have any unsavoury evidence to support the allegations.

Three. Confront Steven Rowntree. Find out what he's done. Ask him to go quietly.

Four. Confront Steven Rowntree. Find out what he's done. Ask him to be discreet.

Alice runs out of options. A lot depends on whether there's any substance to the allegations. And whether Steven has done anything illegal. She knows the only way to find out is to ask him. But it's not a question to be relished. Alice checks the timetable. He should be free after lunch for a double period. Alice peers across the gardens to the music room. It looks unusually empty of pupils. But through the greyness of the gathering storm she can see what looks like Wendy Armitage and Steven Rowntree, deep in conversation. According to Hilda they are having an affair. And dealing in drugs. But not perversion, so far as she can tell.

'Could you come to my office for a minute?' Alice nods politely in the direction of Miss Armitage. 'Hopefully it won't take long.'

Steven smiles mischievously at Wendy. Sensing a conspiracy. Anticipating an initiative. He follows cheerfully along the corridor to her study. But her mood is serious. And when Steven sees the expression on her face, he knows it means trouble.

'This letter arrived in the post this morning. It's anonymous, of course. I wonder what comment you have to make?'

There is a moment's silence.

'It's malevolent', he says. 'Someone who wants to cause me trouble. Not really surprising in this bloody place.'

'It was posted in Aylesbury on Saturday.' Alice hands

across the envelope. 'We have some girls who live out that way. Hilda could provide a list.'

' I hope you won't tell Hilda about this', Steven says. 'It will be just the nail she's looking for to hammer into my coffin.'

'If it's untrue, we can call the police. They probably have procedures to deal with malicious threats and anonymous letters.' Alice waits.

'Of course it's untrue. I'm not a pervert.' He wants to add 'any more than you are' but thinks better of it.

'But would other people take such a view? I mean, is this to do with socialist tendencies, or adultery, or drugs, or what? Are you involved with one of the girls?'

Steven laughs derisively. His hands dig deep into his pockets, his shoulders are hunched with tension.

'Don't worry. I'm not a mad axeman or a serial killer. Or even, much of a philanderer.' He takes a deep breath. 'I'm surprised you don't have any idea. I'm what I think you might call gay. At least, I have a male lover. My first.' He adds with a fair degree of emotion, 'It's all very new to me.'

The women in the paintings look down from faded walls. Dust settles on a line of first editions. Alice feels her heart smack against her chest.

'Do you want some coffee?' She indicates the cafetière on the table by the door. 'I'm whatever is the coffee equivalent of an alcoholic. Will you join me?'

Steven nods. 'I'd prefer a cigarette. Do you have any objections?'

'Not in the circumstances. I might even keep you company for once.' She takes a brass ashtray from the bottom drawer of her desk and puts it on the table by the fire. 'Sit over here. It's not so formal.' They watch each other with embarrassment.

'Who would know about this?' Alice pours herself and Steven a mug of coffee. 'Is it common knowledge among the girls? They seem to know about most things, I always find.'

'I don't think so. Unless they've seen something. Do I suddenly look like a faggot to you?'

Alice blinks. 'I'm not the best person to judge.' She looks away. 'But I can't say I notice much difference, to be honest.'

'I haven't done anything you know. No cruising. No cottaging. No under age sex. I'm squeaky clean in that respect. But I *am* in love. And it does present me with a few dilemmas.'

Alice sips her coffee. 'Me too. To the extent that I'm clearly expected to be shocked.'

Steven smiles. 'Ironic isn't it?'

Alice stiffens noticeably. 'It's not ironic in the least Mr Rowntree. I'm the Headmistress of this school. Parents pay considerable amounts of money to place their daughters in a respectable establishment. I am responsible for their education whilst they are here and for their moral guidance. This is not the kind of place where "anything goes" and I think I'd have great difficulty persuading the parents and the Governors that it should be.'

Steven gets the message. 'I see. No favours. No pack drill.'

'No nonsense, Mr Rowntree. We can't afford to let our personal lives interfere with our professional responsibilities. I'm sure you would agree. It wouldn't do you, or the school, any good to be at the centre of a scandal about homosexuality.'

'I haven't committed any crime, Miss Morrison. I would have thought you at least might understand.'

Steven knows that his appeal to commonality is a risky strategy. Alice Morrison must be so far into the closet she can't remember where she keeps the closet.

'I would prefer you to be totally discreet.' She softens, just a little.

'I have no option. Not until I've sorted out some things at home. I have a wife and a child to think about. Whom I also love.'

'Then stand by them, Steven. It probably isn't too late at this point. You need to get your priorities in order. And exercise a little commonsense.'

'But my priorities tell me I'm gay, Miss Morrison. And that I shouldn't try to live a lie. There are worse things to be.' He wants to say like lonely and afraid . . . a hypocrite.

'But you haven't told your wife! And what about your child? Maybe they'd be glad of a few white lies if it meant they didn't have to lose you.'

'Lead a double life you mean. Pass for straight. Skulk in the shadows with the rest of the misfits and cowards. I don't think that's a tenable position for me. Not in the long term. Others might take a different view.'

'Responsibility and duty are qualities that also deserve some recognition, Steven.'

'You're talking about self sacrifice, I think. Which isn't something to be particularly proud of. Is it?'

'The person who wrote this note wants your head on a block. Make no mistake about that. If I don't take decisive action, the campaign against you – and the school – will escalate. I expect the tabloids will be informed and the Chair of Governors, at the very least. I can't risk putting the good reputation of the school in jeopardy because of you. Especially at the present time. Surely you see that Steven?'

'What can I say? Of course I'll be discreet. But for the

sake of those I love. Not for the school, or to protect the precious sensibilities of right-wing bigots and control freaks. I won't resign. You'll have to sack me. If you know of any just reason, that is. In the meantime I'll do my job to the best of my ability. The way I always have. You might like to consider whether *West Side Story* provides sufficient 'cover' for me as the New Year concert. Suitably safe for a straight audience, wouldn't you say?' Steven stubbs his cigarette out in the ashtray and gets up to leave.

'I'm sorry this is all so unpleasant, Steven. You must give me some time to think. We really can't afford a scandal It's all too messy.'

'This is a scandal.' Steven looks at Alice with straightforward honesty. 'Poisonous letters are a scandal. Hounding me is a scandal. You behaving like a robot is a scandal. Talk to Jack about it. He might have the answer. It'll give you both something to think about as you shovel through the shit in your allotment.'

As the door closes behind him Alice sinks back into her chair.

'Shit', she says. 'Shit, shit and double shit.'

Outside in the lobby the insistent ringing of the bell announces the beginning of afternoon break.

'Jack, you didn't tell me about Steven Rowntree.' Alice has driven round to Jack Greyling's flat after work.

Jack takes a deep breath. 'You'd better come in.'

The space he lives in is like a cell. Grey carpet. White walls. A minimum of stark modern furniture. No dust. Or clutter. Two Hockney drawings on the walls – of Gregory asleep, and Peter naked, looking bored, as if his mind has already retreated from any intimacy with the artist. The sound system plays the blues. Jack places wooden coasters under fragile tumblers of gin and Indian tonic. His long pale fingers stroke the glass thoughtfully.

'You could have told me', Alice says. 'Why didn't you?'

'I wanted to, the other night. But Steven has been quite ambivalent – about his son mostly. And of course, discretion has become habitual with me.' Jack's elegant silence freezes the setting like a lithograph in shades of grey. Alice is staring past the stillness into darkness made real by the glow of neon from a flashing pub sign in the square below. She feels exhausted. Both physically. And in her heart.

'Who would write such a letter?' She turns her eyes towards her friend. 'It's so crude and threatening.'

Jack shakes his head.

'I don't know.' He wants to call up Steven. Make him come over. Reassure him. 'I know he'll chuck the towel in.' Jack moves a book of poetry on the occasional table by his side two centimetres into line. 'This will the final straw.'

'That's not the impression he gave me.' Alice says. 'He was very shocked, it's true. But very emotional about his right to love you – without any kind of shame.'

'But will he want to be his own cause célèbre? He's got a lot to lose.' Jack looks at Alice with an air of resignation.

'We all have', she replies. 'I feel angry with you Jack. With both of you. Sorry, but angry. Why can't you learn to keep things clear? Keep things separate?' She feels the reprimand is probably unfair. Jack is hardly like a dance hall queen. His life – like hers – has been immensely solitary on the whole. With moments of intensity punctuated by loss.

'It's not a deliberate demonstration, Alice. I love the

boy. It's just coincidence that he works for you. Oxford is a small town – in more ways than one.'

'If the press get onto this, they'll have a field day. The Governors' Report is already bordering on the fundamental about moral rearmament and higher standards. You can't imagine what they're like.'

'I thought Steven's appointment had transformed the music and drama department? He's very proud of his success rate – especially as the girls seem to be so enthusiastic.'

'I don't have any problems with his exam results. It's true he's very popular with the girls and quite inspiring. But some people on the staff already regard his influence as dangerous. Many of them are quite traditional in their attitudes.'

'Well they're wrong', Jack says with anger in his voice. 'The world is already overpopulated with mediocre minds and jaded cynics.'

'But that doesn't make it any easier for me', Alice says. 'I have to maintain a united front. I need these people to do their jobs conscientiously. Which they do. I need Steven to keep his private opinions – and his private proclivities – to himself. As I have learned to do.'

'But he is from a different generation Alice. The world outside the window is much more open to ideas about sexual differences these days. It's only in the closed kind of institutions in which we work that closed minds still operate. So we end up policing ourselves. Out of habit, probably. I know I do.'

'I know I can't sack him. He's done nothing wrong – in a sacking sense. But if I do nothing, the letters will continue. And not just to me. We'll be in the middle of a public scandal before the week is out. I can feel it looming.'

'I know.' Jack doesn't want to minimise her foreboding. As Steven would. As Mattie would. 'So what will you do?'

'I don't know. I really don't know.'

'What's your biggest fear?' Jack picks the scrap of lemon from his tumbler and chews it slowly. He watches the tears rise and blur the steady gaze of Alice's grey-green eyes.

'That I'll be next', she says. 'That now there's nothing to stop them coming after me.'

Mattie doesn't ask to come into Alice's bed again and Alice doesn't offer. Alice has grown used to celibacy and, at a time like this, she doesn't want to cloud her judgement with old yearnings. Besides, Mattie is on the mend, and displaying all the early signs of restlessness, which usually indicates the moment of departure.

Alice chooses to say nothing about the letter or about Steven. She needs more time to think. And Mattie would be full of instantaneous indignation and solutions requiring head on confrontation. Besides she's working on a press release for the Campsfield Campaign.

'How is Viv?' Alice asks. She is missing the kind of comfortable contact that has become a feature of their friendship. Light-hearted phone calls when Viv has some news or some enthusiasm to unload. A drink or two after work in the Café Can Can. A shared visit to the opera or to the garden centre. She suspects that Viv must find her boring now that Mattie has arrived on the scene.

'On the turn I would say.' Mattie raises her eyebrows and grins knowingly.

'Into what? A pumpkin at midnight?' Alice is not in the mood for any more catastrophic conversions.

'Don't be dismal, Alice. And don't pretend you don't know what I mean. You don't expect me to believe that it's your power to save her daughter from expulsion that makes Viv Williams so attentive when she's in your company!'

In moods like this Mattie quite enjoys a touch of smut. She strokes Alice's cheek. 'Who wouldn't be?'

Orlando squirms and waits for the air to electrify.

'You could have that woman in your bed any time you choose.' She watches Alice blush with irritation.

'Please stop it Mattie. I'm not in the mood.' Alice gathers up the Oxford Clarion and prepares to retreat out of harm's way.

'Bill sounds like a boring bastard.' Mattie tries a different tack. 'How do these marriages survive? And Viv so lively! It always defeats me.'

The question is rhetorical. Alice takes her newspaper and heads for the study. Of course it's much too soon for any repercussions to appear in print, but nonetheless, she checks the local news pages for any reference to the school or to 'queers in the classroom'. She feels her heart quicken until the scrutiny is over, then tries to think constructively about what action she should take.

Unfortunately for Alice, she is not the only person to be exercised by the prospect of exposing Henley Manor to public debate about sexuality and drugs. Whatever her intentions, which she clearly sees in missionary proportions as being about the pursuit of evil, Hilda is impatient to achieve results. Twice now she has provided

Alice with irrefutable evidence about illegal drug taking and sexual irregularities, on the basis of which, Alice has taken no obvious action. No sign of police activity. No sign of sacking or expulsion. No letter to the Chairman of Governors setting out the details of the crimes. It doesn't take Hilda long – in her impatience – to shift from an explanation based on weakness and incompetence to one based on something altogether more damaging. Alice's complicity.

'She's in cahoots with someone over this. That's my theory.' Hilda has telephoned Marion. Marion can always be relied upon to be at home during the evening. And to have plenty of energy to release on gossip. Marion is eating an enormous roast beef sandwich, packed generously with gherkins, between thin slices of listless, white bread.

'Feed a cold' she says by way of explanation as Hilda says 'pardon' for the third time. 'My mother is a great believer in protecting yourself from flu by sticking to a healthy diet.' When Marion and her mother use the term 'healthy' they don't mean bean sprouts. Marion is quite good at talking with her mouth full. From constant practice. But a dodgy telephone connection like this one serves to inhibit clarity. 'Does Alice Morrison lack authority?'

'She doesn't have to exercise it very often. Not really. Until recently Henley Manor was quite an orderly kind of place. It's more to do with sweeping things under the carpet. I don't trust her.'

'There's no smoke without fire', Marion says.

'Precisely. She's protecting someone. You'd think she'd be pleased to get rid of Clancy Williams. She's been nothing but trouble since the moment she arrived. She looks like you wouldn't believe! If that's school uniform, I'm Princess Diana.'

'Has this girl got anything on Alice Morrison?' Marion readjusts the angle of the sandwich to prevent the occasional spots of mustard and gherkin from splatting on the carpet. 'Sometimes junkies resort to blackmail. They need money to feed their habit. That's what my husband says.' Marion's husband is in damp and woodworm. He puts a lot of store by lurid articles in the daily papers. There's quite a bit of sitting round in vans when you've involved with damp and woodworm, waiting for the chemicals to dry. You tend to drink a lot of tea and gather dubious information from the headlines of the *Sun*. He's now an expert on the behavioural irregularities of petty criminals.

'Not sure.' Hilda considers the possibility. 'Her mother's on the council. The Labour Party.' Hilda speaks the name as though it were a disease. 'She's always ringing up. More often than you'd expect. More often than other pupil's parents.'

'My Frank did a job for Bill Williams the other week. Some problem in the cellar at his factory on the industrial estate. He's stinking rich, my husband says. Nice enough, by all accounts'.

'Is he Labour too?'

'Doubt it. He wouldn't own a factory and vote Labour would he? My husband sees him sometimes at the club.'

'Conservative?'

'No, Golf. Sometimes they play a round together. I don't suppose he's got a clue about his daughter doing drugs. Or his wife pestering Alice Morrison. He's building up his business, just like Frank.'

'And while the cat's away . . .' Hilda beats Marion to the obvious aphorism.

'So who *is* Alice Morrison protecting? Could it be Steven Rowntree?'

'Possibly.'

'Depends what she's got in common with a homo-sexual.' Having discovered the opportunity to speak the term quite freely, Marion rather likes the twist of excitement she derives from using it as often as possible.

'I wouldn't say she has much in common with anyone. But she does seem to approve of Steven Rowntree. I'm sick of hearing about how good his exam results are. And how she thinks he's helped to change the cultural life of the school. A load of prancing about dressed up as thugs so far as I can see. Not to mention swearing.'

'I think *West Side Story* is a bit like that', Marion points out. 'But it has been in the West End for years. I don't think it's quite as bad as some of the modern musicals for showing sex and bare bodies in public.'

Hilda likes to think she knows about culture. Having been a theatre landlady. But she's not impressed by 'animal instincts' especially since she became involved with God. She sniffs disdainfully.

'So what's she like then, your Miss Morrison?' Marion licks the last traces of mustard from her fingers and contemplate a dish of tiramasu before *News at Ten*.

'Lives alone. With a cat called something ridiculous. Never married. No contact with her family, so far as I know. Always been a teacher in a girls' school. A typical spinster, I would say.'

'That's it then.' Marion stands sideways to the mirror in the hall and pulls her stomach in. No point starting on the diet until after Christmas. Anything she takes off now will only go back on again when Frank's sister and the kids arrive. 'All the hallmarks. Birds of a feather. Two of a kind. She's saving her own skin.'

'Do you mean what I think you mean?' Hilda fits the emerging speculation to the pattern of her prejudice.

'Add it up! Two plus two. Another homo-sex-ual is what I think – of the female variety. That's what Clancy Williams has got on her. And that's why she's frightened to expel her. That's why she's covering up for Steven Rowntree. I'd watch out if I were you. You'll be surrounded by them soon.'

Later that evening, another revelation in thick black capitals gets copied onto cheap lined paper, and popped into an envelope marked PERSONAL. This time the recipient isn't already looking through the post with trepidation every morning. Unlike Alice, Michael Duke has experienced little in his life to disturb the confident complacency that he derives from being a Magdalen man, a successful barrister, the driver of a BMW and the prospective Tory candidate for South Oxfordshire. One of God's chosen few, on whom considerable good fortune has been lavished, including the unlikely privilege of being recently elected Chair of Governors at Henley Manor Independent School for Girls.

By Wednesday Alice has finally decided on her course of action, and fortunately for her, she gets to the telephone first. At 9.15 precisely, she rings Michael Duke. Just at the moment when he has digested a rather disturbing message in a manilla envelope, posted on the previous day in Central Oxford.

'Alice, my dear.' He greets her with his usual charm and slick assumption of familiarity. 'I was just about to ring myself, about a small query.'

'I have a matter of great urgency to discuss with

you.' Alice has little time for what she imagines to be pleasantries. 'I don't know what your diary's like for later in the day, or tomorrow morning, but I need to speak to you as soon as possible. I'm happy to come to you, in fact I'd prefer it.'

Michael Duke flicks quickly through his filofax. 'Shall we say 4.30, Alice, over here? If you leave the car keys in reception, someone will park your car in the office compound'.

'Thank you Michael, that will suit me fine.' Alice forces a reluctant familiarity in an effort to keep the power that struggles for ascendancy between them in some kind of equilibrium. 'I'll explain everything when I see you.'

Michael Duke replaces the receiver. He re-reads the note he has just received, puts it in his desk drawer, and turns the key.

On Wednesday lunchtime Mattie is due to drop a press release round at Viv's office in town. But just as she's about to leave the cottage, Viv rings her from a phone box in St Aldgates.

'I'm on my way home for a spot of lunch. Do you want to meet me there I can offer you taramasalata and a glass of genuine retsina.'

'Sounds wonderful. Which number bus is best?'

Mattie arrives in a sprinkling of light snow. The first flutter of the winter. The temperature is falling and already Kent looks like central Russia. In Oxford it's not yet cold enough to settle but sharp enough to engage Mattie's interest in flights to Southern California. The Campus Travel Agent in the Square is offering mid-

December deals, with an option to stay over until New Year. Mattie takes the details and thinks of asking Alice if she'd like to join her, once term is over.

'Excuse the bomb site.' Viv kicks a pair of football boots to one side. 'Come through to the kitchen. The aga makes it feel less chilly.'

She places warm pitta bread and olives and a bowl of taramasalata between them on the table.

'Is retsina all right? Or would you prefer straight wine?'

'I prefer nothing straight', Mattie smiles. 'Present company excepted, of course.'

Viv pours a generous measure of yellow liquid into Mattie's glass.

'We should probably be drinking punch or something hot.'

Mattie can see that Viv is hugely confident but also oddly ill at ease.

'Here's to us!' Mattie's mother's favourite toast.

The conversation meanders skilfully around council politics and cuts in public spending. Viv says how she got involved in the campaign to close down Campsfield. Mattie talks about her stint in Holloway for disturbing the peace at Greenham Common. It's a familiar kind of conversation. The sort you'd come across quite regularly in Jericho and Summertown on any day of the week. The detail might be different. But the context, the commitment to slightly radical concerns, is not out of place behind North Oxford's gentrified façades.

Mattie takes the chance to wash her hands. She can learn a lot from bathrooms. She can tell from this one, for example, that the house is customised by family life. A scrunched up sock squats rejected by the shower, belonging to a child. Philip's walkman is hanging on a peg beside his tracksuit bottoms. A clutch of toothbrushes, in different colours, and in different sizes, flower from a mug celebrating Bill's fortieth birthday. She has no idea how much of a family heirloom the mug has now become, but the junior toothbrushes inside look dusty dry in ways that suggest they're hardly ever used. Except under parental supervision. A shelf beside the window contains a clutter of tubes and plastic bottles announcing hair dye, bubble bath and massage lotion.

It seems intrusive to investigate more private spaces like the mirrored wall cabinet made of pine, the contents of square, polished drawers beneath the flowered, tiled surround of an elaborate Victorian wash stand. But Mattie can't resist. She is intrigued by the domestic intimacy of long term residency and survival in the married state. She notes that Viv prefers French perfume. *Dune* and *Poison*. Showing obvious good taste. That Bill uses an electric razor and Marks and Spencer's aftershave. Predictable and boring. Although it might reflect a present rather than a choice.

She discovers that someone in the house – not Viv she hopes – uses a pink and sticky substance smelling of petroleum, to eliminate the spread of body hair. Mattie has a fondness for the curl of hair beneath a woman's arms, her cunt, the kind of down on strong brown legs that bleaches with the sun. Viv could be deliciously endowed, judging by her thick full eyebrows and long soft lashes. Or bald if this vile smelling concoction has got anything to do with it.

It's a long time since Mattie has actually been this close to condoms. She notices that they are rainbow coloured and flavoured with strawberry and vanilla essence. A pot of jelly predicts 'easy access during coitus'. On a higher shelf there are headache pills and homeopathic sleeping tablets. A cure for haemorrhoids. A preparation to relieve the side effects of thrush. It's a fairly unromantic activity to be involved in, rummaging through the bathroom secrets of a married woman. Mattie consoles herself with the observation that the strawberry flavoured rubbers look about as dusty as the children's toothbrushes. Sex isn't everything in a marriage after all. Not after 20 years when it probably figures very little. Except in Bill's case. And as adultery. Mattie wonders where he keeps his extra marital supplies. And what fruit and ice-cream flavours conspire to disguise the taste of latex and the strong smell of sperm in these surreptitious moments.

She goes downstairs. Viv has by now decided to discuss the real reason for organising this elaborate diversion from the press release in hand. Which, by the way, she hasn't asked to see. And Mattie has completely forgotten to pass over.

'Is it common for women to find you attractive?' Viv is intent on direct action.

Mattie is the one to feel a little thrown. She smiles. She hopes modestly.

'It happens', she says. 'There's always gorgeous babes around. It's the nature of towns at midnight.' Mattie doesn't acknowledge the appropriation of the line from one of her favourite Ferron songs.

'Do they fall in love with you?' Viv is determined to finish what she has now begun. Whether Mattie chooses this conversation – this moment for disclosure – or not.

The light is fading in the large, lived-in kitchen. Bill's golf clubs stand propped in a corner by the door. A pile of well-thumbed cookbooks and recipes betray a lifetime of family communion over food. Three times a day when the kids were little and Bill was still working from home. Special roast on Sunday. Friends by candlelight on Saturday. The patterns of a habit. The details fashioned into routine.

'Do they?'

'Sometimes', she smiles. 'Now and then, I suppose.'

'Do you sleep with them?'

'Who? Everyone that falls in love with me? Hardly!'

'So it happens quite often then?' How tedious to be another one of many. Viv thinks that Mattie is the sexiest woman she has ever met. A view that is clearly not unique.

'When I was younger I thought that every experience was a challenge. A political responsibility.' She laughs 'Part of my personal crusade against patriarchy.'

Viv doesn't understand.

'To steal the woman from the boys. Encourage mass defection. Give out orgasms like bonus prizes at a raffle. Having fun with women is contagious.'

'I've always liked women better than men', Viv says. 'All my best friends are women.'

'That's a start.' Mattie likes to be encouraging.

'What about now? You said when you were younger...'

'Now I'm more discerning. Not all women are wonderful. As a teacher I have to be aware of not using power – with my students, for example.' (God, she can be pompous and a hypocrite.) 'Anyway, younger women seem rather boring to me as I get older.' (So much for her total disintegration as Jess was leaving.)

'I look at the young women students around Oxford', Viv confides. 'They look so full of life and beauty. Isn't that exciting?'

'Sex is often exciting. But not always. Intellect is better. Life experience. Maturity. These days I want to have decent conversations with the women I make love to. Mostly young women don't know enough to interest me.'

'Do you find me exciting?' Viv can't believe she is really saying this. It must be the bottle of retsina on an empty stomach. And the knowledge that this conversation will only happen now – or never.

'I'm not in love with you, if that's the next question. Which doesn't mean to say I don't think you're attractive. And I'm sure that you're exciting.' Mattie likes to leave her options open.

'Are they related though?' Viv wants Mattie to speak the words she has imagined in her head.

'Love has become about the most commonplace of all four-letter words', Mattie knows about the function of romantic language in the creation of illusions, 'which like its more explicit counterpart, gets grossly over used. And loses some of its significance in the process.'

'I think I love you, nonetheless.' Viv feels the edge of her fingernails pressing against the flesh of her inner palms.

Mattie always finds these conversations flattering. Because more than anything, she likes to be the centre of attention. And for Mattie, being central has its sexual dimensions. She enjoys the power which she derives from being idolised. And she finds it relatively easy to play at flirting. Especially with women who are not conversant with the rules. Who think the narrative which they inhabit is original.

'Isn't it rather premature to talk of love? Desire might be more appropriate. Or fantasy. Or lust.'

Viv laughs, a little nervously.

'All right. I desire you.'

'Me? My body? Or my mind?' Mattie has a ready stock

of clichés. And whilst she might be flattered, she isn't tempted. Something about the bathroom cabinet and the football boots has changed her mood completely. She hasn't got the inclination any longer to negotiate around children. Or stray into the kinds of deals that straight women seem to strike with husbands, to create themselves a little space.

'You're very inspiring. I've read almost all of your writing. But I think you have something to teach me about myself.'

'I'm sick of teaching, to be honest.' For once Mattie *is* being honest. But Viv is too preoccupied with painting Mattie into the fantasy she has created to recognise the simple truth she is being offered.

'I don't think I'm what you'd call a lesbian', she continues. 'Not like you. Because I don't think I'm attracted to women on the whole. But there's something different about you which I'd like to explore a little further.'

'The difference is I'm queer. And if you find me attractive maybe you should think more deeply about what that says about you.'

'That's what I mean.'

'What do you mean?' Mattie is now feeling as though she could write the script with her eyes shut.

'Well, my sexuality. What it feels like to sleep with a woman. How being a feminist fits in with a sexual life.' For Viv all these are serious concerns.

'Then why don't you try The Cottage Club? Delia's Disco on a Friday night? It's full of women who could help you out. They wouldn't ask as many questions as me.'

Viv shudders. 'Oh I don't think I could do that. I don't know them do I? I couldn't be sure what might happen.'

Mattie is beginning to feel irritated.

'You don't know me. You don't know what "might happen" if you did sex with me.'

'I was rather hoping we could make love. Not sex. I imagine there's a difference. You could show me what to do.' Viv is beginning to sound like one of the seven foolish virgins. Getting ready to close her eyes and think of England.

'When do your kids get home? What time do you start making Bill's tea?'

'I wasn't thinking about now', Viv answers hastily. 'The boys will be back in less than an hour. And not here. I couldn't do it in this house. I'd feel too guilty.' Viv looks suddenly panic stricken.

Mattie nods. 'So where did you have in mind?'

'Well, your place in London, I suppose.'

'But I'm not living there at the moment, Viv. As a matter of fact I can't bear to be within a 40 mile radius of it. Jess's books are still on the shelf. I can smell her perfume on the sheets.' Mattie feels her eyes fill up with tears.

'Well a hotel then. Except it might be a bit embarrassing when we book in.' Viv giggles at the prospect.

'I stay in hotels all the time when I'm travelling. It isn't embarrassing. It's what people with money do. Including lesbians. If other people are embarrassed, that's their problem. Not mine.'

Viv detects the beginning of another lecture.

'Look, I'm sorry Mattie. This is all rather new to me. I don't mean to imply that being with you would be embarrassing . . . it's just, I don't want to do it here. What about Alice's then? She's out all day. It's quiet. Orlando is discrete I'm sure.'

If Mattie was wanting to make love to Viv she'd do it anywhere. On top of this scrubbed pine table in broad daylight. Five star at the Grand in St Giles. In Alice's bed, even. It wouldn't be the first time. But she doesn't. She doesn't want to be the object of yet another straight woman's effort to discover her identity. Rip off all the years it's cost Mattie to live openly and politically as a dyke. Feed off her accumulated experience like a parasite, and then scurry home to make the old man's tea. Home, where she isn't really what you'd call a lesbian. Just fancies Mattie rotten and wants to be seduced.

'Don't you think Alice might object?'

'Alice? Why should she? You two aren't lovers any more are you? Anyway, she doesn't need to know, if it makes you feel embarrassed.'

'I'm not embarrassed about anything', Mattie looks at her watch. 'But Alice is my friend. I thought she was yours. All of this could seem a little seedy from Alice's perspective. Born out of desperation. Or despair. I don't like lying at the best of times. Especially not to my friends.'

Viv looks away. Now she knows she's foolish.

'You're right. Alice wouldn't like it. But I'm not suggesting that I move in.'

'Just a quickie – so to speak.' Mattie reaches for her coat. 'I think I'd better go. Before this turns into a full scale row. Here's the press release by the way. I hope it will be some use to the campaign.'

Mattie pulls the door securely shut behind her and steps out into the snow. She turns towards the bus stop as the daylight drops to dusk. Southern California – here she comes.

Across the street two schoolboys carrying wet handfuls of snow charge along the pavement in an effort to get home before it melts.

'Mum, Mum it's snowing!' Philip shouts as the door bursts open.

'Get the sledge down!' Boyd drops his duffle coat and sandwich box in the hallway as he rushes through.

In the kitchen Viv starts to clear away the cold pitta bread and empty glasses. She puts potatoes in the sink to peel. If it's Wednesday, it must be shepherd's pie and sprouts, followed by treacle pudding. She turns the radio to Fox FM and fills her head with golden oldies and someone phoning in about dead cats. She isn't imagining it. It was Mattie who, on a previous occasion, began the discussion about women's passion and subversive sexuality. But now she's gone. With clearly no intention of investing her commitment to such activity in Viv. And Viv, first netted then rejected, is left to think about how she could get it all so wrong, like a short-sighted cyberite in a moral maze.

Across the city, in the glow of Christmas lights through leaded windows, and in the solid confidence of a leather sofa, Alice takes a deep breath in the offices of Michael Duke Associates and begins her explanation to the Chair of Governors.

Part Four

Thirteen

There is something to be said for being a private school headmistress, with no dependents, and only fleeting interest in the material world – substantial savings. Alice leaves the meeting with Michael Duke feeling manipulated, humiliated and angry. She crosses the street between the log jam of competing bus services that turn central Oxford into something resembling Piccadilly Circus in the rush hour. And walks briskly through the scatter of children clutching Christmas drawings, office revellers and late night shoppers, towards the sober magnificence of the Grand Hotel. For two pins she'd book in for the duration and pretend to be a passenger on a Caribbean cruise. Run out on her responsibilities. Join the Foreign Legion. Alice chooses a quiet table in the corner of the cocktail lounge, beside an extravagant display of arum lilies and winter roses, sinking herself into the reassuring velvet of an easy chair.

The private dinner guests and early theatre goers are already limbering up for an evening of indulgence and excess. The men in dinner jackets, their wives in taffeta and silk brocade, with milky skin and plunging necklines. Alice can't remember when she has seen so much unrestricted female flesh. Not since she stumbled – quite by accident – into a nudist colony on the Istrian Peninsula in 1985. The less than glamorous severity of ordinary Croatians in those utilitarian times, when communism and Yugoslavia could still be recognised as such, added the convention of plastic shoulder bags, binoculars and woolly ankle socks to otherwise quite naked naturists. It did little to raise Alice's temperature on an already blistering day. But now in candlelight, with shadows stealing to a blur in the middle of the lounge, the unexpected glimpse of women's shoulders and the rise of rounded cleavage beneath taffeta and silk is holding her attention in a way that very little else – in recent everyday experience – has done. For longer than she cares to think about.

'Are you waiting for someone? Or would you like to order?' The girl in a black waistcoat, white blouse and pencil skirt places honey roasted cashews and a plate of canapés on Alice's table. The kind of gratuitous appetisers that imply a suitably extravagant response. Through elegant plate glass windows, hung with brocade and velvet drapes, beautiful and wealthy people stare blindly into the eyes of beggars, huddled on the outside pavement. In Oxford, never very far away. Weighing their chances against the possibilities and opportunities provided by such lucrative surroundings. Before the police are called and in a screeching of brakes some officious constable instructs them to move on.

'I'd like a double gin with lots of tonic', Alice says. She doubts the waitress's enquiry is meant to be remotely existential, but in its innocence, devoid of context, Alice is forced to question why she's sitting here at all. Amidst this affluent, overwhelmingly conventional, display of coupling on a lavish scale. The measure of her marginality.

'I'm not expecting anyone else', she says. 'But I would like to order something to eat – if a place can be found for me at such late notice.'

'The dining room is fully booked, I'm afraid.' The girl can't imagine how anyone could possibly think otherwise. Telephone enquiries, table bookings, cocktails in the cocktail lounge, dinner in the dining room, coffee and brandy in the music room, are second nature to employees of the Grand Hotel. Anyone who doesn't automatically understand such things must – in some quite serious way – be stupid. Fortunately for Alice, the most obsequious of training, and the most particular requirement by the management that staff exhibit patience, means that an alternative arrangement is tactfully spelled out.

'Supper dishes are being served in the bar after 7 p.m. Madam. Would you like to see a menu?'

'Thank you.' Alice takes off her duffle coat and pushes her briefcase under the seat and out of sight. At least her bank account can meet whatever bill the Grand decides to throw at her.

This is the kind of place that Michael Duke is bound to choose, to meet his business associates and cronies. Alice checks the portly, balding men to right and left and hopes that he is safely tucked away at home. Neither allowed the other to display a whisper of emotion in the meeting earlier. Although Alice was shocked to learn that another anonymous letter had been sent – this time addressed to Duke at his Chambers in the town. It linked Steven Rowntree with the drugs incident and effectively exposed both bits of the story she had already determined to discuss. Duke said he found the entire proceedings totally distasteful. Including the unfortunate display of gratuitous sensationalism employed by the anonymous and malicious correspondent. But he was anxious, as was Alice, that the content of the letters should not be further circulated in the pages of the *Oxford Clarion*.

'This matter must be scotched as quickly and as quietly as possible, my dear.' Duke's lugubrious manner and calculated charm could barely conceal a standpoint that was much more ruthless. He was inviting Alice's co-operation in a decisive and uncompromising response. Which had no room for sentiment or prevarication.

'The girls must go, whatever undertakings you have previously negotiated, as a warning to the rest. And Rowntree must be made to understand, in no uncertain terms, that his better interests lie elsewhere. It is fortunate, in the private education sector, that these arrangements can be organised without too much deliberation over contractual arrangements or trade union agreements.'

'He is one of the best teachers currently employed in the school.' Alice took great care to confine herself to statements of actuality. 'He has committed no crime, so far as I understand it.'

'In the eyes of most respectable people – including all our parents, I think you will agree – the exhibition and promotion of homosexual tendencies will be viewed as crime enough.'

'But that is a matter of judgement, Mr Duke. Not a crime. Not unless minors are involved or there is evidence of illegal soliciting.'

'Trust me. Dear Miss Morrison. After 20 years in legal practice I know about such things. Sooner or later the legal and illegal manifestations of this scourge go hand-in-hand. There is a certain inevitability about the attraction, to those with deviant personalities, of moving outside the law. Take it from me. This is a matter which is better nipped in the bud before we find ourselves in deeper water. What is more important, would you say, the sensibilities of a two-penny-half-penny music master, compared to the burgeoning reputation of an extremely popular and successful school? And one which, if I may say so, Alice, you have personally given considerable time and energy in helping to establish.'

Alice was inclined to share his concerns, if not his sentiments.

'Of course, the responsibility for managing this disaster rests with you. That is why we pay you. I can only offer my advice.' He paused. 'At this stage.'

Alice took the point. As if she needed further elaboration. She was only too aware that her authority was at stake. That she must remember her duty and her obligations. She had spent the best part of her life in service to her sense of responsibility. With none of the slippery accommodations, the deals in smoke-filled rooms, the opportunism, she had come to associate with more political evangelists. Of both right and left persuasions.

'It's your responsibility, my dear. And I have every confidence that, having had this opportunity to put our heads together, you will act speedily and with conviction. You can count on my total support on Governor's Day, in maintaining a united front.'

The telephone on Michael Duke's desk interrupted the final flourish of what Alice recognised as his summing up. A conviction he was sure to win, especially as it seemed he had cast himself into the role of judge and jury, as well as spokesman for the prosecution. Alice took the opportunity to leave, alluding to a new agenda for the governors' meeting and declining offers to prolong the present agony with a glass of thin dry sherry. She left his Chambers feeling patronised and furious and desperately in need of alcoholic sustenance from the anonymous, transparent decadence of the Grand Hotel.

By 9.30 Mattie was beginning to get worried. It was unlike Alice to be late. Usually you could set your watch by the rhythm of her routines. Orlando was already sound asleep. Lying in the crook of the sofa, in a state of gay abandon, on her back, with folded paws akimbo, as though a dream required her rapturous concentration.

Mattie contented herself with playing Haydn, and musing on the meaning of a life she had collided with from time to time, but never really known. A life she had always finally dismissed as one preoccupied with taking care, and not with taking trouble to be free. Now, in the stillness of Alice's sitting room, with snow silting into nooks and crannies on the porch outside, and surrounded by her solid furniture, her well-studied and thoughtfully considered books – it seemed as though the measure of that life was set in stone. Like doctrine or the ten commandments.

But it was not always so. At 23 Alice was capable of extraordinary intensity. Which she channelled into introspection. Afraid, in those early days, to own the consequences of her surprising passion.

Mattie was then too ignorant about herself, and Alice, and the world outside the ragged streets of Holderness, to think much about complexity and contradiction when she began to spin her dreams of bright, eventual release. She loved Alice as the symbol of another life. Another world. Another class. A life of intellect and poetry. In which her feelings and her head united in pursuit of truth and meaning, that no one in her family, or even Joyce, could ever hope to understand. Alice was the kind of woman who studied literature and talked about ideas. And looked through grey-green eyes with such intensity that Mattie fully expected her to melt a mountain.

At university Mattie met others who, if not quite so dramatic in their early influence as Alice, presented her with similar possibilities. To move outside her class. Escape her narrow, undemanding preparation for a life of existential boredom. Of learning to make do.

In those days Mattie's enthusiasm for change and hopeless causes both delighted and disturbed the more circumspect and cautious Alice. Although she recognised the passion, Alice had learned to link her self-sufficiently with self-restraint. She understood only too well that no one in her life so far, could seriously be relied on. She had never learned to be gregarious, and whilst she took delight in Mattie's growing confidence, she worried that it seemed insatiable and restless, in ways that confronted Alice with her oldest fears.

There was a moment, now and then, when longing and romance defied Alice's more usual caution. When Mattie, if she had been more sensitive, more generous, less self-absorbed, could have recognised the sea-change and helped Alice well and truly from her closet into a public life they both could share. Instead, she chose these occasions to attend to matters of her own, and saved her exhortations to 'come out, for god's sake' for those moments when she was feeling self-righteous and indignant. And generally pre-occupied with feelings of recrimination.

In the few years after university, when Mattie gave her energy to separatism and sex with women as a point of principle, she and Alice remained intense and greedy lovers. But with disparate dreams. As Mattie grew in confidence, Alice began to shed her inhibitions and her fears. But only in the context of Mattie and monogamy. They talked of moving south. Of Alice changing jobs. Of Mattie writing poetry. Until it seemed one day to be a serious suggestion. The kind of probability which by then filled Mattie with alarm. She didn't want to settle down, to get a job, to feed a mortgage. And she didn't want to tie herself to anyone who might expect she would. She liked the idea of Alice and security. Of unconditional love. Of heaps of praise and little personal criticism. The kind of constancy you hope for from a mother. And from the kind of lover who knows when to suppress her own demands. Who understands about another's freedom. Who takes the chance, from time to time, to share some passion and intensity. But without any expectations of control or feelings of possession.

In retrospect, a less than considerate arrangement. A

pretty ropy deal from Alice's perspective, which was bound to flounder. Which meant that Alice never made it to the big wide world on equal terms. And which after some indulgence in her youth, that passed for experience, brought Mattie stranded, on this snowy night in Oxford, to a chintz chair beside the fire, with a sleeping cat, quite lost inside her dreams. Now feeling that she made some bad decisions. Resorting, as the years went by, to temporary connections with much the same kinds of women – in different contexts but with the same agendas – seeking variously, redemption, energy, excitement. All making similar demands, without much thought for Mattie's feelings in the matter. Treating her like some kind of prize. The proclaimed leader, who should then become their property. Their desired target. Their source of power. Their object of expressed need. Like Viv, for example. Desperate for a new dimension in a boring marriage. Wanting Mattie as a swift solution. With no notion of complexity. Of taking time or tenderness. Too trite. Too altogether obvious. As if the love that lingers in the memory, far longer than it survives experience, could ever be this quick or casual. This readily available. Like instant credit.

So that then, when Mattie displayed her limitations, as she was bound to do, because of course, it is impossible to properly fulfil imaginary dreams, she became rejected in her turn. With multiple recriminations. For failing to live up to expectations. Some kind of fraud. In the messy gamble that gets portrayed as love. By Jess, for one. Restless, irritated. Ready to move on. The learning she had usefully acquired, all done. Making, in her turn, much the same kind of calculation already made by Mattie on a dozen previous occasions. Not only, but most significantly, in her relationship with Alice. Coming now full circle in the greater scheme of things. To a fine irony.

Meanwhile, in solitary contemplation in the Grand Hotel, Alice orders fish. In other circumstances she would have called up Viv. 'Come and join me. I need advice.' Or Jack. A careful listener and an honest judge. But Jack is in love with Steven. And unless Alice is very much mistaken, Viv is more than likely in the arms of Mattie at this moment, not a stone's throw from the Grand Hotel. Alice has a sixth sense for such things. Despite the influence of alcohol. Which derives from years of previous experience. She fights to keep the pain of earlier betrayals under wraps. No point in opening up old wounds. Or becoming even more depressed.

She speculates. Clancy's escapade with marihuana will be the least of Viv's concerns if Bill finds out about Mattie. Alice wonders if she understands the likely repercussions. The challenge to his masculinity. The inevitable, messy argument about custody. All the threats and allegations. Not that Mattie will be seen for dust. When the shit hits the fan. Or even when it doesn't. When she gets tired of subterfuge and when her conquest is complete. When Mattie books her flight to somewhere more exciting. She really ought to talk to Viv about these things. Offer her the benefit of a life's experience. If she was feeling more compassionate and less preoccupied with her own disasters, she might consider it. If she was feeling less betrayed. Instead she orders Muscadet to complement the lemon sole. The waitress allows herself a tiny smile.

Alice thinks how natural it seemed, the other night, to

let Mattie back into her bed again. Mattie, never satisfied until she has taken everything. Still greedy after all these years. Still needing to be central. Still testing Alice, like a child, against some impossible standard of self sacrifice. Still side tracked by the odd, predictable diversion when she's feeling bored. Or in need of reassurance. Still battling for her freedom. Still looking for a home. Still expecting to be wanted . . . once more with feeling. Alice didn't feel abused.

Alice finds it easier to understand Mattie than to forgive Viv. Her friend, so called. Someone from whom she might have expected a little more loyalty. And more commonsense. So easily seduced by Mattie's easy charm, like all the rest. Although she's old enough and wise enough to be more sensible. A world well lost – for sex. It's quite a price.

When Alice thinks about it she hopes that sex is all that Viv has in mind. Any suggestion that she's in love would be the real disaster. Mattie doesn't know the meaning of the word. And Viv? Who knows what fantasies she might construct to justify her burst of curiosity? How unfaithful does a husband have to be? How terrifying is the prospect of an empty marriage, once the kids have gone? How many more years of active service to be tolerated in the line of duty?

If Viv is serious about her disaffection, if loving women seems to be a better proposition (God knows it has taken Alice long enough to understand there might be choice involved, not simply genes) then why not save herself for someone who would listen to her needs? Who'd pay her fears respect? Who'd take her children seriously? And not expect a quick conversion. Alice sips her Muscadet. Someone like Alice. But not Alice, of course. She's not afraid of offering commitment. It isn't lack of commitment that has been her issue. She would have liked the opportunity, in her life, to build a serious relationship. With some expectation that it could last. Alice thinks she's good at staying put and talking on responsibilities. She wouldn't do it lightly. Making a commitment to a woman, she could rely on, would overcome the worry about people finding out. With someone by her side – she could face the flak. And still do her job with pride and proper authority. Maybe more authority. Knowing that, deep down, she wasn't behaving like a hypocrite.

It was always Mattie, in the end, who wouldn't put it to the test. It's true, she always found it easy to be open. She was always good at speeches. Good at rhetoric. She had the capacity to make her life seem like a political crusade. Her selfishness to be the strength that others should indulge. Her acolytes. Her little band of groupies. Heady days for self-appointed stars.

And it's true, it took some courage to confront the bigots – the likes of Michael Duke across the years. She provoked a lot of pompous men and made the difference in a lot of women's lives. But it's no sacrifice to fall in love from time to time. At exciting political moments and in interesting, far away, foreign places. With girls in every port. And with an inbuilt obligation to move on. Good emotional material for one who makes a living from writing poetry. Who thrives on fame and fortune. A captive audience. With adulation the recurring proof that she exists.

Alice's wonders whether her reflections begin to sound a little twisted. She can't imagine who she'd ever say them to if she were sober. They are a measure of her own regrets as much as Mattie's culpability. Reflecting personal history. The diamonds and the rust involved in living on the edge of passion. Of moving through her suffering to some better understanding of what finally counts. Alice thinks she could be wiser now. And as a consequence, more safe, more in control. She suspects that Mattie still has quite a way to travel in the need to understand herself. Which casual affairs to ward off desperation will not circumvent. She will try to have this conversation with her, one more time, before she asks Mattie to leave. But no doubt she'll get it wrong. As usual.

'Will you be taking coffee in the music room?' It seems by now that Alice is regarded as a proper diner by the girl in the black pencil skirt. 'I'm asked to offer you a brandy – with the compliments of the couple in the corner.'

Alice looks across the lounge to recognise a pair of Henley Manor parents, who raise their glasses and smile. 'I may have had rather too much to drink already', Alice says, 'for a respectable headmistress!'

'You only live once', the waitress says, with the sincerity of a true believer. 'No one leaves the Grand Hotel sober when its Christmas. Why should you be any different?'

Alice smiles. 'Is that so?'

She thanks the couple in the corner, and picking up her duffle coat and briefcase, she concentrates on making her exit to the music room, with as much dignity as she can muster, given the circumstances.

The taxi slides to a standstill at Alice's gate.

'Be careful', the driver shouts as she picks her way precariously through the drifting snow. 'It's icing over.'

A white crescent moon hangs in the black sky. And

somewhere in the distance, the train to London rumbles through the silent fields.

Alice opens the door to a breeze of candlelight and music. And Mattie drinking cocoa by the fire, like a permanent and familiar fixture.

'You ok Old Girl?' she comes to greet her. Not seeking information. Merely reassurance.

'A touch the worse for wear.' Alice throws her duffle coat across the chair. 'But sound in mind and body, nonetheless.'

'And still able to make your own decisions?' Mattie puts her hand round Alice's waist and draws her close. Her breath is cold on Mattie's cheek.

'I always make my own decisions. Although on this occasion, hypothermia might affect my judgement.'

'Do you want to come to L.A.? Spend New Year with me in the desert?'

It seems to be a serious suggestion. Alice kisses Mattie on the nose.

'Are you leaving then? Before I get the chance to throw you out?'

'You wouldn't throw me out.' Mattie moves Alice gently through the hallway to the bedroom door. 'Anyway, I want you to come with me.'

'I'll come with you to bed', Alice laughs. 'I was about to make the same suggestion myself. But you beat me to it. The desert you'll have to deal with on your own.'

'I want to make a speech', Mattie says as she gently unfolds Alice from her tartan skirt and cashmere sweater. 'About how much I've come to value you. How I have always loved you. And how I always will. Though never very well.'

'No speeches by request.' Alice runs her hand along the curve of Mattie's back. 'Send me a letter from Los

Angeles. Or better still, a poem – which suitably befits the moment. I'm tired of talking.' She reaches for the nape of Mattie's neck. 'When I first discovered this little spot... just here...', she kisses along the line of silky skin beneath her hairline, 'I thought it was the most beautiful place I'd ever been. I've never found anywhere else that suits me better.'

'I can get a flight on Friday', Mattie says. 'Come and join me when your term is finished. It doesn't have to commit you to anything.'

'God forbid that I should be committed', Alice laughs. 'Shut up Mattie. Shut up, for once. And let me love you like I used to. That's all I want right now. Without any need for speeches.'

'I had a call from Steven. He says you've suspended him.'

It's Friday morning in Alice's study. Alice is looking tired. Viv is looking anxious.

'I've given him some home leave to work on the libretto for the school concert.'

'Isn't that a rather unusual thing to do?'

'These are unusual times, Viv. He needs protecting.'

'Who from?'

'Himself mostly.'

'He told me about the anonymous letters.' Viv is dressed in her finest camouflage. As a local councillor and respectable mother of three. But the strain across her eyes suggests she hasn't slept. And that this meeting with Alice is something of an ordeal. 'So the marihuana episode hasn't gone away?'

'I don't believe it has got anything to do with Steven',

Alice says. 'Except in the closed mind of whoever wrote the letters.'

'Why haven't you told the police?'

'About the letters or the drugs?'

Viv finds it difficult to meet Alice's steady gaze.

'How many people know?'

'Only Steven and the Chair of Governors so far. And now you. But it will be hard to keep the allegations quiet for much longer. I need to tell the police or take some action of my own.'

'What's Duke's assessment? As if I didn't know!' Viv's voice is angry in anticipation.

'He has a right to be concerned. I could feel quite angry myself', Alice says, 'that a member of my staff is being blamed for something that – to be frank – implies an absence of parental supervision. I don't know where the marihuana came from, or the money to buy it, but it didn't come from Steven Rowntree or Henley Manor School.'

'I know. I'm not condoning what Clancy's done, Alice. I feel like strangling her myself. But she isn't the only one, you know. I don't think she'd lie to me. I could provide you with a list of girls in your sixth form at this moment who think it's cool and smart to defy the lot of us. Including Michael Duke's precious daughter Zoe.'

'I do know the solution isn't simply to expel Clancy and the others who were caught. Although that's the instruction I've been given. I also have to consider the wider allegations made about Steven. I'm sure he told you the full indictment in the letters.'

Viv looks distressed.

'He did. It all feels very close to home.'

Alice finds it impossible to disagree.

'It's hard to see how any of us will come out of this

smelling of roses', she smiles ruefully. Not any one of us...'

'Have you spoken to Mattie?' Viv is unsure what Alice knows.

'What about particularly?'

'Well about the letters for a start.' Viv is being cautious. Alice could be kind and put her out of her misery.

'No. There doesn't seem much point. And I can't stand one of her lectures. Anyway, she's gone.'

'She's gone!' Viv is clearly shocked. Her precarious composure finally collapses. Much to Alice's relief. Maybe now they can stop talking like strangers and automatons.

'She caught a plane to California about an hour ago, to spend Christmas in Los Angeles and New Year in the desert. She's not a woman who does things by half, our Mattie. Didn't you know?'

Viv shakes her head.

'No I had no idea. Do you mind?'

'I shall miss her, of course. I always do at first. Like you miss a scratch when it stops itching.' Alice smiles. 'But I'll be glad to have my life back to myself. And Orlando is ecstatic.'

'I had the impression, from something Mattie said the other day, that you and she were, what do you say? Back together – in a way.'

'It's the story of our life.' Alice pours a second cup of coffee. 'I expect she'll keep on turning up from time to time. I expect I'll keep feeling pleased to see her. So long as I don't have to take her too seriously.'

'I thought she was the love of your life?' Viv says.

'She is. No was about it.' Alice looks very dignified and calm. 'But that doesn't mean to say I like having her around. She's a pain in the neck most of the time.'

Viv feels like a total fool.

'I suppose you know what happened?' she says quietly.

'I can guess', Alice says. 'But spare me the details now. We'll talk about it all in good time, no doubt. If we manage to get through this current mess.'

'What are you going to do?' Viv stretches out her hand to touch Alice's sleeve.

'The first thing I'm going to do..' she pushes back her chair decisively, 'is take the rest of the day off. Get myself a decent haircut. And a brand new wardrobe. I feel a change of image coming on. What do you say?'

'There's nothing wrong with your image', Viv looks relieved, 'that a little retail therapy wouldn't cure.'

'Not Laura Ashley!' Alice is determined.

'Not Laura Ashley', Viv laughs. 'But there are other possibilities – if you have the money and the inclination.'

'Are you doing anything this afternoon?' Alice's bravado begins to slip. 'I could probably do with some assistance.'

'Do you trust me?' Viv is looking more relaxed.

'I trust you not to let me make a bigger fool of myself than I already am.'

Viv kisses her quickly on the cheek.

'Come on. Before you change your mind. Tell the dragon on the desk to hold the fort. She'll like that. It'll feed her megalomania.'

'I need to speak to Hilda', Alice hesitates. 'But later. When I'm in a better frame of mind. Let's make a run for it whilst she's dressing down the dinner ladies in time for Governors' Day.'

Fourteen

Alice wakes on Governors' Day with a dream still in her head. She has read somewhere that remembering your dreams is a good thing – it shows your conscious and unconscious mind is doing what it is supposed to do. Build bridges.

In the dream she is visiting Mattie in her life at the university, where Mattie is greatly in demand. Putting on a performance with her students of *West Side Story*. Alice catches a glimpse of Mattie in an Orphelia-type dress. Pre-Raphelite and sitting in a boat, like the Lady of Shallot, with long red hair and candles. At one point they go hand-in-hand into a lecture theatre, brimming with feelings of love, looking for privacy. But students follow them in.

Alice wakes in a state of gentle melancholy. Orlando stalks across the duvet, pausing for a second to stretch her long, thin back and direct a considered stare at Alice, examining her mood. Alice shuts her eyes, wanting to go back into the dream. Dreading the duties of the day. Orlando starts to purr and to butt her gently in the nearest bit of body she can find protruding from the covers. Alice ducks her nose and chin out of range, until she is confronting Orlando eye to yellow eye.

'I know it's time to get up. But I don't want to.' Alice's new haircut is poking, like a tuft of grey thistle, from beneath the duvet. Orlando indicates the door, the Wild, the promise of another life beyond the cat flap. And more immediately, her insatiable demand for diced rabbit and a bowl of milk.

Alice turns on the radio. Rabbi Lionel Blue is giving his 'thought for the day'. Such a sweet man. He always tells a joke. He always says something quite revealing about himself. Not as conceit. But in a self-mocking kind of way which should make others more reflective too. And not take themselves so seriously. He's not afraid to say he's queer. His God – or someone – has given him the courage to be honest.

Governors' Day is an annual event. The high spot of the academic year. The meeting in the afternoon is preceded by a morning of girls showing off their work to doting parents and teachers being on their best – least cynical – behaviour. Once lunch is cleared away the parents and the girls slide out into the Christmas streets of Oxford to shop for seasonal good cheer and celebrate the end of term. Leaving Alice and her colleagues, with

Hilda taking minutes, to lead the complement of governors into the meeting in the library.

Alice chooses chocolate brown. 'The fashionable colour for the winter season, Madam' according to the smart brown-eyed, brown-haired, brown-frocked assistant in a shop which Alice didn't know existed. Until Viv's recommendation. And which painlessly separated Alice from the best part of a month's salary, before releasing her through heavy, plate glass doors back into the narrow cobbled lane, leading to the High Street.

She must admit that *Pickles* turned out to be the perfect choice. She now admires her new image in the wardrobe mirror. Brown woollen jacket, made in Italy, that she can wear with matching trousers or matching skirt. A cream silk shirt and soft brown ankle boots with tiny buttons on the cuff. Today she chooses the skirt. Her grey hair is brushed into a spiky crop and held in order by a touch of gel. She pins a ceramic broach to her lapel and collects a cream scarf and long woollen trench coat from the hall stand, chosen to co-ordinate with chocolate brown. Orlando is impressed and watches from the window ledge with rekindled interest as Alice strides out into the snow.

There is little in the way of elegance that can dislodge Hilda from her usual, curt 'good morning'. But even Hilda allows herself a second, lingering appraisal of Alice's surprising transformation.

'Could you re-order the agenda for the meeting Hilda?' Alice is businesslike and breezy. 'I'll take Mr Duke's Report on behalf of the governors first, followed by my Report and then the paper about finances. You can omit the items entitled School Drugs Initiative and Staff Code of Conduct because I intend to deal with these in the context of my report. Any Other Business will obviously come last. And I wonder if you could make sure that all the governors have copies of the anonymous letters to hand – so they know what I'm talking about.'

'Do you want them circulated in advance?' Hilda rarely manages to include Alice's name these days. 'Or in response to a particular item? I don't think I'll find them in the usual file.'

'Oh dear because they're not there. Sorry Hilda. You'll find them in the bottom drawer of my desk in an orange folder marked "allotment specifications". I think it would be best if you were to circulate them just before I make my report. And could I have some coffee when you have a minute?'

At two o'clock precisely Michael Duke calls the meeting to order. The governors have been suitably impressed by excellent displays of academic and creative work. And suitably relaxed by one of Cook's exceptional buffets and more than generous supply of mulled wine. Duke congratulates the school, the staff and Alice about sporting accolades, Oxbridge entrance, and the general atmosphere of respect and purpose he detects among the pupils. He directs colleagues' attention to the section in the Report which deals with performance indicators and examination targets for the coming year, and to the mission statement at the beginning, underlining the moral and academic context in which all those at Henley Manor must continue to strive for the highest standards in behaviour and achievement.

'I know Miss Morrison will want to add her authority to this statement in particular. The last few weeks have not been plain sailing in this respect. But I have every confidence, having discussed two matters in particular with her in recent days, that she is well in command of the situation. And will be able to reassure us all about the actions she is taking to deal with the unfortunate incidents that have occurred.'

Hilda takes a moment from the minutes to glance around the room. Edwin Crosby's face is very red. His eyes are drifting towards sleep. Professor Inchcape is already anticipating the next appointment in her leather filofax. Alice looks composed. She is extremely nervous. But Hilda lacks the necessary perception to recognise controlled emotion.

Alice thanks Michael Duke for his support, and thanks the governors generally for their attention to detail in the Report.

'It will be extremely helpful to us in the coming year in our continuing efforts to persuade Oxfordshire parents to make an investment with us in their daughter's education.'

She goes on to itemise achievements in artistic and musical excellence which are many, and which are missing from the Governors' summary. And to thank parents, in their absence, for their generous contributions of time and money to the school's extra curricular activities.

'However. It is with the deepest regret that I must bring another matter to your attention. Hilda, could you circulate the copies of the letters, if you please.'

Alice pauses whilst the papers pass from hand to hand and their substance is digested. Edwin Crosby straightens his body in his chair as Professor Inchcape snaps shut her filofax. Michael Duke watches Alice astutely, above the half light of his gold rimmed reading glasses.

'These are copies of two very defamatory letters which have been sent to myself and to the Chairman of Governors in recent weeks. To my knowledge they have been sent to no one else and I must conclude that they originate from someone with a grievance to express about the school. They make two serious allegations about a member of my staff – who, I have to say, is a most admirable young man and a remarkable teacher. They allege and imply professional misconduct, but without any semblance of evidence whatsoever'.

A flutter of dismay rumbles through the rows of assorted Governors and teachers. Mrs Maudling is looking tight-lipped and irritated. Wendy Armitage is horrified.

'Three weeks ago three girls were caught smoking marihuana on the school premises – which to my knowledge is an isolated occurrence – but which I am given to understand could implicate a wider circle of pupils than those who were apprehended. I take the matter very seriously. And I have no intention of adopting a relaxed attitude to such activity, until such times as there is a change in the law regarding recreational drugs. At which point I shall continue to treat the matter with the same severity as I already apply to the prohibition of smoking and drinking on the school premises, in the interests of pupils' health and safety.'

Mrs Maudling nods gently, with a look of pained concern in her pale, dull eyes.

'In consultation with Inspector Roger Bates, from the local constabulary, I am now better informed about police procedures and discretion in relation to the wholesale increase in marihuana smoking by the young and I shall be arranging for all pupils and teaching staff to attend information sessions about the dangers, and potential consequences, of drug-taking. I shall be arranging complementary sessions in the evening for parents facing similar problems on the home front. My feeling is that these are matters which we should all be more informed about, in ways which help us to help our daughters withstand the undoubted pressures they are currently subjected to. After considerable thought, and much soul searching, I am now convinced that this, rather than a knee jerk response – by which I mean summary exclusion – is the best solution.'

'I can also confirm that the allegation made in the letters about Mr Rowntree's supply of drugs to the Upper Sixth is completely unfounded. And if I was him, when the anonymous culprit is apprehended, I should be seriously considering legal action on the grounds of libel.'

All eyes are focused on Alice.

'But if you have caught girls in the act of smoking illegal drugs Miss Morrison, surely it is your responsibility to make an example of them, as a deterrent to the rest. Their corrupting influence on other pupils could be a dangerous one.' Professor Inchcape fixes Alice with a steely eye.

'I think you underestimate the potential in such a reaction for promoting heroines, Professor. A bunch of martyrs to rebellion will merely glamorise the practice. To behave as though we're scandalised and horrified will help to publicise the attraction, in my opinion. I prefer an educational response.'

'If this hits the headlines Miss Morrison . . .' Michael Duke had not been expecting this. At their recent meeting in his office in the High Street he had strongly advised Alice to simply announce the names and the expulsion of the culprits.

'If it isn't contested in an educational and responsible

way, Mr Duke, it will lead to more expulsions. Including, I am led to believe, the daughters of some of our most respected and respectable parents.'

'Who for example?' Edwin Crosby's daughter left the school two years ago. She dropped out of university two terms later because she was pregnant. It isn't something he likes to boast about.

'I don't think it's appropriate for me to answer that question in this context, do you? But I will be contacting any parents whom I think may have reason to discuss this matter with me privately.' Alice looks straight at Michael Duke and allows her eyes to linger in an exchange of meaning for a moment before passing on to the second point she has determined she will make.

'I do not propose to make any comment about the references in these scurrilous letters to Mr Rowntree's private life. So long as his professional competence is in no doubt, I consider that his personal life is no concern of ours.'

Mrs Maudling's pale eyes look out across the white lawns, towards the empty tennis courts and the cricket nets. Her soldier husband is waiting for the call of battle from his armchair in their neo-Georgian town house, somewhere in the quiet suburbs. Their silent children already turning into silent wives.

'However, I am well aware that the purpose of the speculation is to promote the kind of prejudice which leads to discrimination against perfectly decent people, whose way of life is feared and misunderstood in various ways. I am not proposing public education sessions about sexual minorities at the moment . . .'

Edwin Crosby shakes his head energetically from side to side, which Alice takes as a tacit indication of his agreement – if only for the wrong reasons.

'. . . but as one who has spent half a lifetime, in fear of others publicising the truth about me in this respect, I am very familiar with the kind of climate of hatred and denial, in which malicious damage can be done to those of us who are pilloried as being deviant from the norm.'

Hilda puts down her pen and stops writing. Michael Duke is fingering his tie nervously and weighing up the wisdom of a Chairman's intervention, before Alice Morrison goes completely over the top.

Across the stunned silence, Wendy Armitage is smiling, and as she catches Alice's eye for a moment, it provides the confirmation of support which Alice needs to make one final declaration. She can feel her heart pounding in her breast. Her voice challenging the silent, astonished gathering with quiet dignity.

'I never imagined – in a million years – that I would be standing in a meeting like this, and saying what I'm saying. But I am saying it, nonetheless.' She pauses, looking with a gentle authority into the eyes of any who can hold her gaze. Hilda is glued to the detail of her shorthand. Apparently preoccupied. 'If your instruction to me, as my Governing Body, is that I should sack Mr Rowntree, or encourage him to think that "his better interests lie elsewhere", then you must also agree to accept my resignation. You have been most kind in your Report about the school, and about the quality of my leadership during the last eight years – but you must also understand that my professional commitment to high standards in the education of young women is also because I am profoundly committed to the social, political and educational advance of young women, in what is still a far from egalitarian society.'

At some point Alice must have risen to her feet. Because now, she feels the need to sit down. Wendy Armitage wants to clap But she knows enough about the others in the room to understand it may not lead to an ovation.

'Sounds like you're a bit of a feminist, Miss Morrison.' Edwin Crosby looks uncomfortable. 'I'm not sure we should be getting too excited about anything that smacks of feminism.'

Alice takes a deep breath.

'I am a feminist Mr Crosby. I hope we all are in a girls' school.' She takes an even deeper breath, glimpsing in her mind's eye the soft, delicious nape of Mattie's neck. 'But what I am also saying is that I am a lesbian. And if any one of you has any problem with this information, I would be glad to hear about it. Now. Publicly. In this meeting. Because I don't want to receive ghastly, poisonous, grubby little scraps of malice, like the ones we have in front of us today, making allegations about me.'

She looks into the silent faces of her staff and governors.

'Well thank you, Miss Morrison.' Michael Duke smiles a limp smile. 'I want to commend you on your candour. I'm going to take the rather unusual step of declaring a short break in the proceedings. I'm sure your Report has given us considerable food for thought and I propose to adjourn the meeting for 15 minutes to give us all a chance to catch our breath and stretch our legs.'

Alice sinks back into her chair as the room clears.

'Could I have a little word?' Michael Duke is at her side. 'In your office? Do you mind?'

'Please say anything you want to say to me here, Mr Duke. I prefer to stay put for a moment if you don't mind.'

'Just a point, Miss Morrison.' Duke raises his eyebrows into a question. 'Were you, by any chance, referring to Zoe?'

Alice isn't sure about the purpose of his question.

'I do have reason to believe that Zoe could be smoking marihuana, yes. But I haven't had the opportunity to tackle her about it yet.'

Michael Duke leans forward.

'I would be grateful if you would keep this information to yourself, Miss Morrison. Until I have had time to ascertain the truth. I'm sure you understand. I wouldn't want...'

'None of us wants any of this to hit the headlines Mr Duke. That is what I think I was trying to say. There are better ways of responding.'

'Quite. Quite. So I can count on your discretion?'

'It's not a question of discretion Mr Duke. It's a matter of my getting to the bottom of this in an educational and professional way. Our young women have a lot to lose – which they may not be old enough or mature enough to understand at the moment. I need parents and the Governors to give me their full support and to work with me on this one. That's if you have confidence in my abilities. Now that you know I shall no longer be denying the truth about my sexuality.'

Duke doesn't understand the need for public declarations of principle or conviction. Professionally he has made his reputation and his money from the business of exposure. The exposure of his political opponents. And in pursuit of his clients' interests. But he is not an advocate of open government or making personal revelations.

'But will you flaunt it Miss Morrison?'

'Really Mr Duke! Do I look like a woman who is about to chain herself to the school railings?' Alice laughs. If she was younger – with the wisdom she has now – she might consider it.

Duke coughs nervously.

'My sister is a bit of a...' he thinks carefully about the appropriate word to choose '... a bit of a feminist, as a matter of fact. She's never married. Runs a bookshop with a woman in Tiverton. We don't get on all that well. But Zoe likes her.'

Alice nods.

'I'm not ready to stop teaching yet Mr Duke. Or to leave Henley Manor. But I will resign if there is any suggestion that I must get rid of Steven Rowntree.'

Duke polishes his spectacles. The room refills with staff and Governors who are looking like they've had enough and who are wanting to go home.

'Does anyone have anything they would like to add?' Michael Duke is used to guiding meetings through a semblance of democracy towards the kind of closure he is now preparing to impose. 'Because if not, I would like to move on to the Statement of Accounts. I'm sure we've all got homes to go to...' he laughs nervously. 'I for one would like to finish by 4.15.' Duke calls the meeting to perfunctory order as Hilda picks up her pen and continues with the minutes.

Later, in the office, Alice says. 'How did you know the letters weren't in the file Hilda?'

Hilda blinks self consciously.

'I knew they weren't. Because I knew you hadn't given them to me.'

'I'm surprised you even knew that they existed, Hilda. Since no one but myself, Mr Duke and Mr Rowntree were aware of their existence. Mr Rowntree chose to tell Mrs Williams. Who discussed the matter with me. But not with you, I don't suppose?'

'I don't know what you're getting at, Miss Morrison. It seems I'm just the dogsbody around here.'

'Did you write the letters Hilda?'

'No, I certainly did not. What do you take me for? If I don't agree with something I say so. I don't need to go writing anonymous letters.'

'Well I'm glad to hear it. Because if you did, as I'm sure you understand, I would have to tell the police.'

Hilda studies her watch.

'It's past my leaving time, Miss Morrison. I've got a bus to catch.'

'You have until Monday Hilda, to provide me with a credible explanation about how you knew about the letters if you didn't write them.'

Alice takes her trench coat from the hook inside her study door. She must acquire a proper coat hanger if it's not going to end up looking like a duffle coat. She waits for Hilda to zip her anorak, to stop thrusting various personal belongings into a plastic shopping bag, and leave. She turns the light out in the study and the office and shuts the door. Outside the snow is falling thick and deep as Alice walks along the river towards home. She thinks of Mattie in an Orphelia-type dress, sailing through the desert, with long hair blowing in the breeze, her candles smoking in the dry desert air.

The news of Alice's announcements travels fast. Oxford is a small town and gossip circulates. On Saturday she receives a bunch of yellow roses with a note from Viv. 'I'm proud of you', it says. 'You have given us all a lesson in courage and conviction. I don't want to intrude on your privacy – but I'd like to see you. Do phone me if you feel the same.'

Alice has never known the experience of receiving flowers from a possible admirer. She plunges them in hot water and sugar, as the instructions on the expensive label indicate, and allows herself a tiny flutter of self-satisfaction.

Sometime later in the afternoon Jack calls from a phone box near to the allotment.

'I'm digging rocks and blasting nettles', he announces, 'in a massive fit of sublimation.'

'What's the matter Jack? Have you been drinking? It must be freezing out there.'

'No. But I intend to. I wanted to congratulate you, Alice. On your honesty. I don't suppose you've heard the last of it, but it will make any one that challenges you now, look like a rampant bigot.'

'It could also be a three day wonder Jack – once Christmas and the New Year are underway. I'm sure they've all got better things to think about. I feel more exercised by sticking to my guns about the drugs initiative. That will be enough of a shock to the collective system in the staff room. What's the news of Steven? I haven't seen him since I sent him home to work on *West Side Story.*'

'Neither have I. That's why I'm pounding rocks in the snow.' Jack puts more money into the phone box. 'I think he's weakening, Alice.'

'It can't be easy, Jack. I'm sure Steven's disappearance hasn't got to do with weakness. He's probably trying to sort things out at home. He must feel torn apart.'

'No prizes for guessing where that will lead.' Jack is sounding bleak and angry.

'I wouldn't be so sure.' Alice is feeling tired of emotional demands and allegations of betrayal. Wiped out. And wanting peace. A quiet evening on her own, with Mozart playing softly in the shadows, and Orlando curled in reassurance on her lap.

'Do you feel like a drink later?' Jack's voice on the phone is sounding urgent.

'I'm sorry Jack. I've promised myself some peace and quiet for a while. I hope you understand. I'm not really used to all this intrigue and excitement. I need to re-establish my routines.'

As the daylight fades Alice finds some candles and places holly in a vase. Only three more days at work then she can think of taking Christmas leave. In the study the phone is splitting through the early evening chill. Orlando opens her eyes and shuts them lazily. Her mind on matters of subsistence.

'Shift yourself!' Alice lifts her gently to the floor and goes to get the phone. The yellow roses in the hallway catch her mood and cause a second little smile of secret pleasure.

'Is that Oxford three, zero, five, two?' An American telephonist bridges the time and distance with a disaffected drawl. 'I have a collect call for you from Los Angeles, California. Will you accept the charge?'

Alice takes a deep breath and pushes her fingers through the spiky uncombed tangle of her hair.

'Do I have any choice in the matter?' she asks, 'probably not!'

'Go ahead, caller.' The operator flicks a switch. 'You have your connection.'

Silver Moon Books
Publishers of Lesbian Romance, Detective and Thriller Novels

BABY, IT'S COLD, JAYE MAIMAN
The fifth appearance of Robin Miller, this tremendously exciting thriller will keep you guessing right up to the final page.
(£7.99, 256pp, ISBN 1 872642 403).

FIRST IMPRESSIONS, KATE CALLOWAY
A stunning debut thriller from exciting new talent Kate Calloway.
(£7.99, 208pp, ISBN 1 872642 381).

DOUBLE BLUFF, CLAIRE MCNAB
Fast becoming the number one lesbian detective writer, Claire McNab has produced another gripping thriller featuring the stunning Detective Inspector Carol Ashton.
(£7.99, 190pp, ISBN 1 872642 365).

THE FIRST TIME, eds BARBARA GRIER & CHRISTINE CASSIDY
This collection of lesbian love stories is the fourth in the best selling series of short story anthologies from Silver Moon Books
(£7.99, 246pp, ISBN 1 872642 357).

SOMEONE TO WATCH, JAYE MAIMAN
Mystery, lust and betrayal are all here in this fourth Robin Miller mystery from bestseller Jaye Maiman.
(£7.99, 272pp, ISBN 1 872642 349).

DEVOTION, MINDY KAPLAN
A gripping and erotic novel about the dangers of trying to go back to rewrite history; of risking what is - for what might have been; and of the power of love over illusion.
(£7.99, 160pp, ISBN 1 872642 330).

PAXTON COURT, DIANE SALVATORE
A wonderful book about how people learn to live together, overcoming stereotypes and the fear of the unknown. Sexy, moving and very funny it is this fine author's best book yet.
(£7.99, 240pp, ISBN 1 872642 322).

DEEPLY MYSTERIOUS,
eds KATHERINE FORREST and BARBARA GRIER
Cross the best lesbian mysteries with the hottest lesbian romances and what do you get? *Deeply Mysterious* Silver Moon's third collection of lesbian erotic stories.
(£7.99, 304pp, ISBN 1 872642 31 4).

BODY GUARD, CLAIRE McNAB
An unwelcome assignment makes Detective Inspector Carol Ashton body guard to Maria Strickland - a famous American feminist under personal threat from the New Right. The only thing between Maria and her assassin is Carol's courage. Will it be enough?
(£7.99, 192pp, ISBN 1 872642 306).

SECOND GUESS, ROSE BEECHAM
Amanda Valentine who first appeared in *The Garbage Dump Murders* makes a welcome return in this compelling thriller.
(£7.99, 208pp, ISBN 1 872642 276).

DESERT OF THE HEART, JANE RULE
Told with all the wit and skill at the command of this fine novelist, *Desert of the Heart* stands as a classic of lesbian literature.
(£6.99, 224pp, ISBN 1 872642 21 7).

CONFESSIONS OF A FAILED SOUTHERN LADY,
FLORENCE KING
From her first tentative steps in school, to her college days where she discovers women in the form of the beautiful Bres, Florence King's sensationally funny autobiography reads like a novel and is a treat not to be missed.
(£6.99, 272pp, ISBN 1 872642 23 3).

CAR POOL, KARIN KALLMAKER
Anthea Rossignole is good looking, successful, possessor of a great house and a fast car. She is comfortable in her closeted world until she meets Shay Sumoto. A captivating and erotic lesbian romance from the very popular author of *Paperback Romance*.
(£7.99, 272pp, ISBN 1 872642 24 1).

DIVING DEEPER,
eds KATHERINE V. FORREST and BARBARA GRIER
Silver Moon's second anthology of erotic lesbian short stories takes over where its predecessor *Diving Deep* left off.
(£6.99, 304pp, ISBN 1 872642 22 5).

CRAZY FOR LOVING, JAYE MAIMAN
Romance and mystery with detective Robin Miller loose in New York. Jaye Maiman at the top of her form in this sequel to the very popular *I Left My Heart*.
(£6.99, 320pp, ISBN 1 872642 19 5).

PAPERBACK ROMANCE, KARIN KALLMAKER
Literary agent Alison, romantic novelist Carolyn, and the enigmatic conductor Nicolas Frost – who is *certainly* not what he seems – come together in this fast moving, erotic lesbian love story.
(£6.99, 256pp, ISBN 1 872642 13 6).

THE GARBAGE DUMP MURDERS, ROSE BEECHAM
A monster is on the loose – his victims a grisly jigsaw puzzle of anonymous body parts left around the city. Set against him is Amanda Valentine, a tough and unusual cop. Unpredictable, passionate and, as adversaries and lovers quickly learn, very much her own woman.
(£6.99, 240pp, ISBN 1 872642 15 2).

LOVE, ZENA BETH, DIANE SALVATORE
The novel all lesbian America is talking about. The story of Joyce Ecco's love affair with Zena Beth Frazer, world famous lesbian author. Zena Beth is sexy, witty, outrageous and recovering from her sensational love affair with sports superstar Helena Zoe. A passionate novel of love and jealousy which has the ring of truth.
(£6.99, 224pp, ISBN 1 872642 10 1).

CHASING THE SHADOW, LAUREN WRIGHT DOUGLAS
As the action builds to its nerve tearing climax Caitlin Reece must face a moral dilemma which nearly costs her her life. A hard-hitting and hugely entertaining thriller which packs a heart-stopping sting in its tail.
(£6.99, 224pp, ISBN 1 872642 09 8).

COP OUT, CLAIRE McNAB
A bestseller from this very popular author. The story of the Darcy family – a family at war – and the killer who menaces it. Can Carol Ashton find the murderer before it is too late?
(£6.99, 191pp, ISBN 1 872642 08 X).

A THIRD STORY, CAROLE TAYLOR
A fine novel about the pain of hiding, and the joy of coming out told with great humour and compassion.
(£5.99, 133pp, ISBN 1 872642 07 1).

FLASHPOINT, KATHERINE V. FORREST
A contemporary novel in which Katherine V. Forrest brings together all the skill and passion that have made her the most popular lesbian author writing today.
(£6.99, 240pp, ISBN 1 872642 29 2).

STILL CRAZY, JANE THOMPSON
A moving and passionate debut novel from an exciting new lesbian talent.
(£6.99, 176pp, ISBN 1 872642 20 9).

UNDER MY SKIN, JAYE MAIMAN
Following on from the success of *I Left my Heart and Crazy for Loving*, this third book in award-winning Jaye Maiman's highly-charged mystery series is the best yet.
(£6.99, 285pp, ISBN 1 872642 26 8).

DEAD CERTAIN, CLAIRE MCNAB
Faced with the exposure she has always feared, her integrity and objectivity questioned as never before, Detective Inspector Carol Ashton finds her professional and emotional life spinning out of control in this scorching thriller.
(£6.99, 206pp, ISBN 1 872642 28 4).

SILENT HEART, CLAIRE MCNAB
A moving and erotic love story from the author of the bestselling *Under the Southern Cross*.
(£6.99, 173pp, ISBN 1 872642 16 0).

A TIGER'S HEART, LAUREN WRIGHT DOUGLAS
A sizzling thriller from the author of bestsellers *Ninth Life* and *Chasing the Shadow* to keep you on the edge of your seat until its gripping final page.
(£6.99, 220pp, ISBN 1 872642 12 8).

DIVING DEEP,
eds KATHERINE. V. FORREST and BARBARA GRIER
Silver Moon's first short story anthology brings together stories of love, desire, romance and passion.
(£6.99, 218pp, ISBN 1 872642 14 4).

UNDER THE SOUTHERN CROSS, CLAIRE McNAB
Claire McNab departs from her famous Detective Inspector Carol Ashton series to bring her readers this passionate romance set against the majestic landscape of Australia.
(£6.99, 192pp, ISBN 1 872642 17 9).

I LEFT MY HEART, JAYE MAIMAN
As she follows a trail of mystery from San Francisco down the coast travel writer and romantic novelist Robin Miller finds distraction with sexy and enigmatic Cathy. A fast paced and witty thriller from an exciting new talent.
(£6.99, 303pp, ISBN 1 872642 06 3).

NINTH LIFE, LAUREN WRIGHT DOUGLAS
Introducing Caitlin Reece, uncompromising, tough, a wisecracking lesbian detective who takes no nonsense from anyone.
(£5.99, 242pp, ISBN 1 872642 04 7).

BENEDICTION, DIANE SALVATORE
A wonderful story of growing up and coming out. Its progress through love, sexuality and friendship will awaken so many memories for us all.
(£5.99, 260pp, ISBN 1 872642 05 5).

DEATH DOWN UNDER, CLAIRE McNAB
Detective Inspector Carol Ashton returns in the most formidable, baffling, and important homicide case of her career.
(£5.99, 220pp, ISBN 1 872642 03 9).

CURIOUS WINE, KATHERINE V. FORREST
An unforgettable novel from bestseller Katherine V. Forrest. Breathtakingly candid in its romantic eroticism – a love story to cherish.
(£6.99, 160pp, ISBN 1 872642 02 0).

LESSONS IN MURDER, CLAIRE McNAB
A marvellous tale of jealousy, murder and romance featuring the stylish Inspector Carol Ashton.
(£5.99, 203pp, ISBN 1 872642 01 2).

AN EMERGENCE OF GREEN, KATHERINE V. FORREST
A frank and powerful love story set against the backdrop of Los Angeles, this passionate novel pulls no punches.
(£6.99, 270pp, ISBN 1 872642 00 4).

Silver Moon Books are available from all good bookshops. However, if you have difficulty obtaining our titles please write to Silver Moon Books, 68 Charing Cross Road, London WC2H 0BB

SILVER MOON BOOKS
LESBIAN PUBLISHING FOR THE 1990s

What the press have said

" If you thought lesbian fiction was worthy but unskilled writing for an oppressed minority, move over darling. Today Silver Moon Books launch Friday Night Reads, a series of fun books for lesbians"

THE GUARDIAN

"Shine on Silver Moon"

THE OBSERVER

"...much welcomed new lesbian publishing house"

TIME OUT

"Silver Moon's first two books are indeed fun and erotic"

EVERYWOMAN

"Publishers with a mission to rescue lesbian readers across the nation from...tedium"

THE GUARDIAN

SILVER MOON BOOKS publish lesbian romance, detective and thriller stories. The accent is on FUN, our books are ideal for weekends at home or journeys away. So, when you want entertainment think of us first.